THE
COLOR OF
BEE LARKHAM'S
MURDER

THE
COLOR OF
BEE LARKHAM'S
MURDER

A Novel

SARAH J. HARRIS

ATRIA PAPERBACK

New York London Toronto Sydney New Delhi

ATRIA
PAPERBACK

An Imprint of Simon & Schuster, Inc.
1230 Avenue of the Americas
New York, NY 10020

Originally published in Great Britain in 2018 by HarperCollins UK

First Atria Paperback edition February 2019

ATRIA PAPERBACK and colophon are trademarks of Simon & Schuster, Inc.

For information about special discounts for bulk purchases, please contact Simon & Schuster Special Sales at 1-866-506-1949 or business@simonandschuster.com.

The Simon & Schuster Speakers Bureau can bring authors to your live event. For more information or to book an event contact the Simon & Schuster Speakers Bureau at 1-866-248-3049 or visit our website at www.simonspeakers.com.

Interior design by Jill Putorti

Manufactured in the United States of America

10 9 8 7 6 5 4 3 2

The Library of Congress has cataloged the Touchstone edition as follows:

Names: Harris, Sarah J., 1971– author.
Title: The color of Bee Larkham's murder : a novel / Sarah J. Harris.
Description: First Touchstone hardcover edition. | New York : Touchstone, 2018.
Identifiers: LCCN 2017044321| ISBN 9781501187896 (hardcover) | ISBN 9781501187902 (softcover)
Subjects: LCSH: Teenage boys—Fiction. | Synesthesia—Fiction. | BISAC: FICTION / Literary. | FICTION / Coming of Age. | FICTION / Mystery & Detective / General. | GSAFD: Bildungsromans. | Mystery fiction.
Classification: LCC PR6108.A766 C65 2018 | DDC 823/.92—dc23
LC record available at https://lccn.loc.gov/2017044321

ISBN 978-1-5011-8789-6
ISBN 978-1-5011-8790-2 (pbk)
ISBN 978-1-5011-8791-9 (ebook)

For Darren, James, and Luke
With love also to Mum, Dad, and Rachel

"I could tell you my adventures—beginning from this morning,"
said Alice a little timidly: "but it's no use going back to yesterday,
because I was a different person then."

—LEWIS CARROLL, ALICE'S ADVENTURES IN WONDERLAND

synesthesia (sɪnəs'θiʒə)
noun
1. physiology
a sensation experienced in a part of the body other than the part
stimulated
2. psychology
the subjective sensation of a sense other than the one being
stimulated. For example, a sound may evoke sensations of color

—COLLINS ENGLISH DICTIONARY

1

TUESDAY (BOTTLE GREEN)

Afternoon

Bee Larkham's murder was ice blue crystals with glittery edges and jagged silver icicles.

That's what I told the first officer we met at the police station, before Dad could stop me. I wanted to confess and get it over and done with. But he can't have understood what I said or he forgot to pass on the message to his colleague who's interviewing me now.

This man's asked me questions for the last five minutes and twenty-two seconds that have nothing to do with what happened to my neighbor, Bee Larkham, on Friday night.

He says he's a detective, but I'm not 100 percent convinced. He's wearing a white shirt and gray trousers instead of a uniform and we're sitting on stained crimson sofas, surrounded by cream-colored walls. A mirror's on the wall to my left and a camera's fixed in the right-hand corner of the ceiling.

They don't interrogate criminals in here, not adult ones anyway. Toys sit on a shelf, along with an old *Top Gear* annual and a battered copy of the first Harry Potter book that looks like some kid tried to eat it. If this is supposed to put me at ease, it's not working. The one-armed clown is definitely giving me the evil eye.

Would you describe yourself as happy at school, Jasper?

Are you friends with any Year Eleven boys?

Do you know anything about boys visiting Bee Larkham's house for music lessons?

Did Miss Larkham ask you to deliver messages or gifts to any boys, for example, Lucas Drury?

Do you understand what condoms are used for?

The last question's funny. I'm tempted to tell the detective that condom wrappers look like sparkly sweets, but I recently learnt the correct answer.

It's SEX: *a bubble-gum pink word with a naughty lilac tint.*

Again, what does that have to do with Bee and me?

Before the interview began, this man told us his name was Richard Chamberlain.

Like the actor, he said.

I haven't got a clue who the actor Richard Chamberlain is. Maybe he's from one of Dad's favorite U.S. detective TV shows—*Criminal Minds* or *CSI*. I don't know the color of *that* actor's voice, but this Richard Chamberlain's voice is rusty chrome orange.

I'm trying to ignore his shade, which mixes unpleasantly with Dad's muddy ocher and hurts my eyes.

This morning, Dad got a phone call asking if he could bring me down to the station to answer some questions about Bee Larkham—the father of one of her young, male music students has made some serious allegations against her. His colleagues plan to interview her too, to get her side of the story.

I wasn't in any trouble, Dad stressed, but I knew he was worried.

He came up with the idea of us taking in my notebooks and paintings. We would tell the police that I stand at my bedroom window with binoculars, watching the parakeets nesting in Bee Larkham's oak tree. And about how I keep a record of everything I see out of my window.

It's important the police think we're cooperating, Jasper, and not attempting to hide anything.

I didn't want to take any chances, so I stacked seventeen key paintings and eight boxes of notebooks—all filed correctly, their boxes labeled in date order—by the front door.

I hated the thought of them all together in one confined dark place:

the boot of Dad's car. What if the car crashed and burst into flames? My records would be destroyed. I helpfully suggested we divide the boxes and travel in two separate taxis to the police station, like members of the Royal Family who aren't allowed to travel together on one plane.

Dad vetoed this and muttered: "It might be a good thing if these boxes did go up in flames."

I screamed glistening aquamarine clouds with sharp white edges at Dad until he promised never to harm my notebooks or paintings. But the damage was done and I couldn't shake his threat or the colors out of my head; they mixed spitefully behind my eyes. I couldn't bear to look at Dad or think about the terrible things he was capable of doing.

What he had done already.

Returning to the den in the corner of my bedroom, I rubbed the buttons on Mum's cardigan until I felt calmer. When I crawled out again, twenty-nine minutes later, Dad had packed the car without me. He'd replaced some of my numbered boxes containing records of the people on this street with much older ones from the loft.

You've made a mistake, I told him. *These are my notebooks from years ago, listing Star Wars characters and merchandise.*

Dad said not to worry; the police would probably still be interested in the range of my work, and the selection of notebooks could help distract them.

I disliked his explanation. Worse still, when I looked closer in the boot, I realized he'd put box number four on top of box number six.

"Number four's carrot orange and sneaky!" I said. "It can't go on top of dusky pink and friendly number six. They don't even remotely belong together! How can you not know that by now?"

I wanted to add: *Why can't you see what I can see?*

There was no point, there never is. Dad's blind to a lot of things, particularly involving me. When I was little it was always Mum who understood my colors. But Mum's gone now and Dad doesn't want to know.

He let me go back inside so I could spin on the chair in the kitchen rather than run to my den again. We didn't have time, but we both knew I had to avoid more upset. I felt like an actor, walking around in the shoes belonging to me—Jasper Wishart—ever since the night Bee Larkham . . .

I couldn't go there. Not yet.

I had to get the long, snaky ticker tape in my head in order. It had tangled up, with vital bits damaged or jumbled together. I couldn't figure out how to rejig what had happened back into place.

Being late freaked me out even more. Dad said it'd be OK and not to worry, but that's what he says whenever we get late-payment reminders for our electricity bills. I'm not sure I can trust his judgment anymore.

After I'd double-checked my boxes were settled in the boot, we made sure our seat belts were fastened, because people are thirty times more likely to be thrown from a vehicle if they're not wearing one.

When we finally arrived, we were fifteen minutes and forty-three seconds late. The desk sergeant told us this wasn't a problem and we should take a seat, a detective would see us soon.

The desk sergeant's voice was light copper. I tried not to giggle at the irony. No one else in the police station would understand the joke, apart from Dad, who wouldn't laugh. He doesn't find my colors funny.

I longed to fly around the waiting room like a parakeet. Instead, I folded my arms tight and pretended I was *a normal thirteen-year-old boy*. I stared at my watch. Counting.

Five minutes, fourteen seconds.

The door beeped open, *light grayish turquoise circles,* and a man in a gray suit came out and shook Dad's hand without glancing at me.

"Hello, Detective," Dad said. "Are you in charge of the investigation into Bee and these boys?"

The man took Dad aside and spoke quietly in muted gray-white lines. He didn't talk to me or stare.

I overheard Dad tell the detective he doubted I could help because I don't recognize people's faces. Something to do with my *profound learning difficulties,* Dad suspected. He'll get that assessed at some point.

Did the detective still want to go ahead with the interview? It could be a waste of everyone's time.

"Jasper sees colors and shapes for all sounds too, but that's not much use to anyone either," Dad added.

How dare he say that? It's useful to me because the distinctive colors of people's voices help me recognize them. Plus, it's not just useful, it's wonderful—something Dad will never understand.

My life is a thrilling kaleidoscope of colors only I can see.

When I look out of my bedroom window, chaffinches serenade me with sugar-mouse pink trills from the treetops and indignant blackbirds create light turquoise lines that make me laugh.

When I lie in bed on Saturday mornings, Dad bombards me with electric greens, deep violets, and unripe raspberries from the radio in the kitchen.

I'm glad I'm not like most other teenage boys because I get to see the world in its full multicolored glory. I can't tell people's faces apart, but I see the color of sounds and that is so much better.

I was desperate to tell this police officer that while he and Dad can see hundreds of colors, I see millions.

But there are also terrible colors in this world that no one should ever have to witness. Since Friday night I haven't been able to get some of these ugly tints out of my head, however hard I try.

I longed to disobey Dad and tell this detective that whenever I close my eyes at night the palette becomes even more vivid, more brutal.

That's because I can't stop seeing the color of murder.

2

TUESDAY (BOTTLE GREEN)

Still That Afternoon

Before we came to the station, Dad had instructed me to avoid talking about Friday night; I had to stick to what we'd discussed. But when we got there, he was the first person to divert from the plan, not me. Even though they were on the other side of the waiting room, I could hear him firing question after question at the police officer.

"Is this a formal interview?" he asked. "About young boys visiting Bee's house?"

Low murmurs rippled from the detective, gray-white noise in the background that floated away as if it didn't want to draw attention to itself.

"Oh, OK. Not formal, but a first account about Bee and her relationship with Lucas Drury in particular? That's it? I've tried to explain to Jasper what you might want to ask him, but it's difficult for someone like him."

Gray-white lines turned into fluffy clouds and drifted off.

"Have you tried to get hold of Bee yet?" Dad went on.

More muted-colored murmurs as the detective's head moved up and down—something about the police not being able to locate her yet for questioning.

What was a First Account? Why was I really here?

I looked from one man to the other but discovered no clues stamped on their faces. Did Dad and the detective want me to talk about my first impression of Bee Larkham's voice?

Sky blue.

My memory of our first meeting?

I have a feeling we're going to be great friends.

Or did they want to know about her first threat?

Do this for me tonight or I won't let you watch the parakeets from my bedroom window ever again. I'll stop feeding them unless you do exactly as I say.

I wanted Dad to explain what they were discussing, but he had to fetch the boxes from the car. While we waited, I watched the light dove gray tapping of my foot and felt the detective's eyes slice like a knife through my forehead and into my brain as if he knew every detail from beginning to end. The whole ghastly-colored story with no edits.

The waiting room walls closed in on me. I couldn't breathe. I couldn't hear anything or see any colors. I forgot the story I had to tell, the one Dad and me had rehearsed for hours at home. Instead, I walked over to the detective, took a deep breath, and began to confess while I had the chance. He remained silent as I told him all about the ring-necked parakeets nesting in Bee Larkham's oak tree.

They're incredibly intelligent and musically colorful like a vibrant orchestra. They've already got me into trouble with the police and our neighbors but are still my favorite birds in the world.

More important I said very loudly and clearly: "Ice blue crystals with glittery edges and jagged silver icicles."

I didn't have time to explain these were the colors and shapes of Bee's screams on Friday night because Dad returned, carrying the first two boxes.

"Don't talk without me here, Jasper," he said. "Sit back down over there."

A deep line appeared between his eyes. He was annoyed or angry or anxious because I'd launched into the story without him. Dad needn't have worried. I'd spent three minutes and twenty-three seconds describing the parakeets and their glorious colors but hadn't got to the part about hurting Bee Larkham with the sharp, glinty knife and all the blood yet.

Dad's left eye twitched as he turned to the man in the suit. "Art's his favorite subject at school. He'll get carried away talking about colors and painting if you let him."

His muddy ocher voice transmitted a secret warning to me:

Keep quiet or someone will carry you away to a different world.

I returned to the bright orange plastic chair while the detective punched silver coin-shaped numbers into the door panel and disappeared. Dad came back and forth with boxes. I unfolded my arms in case Light Copper thought I looked defensive and had something to hide.

Dad always says that first impressions are important:

Focus on a person's face and make eye contact, otherwise you'll look shifty.

If this is too difficult, fake eye contact by staring above a person's eyebrows.

Try to act normal.

Don't flap your arms.

Don't rock.

Don't go on about your colors.

Don't tell anyone what you did to Bee Larkham.

Remember, that's not the reason they want to speak to us today.

I was sure I'd impressed the detective. I'd told him the absolute truth. Well, 66 percent of it. I hadn't told him everything. I didn't want to think about the missing 34 percent.

After three minutes and fifteen seconds, the desk sergeant buzzed us through the door. Dad heaved the boxes into a small room.

A man in a white shirt entered ten seconds later. He looked at me and then up at the camera.

"Hello, Jasper. Thank you for coming here today. For the record, I'm D.C. Richard Chamberlain. Also present is Jasper's father, Ed Wishart. It's Tuesday the twelfth of April and we're here to discuss an allegation made against your neighbor Bee Larkham."

His voice was a gross shade of rusty chrome orange.

"What was your name again?" I said, shuddering.

"Richard Chamberlain—like the actor," he replied. "My one and only claim to fame. Shall we get started?"

We sat opposite each other on the sofas, me shuffling almost off the edge to avoid the vomit-looking stain and Dad yanking me backwards with a hard grip.

My heart had dropped like a huge, glass lift. This wasn't the first detective I'd met in the waiting room, who listened carefully and only spoke in reassuring white-gray murmurs.

This was Rusty Chrome Orange, possibly named after a mysterious actor from some American TV crime show.

I took an instant dislike to him due to

a. his color (obviously)
b. he talked about dumb actors and claimed to be famous
c. he stared directly at me

Without warning, he launched into a series of baffling questions about school, my friends and teachers, gifts for boys, and condom wrappers that can be disguised as sparkly sweets. But his questions were all wrong from the start—and they haven't improved.

Where's the gray-suited man from the waiting room?

"I don't want to be rude, but I hate your color and I don't want to talk to you."

"Jasper! We discussed this, Son—about being polite and respectful when you answer questions."

"Yes, but perhaps the police officer who had gray-white whispers can come back? He seemed to get me. I don't want Richard Chamberlain *like the actor.* I want the first detective from the waiting room."

Silence.

People say silence is golden. They're wrong. It's no color at all.

Rusty Chrome Orange speaks again. "That was me, Jasper, in the waiting room. You talked to me about colors and parakeets."

"What?"

He picks up his notebook. "Ice blue crystals with glittery edges and jagged silver icicles. You also said that parakeets are incredibly intelligent."

I glance at Dad to verify Rusty Chrome Orange's story.

His head moves up and down. "You were speaking to D.C. Chamberlain while I got the boxes from the car."

I can scarcely believe it. I can't look at Dad or the detective from the waiting room who has morphed into Richard Chamberlain a.k.a. Rusty Chrome Orange. I stare at the gray jacket lying next to the detective on the sofa. He's taken it off. I didn't notice him carry the jacket in here.

"Oh." I can't think of anything else to say. *Oh* is a small word, exactly how I feel.

Tiny. Insignificant.

Oh. A color that people can't see.

"Sorry, I forgot." It's a lie, of course, but a useful one. Like *Sorry, I didn't see you.* I trot it out at least once a day when I don't recognize someone I'm supposed to.

"I did try to warn you," Dad's muddy ocher voice says to Richard Chamberlain. "He doesn't recognize me if I turn up at his school unexpectedly."

He's right.

I don't remember Dad's face.

Richard Chamberlain's face.

Anyone's face.

I see them, yet I don't. Not as complete pictures.

I close my eyes. I hear the muddy ocher of Dad's voice but can't draw together the image of his face in my mind. I couldn't pick him out of a lineup of men wearing blue jeans and blue shirts—his usual uniform. Is that what Dad's got on today? I can't remember. I haven't paid enough attention.

When he speaks, the rusty chrome orange of Richard Chamberlain's voice pummels my eyeballs, but if he walked up to me in the street I wouldn't be able to recognize him unless I'd memorized a distinctive detail: the make of his watch, a hat, socks featuring a character like Homer Simpson, or the color of his voice. Those are the kinds of things I look for first, rather than hair color or styles that change whenever people run their hands over their heads.

I open my eyes again. None of the usual clues helped me today. Rusty Chrome Orange wasn't wearing unusual clothes. He tricked me by taking off his gray jacket and whispered, which disguised the genuine color of his voice with white and gray lines.

Whispers are always frustrating for me because they completely change the hues of people's voices. Coughs and colds play the same mean trick, which is really sneaky too.

More colorless silence.

It lasts longer than before. I count ten teeth with my tongue before Richard Chamberlain clears his throat, creating an offensive ocher shade.

"You've gone to town on this," he says, pointing at my boxes as I perch with one buttock hovering in midair over the fried-egg-shaped splodge on the sofa.

I sigh. "We didn't go to town. We came straight here otherwise we'd have been even later."

"Okaaaaaaaay." The rusty chrome orange stretches into an equally unpleasant brownish mud color.

Richard Chamberlain—*call me Richard*—clarifies that he's surprised by how many notebooks I keep and stresses *there was no need to bring so many today.* He only wants to know if anything I've seen might help the investigation.

Before Dad can stop me, I pull out the crucial notebook from box number six and turn to January 22. This isn't the true beginning, but it's an incredibly important day in the sequence of events that followed:

7:02 A.M.
PARAKEETS LAND IN THE OAK TREE AT 20 VINCENT GARDENS.
HAPPY, BRIGHT PINK AND SAPPHIRE SHOWERS WITH GOLDEN DROPLETS.

7:06 A.M.
MAN WEARING CABBAGE GREEN PAJAMAS OPENS UPSTAIRS WINDOW OF HOUSE NEXT TO BEE LARKHAM'S. SHOUTS PRICKLY TOMATO RED WORDS AT PARAKEETS. CLUE: NUMBER 22 BELONGS TO DAVID GILBERT.

"Can we skip forwards?" Rusty Chrome Orange interrupts, setting my teeth on edge. "I'm not sure this is getting us anywhere."

I sigh. We're back to where we started, with Rusty Chrome Orange asking the wrong questions again.

If he were a proper detective, he'd have asked me to rewind and start even earlier, from the day it all began: January 17.

The day Bee Larkham moved into our street.

I guess I understand Rusty Chrome Orange's impatience. It's been four days since her murder and he still doesn't seem to realize she's dead, but he needs to follow the correct order. I try again with my entry from January 22, since this part is clear in my head. It's not confused at all:

8:29 A.M.
CHERRY CORDS WITH A DOG BARKING YELLOW FRENCH FRIES TALKS TO DAD ON STREET. SMOKING BLACK DUFFEL COAT MAN ARRIVES BUT I DON'T HEAR HIM SPEAK.
    CHERRY CORDS THREATENS TO KILL PARAKEETS USING A SHOTGUN. THE COLOR OF HIS TROUSERS, THE DULL RED, GRAINY VOICE, AND THE DOG GIVE ME CLUES—THIS MUST BE DAVID GILBERT FROM NUMBER 22.
    I DON'T KNOW THE COLOR OF BLACK DUFFEL COAT MAN'S VOICE. I DOUBLE-CHECK HIS IDENTITY LATER AND DAD SAYS IT WAS OLLIE WATKINS. I HAVEN'T SPOKEN TO HIM BEFORE. HE MOVED BACK TO THE STREET A COUPLE OF WEEKS AGO TO LOOK AFTER HIS MUM, LILY WATKINS, WHO IS DYING OF CANCER AT NUMBER 18.

I pause and wait for Rusty Chrome Orange to catch up, because this is the first sign a murder's going to happen on our street. But he's hitting his knee with a pen and has missed the vital clue.

Tap, tap, tap.

A light brown sound with flaky blue-black edges.

I ignore the irritating color and jump ahead by nine minutes.

8:38 A.M.
SET OFF FOR SCHOOL WITH DAD, WORRYING ABOUT DAVID GILBERT. HE'S LIVED ON OUR STREET AS LONG AS MRS. WATKINS. I ASK DAD WHY HE MENTIONED THE SHOTGUN. DAD SAYS HE'S A RETIRED GAMEKEEPER AND STILL GOES PHEASANT AND PARTRIDGE SHOOTING EVERY YEAR.

WHY OH WHY ISN'T SOMEONE TRYING TO STOP THE POTENTIAL MURDERER, DAVID GILBERT?

9:02 A.M.
ARRIVE AT SCHOOL. LATE. DAD TELLS ME NOT TO WORRY. HE'S SORRY. SHOULDN'T HAVE MENTIONED DAVID GILBERT'S HOBBY AND FORMER OCCUPATION. FORGET ABOUT IT.

9:06 A.M.
MUST SAVE PARAKEETS. CONCENTRATE ON POTENTIAL FUTURE MURDERER, DAVID GILBERT FROM NUMBER 22. DIAL 999 ON MY MOBILE PHONE IN TOILET AND REPORT DEATH THREAT.

9:08 A.M.
OPERATOR SAYS-

"Let's take a break there, Jasper," Rusty Chrome Orange interrupts. "I think we should cover this. I can see from our log, this was one of a number of 999 calls you've made to the police recently." He stops talking and starts again. "These calls weren't emergencies. Unnecessary 999 calls take up police resources, which could be used for proper emergencies. They waste police time."

Who is this idiot? He's wasting my time right now, when I could be watching over my parakeets. Maybe the actor Richard Chamberlain is brighter.

"Of course it was necessary. It was an emergency that day. Don't you see? I was reporting an imminent threat to life. One you should have taken more seriously if you'd wanted to stop a murder."

"Jasper—" Dad starts.

"That's OK." Rusty Chrome Orange holds up his hand like he's directing traffic.

I hope he's better at that than interviewing me about serious crimes.

"Your dad's already explained you suspect someone on your street has killed a few parakeets that nest in Miss Larkham's front garden."

"I *know* twelve parakeets are dead. Thirteen, if you count the baby parakeet, which died on March 24, but that was an accident. The other deaths were definitely deliberate."

Rusty Chrome Orange's head bounces up and down. "I understand you've found recent events hard to come to terms with."

"Yes," I confirm. "Murder upsets me."

"Stop it, Jasper!" Dad warns.

Rusty Chrome Orange stops cars again with his hand. "It's OK, Mr. Wishart. I can handle this."

He leans towards me and I almost fall off the cushions to escape from him.

"Don't worry, Jasper. We can certainly discuss your concerns about the death of the parakeets. But first, I'd like to talk about your friends: Bee Larkham and Lucas Drury."

Where did the Metropolitan Police find this man? Is he the last human survivor of a zombie apocalypse? Honestly, I thought this was what we were talking about before he changed the subject abruptly and brought up the massacre of my parakeets.

I should give him another chance, I suppose, even though he's stupid enough to think Lucas and me are friends. We've never been friends. We were Bee Larkham's friends. Her willing accomplices.

I try again to make him understand. "Ice blue crystals with glittery edges and jagged silver *icicles*." I emphasize the icicles because that's important. It's the one thing about Friday night that sticks in my mind. The rest is too blurry; too many blanks and curly question marks, but the icicles' jagged points remind me of the knife.

"You've told me that twice already, but I'm afraid artists' colors don't mean a lot to me," Rusty Chrome Orange says. "Look, I'm sorry if I've confused you. Let's be clear, none of the boys we're speaking to are in any trouble or danger. We're trying to establish a few background facts before we track down Miss Larkham and speak to her ourselves."

I'm attempting to tell him he'll never be able to speak to Bee Larkham, but he's not interested. His voice grates like nails down a blackboard.

"I want to go home."

"Please, Jasper. Concentrate. It's not for much longer." Dad's muddy ocher has a yellowish pleading tone.

"I can't do this. I'm too young. I can't do this. I'm too young."

I speak loudly, but Dad doesn't hear.

"Jasper's hardly an ideal witness in your investigation," he says. "There must be other boys at his school who can assist you? Boys who don't have as many special needs?"

I *need* to go home. That's my special need. My tummy's hurting. No one's listening. They never do. It's like I don't exist. Maybe I've melted away beneath my fingertips into nothing.

"I understand your concerns, Mr. Wishart. I'll raise them at our case meeting this week, but we need to look closer at Jasper's relationship with Miss Larkham and Lucas Drury. We believe he may have information that could assist our inquiries. He may have made notes of important times and dates in their alleged relationship."

"I doubt it."

A fluttering of pale lemon.

One of my notebooks protests against Dad's probing fingers.

"Look at this entry. The people going in and out of Bee's house have only basic details: Black Blazer enters, Pale Blue Coat leaves, et cetera. Jasper has no sense of what they look like, even if they're teenagers or adults. I doubt he'd be able to identify Lucas or any other boy."

Dad flicks through my notepad.

"Most of Jasper's entries don't even record people. They're his sightings of the parakeets nesting in Bee's tree and other birds. He's a keen ornithologist."

Rusty Chrome Orange's hand dips into a box and pulls out a steel blue notebook with a white rabbit on the front.

"That's not right," I say, surprised. "The rabbit doesn't belong there."

"OK, sorry," Rusty Chrome Orange says.

The white rabbit notebook returns to its hiding place in the box.

"Look at this notebook," Dad says, holding up another. "It's all about his colors. How's that interesting to you? To anyone?"

I want to scream and kick and flap.

Dad doesn't see my difference in a good, winning-the-*X-Factor* kind of way. He doesn't look for the colors we might have in common, only those that set us apart.

I need to hold on. I have to focus on the color I love most in the world: *cobalt blue.*

That's all I've got left of Mum—the color of her voice—but after Bee Larkham moved into our street the shade became diluted. It happened gradually and I never noticed until it was too late.

"Take me home!" I say. "Now! Now! Now!"

The color and ragged shape of my voice shocks me. It's usually cool blue, a lighter shade than Mum's cobalt blue. Today it looks strange. Is it actually a darker shade than Mum's? More grayish? I can't remember. I need to remember her. I want to paint her voice.

"I have to leave!"

It's too late. Her color's slipping from my grasp, sand through my fingertips. I plaster my hands to my eyes. I want to keep the cobalt blue, vivid, reassuring, behind my eyelids.

Rub, rub, rub.

I want her cardigan. I forgot to bring one of the buttons to rub because I was concentrating on making sure my boxes were correctly ordered.

I glance across the room and the back of my neck prickles. Rusty Chrome Orange told me the mirror was ornamental, like the ship picture on the far wall. He insisted there's no one behind it, but I can't trust his color.

Someone *is* standing behind the mirror, scrutinizing my face, my mannerisms, and laughing at my mix-ups. There are three strangers sitting on crimson sofas on this side of the mirror.

I don't recognize any of them.

The smallest, the one with dark blond hair who is rocking backwards and forwards, opens his mouth and screams.

Pale blue with violet-tinged vertical lines.

He vomits on the sofa.

Dad's silent. He doesn't flick on Radio 2 or tap his fingers on the steering wheel. I guess it's not surprising, considering the whole embarrassing vomit thing. He's still angry with me even though Rusty Chrome Orange said not to worry. Lots of kids throw up in that room; the police service employs someone to scrape up their sick. Dad says that's the deadbeat career I'll end up with if I don't work harder to control myself.

The sofa had definitely seen a lot of sick action. What does Rusty Chrome Orange expect when he hangs a trippy mirror on the wall? One minute you think you're alone and the next you're surrounded by strangers.

He showed me behind the mirror after I'd calmed down; it was a normal wall.

No hidden window into another room.

No hidden recording devices.

I attempt to block out the dark colors and harsh shapes of the lorries and cars rumbling past. Dad hasn't said a word since he turned on the engine, *marmalade orange with pithy yellow spikes.* Maybe he's not angry with me. Maybe he's thinking about Bee Larkham.

He knows we both need time to think about what's happened—me without distractions of unnecessary colors and shapes, him without me banging on about my colors and shapes.

I should try to make him feel better, considering everything he's done for me. He hasn't forced me to come out of my den over the last three days except to visit the police station. He rang my school yesterday and said I had a bad tummy ache. At least that wasn't a lie.

"Don't worry, Dad," I say finally. "I think we did it."

"We did what?" he asks, without glancing back.

"We got away with murder. Richard Chamberlain—like the actor—knows nothing."

Dad spits out a yellowish cat-puke word.

I hate swearing. He knows I hate swearing.

He's getting back at me for throwing up over Rusty Chrome Orange's sofa.

"I'm sorry, Jasper. I shouldn't have used that word. Have you understood anything I've told you? Is that what you think's happened?"

I screw my eyes tightly shut and curl into a ball beneath the seat belt.

Yes, I do. Think. That's What Happened Back There.

Despite his repeated warnings to keep quiet, I tried to confess. Honestly I did, because I'm very, very sorry about what happened in the kitchen at 20 Vincent Gardens. I deserve to be punished.

Rusty Chrome Orange wouldn't listen. I doubt he's going to start looking for Bee Larkham's body.

Which gives me time.

Time to protect the surviving parakeets. I need longer, around four days until the young begin to abandon the nests in Bee Larkham's oak tree and eaves and fly far, far away from the dangers lurking on our street.

But I can't leave.

I can't ignore the colors anymore.

I have to face the truth. I have to remember what happened the night I murdered Bee Larkham.

3

TUESDAY (BOTTLE GREEN)

Evening

Lying in bed that night, I trace my index finger over the ring-necked parakeet photographs in my *Encyclopedia of Birds*. The adult male parakeet is easily identifiable because of the pink-and-black ring around its neck. Females also have these rings, but they're similar shades of green to their bodies and harder to pick out.

Twelve deaths in total.

Bee Larkham didn't tell me how many males versus females were slaughtered before she died. I must start a new census before it's too late. Before the nests are abandoned.

After we got home from the police station, Dad didn't ask if I felt up to afternoon lessons. While he made cheese toasties and looked for painkillers for my tummy, I grabbed my half-empty bag of seed. I managed to get to the hallway before he stopped me.

Don't go over to Bee Larkham's house to feed the parakeets.

Promise?

Don't put pieces of apple on the ground in our front garden for the birds. It'll attract rats.

Promise?

No more 999 calls.

Promise?

It's a pinkish gray word with curly edges, which always gives me a strange, achy feeling inside my tummy—not on the outside, where it currently burns like dry ice and looks like a half-open mouth.

I agreed, but I had my fingers crossed behind my back, which means it didn't count. Someone has to feed the parakeets because Bee Larkham can't do it anymore.

Dad doesn't realize it yet, but Bee Larkham's house is already attempting to grab attention. The six bird feeders in her front garden have been empty since Friday night. She hasn't strung up any peanuts or put out plates of sliced apple and suet. Bee Larkham didn't turn on her music to full blast as usual. The parakeets weren't serenaded and the neighbors didn't complain about the noise. Earlier today, she didn't open her front door to the piano and guitar pupils who are allocated forty-five-minute slots after school from 4:00 P.M. onwards. The house has remained dark and silent since Friday—the Indigo Blue day Bee Larkham died.

I know these Important Facts because I barricaded myself in my bedroom after Dad stopped me leaving the house to feed the parakeets. At first, I concentrated on painting Mum's voice, but the shades were off. The colors were uncooperative and churlish. That's the way Dad describes me.

Difficult.

He said he was working from home for the rest of the day, but I could see the color of the television downstairs while I painted. Half an hour later, when Mum's true cobalt blue refused to reveal itself and the black-and-silver stripes of the TV became too distracting, I had abandoned my tubes of blue paints and stood at the window with my binoculars.

As usual, I had kept a record of all the relevant activity and used a fresh cornflower blue notebook. I started it especially because it seemed like the right thing to do—to keep my "after" notes separate and uncontaminated from the "before" notes.

3:35 P.M.-MALE PARAKEET FLIES INTO BRANCHES, BERRIES IN BEAK.
4:02 P.M.-BEE'S PIANO LESSON. KINGFISHER BLUE COAT BOY TWO
MINUTES LATE. RUNS UP PATH. LOOKS AT EMPTY BIRD FEEDERS.
BANGS CARDBOARD BOX COLOR ON DOOR. DOOR DOESN'T OPEN.
KINGFISHER BLUE COAT BOY WALKS DOWN STREET.
4:11 P.M.-FIVE YOUNG PARAKEETS TOGETHER ON BRANCH.

4:45 P.M.-BEE'S GUITAR LESSON. SEA GREEN COAT BOY TAPS LIGHTER, DUSTY BROWN. DOOR DOESN'T OPEN. SEA GREEN COAT BOY GETS BACK INTO BLACK CAR.

Bee Larkham also had an unexpected appointment that wasn't on her usual teaching schedule.

5:41 P.M.-DARK BLUE BASEBALL CAP MAN.

Bang, bang, bang.

"Open the door, Bee! We need to talk!" *Clouds of dirty brown with charcoal edges.*

I was tempted to lean out of my window and shout: *Go away and take your clouds with you!*

Of course, I couldn't. I was too afraid of the Dark Blue Baseball Cap Man. I wasn't sure if I'd seen him before, but I knew I didn't like his colors. Or his baseball cap.

I had scanned the tree with my binoculars. The parakeets remained hidden in the highest branches; even the youngest didn't draw attention by squawking noisily. *Clever birds.*

5:43 P.M.-DARK BLUE BASEBALL CAP MAN WALKS BACKWARDS DOWN PATH, STARING UP AT BEE'S BEDROOM WINDOW. TURNS AROUND-

The pen had fallen from my hand, making droplets of light, flinty brown on the green carpet. I dived into my den and buried myself beneath the blankets. I stayed in the dark, warm cocoon, running my fingers around the buttons on Mum's cardigan and smelling the rose scent.

Finally, I crawled out and peeped outside my window. The Dark Blue Baseball Cap Man had gone. 6:14 P.M. I know, because I had double-checked on both my watch and the bedside clock. It's important to be precise about the details.

I have to record the rest now, one hour and forty-two minutes later, at 7:56 P.M., otherwise I'll never be able to sleep, knowing my records are incomplete. I pick up the blue fountain pen I keep at the side of my bed and start the sentence again. It looks better that way, when my handwriting isn't panicking and attempting to run off the page. I write:

5:43 P.M.-DARK BLUE BASEBALL CAP MAN WALKS BACKWARDS DOWN PATH, STARING UP AT BEE'S BEDROOM WINDOW. TURNS AROUND AND SEES ME WATCHING HIM WITH BINOCULARS. HE STRIDES TOWARDS OUR HOUSE.
??????????????????????????????????????
6:14 P.M.-DARK BLUE BASEBALL CAP MAN GONE.

What happened while I hid for thirty-one minutes in my den? I can't answer the thirty-three question marks I've jotted down.

Did the Dark Blue Baseball Cap Man plan to confront me about my snooping then change his mind? I didn't hear Dad open the front door. I'd stuck my hands over my ears and sung Taylor Swift's "Bad Blood" loudly. Still, I'd have heard, wouldn't I? I'd have seen dark brown shapes, the rapping on our front door.

I'd have heard the color of voices.

I update my notes:

WHO WAS DARK BLUE BASEBALL CAP MAN AND WHAT DID HE WANT WITH BEE LARKHAM?

4

TUESDAY (BOTTLE GREEN)

Still That Evening

After updating my records, I push the notebook beneath my pillow and return to tracing my finger over the male parakeet photo. I don't want to think about the Dark Blue Baseball Cap Man. I may get nightmares again and they hurt my tummy even when I've taken Dad's painkillers.

I don't want to think about the blood either, but I can't help worrying. It hasn't gone away. Dad's probably stuffed the knife and my clothes from Friday night behind the lawn mower in the shed at the bottom of our garden. That's where he hides the sneaky contraband he thinks I don't know about—emergency packets of cigarettes even though he's supposed to have given up smoking.

"Everything OK in here?" *Muddy ocher.*

The encyclopedia tries to escape off my duvet. I manage to catch it in time, ramming my elbow on the pillow to protect my notes. Dad mustn't find out I'm continuing to make records; I'm keeping secrets. He won't like to hear about the things I'm remembering.

It's 7:59 P.M. Dad's come to say good night earlier than usual. A new episode of *Criminal Minds* must be about to begin on TV.

"It's been a tough day, but it's over now," he says. "I don't want you to get worked up about the police. I've spoken to D.C. Chamberlain this evening and taken care of everything. Bee's someone else's problem now, not ours."

I concentrate on the parakeet photos.

"What about her body?"

Dad sucks in his breath with smoky ocher wisps. "We've been

through this a million times. I sorted everything with Bee. You can stop worrying about her."

"But—"

"Look, I'm telling you she's not going to bother either of us again. I promise you."

Silence. *No color.*

"Jasper? Are you still with me?"

"Yeah. Still here." *Unfortunately.* I wish I wasn't. I wish I could be a parakeet snuggled deep in the nest in the oak tree over the road. I bet it's cozy. It used to be a woodpeckers' nest after the squirrels left, but the parakeets took over the old drey. They always force out other nesting birds like nuthatches, David Gilbert said.

"Jasper. Look at me and focus on my face. Concentrate on what I'm about to say."

Don't want to.

I drag my gaze away from the book in case Dad tries to take that away as well as the bag of seed. I pull his features into a concise picture inside my head—the blue-gray eyes, largish nose, and thin lips. I close my eyes and the image vanishes again like I'd never drawn it.

"Open your eyes, Jasper."

I do as I'm told and Dad reappears as if by magic. His voice helps. *Muddy ocher.*

"I've told you already, the police aren't going to find Bee's body because there's no body to find."

Now it's my turn to make a funny sucking-in color with my breath. It's a darker, steelier blue than before.

He's trying to distance us both from what happened in Bee Larkham's kitchen on Friday night. Maybe he thinks Rusty Chrome Orange has bugged my bedroom. He could have planted listening devices throughout the whole house. The police do that all the time on *Law & Order*.

I picture a dark van parked outside our house—two men inside, headphones clamped to their ears, listening to Dad and me talking, hoping we'll let slip something incriminating about Bee Larkham.

I have to stick to our story.

There is no body.

I repeat the words under my breath.

The police can't find Bee Larkham's body if they don't look for the body, and the police aren't looking for the body, dense Rusty Chrome Orange has proven that. He's trampled over the Hansel-and-Gretel-style trail of crumbs I left for him, never noticing they lead to the back door of Bee Larkham's house. They continue into her kitchen and stop abruptly.

I don't know where the crumbs reappear. Dad hasn't told me what happened after I fled the scene. Her body could rot for months before it's found.

If it's ever found.

There's no body to find.

"OK, Dad. If you're sure about this?"

"I am. Stay away from Bee's house and stop talking about her. I don't want to hear you mention her name again. I want you to forget about her and forget what happened between the two of you on Friday night. No good can come from talking about it."

I move my head up and down.

Dad's supposed to know best because he says he's older and wiser than me. The problem is, whatever Dad claims, it still feels wrong.

I pull out a photo from beneath the book on my bedside table. It's a new one. Not new, as in someone just took a picture of Mum, which would be impossible. She died when I was nine. I wasn't allowed to go to the funeral because Dad said I'd find it too upsetting. I haven't seen this photo before—not in the albums or in his bedside drawer. I found it at the back of the filing cabinet in his study.

I stare at the six people standing in a line. "Which one's Mum?"

"What?" Dad's checking his watch. I'm keeping him from important FBI business. The plots are complicated. He'll never catch up.

"Which one's my mum?" I repeat. "In this photo?"

"Let me see that."

I hold the picture up but don't let him take it off me. He might leave a smudgy fingerprint, which would ruin it.

"God, I haven't seen that photo in years. Where did you find it?"

"Er, um." I don't want to admit I've been rummaging in his filing cabinet again and the drawers in his study.

After the parakeets and painting, my next favorite hobby is rooting through all Dad's stuff when he's not around.

"It was stuck behind another photo in the album." It's only a small lie in the grand scheme of things.

Dad's eyebrows join together at the center. "Wow. This brings back memories. It's Nan's seventy-fifth birthday party."

Interesting, but he hasn't answered my question.

"Which woman is Mum?"

He sighs, *smooth light ocher button shapes.* "You honestly don't know?"

"I'm tired. I can't concentrate properly." It's that useful lie again, a trusty friend, like dusky pink number six.

"She's that one," he says, pointing. "At the far right of the photograph."

"She's the woman in the blue blouse with her arms around that boy's shoulders." I repeat it to myself to help memorize her position in the photo.

"*Your* shoulders. She's hugging *you*. You're both smiling at the camera."

I stare at the strangers' faces.

"Who's that?" I point at another woman, further along. She's also wearing a blue top, which is confusing.

"That was your nan. She passed away a month . . ." His muddy ocher voice trails away.

I finish the sentence for him. "A month after Mum died. Her heart stopped beating from the grief and shock of losing her only daughter."

Dad inhales sharply. "Yes." His word's a jagged arrow, whistling through the air.

I bat away his unprovoked attack. "She knew she couldn't replace Mum. That would have been impossible."

"Of course she couldn't replace Mum. You can't replace people like possessions. Life doesn't work like that, Jasper. You understand that, right?"

Deep down, he must know he's a liar, but I don't want to think about that now.

"What color was Mum's voice?" I say, changing the subject.

Dad checks his watch again. He should have pressed pause on the remote before he came up to say good night. He's missed six minutes and twenty-nine seconds of *Criminal Minds*. A serial killer has probably struck already.

"You know what color she was. It's the color you always say she was."

"Cobalt blue." I pinch my eyes shut, the way I did in the police station. It doesn't work. I open my eyes and stare at my paintings. I've lined them up under the windowsill, below my binoculars. They stare back accusingly.

"Mum's cobalt blue. That's what I want to remember about her. Shimmering ribbons of cobalt blue."

"That's her color," Dad says. "Blue."

"Was she? Was she definitely cobalt blue?"

His shoulders rise and fall. "I have no idea. When Mum spoke, I saw . . ."

"What?" I bite my lip, waiting. "What did you see?"

"Just Mum. No color. She looked normal to me. The way she looked normal to everyone else. Everyone apart from you, Jasper."

He turns away, but I can't let Mum's color go.

"I used to talk about Mum being cobalt blue when I was little?" I press. "I never mentioned another shade of blue? Like cerulean?"

"Let's not do this now. It's late. You're tired. I'm beat too."

He means he doesn't want to talk about my colors again. He wants me to pretend I see the world like he does, monochrome and muted. *Normal.*

"This is important. I have to know I'm right." I kick off the duvet, which is strangling my feet.

"What am I thinking? Of course she was cobalt blue." Dad's voice is light enough to be swept away by a gentle summer breeze. "Don't get het up about this before bedtime. You need to go to sleep. It's school tomorrow and I've got work. I can't take another day off. You have to stop thinking about Bee and start concentrating on school. Your stomach looks a lot better, but you need to get your head straight. OK?"

He comes back, leans down, and kisses my forehead. "Good night, Jasper."

Four large strides and Dad's at the door. He closes it to the usual gap of exactly three inches.

He's told yet another lie.

This isn't a good night. Far from it.

I wait until I hear the dark maroon creak of the leather armchair in the sitting room before I leap out of bed and snatch up the paintings of Mum's voice again.

Her exact shade of cobalt blue doesn't come ready-mixed in a tube. It has to be created. I've tried to change the tint by adding white and mixed in black to alter the shade, but everything I attempt is wrong.

If these pieces of art are misleading me, are my other paintings a series of lies too? I sift through the boxes in my wardrobe and retrieve all the paintings from the day Bee Larkham first arrived and onwards. There are seventy-seven in total, which I sort into categories: the parakeets; other birdsongs; Bee's music lessons; everyday sounds.

I'm not worried about these pictures. Their colors can't harm me.

Not like the voices, which I arrange into separate piles to study their colors in more detail: Bee Larkham. Dad. Lucas Drury. The neighbors.

All the main players.

I painted them to help remember their faces.

Some paintings refuse to get into order. The colors of conversations bleed into each other and transform into completely different hues.

That's when I finally see what was never clear before. It's where my problems began and it's why I can't get Mum's voice 100 percent right: I no longer know which voice colors are right and true, which are tricking me, and which are downright liars.

I need to start again. I'll never know what happened unless I get them right. Until I sort the good colors from the bad.

I wet a large brush and mix cadmium yellow with alizarin crimson paint on my palette.

I feel calmer and stronger. I'm in control. I'm going to paint this story from the beginning—from January 17—the day it began. My first painting is called *Blood Orange Attacks Brilliant Blue and Violet Circles on canvas.*

I will force the colors to tell the truth.

One brushstroke at a time.

5

January 17, 7:02 A.M.
Blood Orange Attacks Brilliant Blue and Violet Circles on canvas

The grating blood orange tinged with sickly pinks demanded my un-
divided attention as three magpies argued noisily with an unidentified
bird in the oak tree of number 20's overgrown front garden. The house
had been empty since we'd moved in ten months ago and various species of birds had staked claims to the trees and foliage.

I watched the magpies spitefully flutter and fight through the binoculars Dad had bought me for Christmas. Normally, I used them to
spot the birds making colors in Richmond Park during our Sunday afternoon walks: the lesser spotted woodpeckers, chiffchaffs, and jays. I
couldn't see what bird the magpies argued with, but I already respected
it. Although outnumbered, it bravely held its ground. The bird remained
hidden behind a branch, its voice color drowned out by new, spiky gin-
ger brown shapes.

A large blue van had pulled up outside the house, but the magpies
didn't break off from their vicious attack. A man wearing jeans and a
navy blue sweatshirt climbed out and walked up the path to the front
door. I thought just one man heaved furniture to and from the van, until
I saw two men in jeans and navy sweatshirts carrying a chest of drawers.

I didn't pay too much attention because two more magpies had
landed in the tree. The three bullies had called for backup.

Then, something extraordinary: a parakeet shrieked at the magpies—
brilliant blue and violet circles with jade cores—and soared into the sky.
Come back!

I opened my mouth to shout, but my throat was dry with excitement and no words came out. I'd only ever seen parakeets in Richmond Park, never here on my street.

I put my binoculars down and made a note of the parakeet in my light turquoise notebook, where I recorded all the birds I spotted in the park and on our street. I didn't bother with the magpies. I've always disliked their pushy colors.

Across the road, the men continued with their work. *Backwards and forwards.* They lugged mattresses and boxes out of the house and squeezed them into the back of the van.

I scanned the branches with my binoculars, but I couldn't spot the parakeet in the trees further down the road. The magpies had flown off too, proving the pointlessness of their territorial battle.

I continued to watch the tree, furious I may have missed another glimpse of the parakeet. When Dad told me it was time for school, I wouldn't budge from the window. He tried to pull me away, but I screamed until my nose bled down my chest. I didn't have a clean white shirt because Dad had forgotten to put a wash on again, so we agreed I could stay off school while he worked on a new app design in the study.

Long after the men's unpleasant-colored shouts and the sharp yellow spines of the van's revving engine had died away, the street remained strangely quiet. I didn't hear the color of a single chaffinch or sparrow, a car horn beeping or a door slamming.

Maybe I blocked out other noises as I stood guard at the window. I focused on the tree in the front garden of 20 Vincent Gardens, not the house, but I don't think anyone went in or out.

Nothing happened.

It was the calm before the storm; the whole street waited with bated breath for the parakeet to return.

That evening, 9:34 P.M.
Carnival of the Animals with a Touch of Muddy Ocher on canvas

The windows of 20 Vincent Gardens swung open and loud music poured out, like a long, windy snake trailing across the road and up to my bedroom, tap-tapping on the window. Tap-tapping on all the windows in the street.

I'm here. Notice me.

The colors arrived with a bang and drifted into each other's business, disrupting everything.

Some might call them a nuisance. They certainly did that night and in the weeks and months to come.

The glossy deep magenta cello; the dazzling bright electric dots of the piano, and the flute's light pink circles with flecks of crimson formally announced that someone new had arrived on the street.

A person as well as a parakeet. They wanted to be seen. They loved loud, bright music as much as me.

Later, much later, I discovered this glorious music was called *The Carnival of the Animals*. Fourteen movements by Camille Saint-Saëns, a French Romantic composer, who wrote music for animals: kangaroos, elephants, and tortoises. I loved the colors of "Aviary," birds of the jungle, the most, but that evening was the turn of the Royal Lion.

As soon as the colors started, I jumped off my bed and raced to the window, tearing open the curtains. A woman with long blond hair held a glass while she threw herself around the sitting room. She danced like me, not caring if anyone else watched. Not caring if she spilt her drink.

Whirling, twirling, she wrapped herself in a brightly colored shawl of shimmering musical colors, hugging it close to her body.

The colors overlapped and faded in and out of each other on a transparent screen in front of my eyes. If I reached out, it felt like I could almost touch them.

"Jasper! Turn it downnnnnnnnnn . . ."

The last word was long and drawn out because the sentence never finished, like a lot of Dad's sentences when he talks to me.

He walked towards me, but I couldn't turn around. The pulsating music pushed absolutely everything out of my mind. Our house could have burnt to the ground and I wouldn't have shifted voluntarily.

I thought it was the most perfect combination of colors I'd ever seen. I was wrong, of course. Much better was to come when the pandemonium of parakeets arrived. But I couldn't know that then.

I focused my binoculars on the house opposite. The colorful music had squeezed out most of the furniture from the sitting room. The sofa, a small table, and chairs were pushed up against the walls by the side of a piano. A green beanbag remained, along with an iPod on a stand.

I recognized the dark brown curtains and grayish white nets that usually hung at the windows folded neatly into squares and placed on the table. They'd been sacked, *made redundant*.

"Good God." Dad snatched the binoculars off me. "What will people think? You mustn't do that, Jasper. No one likes a spy."

I didn't bother to ask what people would think. I'd given up trying to guess the answer to that particular puzzle long ago.

Normally Dad's grabby hands would have outraged me—it's rude to snatch. That's one of the rules he's taught me. I didn't remind him because the depth of colors had transfixed me.

They dazzled against the whiteness of the woman's arms in the background as she waltzed around and around, her floral dressing gown flapping open as if she'd been caught in a sudden breeze.

I couldn't pull my gaze away to look at Dad.

He was about to explain what I'd done wrong when the music stopped.

"No! Wait!" I cried.

The colors vanished as fast as the parakeet from the oak tree. They didn't drift off or melt away. Gone. Like a TV switched off. But then . . .

A few minutes later, 9:39 P.M.
Martian Music and Warm, Buttery Toast on canvas

The woman must have heard my shout.

She darted across the room to the beanbag. Bigger, bolder, glittering neon sounds belted out from the iPod.

Martian music.

These colors are alien visitors that only I can understand—colors that people like Dad don't know exist. They don't look like they belong in the real world. They only exist in my head—impossible to describe, let alone paint.

Silver, emerald green, violet blue, and yellow simultaneously, but somehow not those colors at all.

"She likes her house music, doesn't she?" Dad said. "The neighbors *will* be thrilled."

It sounded like a question, but I had no answer. I didn't know who "she" was or what "she" was doing at 20 Vincent Gardens.

Dad's other choice of words was accurate for once. *I* was thrilled, along with all the neighbors. Not only did "she" like dancing and loud classical music but she loved Martian music even more.

I sensed we could be friends. *Great friends.*

"This won't go down well," he said. "She's already wound up David by parking directly outside his house."

"Who is she?" I asked. "Why doesn't she have any proper clothes? Why did the men take away her furniture in a van?"

Dad didn't answer. He watched her wild dancing, throwing her hair from side to side. I think he felt sorry for her because she couldn't afford furniture or curtains. She wore a slippery bright floral dressing gown, which kept wriggling down her shoulders and falling open at the waist. It felt wrong to look at her bare, alien-like skin, with or without binoculars.

This wasn't the elderly woman Dad said used to live here. This "she"—the Woman with No Name—didn't remind me of an old person. *At all.* I don't normally pay too much attention to hair, but hers was long and blond and swinging. She moved gracefully around the room, twirling like a ballet dancer or a composer, conducting an orchestra of color.

"Who is she?" I repeated.

"I don't know for sure," he replied. "Pauline Larkham died in a home a few months back. This woman could be a friend or a niece or something. Or maybe she's the long-lost daughter. I don't know her name. She'd be about the right age. David mentioned her a while ago. Said she never bothered to come back for Mrs. Larkham's funeral."

This was news to me. I didn't know the old woman who used to live over the road was called Pauline Larkham or that she'd died in a new home. Maybe she didn't like this one much.

"Well, which one is this woman? Is she a friend or a niece or a long-lost daughter who didn't come back for the funeral and doesn't have a name?"

Dad was infuriating. He didn't grasp the importance of getting the facts straight. I knew one woman couldn't be two or three people at the same time. She was either someone's friend *or* someone had lost her and needed help finding her again.

"I don't know, Jasper. Do you want me to ask her for you?" He fiddled with the strap of the binoculars, which made me itch to snatch them back before he scuffed the leather. "It would be neighborly of us to welcome her to our street, don't you think? To help her find her feet?"

I stared out of the window, confused. It was obvious where her feet were and she didn't need his help finding them. She flitted about on the tips of her toes.

I didn't want to point out the stupidity of his question. Instead of concentrating on her feet, he should have run out of our house and up the path to hers. I could have watched from the window because it was too soon to meet her in person. I hadn't had time to prepare for the conversation.

Too late!

A man walked up the path to 20 Vincent Gardens, wearing dark trousers and a dark top. I guessed he was a thrilled neighbor, welcoming the new arrival to our street.

He banged hard on the door. *Irregular circles of mahogany brown.*

The music stopped abruptly.

I instantly disliked this visitor. He'd prevented Dad from introducing himself to the Woman with No Name. Worse still, he'd disrupted her palette of colors.

"Uh-oh," Dad said.

"Uh-oh," I agreed; this man looked like bad news.

The Woman with No Name tied up her dressing gown. Hard. Like she was fastening a parcel at Christmas to deliver to the post office. Fifteen seconds later, she appeared at the front door. Her mouth opened wide as if she'd sat down in a dentist's chair. She took a step backwards, further away from the door. Maybe he wasn't a thrilled neighbor after all. I didn't like the way he'd made her mouth change into an O shape.

"Why is she walking backwards?" I asked. "Has he frightened her? Should we call the police?"

"No, Jasper. That's just Ollie Watkins from number eighteen. He came home last week to look after his mum. Mrs. Watkins is very poorly so I doubt you'll see much of him on the street."

"Are you sure the woman over there's OK?"

"Absolutely. Ollie doesn't mean her any harm. He's taken her by surprise, that's all. She probably wasn't expecting any visitors on her first night here."

Again, my hands longed to rip the binoculars back. Dad gripped them hard. He didn't want to let go, but they didn't belong to him. They were *mine*. I was about to point out this Important Fact when the man's hand lunged out. I gasped. I took a step back too, convinced he was about to grab the belt of the Woman with No Name.

"Don't worry, Jasper. He's not threatening her or anything like that. He wants to shake her hand. Remember, people do that when they're introducing themselves to each other for the first time. It's polite."

The woman didn't want to shake his hand. Perhaps she didn't know Dad's rules about what to do in social situations. She folded her arms around her body as if she needed to tie up the parcel even tighter, with especially strong brown vinyl tape, for the long journey ahead.

"Ha! That went well," Dad said.

"I know. It means we can't welcome her now that he's welcomed her." The crushing disappointment felt like a huge weight on my shoulders, drilling into the carpet, through the wooden floorboards, and plunging me into the sitting room below. The man had stolen our introduction.

"I doubt he's the welcoming committee," Dad said. "I mean, he probably has welcomed her to the street, to be polite. I don't think that's his real reason for visiting tonight."

"Why? What is it?" I stared at the mysterious man, Ollie Watkins, with the mysterious motive for wanting to jump the queue and meet the Woman with No Name before us.

"He probably wants to have a chat about the music. The noise passes right through the walls of terraced houses. He and his mum must be able to hear everything magnified in Technicolor."

That's when I felt another, strange emotion.

Jealousy. The word's a wishy-washy pickled onion shade.

Ollie Watkins and his mum didn't suffer an annoying dilution of color. It could absorb through the walls into their front room.

"Lucky, lucky them," I said.

Dad accidentally breathed in and out at the same time, making an ink-shaped blob of mustard and brown sauce.

"Not everyone appreciates loud house music like you, Jasper. I'm sure he's asking her to turn the volume down. It's a residential street, not Ibiza."

Why would Ollie Watkins and his mum want the colors to disappear? Ibiza sounded like a fun place to be.

The front door closed and the man walked back down the path again. He looked up and raised a hand at us. Dad raised his hand back, a secret gesture.

"You have to feel for Ollie," Dad said. "He's having a rough time with his mum. It won't be long now. She doesn't have much time left."

Dad was wrong yet again. I didn't feel anything at all for Ollie Watkins. I didn't know who he was, where he'd come from, or the color of his voice. I'd never seen him before—at least I didn't think I had. I didn't recognize his clothes.

All I knew for sure was that Ollie Watkins didn't like loud music and had stopped all the lovely colors.

That was a black mark in my book. Not pure black, but a dirty smudge of a color with traces of grainy gray that would deliberately stain anything it touched.

I tried to focus because I could feel myself getting distracted by the shades. Dad was right about one thing—the man walked along the pavement and up the path to the next-door house, 18 Vincent Gardens. This was definitely Ollie Watkins, going back to his mum, who didn't have much time left. *For something or other.*

"That's it, Jasper." Dad wrapped the strap around the binoculars. "Time for bed. It's school tomorrow. No more raves. No more excitement on our street tonight." He sounded as disappointed as me that the show was over.

I bit my lip and closed my eyes. I didn't want to let the Martian colors go; I could forget them in my sleep. My alarm clock would go off at 6:50 A.M. as normal, but I had to paint them straightaway.

I needn't have worried. The Martian music dramatically returned a few seconds later, a fraction quieter before it cranked up again. Louder. Louder than ever before.

My eyes flew open. The Woman with No Name was back in the sitting room, twirling, her dressing gown lifting and blowing as if the breeze had grown stronger.

I couldn't help myself. I knew Dad hated my dancing, but I flapped my arms and leapt about, swimming in the colors. I danced in solidarity with her, a perfect blending of shades.

Defiant colors that didn't care what anyone thought or said.

Dad didn't tell me off or demand I stop dancing as usual. He stood at the window, staring at the Technicolor rebellion.

"Here comes David Gilbert to complain about the noise too," he murmured. "It won't take him long to lay down the law. She'll regret moving in next door to him."

That evening's second visitor, David Gilbert, strode up the garden path. He came from the house on the other side, number 22. If I hadn't seen this and Dad hadn't given me his name, I'd have guessed Ollie Watkins was back. Wearing a hat.

"I don't think she'll turn the music down for Ollie Watkins or David Gilbert," I said. "I don't think she can. This music has to be played loud. The neighbors will get used to it."

There was a rolling, darkish ocher color as Dad chuckled to himself.

"I wouldn't want to take on David. I think he's going to have his hands full with this one. Whoever she is, Jasper, she's going to be a troublemaker."

"Really?"

She didn't look like a troublemaker to me. Troublemakers covered their faces with scarves and spray-painted graffiti on walls at weekends. They hung around street corners, aiming kicks and punches at anyone who strayed too close.

Dad didn't sound worried about the Woman with No Name or the fact she was transforming into a Troublemaker. He studied her through my binoculars even though *No One Likes a Spy.*

"Mmmmmm." *His voice was the color of warm, buttery toast.*

6

TUESDAY (BOTTLE GREEN)

Later That Evening

I line up my brushes by the bathroom sink. I don't want to alert Dad to the fact that I'm up at 11:47 P.M. I turn on the tap slowly, making a trickle of water.

Small circular clouds of kingfisher blue.

I love this color. It's happy, without a care in the world.

Shivers of excitement play trick or treat up my back, the way they do whenever I open a fresh tube of paint. I love gently squeezing the smooth tube. Too hard and the paint spurts out, wasting it; too little and it's impossible to tell a proper story from beginning to end.

A small dot of paint is always the best place to start. I can add to the splash of color and make it grow in size until it becomes the perfect amount. I've remembered enough for one night—how excited I was about seeing the mystery woman for the first time and how I longed for the right moment to meet her in person.

When the music eventually stopped that night, after a visit lasting three minutes and thirteen seconds from David Gilbert, I began planning for the day when I could meet our new neighbor. I had to memorize what she looked like (*long blond hair, not many clothes*) and come up with the perfect introduction.

Both these things were important. I didn't want her to think I was a stupid weirdo, like everyone else.

I had hope: *a tomato-ketchup-colored word.*

Hope she would get me. How couldn't she? She loved loud Martian music and dancing wildly. The only difference between us was I didn't like the cold and still don't. I only ever dance with my clothes on.

The same scarlet-in-a-squeezy-bottle color embraces me as I tiptoe back to my bedroom with damp paintbrushes, dabbed dry on an old hand towel. The TV in Dad's bedroom buzzes gray grainy lines, but tomato ketchup's in my head.

As soon as I climb into bed, I remember it's school tomorrow and popcorn yellow dread crawls under the duvet with me. It rudely refuses to budge, however hard I try to kick it out and replace it with tomato ketchup.

Dread's my usual unwelcome bed guest on Sunday nights, reminding me of the break-time gauntlet—waves of anonymous faces surging towards me along the corridors.

Some could turn out to be friendly, others will not. Good and bad aren't stamped on pupils' foreheads to help me sift through their identical uniforms.

This time it's different. Tomorrow's Wednesday (toothpaste white) and dread is a far harsher color because I have to face Lucas Drury again, for the first time since *IT* happened.

He was mad at me last week for my *Big, Dumb Mistake*. He's going to be even madder now the police are involved.

He'll yell shades of thorny peacock blue at me.

I jump out of bed and pull the curtains tighter together to get rid of the crack of light and the blurry purply black lines of a passing motorbike.

The windows of Bee Larkham's house stare reproachfully at me through the duck egg blue curtain fabric.

However many times I apologize, the panes of glass will never forgive me.

Lucas Drury won't either, if he finds out what I've done to Bee Larkham. I wish I could avoid him at school tomorrow, but I can't.

It's impossible to hide from someone you don't recognize.

7

WEDNESDAY
(TOOTHPASTE WHITE)

Morning

I say hello to the young parakeets through the crack in the curtains—our daily routine. I estimate these small birds are just over six weeks old. They usually caw playful shades of cornflower blue and buttercup yellow balloons back. Today, they preen their feathers and chatter among themselves. They're ignoring me because I didn't protect them. Only two in the tree and five adults—far, far fewer birds than usual. One's pecking at the empty feeder, willing it to spew out seed. It can't understand what's gone wrong.

I don't open my curtains completely in case Richard Chamberlain's eavesdropping men are watching me. I take a quick peek. Two little girls in blue uniforms run out of number 24: Molly and Sara live at this address. A woman chases after them—probably their mum, Cindy. She always dresses the girls in similar clothing—even at the weekends—so I never know which one's Molly and which one's Sara from up here.

I can't see any vans on our street. Or police cars. No detectives banging on the front door of Bee Larkham's house.

The house looks exactly the same as last night:

Deserted.

Reproachful.

Vengeful.

I keep the curtains shut and pull on my school uniform, carefully, making the least amount of movement possible. My tummy sings prickly stars. I'm not sure if I've got an infection, we still haven't seen a doctor. Dad's looking after me instead. That's safer.

A doctor would ask us both too many difficult questions.

I tuck one of Mum's buttons in my trouser pocket. I cut it off her cardigan and carry it around with me, which means she's never far away whenever I get stressed.

Next, I stick a five-pound note into my blazer pocket. It's dog-eared and torn, making my scalp itch, but I can't replace it. I have no pocket money left.

Without looking, I stick my hand under the bed. I know the exact spot to aim for. My fingers clasp around something cold and unforgiving: a disfigured china lady. I was too ashamed to return her to Bee Larkham two months ago and now it's far too late to own up.

I hide the broken ornament under my blazer—she's unable to return home but can't stay in my bedroom either. Not anymore. That wouldn't be right.

I check the forget-me-not blue blanket hangs down properly, sealing the entrance to my den, and pull the bedroom door shut. Twice. To make sure it's closed. Only then can I go downstairs.

Dad's frying bacon in the kitchen. He doesn't turn around. I use the chance to stuff the ornament into my school bag, next to the maths worksheets for Mrs. Thompson. They sting my fingers reproachfully. She gave them out last Thursday and I haven't got round to them yet.

Dad never cooks a fry-up on a school day. We only have bacon on Sunday mornings before football practice, which he makes me go to. I didn't play football this weekend or sit on the bench in Richmond Park, which is inscribed with Mum's name. Dad didn't go for a run. If anyone had watched *us*, they'd have realized the Wishart family routine—as well as Bee Larkham's—was off.

My legs want to bolt and not stop running until I'm covered in blankets in the corner of my bedroom.

"Grab a plate, Jasper. It's almost done. We both need a good breakfast today."

Good. It's that dumb word again.

A *good* night. A *good* breakfast. A *good* day. It's not a *good* color; it's brash yellow with a slushy dark purple core.

I don't want the bacon Dad forgot to fry on Sunday.

I pick up my favorite blue-and-white striped bowl and reach for the cereal packet.

Rustle, rustle. *Crinkly dashes of iceberg lettuce.*

The pieces drop into my bowl, up to the lip of the second stripe. I pour in the milk until it reaches the gray crack in the enamel. It's a delicate operation. Above the crack, the cereal is ruined and I have to throw it away and start again.

Dad doesn't turn around. He tuts light brown dots. "Have it your own way. All the more for me."

Using tongs, he picks up the bacon from the pan and piles the pieces onto his plate. He sits in his usual seat at the table, opposite me, which he says encourages me to practice eye contact and my conversational skills.

I will his chair to magically sprout wings, soar into the air, and fly out of the kitchen window.

I pick up my spoon and stare at the seven Cheerios floating like mini life rafts in the milk. My throat tightens. I drop five of the Cheerios back into the sea.

"You're feeling OK today, Jasper, because I've got meetings all day at work."

I can't detect a question mark in that sentence. It sounds like a statement.

"Yes." It's another lie, but it's what he wants to hear. I can say things I don't mean if it helps Dad. He does the same for me.

He's going through a lot. Like me. Except he doesn't have Mum's cardigan to rub.

"Good news." He breathes out. "I've got a late conference call. You'll need to let yourself in with the spare key."

I cough as a Cheerio catches in my throat. The cereal tastes wrong. Off somehow. The milk too. I check the labels in case Dad's accidentally bought the wrong brands. They're the same as usual. It must be me. *I'm different this morning.*

Will my classmates notice? Will the teachers? Has Dad?

"You can do that, right?" he asks. "It's not a problem, Jasper? The key's in the usual place. Under the flowerpot."

I push my bowl away, brandishing the spoon like a weapon.

Too much. I can't do this.

Three Cheerios are drowning. I can't make up my mind whether to save them or not. They should have learnt to swim, but it's wrong not to help. It'd be like failing to make a 999 call.

"Yes. I can do that. Right. It's not a problem."

It *is* a problem. *My problem.* I don't want to be alone here, watched by the windows in Bee Larkham's house.

"I meant what I said last night," he says, biting into the bacon. "We both need to move on. You're to stay away from Bee's house. You're not to go anywhere near it." He chews, making his jaw click baby pink. "I don't want to find out from one of the neighbors you've been feeding the parakeets after school. Do you understand? Her front garden's a no-go zone, along with the alley at the back."

The spoon drops from my hand, a red-tinged clattering. "Which neighbor would tell you I've fed the parakeets?" My five-pound note crackles as I shift uncomfortably in my seat. I'm glad he can't see the grayish mint color coming from my pocket, that he can't see any colors. He can't see me. Not properly, anyway.

Dad laughs deep, mellow ocher.

"I'm not going to say who my spies are on the street. That would blow their cover."

This is news to me and not of the good variety, like winning the lottery or discovering a cure for cancer. There are spies on our street, spies other than me who look out of their windows with binoculars and make notes about people. Spies other than the ones in the blacked-out van that forced Dad and me to speak in code about Bee Larkham's body.

Is David Gilbert the treacherous spy? I bet it's him.

I always thought David Gilbert was only observing the parakeets, waiting for the chance to kill them.

He tricked me into watching the wrong suspect all along.

"Yes, Dad. We both need to move on." Like the van from last night, which will probably return later to check up on me.

"Good boy. Now eat up. You need to build up your strength." He nudges the bowl towards me, spilling milk.

"I'm not hungry."

"I'll make some toast. Or I could defrost a bagel?"

I push my chair back and walk into the hall. Slowly, I ease my arms into my old winter coat. That's all I can find to wear.

"What is it, Son?"

Dad's followed me into the hall.

At first I think he's got X-ray vision and plans to frisk me for the five-pound note, but he ignores the blazer and peers under my shirt even though I tell him I've changed the dressing.

"It's looking better," he says. "Remember, don't show anyone your stomach and don't run around in the playground. It could make it a lot worse."

"I won't run unless someone's chasing me and I have to get away," I point out. "It's the only logical thing to do. I can't stand still and be caught. That would be madness."

"Jasper . . ." His eyes burn into my forehead.

"Yes?"

"We're going to get through this, I promise."

Dad's promised a lot lately. I won't hold him to this on top of everything else. I take a deep breath and open the front door. Dad can't take me to school this morning because he has a busy day at work. He walks to the end of the garden path. I know what he's doing—he's making sure I don't cross the road and walk past Bee Larkham's house. Worse still, I might go through the gate to refill the bird feeders. But I can't do that because he's hidden my bag of seed.

I check over my shoulder. Once he's gone back into the house, I break into a run that stabs my tummy. I have to get off this street ASAP. I'm careful after Dad's warning, making sure David Gilbert doesn't follow me along Vincent Gardens and right into Pembroke Avenue.

When I reach Harborne Street, 100 percent positive I'm alone, I pull out Bee Larkham's mutilated ornament. She was the first china lady to be smashed. I tried to glue her back together, but she hates the way she looks now: the blemished face, the ruined gown and broken parasol.

Pieces are missing.

She blames me.

I chuck her in a rubbish bin and hurry towards school.

I feel guilty, but it was the kindest thing to do.

I couldn't help her.

I couldn't make her whole again.

8

WEDNESDAY
(TOOTHPASTE WHITE)

Later That Morning

I'm safe in maths first period. Lucas Drury won't be able to find me in 312b. We don't share any lessons; he's in Year 11. I like this class even though it's tough. I'm behind because I haven't done my homework from last week. It's only a few pages, but it feels like they've covered a whole new syllabus.

Mrs. Thompson has promised to help me catch up. She's my favorite teacher by far. She has a lovely, dark navy blue voice and helpfully rotates her tops to match her black trousers on a strict regime. Today's Wednesday, which means it's the turn of the racing green blouse.

None of the other female teachers dress like her. They have a weird aversion to color and routine, like the male members of staff, who stick to gray, blue, or black suits.

Apart from her easy-to-identify appearance, the best thing about Mrs. Thompson is that she insists on a seating plan. Everyone has to sit in the same place, every single lesson. No discussion, no arguments.

I always sit at the back, fourth seat from the left, which means I've had the chance to memorize the backs of people's heads and place them in a grid.

It goes something like this:

Row 1, seat 3: Susie Taylor, dome-shaped skull, shoulder-length blond hair
Row 2, seat 4: Isaiah Hadad, acne scars on back of neck, short, black hair

Row 3, seat 1: Gemma Coben, dandruff on blazer, greasy, mousy
    blond hair
Row 3, seat 2: Aar Chandhoke, gray turban
Row 3, seat 3: Jeanne Boucher, black cornrows

It's like playing Guess Who? backwards, but unlike other games
this one I actually have a chance of winning. Unless my classmates
turn around, of course, or I'm asked to recognize the students in my
row, further along to my right. I can't remember what they look like. I
haven't been able to memorize their heads from this position.

"Algebraic equations can be written in the form y equals mx plus
c," Mrs. Thompson says. "We can draw a straight-line graph. Everyone
make a start before the bell and we'll pick up from here next time."

I've left my ruler at home and have to use the edge of my folder to
draw the line. It's wonky, the way I feel this morning.

An orange juice color erupts from row 2, seat 5: curly-red-haired
Lydia Tyler is arguing with Mrs. Thompson.

"That's God's honest truth, I swear," she says loudly.

"Make your mind up, Lydia." Mrs Thompson snaps like an angry
turtle. "I'd suggest you get your story straight before you earn another
detention this week."

Straight lines.

Straight stories.

Those are the best stories, but also the hardest to tell.

Will Lucas Drury tell the truth to Richard Chamberlain about Bee
Larkham? What has *he* told the police already? I don't understand how
they got involved. Lucas said he'd sorted everything last week.

*My dad believes my story. I think I've got away with it, but warn Bee
not to try and contact me. Got that, Jasper?*

"Are you feeling OK, Jasper? Do you want to borrow my ruler to
help you draw a proper straight line?"

Mrs. Thompson has finished her argument about straight stories with Lydia. I expect she won; you have to be smart to be a maths
teacher. She's standing beside my desk, staring down at my pathetic
graph. It curls up in shame under her hard gaze.

Silvery yellow dancing lines ring through the air.

"Saved by the bell," Mrs. Thompson says.

She's wrong. I haven't been saved at all. It's first break. I can't hide in her class any longer. I have to brave the corridors.

"Is everything all right, Jasper? You're trembling."

Mrs. Thompson and me are always on the same wavelength. She understands patterns and the need for order. I want to tell her there's a slit in my tummy, like a mouth. As I stand and push my chair back, it opens and closes again; the pain makes silver, pointy stars dance on my skin.

Don't tell anyone what you did to Bee Larkham.

Keep your mouth shut.

I leave the classroom without replying because I don't want to lie. I can do it to other people, but not to Mrs. Thompson. The truth is, I don't know how I got hurt. I can't remember what happened to my tummy. I only recall parts of Friday night. My brain's blocked out the rest. It's fuzzy and no distinct color becomes clear.

My best guess?

I accidentally slashed myself with the knife when I murdered Bee Larkham.

A hand stretches out from the bundle of black trousers and black blazers traveling down the corridor. It thrusts me against the wall. To be honest, I'm surprised I've made it this far without being caught.

The boy's face is indistinguishable from the Blazers accompanying him. I concentrate on his hand instead. It has a telephone number written in blue Biro on the skin. Would Lucas Drury's dad pick up if I rang it? Or his younger brother, Lee? Lee used to have electric guitar lessons with Bee Larkham. I enjoyed the range of his colors.

"Don't worry," I say. "I didn't tell the police anything about you and Bee yesterday, I promise. They only asked me about school friends and condoms."

"Are you having a laugh?" The boy's face looms at me, his voice a dark nutmeg brown. "Why are you talking about bees and condoms?"

I flinch at the spiky turmeric swearword that follows.

"I—I, don't know anything," I stutter.

The Biro hand doesn't belong to Lucas Drury; his voice is the wrong color. I have no idea who this is. His shade is similar to lots of boys' voices in this school. *Dull brown, not interesting enough to paint.*

I look up and down the corridor, hoping to see someone who isn't wearing a uniform. I draw a blank. I wish Mrs. Thompson would appear, but she's probably at her desk, marking books. She's hardworking like that and dead brainy and organized.

"Damn right you don't know anything." The boy's hand dives into my blazer pocket and pulls out my five-pound note. It's as if he knew exactly where to find it. How is that possible?

"That's mine," I whisper.

"Pardon?" Biro Hand's face looms closer. Pasty and acne-scarred.

I hadn't noticed those details before. I glance away, my eyes pierced by daggers. I need the money to buy seed from the pet shop for the parakeets, but I can't find my voice. I can't tell Biro Hand anything.

"Think of this as a retard tax. It's money you owe me for getting in my way." He pats my pockets down again. "Let's see. Nah. Thought not. As if you'd have condoms! You couldn't even get a pity shag."

He pockets my money, whistling yellow-brown spiraling lines, and returns to the Blazers. The gang has swelled in size. Their giggles and taunts are thunderclouds of dark gray with streaks of cabbage green.

I don't try to stop him. *No point.* He's twice my size and I won't be able to wrestle my money off him. Now what am I going to do? I've got less than half a bag of seed hidden somewhere at home and no more cash left. I can't borrow money from Dad; he'll ask what I want it for.

I can't admit I'm planning to disobey him and feed the parakeets. I'll head back to Bee Larkham's house while he's working late. Well, technically not her house. Her front garden. I'm not brave enough to go inside. I'm afraid of what I might find.

I walk down the corridor, away from Biro Hand. *Too slow.* Within seconds, he's caught up with me again. This time he puts his hand on my shoulder, making me jump. I don't look at him. His pockmarks make me think of moon craters. If I stare at them, they'll swallow me up and I won't be able to climb out again.

"I don't have another five-pound note," I say.

"I don't want your money, Jasper." He hisses whitish, almost translucent lines. I can't identify the true color. I look down at his right hand. It doesn't have a phone number written on it.

This isn't Biro Hand.

He whispers in my ear: "I want to know what you've told the police about me and Bee Larkham."

I don't need to study his face or ask him to raise his voice so I can see the genuine shade. *Lucas Drury.*

This is the boy at the center of everything, whose voice is blue teal when he's not whispering.

It was Bee Larkham's favorite color; she liked it far more than my cool blue.

Another uncomfortable truth that revealed itself to me when I least expected it.

"I know you were at the police station yesterday, Jasper," he says quietly. "There's no point denying it. My dad called a copper for an update. He said you came in for a chat with your dad."

Light Copper makes me laugh, but it could have been Rusty Chrome Orange.

"This isn't funny, you idiot. My dad's gone ballistic."

"You told me that last week. You said you were pulling the duvet over his eyes."

"The wool, you idiot, and he worked it out. He found my Facebook password and guessed *BL* is Bee Larkham. He got straight on to the police on Saturday morning and claimed Bee's a pedophile: a serial offender who preys on young boys. *My two sons. Probably more victims.* Those were his exact words."

I breathe out cool blue with white circles. "Was he right? Was Bee Larkham a pedophile who preyed on young boys including Lee?"

"Of course not," he says louder. "She was in love with me. No one else, but . . . Never mind about that now. We don't have time. We're both in trouble. We have to—"

The bluish green is cut off by shiny conker brown.

"Lucas! What are you doing? Hurry up!"

Lucas glances over his shoulder as two boys approach. They look like identical twins and must be his friends. They're not smiling. I'm not sure about Lucas. I haven't looked at him since he grabbed me. His hand drops from my shoulder as if it's been burnt.

"I have to go, Jasper. I'll meet you in the usual place at lunchtime, OK? We need to get our stories straight before either of us speaks to the police again. Deal?"

I move my head up and down because I agree with him about straight lines and straight stories.

Those are the stories we both need to tell, but I'm not a total fool. Lucas Drury has to go first. He owes me that after everything I had to do for him and Bee Larkham.

9

MUM'S STORY

This is Mum's straight story, not mine. I was only three or four. I sat with her in the back garden of our house in Plymouth on a late summer evening. Dad wasn't there. He was with the Royal Marines in Afghanistan or Iraq. I'm not sure which country. No matter. We didn't need him in the picture when we had each other.

The grass felt warm beneath our bare feet. I don't remember wriggling my toes in the sunburnt yellow grass, but that's what Mum said we both did while we played with my red pickup truck. It had come to rescue the battered yellow car that crashed into Mum's foot and overturned.

She told me this story over and over again because I was too young to remember it actually happening. She remembered it for me and it became our favorite bedtime story.

"What's that?" I asked.

"Do you mean the starlings? Look, they're the noisy birds in the tree over there."

"No. I don't mean those birds. They're reddish pink. I mean the other sound. Short blue lines."

A robin hopped out of the hedge, chirping. "That one," I exclaimed. "That's the color. A short blue line with moving lemon bits."

"You see colors?" Mum asked. "When you hear sounds?"

I said yes, of course I did. *Didn't everyone?*

Mum kissed the top of my head over and over again.

"Not everyone," she said, when we finally stopped laughing. "Not everyone understands the wonderful way we both see the color of sounds, Jasper. Which is a shame. A shame for them, not for us, because we share an amazing gift."

We ran through a list of things, starting with noises we could hear in the back garden, like a lawn mower, a car revving, an aeroplane passing overhead, and radio music blasting out of a neighbor's window. I told Mum the colors I saw for every sound.

Lawn mower: *shiny silver*
Car revving: *orange*
Aeroplane: *light, almost see-through green*
Radio: *pink*

We moved on to other things. The sound of the fan Mum had put in my bedroom to help keep me cool at night (gray and white with flashes of dark ink blue).

Dogs barking: *yellow or red*
Cats meowing: *soft violet blue*
Dad laughing: *a muddy, yellowish brown*
Kettle boiling: *silver and yellow bubbles*

We talked and talked about my colors and I'd never looked happier, Mum said. My smile stretched from ear to ear.

We could have chatted and played forever, but Mum said it was late and time to have a bath and get changed into my dinosaur pajamas.

"Roar!" I shouted. "What color are dinosaurs' roars?"

We both decided they were probably shades of purple because that's the colored sound my T-Rex made whenever you squeezed his tummy.

Mum swung me up and I settled into my favorite position on her hip.

"Thank you for letting me into your secret, Jasper," she said. "Now can I tell you something?"

"Yes!" I shouted. "T-Rex wants to hear too!"

"For me, the starlings are bluish green, the robin is bright yellow, and the kettle boiling is dark gray with orange bubbles." She kissed me quickly on my cheek. "Daddy doesn't like me talking about the colors, so when he gets home you don't need to tell him about yours either. He'll be sad he can't see the world like us, Jasper. Not everyone's built the same. We're the lucky ones."

She was right, but my luck eventually ran out. When Mum died, I lost the one person in my life who could see the world like me.

She loved hearing about my different hues and discovering how they compared to hers.

My colors miss her. They long to be shared with someone who appreciates them as much as I do. But I still have to talk about the shades I see—even to Dad—because a part of Mum lives on through them.

That's my straight story.

I hate the ending but I can't change it.

10

WEDNESDAY
(TOOTHPASTE WHITE)

Afternoon

"It's this way to the science lab, thicko." A hand grabs my collar and hauls me back as I dash out of the dining hall. "Lucas said you might make a run for it after lunch. He needs a word."

I'll call this boy X.

His evil twin, Y, hovers in the background in case I'm a secret ninja who can kick-box his way out of any situation.

I'm not and I can't.

They don't touch me—that would be assault. I'm silently escorted down the corridor. X walks in front and Y behind. No one notices I'm being taken against my will because I'm not screaming. That would be pointless. I doubt anyone would help. Not even the girls who walk past. *Especially them.* They'd probably laugh buttercup yellow.

When we reach the science lab, Y opens the door and pushes me inside. A boy's perched on the bench. His lip is cut and there's a pale green bruise on his cheek and a long, red mark on his hand.

It could be Lucas Drury. Lucas Drury after a fight with a tornado, which has messed up his hair, split his lip, and scratched his hand. I didn't look at his face when we spoke in the corridor earlier, so I can't know for sure this is the same boy. I don't say anything. It's safer that way.

"Did anyone follow you here?" His voice is quiet and low. A dark greenish blue color. *Lucas Drury's color.*

"Dunno," Y says. "Don't think so."

"Then what the hell are you looking at? Get out!" *Blue teal.*

It's definitely him.

X's and Y's shoulders go up and down. They slam the door behind them.

I shudder, not only at the unpleasant squashed beetle color of *hell* but also at the worrying development. I had no idea spies were here at school and on our street—people like David Gilbert who could search for damaging evidence about Bee Larkham and me.

Now I'm certain of one thing: there are spies everywhere.

I gaze at Lucas Drury. He's trembling with rage at what I've done, all the mistakes I've made. I rub Mum's button in my pocket harder as he strides towards me. He's going to pin me against the wall, like last time. Instinctively, I move backwards. My head is slap bang in the middle of the periodic table poster again. Thulium is on my left, rubidium on my right.

He stops in front of me. "Tell me everything."

I can't. I don't want to think about *that*. I turn my head to look at the poster.

Mendelevium, Nobelium, Ytterbium, Thulium.

"Hurry up, Jasper. Before someone finds us in here. We need to agree what we tell the police before they question us both again."

"Rusty Chrome Orange," I say, before I can stop myself.

"What?"

"He's a detective like the famous actor, Richard Chamberlain," I blurt out.

"Wait. You're confusing me. Who have you spoken to?"

"Richard Chamberlain wanted a First Account about Bee Larkham, whatever that means. He didn't explain."

"What did he ask you? Did he mention me?"

I reel off the weird questions about Year Eleven boys and Bee Larkham and condoms.

"What did you tell him?"

"I told him about the death of my parakeets and my neighbor David Gilbert, who's a bird killer, but he wasn't interested."

"Fuck the parakeets, Jasper."

My scalp prickles at the sharp, ugly-colored word.

"Jasper! Open your eyes! You can't pretend this isn't happening. This is real. For both of us."

I don't want to open my eyes. I don't want this to be real. I want to shut out the unpleasant colors.

"I'm not interested in the parakeets and neither are the police. Lee got scared last week and coughed up to Dad about other letters he found in our bedroom. He told him you pass me stuff at school and spy on Bee with binoculars. That makes you a *witness* in all this."

He's lying. I wasn't spying on Bee Larkham. I was watching her oak tree and making notes of who visited her house and the neighbors' houses. I thought that would help me build a case against David Gilbert.

"Please, Jasper. Concentrate. What did you tell the detective about Bee and me? Did you say you'd seen me visiting? Through your binoculars? That you'd seen us together, you know that time . . ."

Uncomfortable colors nudge around the corners of my brain. I daren't let them in. Finally, I open my eyes and avoid looking at Lucas. He sounds like Dad. I hate him for that.

Concentrate. Act normal. Don't flap your arms like a parakeet.

I can't ever tell him that while he broke a grown-up woman's heart into millions of tiny, sharp silver pieces, I did something far, far worse to her on Friday night.

Something unforgivable.

"I didn't tell Richard Chamberlain, like the actor, anything about you and Bee Larkham." *That's the truth.* "I warned him about the death threats to my parakeets, but my notebooks were out of order. He told me to stop making 999 calls. They waste police time. I screamed and threw up all over his sofa."

"Great. Well done. Whatever you're talking about. Weirdo."

He punches my arm, not hard. It doesn't make me cry. Not like when the bigger boys do it after school.

"Listen, Jasper. I'm denying absolutely everything. The police have nothing, just what Lee thinks he knows and Dad's suspicions after he found some messages and pics from Bee on Facebook. That's all. I'm sticking to my story that the note you delivered last week was a prank. It was a dumb girl at school having a laugh."

"A prank," I repeat.

"Yes, a prank. Bee didn't sign the letter with her name. She used initials as usual. They've got no proof unless you tell them she gave it to you. You haven't done that, have you, Jasper?"

"I didn't tell the detective anything."

"You see. No proof. Dad says the police haven't been able to get hold of Bee yet and they won't be able to analyze her handwriting because I ate the letter."

"You. Ate. The Letter."

"Yup. I tried to make a joke of it when Dad waved it in my face. I grabbed it off him, chewed it up, and washed it down with a glass of water before he could pull it out of my mouth. Dad didn't laugh." He touches his split lip. "He didn't find it funny when I refused to tell the police anything about Bee at the weekend."

"What did it taste like? The letter, I mean?"

"You're missing the point, Jasper. I ate it because I needed to get rid of the evidence. I had to protect Bee. Without that note, Dad has nothing concrete. Nothing that proves we were ever together."

"I'm glad you ate it." I'm still curious what it tasted like, but Lucas isn't interested in sharing the details.

"You have to deny everything too, if they speak to you again," he continues. "Say the note was from some random girl at school. You don't know her name. You found it stuffed in your bag or dropped on the pavement outside your house. Or talk gobbledygook about parakeets again to throw them off the scent. Just don't tell the police the truth about the letters or the time you . . ." He stops.

I can't look at him.

I don't want to think about *that*.

I want to be absorbed into the periodic table and create a chemical explosion that annihilates me, Lucas Drury and Bee Larkham, and all the putrid colors we created together.

Bang!

Bright flashing lights, splintering acrid yellows and oranges.

I rub Mum's button harder in my pocket.

"Look at me, Jasper," Lucas says. "You have to do this for me. You have to fix this mess because it's your fault. My dad's threatening Bee with all kinds of things. She could lose her job and go to prison, all because you cocked up. It's over between us, but she needs cash from her music lessons more than ever right now."

He curls up his fist. I close my eyes and wait for him to punch me. I deserve to be hit because I've hurt Bee Larkham far worse than his dad ever could. *I* deserve to go to prison. Maybe this is a trick and Lucas has already guessed what I've done.

Maybe her death is written all over my face.

Nothing happens.

I look up. Lucas has walked over to the window.

"Life sucks," he says, wiping a tear from his face. "I wish I could go back in time. I'd change everything."

I agree about time traveling. My life totally and utterly sucks too. I want him to stop crying. Then I'll pretend I never saw anything; he'll pretend he never did anything. We'll both pretend we haven't seen anything or done anything or know anything about each other.

Most important, we'll both pretend we don't know anything about Bee Larkham or what went horribly wrong last week.

"What am I going to do?" Lucas asks, running his hands over his face. "I don't know what to do."

I have absolutely no idea. If we were both in a swimming pool, I couldn't throw Lucas a life buoy because I'm drowning too. I can't help myself, let alone him.

Lucas doesn't wait for my nonexistent advice.

"I'm only fifteen. I can't do it. We were careful—we used protection." He looks back at me. "Do you think the baby's even mine?"

11

WEDNESDAY (TOOTHPASTE WHITE)

Still That Afternoon

We split up like an apple sliced down the middle, spitting out its shiny black pips. I suggested Lucas leave the science lab first to prevent any spies reporting our clandestine meeting to the head teacher or police. I waited four minutes, fourteen seconds before heading straight to medical, the only possible destination.

I vomited as soon as I walked in, before the nurse had time to stand up from behind her desk let alone pass a paper bowl. That made me feel even worse, because lately I've caused a lot of sick-clearing-up work for people.

I make trouble everywhere I go.

The nurse and me have been arguing for the last five minutes, her dark marigold versus my cool blue.

I can't let you go home alone. I have to get hold of your dad first.

Dad has an important meeting and can't be disturbed.

I'll try again.

He'll have his phone turned off. I have a key. I can let myself in. I do it all the time. I have neighbors who look out for me.

That's a lie, but it's highly unlikely she knows anyone who lives on my street.

I want to hide in my den, away from the accusing windows of Bee Larkham's house until the bright colors stabbing my brain no longer flash.

I need to get rid of the picture in my head of the baby inside Bee Larkham's tummy, the baby I killed when I killed Bee Larkham. I'd murdered two people that day, not one like I thought.

I can't tell the nurse, of course. She's trying Dad's number again. My voice is a higher pitch, a whiter, flakier blue.

My tummy hurts. I'll tell Dad to take me to the doctor's this evening. We'll get a sick note. Medicine. I promise.

Bad, horrible thoughts chase each other around my head and make me want to claw at the hole in my tummy while she leaves another message on Dad's mobile. I can't get a doctor's note to fix those feelings.

The truth is, I can't confess to the nurse. Words jam in my mouth; random thoughts are lodged in my brain. Some can't get out and others won't own up to what they've done and reveal their true colors.

She won't understand, how could she?

Her phone rings bubble-gum pink and she starts talking again.

I have to get to my den and burrow beneath the blankets. I'll close my eyes and wrap Mum's cardigan around me and pretend she's lying next to me, talking about the colors and shapes she sees when she listens to classical music alone at night while Dad's away.

The nurse puts the phone down. "Wait here, Jasper. A pupil with asthma needs me right away. I'll find a teaching assistant to stay with you until your dad gets here."

I do as I'm told.

The door closes and I wait twenty seconds.

I don't do as I'm told.

I run.

I don't know how I've managed to arrive here. Not at this terrible point in my life, aged thirteen years, four months, twenty-seven days, and five hours. I mean the physical journey to my house after running through the school gates—the roads crossed and people passed. I'm grateful my legs kept marching like soldiers rescuing a wounded comrade from behind enemy lines. They moved without me shouting orders.

They carried me all the way back here, to Pembroke Avenue, where I finally stop and catch my breath. My breath is short, ragged lines of sharp blue. My hand and knee throb. A quick inspection reveals I've torn my trousers. There's blood on my knee and a graze on my palm. My tummy's on fire with pointy silver stars.

I don't remember tripping and falling over. Or standing up. Or running again.

It doesn't matter though, because I'm almost home. I'm holding my button; I didn't drop it when I fell. I turn the corner into Vincent Gardens and spot it immediately: the police car parked outside Bee Larkham's house.

My legs grind to a halt, abandoning the rescue mission. They can't go any further. It's too much to ask of any soldier, even a Royal Marine.

Surrender.

That's what my legs silently scream at me.

Give yourself up without a fight.

Dad once shouted that order at an enemy soldier.

I lean against a lamppost to help gather my strength and set off again on my fateful expedition. It's going to end a few meters away, with the blond ponytail policewoman standing next to the car. I stagger towards her.

She doesn't realize it yet, but she's going to solve the mystery of why no one can find Bee Larkham.

Blond Ponytail Policewoman doesn't see me approach; she's talking into her radio, probably checking in with Richard Chamberlain. Giving him a rundown on the situation. Another police officer strides up the path to Bee Larkham's front door and knocks loudly.

"Miss Larkham. It's the police. Are you there? Open up, please. We urgently need to talk to you."

Behind the front door is a hallway, painted cornflower blue, with overflowing coat pegs; a black suitcase, which Bee said she'd packed full of sparkly clothes especially for the hens; and a "who invited you?" mat.

"Erm. Hi, Jasper." A man appears in front of me, blocking my path with his custard yellow words. He drops a cigarette, stubbing it out with a black suede shoe. "I've seen you out and about with your dad. Do you know who I am?"

My throat constricts. I gag. This man's in serious danger of becoming collateral vomit damage if he doesn't get out of my way. I try to skirt around him, but he moves again.

"Are you feeling all right? You're as white as a sheet."

That's not remotely possible. I can't look like stretched cotton material.

His hand reaches out. I don't know what he's going to do with it. I shrink away. He could be planning to attack me.

I glance at him again. He's probably a plainclothes detective, working with the two police officers in uniform. They've come for me while Dad's at work, which is sneaky. I wonder if a lawyer from one of Dad's TV shows would shout: *Inadmissible!*

"Did Richard Chamberlain send you?" I ask.

"Who?"

"Did he send you here to arrest me?"

"What? No. Don't you recognize me?"

I move my head from side to side to signal *no* because I don't know anyone with a custard yellow voice who wears black suede shoes and distinctive red and black spotty socks.

"Sorry, we haven't been properly introduced. I'm Ollie Watkins. I'm staying over the road while I sort through my mum's stuff and sell her house."

He points to the house with a large, ornate knocker in the shape of an owl on the door.

"I saw you and your dad on the street a few months ago when David complained to Bee about the noise of the parakeets," he says. "You probably won't remember—I haven't got to know many of the neighbors. I've been a bit out of it."

I do remember. This is Ollie Watkins who doesn't like loud music or Ibiza and doesn't get out much because he's been nursing his terminally ill mum, Lily Watkins. She lived at number 18 and was friends with Bee Larkham's mum, Pauline, at number 20.

I haven't seen anyone go in or out of number 18 for ages, but I know someone's still there because the lights go on and off. Mrs. Watkins is dead now so maybe that's why Ollie Watkins has been allowed out again.

I saw the hearse parked outside 18 Vincent Gardens eleven days ago, filled with white and delicate pink flowers. Not my favorite colors. I didn't pay too much attention because that was the day I saw the baby parakeets up close for the first time.

"My mum died of cancer," I tell him. "She was cobalt blue. At least I think she was. That's what Dad says I remember. I'm not sure he's telling the absolute truth about that."

About anything.

"I'm sorry," Ollie Watkins says. "Your dad told me."

"About my mum's color? That it was cobalt blue? Is that what he said? For definite?"

"No, I don't know anything about that. I meant we were talking about your mum's death. He was kind when my mum passed away. It's tough when you lose your mum, whatever age you are."

"Kind?"

"He was helpful, too, you know, with the logistics of death: arranging the paperwork and the funeral notice in the local paper. He'd done it before, of course, whereas I didn't have a clue where to start."

The logistics of death.

I've never heard it explained that way.

"I'm not allowed to go to funerals. I might upset people and that would be bad. For them."

He coughs. "Excuse me."

"Smoking makes you cough."

"Actually, I had a chest infection a few months ago. Hopefully, it's not coming back. But you're right, Jasper. I should give up smoking. I started again when I came over to look after Mum. Stress and all that."

"Smoking causes cancer," I point out. "That killed your mum. Cancer will probably kill you too."

The man doesn't say anything.

I walk away. His silence means the conversation is over and I don't need to act normal anymore.

Blond Ponytail Policewoman no longer stands on the pavement, waiting to arrest me. She's back inside the car, sitting in the driver's seat. The policeman climbs in next to her and shuts the door.

Bang. *A dark brown oval with layers of gray.*

The engine revs orange and yellow spears.

I walk faster. I have to stop them. Dad's wrong about this. He's wrong about everything. I can't forget. I can't pretend it hasn't happened. I have to confess. I have to tell the police what I've done.

It's the only way. I can't carry on like this.

"Jasper."

I turn around. This man is wearing black suede shoes, red and black spotty socks and has a custard yellow voice. It's Ollie Watkins from number 18. I'll make a note of those details in my notebook to help me remember him.

"Is something wrong?" he asks. "Should I call your dad? Shouldn't you be at school?"

"No!"

The police car pulls away. I've missed my chance, but there has to be another opportunity to confess. Rusty Chrome Orange will send the car back. Today. Or maybe tomorrow. He'll figure out what I've done, won't he? Eventually.

"You're friendly with Bee, aren't you?" Ollie Watkins asks.

That's an impossible question to answer. I don't open my mouth. I rub the button between my fingers instead.

One, two, three, four, five times.

"Do you know what the police want with her? It's the fourth time they've called at her house since the weekend."

I step away again because his clothes need washing. The stale tobacco smell makes my tummy hurt.

"I wonder what she's done this time," he says.

My head's shaking hard. I may take off like Dumbo and soar over the houses. I'll fly far away from here, leading the pandemonium of parakeets. I'm sure they'll follow me. They won't want to be left here, where it's hard to know which people to trust.

"The police knocked on *my* door this morning while I was clearing out Mum's loft and asked if I knew where she was."

He likes to talk. *A lot.* He's stopping me from reaching my den. I can't be rude. I can't draw attention to myself. I have to act normal for a few more minutes.

"They've knocked on the doors of several houses along this street. David's too." Why won't he stop talking? Maybe he's lonely after his mum died. Like me.

"The policewoman wouldn't tell *him* what she wanted with Bee either, but we both think it's about the loud music. I told her I thought Bee must have gone away. The house was quiet all weekend. I reckon she'll be slapped with that noise abatement order David's been threatening when she gets back."

Slapped. I don't like the way the fizzy lemon sherbet word rolls around his tongue. I change the subject.

"Hens are female chickens. Did you know chickens have as good memories as elephants? They can distinguish a face from more than one hundred other chickens. Except I'm not sure it's technically correct to say a chicken has a face. Do you know?"

"I've no idea," Custard Yellow admits. "I hear you've got a good memory for facts and recognizing voices, not so much for faces. Is that right?"

"Who told you that?"

"David. He was talking to your dad at the party Bee threw to get to know the neighbors. Do you remember? I left early to look after Mum, but it was quite a raucous night. David was a tad worse for wear afterwards. So were a lot of people, I hear."

I shudder. That's when Dad . . .

I force the horrible picture out of my head. The party's high up on the list of things I don't want to paint, after Friday night. It's not in order anyway. There are other pictures to re-create before that. My fingers itch at the thought of my paints, impatiently waiting for me in my bedroom. Maybe I'll be brave and use them instead of crawling inside my den.

"The Martian music vanished and Bee Larkham never fed the parakeets."

"At the party?" he asks.

"Over the weekend. No Martian music. All the bird feeders are empty. No peanuts or plates of apple and suet."

"Martian music? You're right. It actually sounds like aliens are rattling the plates on Mum's dresser when she turns up the volume to full blast. Mum would beg me to do something about it because she couldn't get out of bed to ask Bee herself."

I suck in my breath as he swears a norovirus vomit color about the music.

"Sorry. I'm not used to being around kids. I don't have any of my own. No nieces or nephews either."

My tummy spits silver stars. "I have to go."

"Wait a minute, Jasper. You're right about the parakeets. I hadn't noticed. Bee hasn't refilled the bird feeders. She's definitely away. I'll tell the police if they come back again."

"I'm sorry."

It's my fault the parakeets have no food and a dozen died. It's my fault a baby's dead. I have no idea how to start making amends for everything I've done.

"You feel sorry for the birds?" Custard Yellow asks. "Of course, I forgot. You're a bird lover, like me. I've seen you help Bee top up the feeders. Quite the young ornithologist, aren't you? I was the same at your age."

I don't want to think about Bee Larkham, the parakeets, and me. I don't like that triangle. I block her out of the picture and focus on the parakeets and me instead.

"I have half a bag of seed left, but Dad says I must stay away from Bee Larkham's house," I say. "She's a troublemaker and a silly little tart and a basket case. I'm not allowed to touch the feeders. He has spies on the street. They'll tell him if I refill them."

"Ha, let me guess. David? Right?"

"His favorite hobby is shooting pheasants and partridges. Bang, bang, bang."

"Well, he's out walking his dog. I chatted to him after the police came around. He's knocked on Bee's door too today. She's in demand this morning."

I bite my lip and stare at the pavement.

"Are you thinking what I'm thinking?" Custard Yellow asks.

"Why can't bird-killer David Gilbert leave Bee Larkham alone?"

She hated his visits. I heard her tell him to go away and never come back on February 13. He'd turned up the day before Valentine's Day with a bunch of flowers while I studied the parakeets from her bedroom window. She didn't want the flowers.

I should have called the police that day. Before it was too late.

I watch the starlings arguing in a tree further down the street, attempting to get my attention with their coral pink trills. Their colors can never compete with the parakeets. They should give up. I'm not going to paint them.

"I meant your dad didn't ban *me* from feeding the parakeets, did he? Bird lovers like us have to stick together," he says.

I wonder what he means. Sticking together sounds permanent, like using superstrength glue, yet I don't know anything about this man apart from the fact we're both bird lovers and lonely and our mums died of cancer.

I don't want to argue with him. My tummy, knee, and hand hurt. I want to go home.

"Why don't you give the bag of seed to me and I'll feed them for you? That way you won't be doing anything wrong. You won't get into trouble with your dad."

I think about this for seventeen seconds. "What about the men in the van? Will they tell my dad?"

"What van?" Custard Yellow looks up and down the street.

"I'll find the seed," I say, ignoring the question. The men in the van are only interested in me, but it's best he doesn't draw attention to himself. "Do you promise you won't tell Dad? Or David Gilbert?"

"Cross my heart and hope to die."

He doesn't mean that. No one ever does.

I want to tell him enough people have died on our street.

I don't.

I say nothing at all. It's far safer that way.

We cross the road in silence and walk over to my house. Custard Yellow stays on the pavement, by the gate, as I tip up the large marble flowerpot and retrieve my key. I let go before it smashes down and crushes my fingers.

After letting myself in, I concentrate on looking for the bird seed before I get distracted and forget what I'm supposed to do.

I find the bag in the kitchen cupboard, behind the cereal packets. Dad's never any good at hiding things. Maybe they didn't teach that skill in the Royal Marines. I run out the door and down the path. I thrust the bag into the man's hands and dash back into the house, slamming the door.

From the sitting room window, I watch Custard Yellow cross the road, bag swinging in his right hand. He pushes open the gate to Bee Larkham's house and stops, looking over his shoulder. A man walks towards him. His dog barks. There's only one man on this street with cherry cords, a brown flat cap, and a dog that barks yellow French fries.

My hand dives into my pocket and finds Mum's button.

Rub, rub, rub.

This must be bird-killer David Gilbert—out walking his dog and back sooner than expected. He's outside 20 Vincent Gardens again. He's caught a fellow bird lover. He has a shotgun and he's threatened to use it before. He threatened Bee Larkham.

Run away from bird-killer David Gilbert!

Custard Yellow doesn't move. He can't. He's being kidnapped. He must know about the gun and doesn't want to risk making a run for it. He manages to hide the bag of bird seed behind his back before he's frog-marched away, like I was by X and Y at school. They walk up the path of the house next door.

It's 22 Vincent Gardens, David Gilbert's house. I was right about the man with the dog. His hand's on Custard Yellow's shoulder as they enter the house. He's forcing him inside, whether he wants to go or not, the way I was pushed into the science lab.

No one helped me.

No one's here to help Custard Yellow. The street's empty.

No eyewitnesses, except me.

David Gilbert will punish him for trying to feed my parakeets. I'm afraid, extremely afraid. I need to act. Someone's in danger, the type of terrible danger you can't ignore.

I don't listen to Dad's voice in my head, ordering me not to draw attention to myself, to what we've both done.

I ignore Rusty Chrome Orange's voice in my head, which tells me to stop making unnecessary emergency calls.

I ignore the call of my den, my paints, and the pain in my tummy, which is getting louder and louder and brighter and brighter like a silvery hot spiky star.

I grab my phone and dial 999. I tell the operator I need the police, not the fire service, because I haven't seen flames. *Not yet, anyway.*

"Last week a horrible murder happened on our street and now a man's been kidnapped," I tell the woman in the control center. "He's been taken against his will into a house. He's in great danger."

I give her David Gilbert's address. She asks a lot of irrelevant details about me: Why am I ringing from home? Why aren't I at school? Have I rung 999 before? Where are my parents? Do they know I'm at home alone?

She should question me about the kidnapping. She should demand info about David Gilbert. He's the true villain in this painting.

"Richard Chamberlain, like the actor, knows me," I say. "He told me to stop ringing 999, but he can't expect me to ignore another person in terrible danger on this street. This is an absolute emergency." I repeat myself, in case she didn't hear the first time. "There's been a kidnapping, which shouldn't be confused with a murder."

I hang up the phone and wait by the window for the police. They need to hurry. The parakeets are shrieking green and peacock blue cut glass in Bee Larkham's oak tree.

They're scared, like me.

12

WEDNESDAY
(TOOTHPASTE WHITE)

Still That Afternoon

The police car doesn't screech to a halt with its siren blaring bright yellow and pink zigzags outside David Gilbert's house. The driver slowly reverses into a parking space. A blond woman in a black uniform climbs out, followed by a man. He opens his mouth wide and stretches his arms above his head. To be honest, they're taking this emergency at a frighteningly leisurely pace.

The policewoman could be the one I saw outside Bee Larkham's house earlier. I'm not sure. She walks up the path (*why isn't she running?*) and knocks dark brown shapes on the front door. After thirty-one seconds, the door opens. A man appears, they talk for forty-four seconds, and she goes inside. Her colleague waits by the car.

I'm not an expert in hostage situations, but shouldn't she be more careful? She didn't even have her weapon drawn (*if she's even carrying one*) and she's alone in a stranger's house, which isn't a good idea. People have a habit of turning on you when you least expect it. Her colleague can't help. His finger's stuck inside his left nostril.

After three minutes and two seconds, the policewoman steps out of the house with two strangers. They all walk down the path and stop on the pavement, next to the second police officer. Their faces turn and look in my direction.

Why isn't the man in cherry cords wearing handcuffs?

David Gilbert should be locked up in prison. That's where he belongs.

They walk towards my house. I don't like this. Why are they coming here when they should be going to the police station? I back away from the window. I can't hide. There's no point. They know I'm here. I called 999 on my mobile. Not because I wanted to, because I *had* to.

No one else stepped in to help.

I'm a reluctant witness, a reluctant helper—the roles I'm used to playing.

One member of this group knocks blobs of light brown with streaks of bitter dark chocolate. I can't be sure which one, because I've moved far away from the window. I'm hiding behind the front door, counting my teeth with my tongue.

"Hello, Jasper," the policewoman says in viridian blue when I've finished my teeth count and opened the door. "My name is P.C. Janet Carter and this is my colleague, P.C. Mark Teedle. I think you recognize your neighbors."

She gestures to the two men standing behind her. Obviously, she couldn't be further from the truth if she tried, but I have useful clues to help me. One man is wearing cherry cords and has come from David Gilbert's house. His dog is barking angry yellow French fries at being left alone in 22 Vincent Gardens. The other guy has black suede shoes, red and black spotty socks, and is clutching half a bag of bird seed.

They're the kidnapper and his hostage.

The policewoman glances at the men behind her. "We wanted to let you know everything's OK," she says. "There hasn't been a kidnapping or a murder. Your neighbor Mr. Watkins wasn't forced into Mr. Gilbert's house. He was paying a friendly visit."

"It's true," Custard Yellow says. "I was about to refill the bird feeders when David asked if I could help shift a piece of furniture in his kitchen. It was too heavy for him to do alone."

I'm not entirely certain about this turn of events. It's unexpected and I don't like unexpected. It's a waxy, Crayola orange word.

"He had his hand on your shoulder," I point out, taking a step backwards. "Even X and Y didn't do that to me earlier. They stood one in front and one behind, but they didn't touch me because that would have been assault and they'd have been expelled."

"I went with him willingly, Jasper. It wasn't a problem. I don't mind helping out someone who's in trouble. It's what neighbors do for each other on this street. That's what Mum always said."

I feel a jab of pain in my tummy and the back of my neck is cactus prickly.

"You'd help a neighbor even if you knew he was a serial killer or had helped a serial killer?" I ask.

The policewoman's mouth widens into an O shape, the way Bee's did on her first night here. I guess she's as curious as me to know the answer.

David Gilbert looks at the police officers. "Do you see what I mean? These wild accusations have to stop. The lad's gone too far this time. He's a total basket case."

Like Bee Larkham.

That's how he described her. When she was alive.

"You're a bird killer," I clarify, because that's only fair as he doesn't have a defense lawyer with him. "I didn't accuse you of killing Bee Larkham."

"I should think not!" he says loudly. "What's he going on about? What does any of this have to do with Beatrice? She's going to have a lot to answer for when she finally bloody well shows up again." He directs his grainy red words at the two uniformed police officers. "I want something done about him. This is victimization. He makes slanderous accusations about me *all the time*. I have witnesses like Ollie here, who'll back me up. Isn't that correct?"

The man standing next to him moves his head and arm. I'm not sure what the gesture means. Is he silently signaling he will back David Gilbert up or is he refusing to? It's hard to tell.

Instead, I concentrate on *victimization*. It's an interesting color, almost translucent with a slight violet hint.

The word builds on the singular *victim*. You can turn it around and around in your head to mean different things. Perhaps that's not simple to understand either, who the victim is supposed to be.

"We can deal with this from here on, sir," P.C. Carter says. "Perhaps you could both go home and we'll have a chat with Jasper alone?"

Cherry Cords stalks back to his house, to Yellow French Fries, but the other man, Custard Yellow, doesn't move.

"I can stay with him if you want, since his dad doesn't seem to be around." His body shifts in my direction. "Would you like that, Jasper?"

"Bee Larkham hasn't fed the parakeets since Friday. The bird feeders have been empty all weekend."

The policewoman turns to him. "It's best if you leave, sir. We'll call on you if we need any help."

"If you're sure."

He doesn't move, which is annoying.

"You can refill the feeders with the bag of seed I gave you, but you'll have to buy more. You'll need to keep feeding the parakeets from now on. Twice a day. Also plates of apple and suet. Please don't forget."

"Of course. Whatever you say." He strides away, bag swinging against his thigh.

"Can we talk, Jasper?" P.C. Carter asks.

"In one minute or maybe ninety seconds." I watch as Custard Yellow returns to his original mission. The plastic bag billows in the breeze as he turns it upside down and empties the seed into the feeders. There's not enough to go around all six, but at least three have been half topped up.

Job done.

Custard Yellow sticks his thumb in the air and walks back to his mum's house.

"I'm ready to go to the police station now," I say, turning to the policewoman. "I have to tell you everything that's happened. I want to confess."

"No need for that." She talks in small viridian blue staccato sentences. "We can talk here. Can we come inside? It's nothing to worry about. You should have someone with you. You're on your own, right? Is there someone you want to be here?"

"I want my mum. She's the only person I want right now."

"That's OK. Is she at work? We can call her for you. Have you got her telephone number to hand?"

"You can't call her. She's cobalt blue, but the color's fading." I burst into tears. I can't help myself. Truly, I can't. "That's all Bee Larkham's fault. She diluted Mum's color for Dad, mainly Dad, but me too because I didn't realize what was happening. By the time I noticed it was too late to do anything about it and I'd lost her."

"It's all right, Jasper. Don't get upset. I'm sorry I upset you. How can we get hold of her?"

"I don't know how to bring her back. I don't know how to bring anyone back from the dead."

"Jasper—"

"I want to bring her back, the baby too. I can't! I don't know where the bodies are. Please help me! Help me! I can't do this. I'm too young. I want to get out of here."

Her face looms towards me. Then another. I don't recognize either. A man's mouthing loud words and unpleasant colors at me, but I don't know what they are or who he is. I don't want to study the shades in detail, because I know I'll hate them. I've blocked them out.

His mouth is thin and red, like a gash. It's opening and closing.

I see ice blue crystals with glittery edges and jagged silver icicles again.

They're going to hurt me. Hurt my tummy.

I scream and scream until the icicles smash and fall away into tiny pieces.

I see nothing.

Nothing except blackness, all around me, pulling me down.

13

WEDNESDAY
(TOOTHPASTE WHITE)

Later That Afternoon

I'm back in my den, entrance sealed shut by the forget-me-not blue blanket, clutching Mum's cardigan. It was a terrible mistake to leave my safe place, her buttons and rose scent that *almost* masks the lingering hospital smell in my hair and clothes.

Except that's another lie. It's not *her* perfume. Dad accidentally washed the cardigan after I was sick on it eighteen months ago. He bought another rose perfume from a department store and sprayed it on to help remind me of Mum.

He said it would smell the same.

He was wrong. It doesn't. It's *almost* Mum's scent, but not quite, like my paintings of her voice. They haven't captured her accurately, not in the whole.

I run my fingers over the buttons.

Round and round the garden like a teddy bear.

That's what Mum used to say when I was little. She drew the line over my hand again and again when I lay in bed, looking up at the fluorescent stars she'd stuck on my ceiling.

The buttons are as smooth as her shiny pink nails.

One step, two steps, tickle you under there.

Except Mum never used to tickle me anywhere, because she knew I hated it. She let me tickle her under the chin instead. That used to make us both laugh.

I didn't stay long in hospital—only until the male doctor finished examining me and the police tracked down Dad. *Two hours, maybe three*. It's hard to tell since my watch stopped working when I fell outside the front door and I lost track of time because the clock in the ward was slow.

I know this Important Fact: it was long enough to cause Dad and me a whole stack of trouble. The policewoman panicked after I blacked out and radioed for an ambulance. If I'd been conscious, I'd have stopped her. I wasn't. I couldn't. It was out of my control, like a lot of things that have happened to me recently. Dad doesn't understand.

You shouldn't have run away from school.

You shouldn't have dialed 999.

The doctor examined me and saw the hole in my tummy. He fixed it with small pieces of tape because it was too late for surgical stitches. He gave me tablets to stop infection and put on stingy antiseptic cream. I didn't tell him how I hurt my tummy. I didn't tell him anything. It made no difference whether I spoke or not, because the policewoman did all the talking for me. She told the man my name, age, and where I live. She had it on record somewhere, probably from Rusty Chrome Orange.

By then, she knew my next of kin was Dad; he was my only living relative and she couldn't call Mum because she was dead and buried, like the baby parakeet.

Like Nan and Bee Larkham's mum and Ollie Watkins's mum.

Another woman appeared at the hospital. She talked to Dad in private when he finally showed up, out of breath and sweaty. He'd been dragged out of an important meeting. She was a social worker. We'll see her again soon, now the doctor's had a good look at my tummy, Dad said. We're probably going to see a child psychologist too, as well as all the police officers.

There's no point talking to any of them: Rusty Chrome Orange, the viridian blue policewoman who radioed for an ambulance, the social worker, or the child psychologist.

None of them can help me. They hear what they want to hear, see what they want to see, and they still haven't found Bee, they don't even listen when I repeatedly try to tell them she's dead.

I don't want to speak to Dad either. I can't tell him about the baby.

Bee Larkham's baby. Not yet. I don't want to roll the pithy orange *baby* word around my tongue.

I see grayish green as Dad turns on the radio in the kitchen downstairs. It booms greenish vertical lines that fleck repetitively up and down. The colors wash over me ambivalently. I neither like nor dislike them. I'm neutral. They're shades I'll use in pictures if I feel like it, but I won't be heartbroken if I run out of paint and can't squeeze enough out of the tube. It wouldn't be like running out of my favorite blue colors—on a disaster scale of one to ten that would probably be a nine.

Nine point five.

The track changes in midcolor as Dad switches to a new radio station. The colors make me cry. Not with sadness this time, but with joy. Joy at the colors.

It's Rihanna's "Diamonds," except I don't see diamonds in the sky the way she does. I see exploding stars of gold and silver, rippling and expanding into seas of flamingo and watermelon pink. The pink changes constantly, beautifully, to violet and back again, with underlying yellow lines.

It makes me forget the hospital, Dad, and all the police officers and doctors and social workers. I crawl out of my den and feel the colors embracing me, comforting me. I want to dance. I have to dance, the way Bee Larkham used to.

I throw my arms around. This is how I like to dance, all my limbs moving at once. It's selfish not to share the colors. I stick my hand beneath the curtains and open the window. I want the parakeets to enjoy the music; they haven't heard any since Bee Larkham died. They must be missing the colors and tones and shapes.

They need to realize life won't be the same again, but it does go on. I'll protect the remaining parakeets. The bird feeders will be refilled again and again by the man who temporarily lives next door to Bee Larkham's house. They have to feel welcome, otherwise they'll leave me.

I hadn't fully understood how much I wanted to hear music again. I peek between the curtains. Have the parakeets heard? Three argue noisily over the serenade.

Deep cornflower blue with yellow hiccups.

More parakeets land in the tree and join in the chorus of bickering. They're arguing about what's happened, taking sides.

David Gilbert versus me and Bee Larkham.

Me versus Bee Larkham.

My arms fall back into place, where they belong. My legs stop moving. I stand still as another urge takes hold that is much stronger than the will to dance. I pick up my brush because the need to paint the truth is bright and sparkly like golden Christmas tinsel.

I'm ready.

The parakeets can't tell anyone about the massacre of their pandemonium. They can't explain how they fell into the trap.

They need someone to tell their story. I have to pick up from where I left off, because it's getting close to the day of their arrival.

I pull out a fresh piece of paper and admire the satisfying whiteness. I select my paints: burnt sienna, cadmium red, and yellow, before moving on to my favorite tubes of blue.

It's time to paint the next scene.

14

January 18, 6:50 A.M.
Marmalade with Cobalt Blue and Crimson Stars on paper

The morning after the Woman with No Name moved in and played loud Martian music, I saw jagged dark orange marmalade.

I jumped out of bed, grabbed my binoculars, and stood at the window. First I checked the oak tree, but the parakeet still steered clear after the unprovoked magpie attack. Two pigeons had landed, unaware of the previous ambush.

I scribbled the time in a notebook as my alarm beeped soft pink bubbles across my bedroom as usual. I was definitely going to school.

No arguments.

The pigeons flew off, disturbed by spiky, unnatural shapes.

Another truck arrived with more brutish orangey red colors than the vehicle from the day before. It didn't take furniture away either. Instead, it unloaded a skip outside 20 Vincent Gardens.

A car beeped its horn, glittery crimson stars, as a man swung open the door of the truck and jumped out without warning. His friend flicked his fingers at the driver, who retaliated with another bright scarlet toot.

The starlings had also arrived in our neighbor's tree, along with a robin. Its shy trills were light blue wavering lines beneath cocky coral pink. The times are all recorded in my notebook.

The Woman with No Name flew out of the house, barefoot, wearing a shiny blue dressing gown, which made a low V shape. The men opened their mouths to form words. I don't think anything came out because their lips didn't change shape. The color of her dressing gown took my breath away too.

Cobalt blue.

Ohmigod, ohmigod, ohmigod!!!!!!

I drew a line under those words in my notebook and added six exclamation marks.

It was the exact color of cobalt blue, the color that misled me much later. I have to own up to my error, the first of many to do with Bee Larkham. First impressions can be wrong. I know that now. I wish I didn't.

When I saw the cobalt blue of the dressing gown, I also heard Mum's voice in the back of my head.

Love you to the moon and back.

Love you always.

The vividness of Mum's voice took my breath away. It was bright and loud, as if she stood in the room, looking out for me, even though she'd never lived in this house. I thought I'd lost her forever, that we'd left her behind in the graveyard in Plymouth.

In that fraction of a second I felt an essential truth: Mum had vowed never to leave me.

She'd kept her word.

She'd found me again.

Here, in Vincent Gardens.

My knees crumpled and I hung on to the windowsill. I knew that if I let go, nothing could stop me from falling. Not to the floor, way beyond that. I felt a bottomless pit yawning open across the carpet, trying to swallow me up.

I couldn't hear what the Woman with No Name said to the men from the truck, but it must have been hilarious. They threw their heads back and laughed marmalade bubbles as she wrapped her long blond hair in knots around her finger.

As they climbed back into the truck, she tied her dressing gown tighter at the waist. It was low at the front, but she didn't mind the cold.

The truck pulled away down the street and tooted shooting stars of deep crimson with gold edges. The Woman with No Name stared at the skip for fifteen seconds before picking a flower, a daisy, I think, from her garden. She walked back towards the front door. Instead of going inside, she swung around.

She looked directly at me and waved gracefully, like a princess. Her dressing gown sleeve slid down her arm.

I crouched beneath the windowsill.

Too late. The Woman with No Name had seen me watching her with binoculars.

That was the first time she noticed me at my bedroom window.

I was worried she'd be upset and wouldn't want to get to know me. She'd complain to Dad or laugh about me with her new neighbors.

She'd call me a Peeping Tom. Or Peeping Jasper, if she wanted to make a joke.

The funny thing was, the thing she told me much later on, when we became Great Friends, was that she liked it.

Being watched, I mean.

She honestly didn't mind. She enjoyed having an audience. She said it made her feel alive.

Later that morning, 7:45 A.M.
Cinnamon Blocks on paper

My parakeet watch continued.

I held binoculars in one hand and a notebook in the other, calculating a chance of less than 13 percent that my favorite breed of bird would return before I left for school. The ugly colors had kept it away. They'd already scared off the other birds. I couldn't see any of their colors in our street. I didn't scribble a single note.

The Woman with No Name probably didn't realize it, but she was accidentally deterring the local wildlife by hurling her belongings into the skip: a bookshelf, books, chairs, ornaments, pots and pans, newspapers, lampshades, and curtains.

Bang. Thud. Cinnamon block shapes that transformed into orangey brown shades.

Backwards and forwards, the woman walked in and out of the house, pulling out things she didn't want. More and more cardboard boxes ended up with the rubbish. I wanted her to get a move on—the sooner she finished throwing everything out, the greater probability the parakeet would put in another appearance before school.

Possibly a chance of 22 percent.

Through my binoculars, I could see some of the boxes were taped up. I had no idea what they'd done to upset her, but she didn't like any of them. She didn't want to see their contents. The net curtains also ended up in the skip. They'd offended her for unknown reasons and had to be abandoned.

I watched the oak tree in the front garden of 20 Vincent Gardens for signs of parakeet life for fourteen minutes and twenty-five seconds, before Dad knocked light tan circles on my bedroom door. He wanted to double-check I was getting ready for school.

Of course I was. We'd discussed this last night. *We all have to do things we don't want to.*

"Who is she?" I asked him again. "That woman down there? Why doesn't she like furniture?"

"She must be a relative," he replied, "because she's clearing out the house. David met her last night. I'll ask him later, when I get back from work if you like? He'll have all the gossip, as usual."

I signaled I liked his idea by shifting my head into the correct position. I hoped Dad wouldn't mess up again. The first meeting was crucially important because this was when he said impressions were formed. She might not like me if she didn't like him.

"She doesn't want to keep anything," I observed. "Not a single item. She's turning Mrs. Larkham's house inside out. There'll be nothing left soon."

Dad admitted he'd seen the woman from the sitting room window—two people from the same house watching her at the same time. Only I had binoculars.

"It's amazing the things people throw away," he said, edging closer to the window. "She should have hired a house clearance company to come around and sort through everything. She'd have made some money. There's good stuff in the skip."

"Maybe she doesn't want anyone else to own anything that's been in the house. Maybe she hates the idea of someone else using it or looking at it."

"Good point," he said, "but that's not going to stop people having a good forage for valuables to take for themselves or sell on. A dealer will want those chairs. They look in good nick."

A drug dealer?

"Is that allowed? Isn't that theft?"

"Well, you can't exactly stop anyone if you're throwing it away," he pointed out. "It's not your property any longer if you've left it lying about for others to take."

I could stop the skip thieves and the drug dealers. I had to. What if the Woman with No Name changed her mind and wanted to keep one of the boxes or chairs?

This wasn't the first or the last time I'd rung 999 to ask for help, but it was the first emergency call I'd made to do with Bee Larkham.

I turned on my mobile and punched in the three numbers, and while Dad read a newspaper in the bathroom, I reported a theft from the Woman with No Name.

A potential future theft from the skip outside her house, 20 Vincent Gardens.

Drug dealers shouldn't be allowed to drive her out, the way the magpies had scared off the parakeet.

The operator asked me to put Dad on the phone. I apologized and told her I couldn't. He was doing a number two and didn't like to be disturbed. She insisted I try. I knocked three light brown circles and made him unlock the door. I passed the phone through the gap. They chatted for a few minutes while Dad sat on the loo.

I'll talk to him again, I promise. I'm sorry. He gets overexcited about things. He thinks they're more significant than they are. I know. I understand.

More apologies. I heard the light pink-gray rustle of toilet paper and the silvery blue spangles of the flush.

I grabbed my school bag and ran out before I had to listen to another of his lectures. I didn't want to talk to him. Why didn't he defend me to the police operator?

He watched TV crime shows most nights and had to know that stealing was evidence of a flawed character.

Because if someone stole, they would probably be prepared to do something much, much worse.

I found it hard to concentrate at school for the rest of the day—far more than usual. The background colors and blur of anonymous faces weren't responsible this time. It was due to the Woman with No Name.

I jotted down Important Facts about her in the inside cover of my maths book:

1. She enjoys Martian music.
2. She likes cobalt blue.
3. She likes to dance.
4. She doesn't like anything that belonged in the house before.
5. She's a relative or friend of Pauline Larkham, who died in another home.
6. She's going to be a troublemaker (Dad's opinion).
7. She plays music too loud (David Gilbert's and Ollie Watkins's opinion).

Most of all, I wanted to know the two things missing off my list:

What's her name?
What's the color of her voice?

Was it blue? It had to be a shade of blue. She looked like she had a blue voice. I hoped she did. It couldn't be a crinkly yellowish brown or brash orange voice.

It'd be like discovering a rotting bouquet of flowers—it had the potential to smell sweet and be dazzling but had become faded and brown, unfit for anything except the inside of a bin.

It'd ruin everything.

I brooded about her color all day and didn't speak much, not even to my friends Jeanne and Aar, who found me at my usual seat in the canteen at lunchtime—far right-hand table, third seat from the end.

"Has someone upset you again, Jasper?" Aar (goldfish orange) asked.

"Yes," I said. "They have."

That was the truth.

"You should talk to a teacher, Jasper," Jeanne (sunset yellow) said. "You shouldn't have to put up with being bullied every day."

I remember I was quick to jump to the Woman with No Name's defense. She couldn't help it *if* she had a rotten-colored voice and I didn't know that for sure yet. I was jumping to conclusions without all the Important Facts lined up in front of me.

"It's not her fault," I pointed out. "Some things you can't help, whoever you are. They're out of your control."

"No, they're not, Jasper," Jeanne insisted. "The kids who give you stick know exactly what they're doing. It's not out of their control. That's what they want you to think, that it's your fault, when it isn't. It's theirs. They're the losers."

I stabbed the broccoli on my plate with a fork. Jeanne's sentence was puzzling. No one had tried to give me a stick today.

"Think about it," Aar said. "Taking action is better than sitting around feeling miserable."

Aar was right.

I had to take action. I couldn't leave the important job of discovering my new neighbor's name to Dad. He'd probably mess it up again. He couldn't tell me the color of her voice either, since he wouldn't be able to see it.

I had to be prepared. After lunch, I made a list of the openings to possible conversations, the way Dad had taught me, and memorized them during history class. The repeal of the Corn Laws had already happened. It could wait.

Hello. I'm Jasper Wishart.

Hello. I'm Jasper. What's your name?

Hello. Who are you? I'm Jasper.

How old are you? I'm thirteen years, two months, one day, and four hours old.

I fleshed out my introduction again and again until I was sure it was exactly right.

Hello. Welcome to our street. I'm Jasper Wishart. I'm thirteen years old and live at 19 Vincent Gardens. I'm a pupil at St. Alton's High School and I like to paint. What's your name?

This was relevant and to the point. It contained all the important information and passed the baton to the Woman with No Name to provide a similar description of herself.

I couldn't think about anything else. I repeated the words over and over in my head all day. Whenever the teacher asked me a question, I blocked it out and silently answered:

Hello. Welcome to our street, et cetera.

By home time, I'd memorized it perfectly. I was prepared to meet the Woman with No Name.

15

January 18, 3:31 P.M.
Sky Blue Meets Cool Blue on canvas

A woman appeared in the doorway of 20 Vincent Gardens, surrounded by cardboard boxes and bulging black bin bags. I'd knocked
loudly once, only after the colors of the piano notes had faded. I hadn't
wanted to interrupt the raindrops of electric blue and waves of elegant,
shiny navy. Waiting also enabled me to knead the stabbing pain in my
side after the Blazers had chased me two-fifths of the way home.

She arrived within one minute and twenty-five seconds, which I
appreciated almost as much as the musical colors. I like people who
don't delay doing important things.

I studied the figure. This looked like the Woman with No Name,
except she was smaller than I'd expected and reminded me of a baby
bird. She was thin, like me, and only a few inches taller.

She'd pushed her blond hair behind her ears, showing off tiny silver
swallow earrings. Her sweater had a deep V-neck, which was in a race
to reach the waistband of her long skirt. I watched the tassels at the
bottom of the material tickle the floor.

Swish, swish, swish.

I wanted to study her earrings further, but that meant seeing the
V-neck again, which looked alien, like on the first night.

"Hello. Can I help you?"

Sky blue.

*A bright, cloudless sky blue, the kind you see on a perfect, hot summer
afternoon on a beach—a mixture of ultramarine and cerulean.*

Her voice was almost cobalt blue, like Mum's but not quite. Yet it was close enough, more than I'd ever hoped, more than I'd thought possible. No one I'd met since Mum died had ever come as near as this to her hue.

My mind went blank and I forgot everything I'd memorized about myself.

"Jasper's a semiprecious stone," I said.

She laughed dazzling sky blue with ultramarine edges. "You're absolutely right. Jasper's one of my all-time favorite stones. Did you know it's believed to have strong healing powers?"

I looked up from her tassels as she continued talking.

"It provides comfort, security, and strength as well as great joy." She flicked her hair behind her shoulders. I wanted her to wipe her forehead, which had a streak of gray dust. "Why do *you* like Jasper?"

"I'm Jasper. How old are you?"

"Ha! I see. You get to the point, don't you? You do realize you can never ask a woman a personal question like that?"

"Why not? I live over the road from you." I pointed to my window. "My bedroom's up there. That's where I sleep."

"Ah, the boy with the binoculars. The one with the handsome dad in the window."

I didn't know about this last bit, as I'd never heard Dad called this before, but confirmed I was the Boy with the Binoculars. I doubted there could be another on this street; well, not one I'd noticed.

"I use the binoculars for bird-watching," I explained.

"That's one way to describe it." She giggled light blue with white margins. I didn't join in because bird-watching isn't funny. It's a serious pursuit, watching and logging every bird I see. It takes time to learn all the species in the United Kingdom, let alone the whole world.

"Are you going to die soon? Is that why you don't want to tell me how old you are?"

"What? I should hope not. You do ask funny questions!"

"Thank you."

"You're an unusual boy," the woman said. "I don't think I've ever met anyone like you before."

I moved the edges of my lips upwards into a curve because she made being unusual sound like a good thing. I began my introduction all over again, because I'd messed up on my first attempt—the way I do when I get distracted and put too much water on my paintbrush.

"That's an impressive introduction," she replied when I'd given it. "Thank you."

"Can I hear yours?" I prompted.

"Well let me see. I've come back from Australia for a friend's wedding and to deal with the house. I'll have to live in this shithole until I decide what to do with it. It'll need a lot of work before I put it on the market."

I tried to focus on the overall color of her voice rather than the mushy tangerine swearword.

"Are you a niece, a friend, or Pauline Larkham's long-lost daughter?" I asked, attempting to fit the piece into the jigsaw puzzle. The Australian part surprised me. She didn't have an accent.

"A long-lost daughter?" The woman's tassels swished again as she laughed bright sky blue. "I'm not sure about that. I was never lost. I guess I never wanted to be found, you know? I wanted to disappear. Nobody was going to come looking for me, least of all my mum."

"Like all that stuff?" I glanced over my shoulder. "Do you want it to be found? Or do you mind if someone takes it?"

Not that they'd be able to, now I'd alerted the police. I'd made sure of that.

The boxes were piled high in the skip. The Woman with No Name must have worked hard all day, clearing the house.

"Out with the old and in with the new, that's my motto," she said. "I don't want to hold on to the past. I'm trying not to keep too much of Mum's old stuff. There's hardly anything worth saving anyway, apart from a few pieces of furniture and old cookbooks."

I don't want to hold on to the past.

I pretended I agreed by moving my head up and down, but I knew she was wrong. You can't hold on to the past, even if you want to; it has a habit of slipping from your grasp.

"I saw you watching me this morning," she continued. "I was hoping you or your hunky dad would come over and help me clear this stuff out. The boxes are heavy."

"I was watching your oak tree," I corrected, ignoring her reference to my dad. "We don't have trees in our front garden. Lots of birds visit your tree. I want to see the parakeet most of all."

"You've seen a wild parakeet?"

I confirmed its Latin name: *Psittacula krameri.*

"Cool. I used to see budgies all the time where I lived in Australia. They're the same, right?"

"They have the same characteristics as parakeets, like curved bills and zygodactyl feet—two toes pointing forward and two pointing back."

"Wow. I'm living opposite an expert. How exciting."

I felt my cheeks warm.

"I'll make sure I keep an eye out for it." The woman gazed down at her boxes. "I have to get through a lot today, making the sitting room look presentable for visitors. I should go back to it. It's been a pleasure though, kid."

"You didn't finish your introduction." I was anxious for her to continue, because now I knew the color of her voice, I needed a name to put to the color.

Hazy sky blue shimmers. "Hmmm. I thought we were saying goodbye! Let me see. I'm a professional musician. At least, I was in Australia, but now I'm planning to work as a piano and guitar teacher until I get the house sorted. Because I love music. I love it more than anything else."

"Loud music," I said, moving my head up and down. "That's the way it should be played."

"Ha! We're on the same wavelength, right? I'm not sure Mum's neighbors feel the same. I mean it's an old street, isn't it? I can't believe the ancient faces that are still here. I'm used to being around *young* people, not the elderly and the dying."

"I don't know much about people's ages," I admitted. "You could ask David Gilbert, who lives next door on that side." I pointed to his house. "Dad says he's the fount of all knowledge. Or the fountain. I can't remember the right word."

"Thanks for the tip, but I knew him as a kid. Like I said, I'd hoped the old git had moved away by now. I'm planning to avoid him like the plague. The prodigal son too."

I kept quiet because *git* was a snot-colored word and the *old* didn't improve its shade. Plus, I didn't want to admit I didn't know the identity of the prodigal son. I couldn't tell for sure if she was worried about David Gilbert spreading a plague. I suspected she wasn't.

She appeared to be smiling like she'd told a funny joke about pestilence and pandemics, but my knowledge of infectious disease outbreaks was limited to what I've learnt about the Black Death and the Great Fire of London at school.

"Who *are* you?" I blurted out.

"Sorry! My name's Bee Larkham, the Bee spelt with an *e*, not an *a* like other people."

"I'm glad," I said, "because I love the color of bees."

"Yes! Brilliant minds think alike. They're such a lovely golden color. I have a feeling we're going to be great friends."

She was wrong on two counts: the word *bee* is a smoky blue with a splash of pale lemon while their buzzing sound is spotty blue with wavering, intermittent orange and yellow stripes.

Bee Larkham with an *e* not an *a* was right about us becoming Great Friends though.

"Can I come in?"

"Not today, if you don't mind. I'm about to go out. Maybe tomorrow or something like that?"

She had a lovely colored voice, almost as beautiful as Mum's, and a truly terrible memory. She was supposed to be going through things and making her sitting room look presentable for visitors.

I looked down, pondering her lapse in concentration, and noticed the doormat.

WHO INVITED YOU?

"Tomorrow," I said, confirming our appointment.

I repeated the word twice, once out loud and a second time under my breath for good luck.

That's what Mum taught me to do shortly before she died. She wanted to help me memorize the times of meetings with a teaching assistant at school when she'd no longer be there to remind me herself.

"Goodbye, Bee Larkham."

"Thanks for coming round to say hi, John. Goodbye."

John?

16

NAN'S STORY

After Mum's funeral, I didn't move or speak for two weeks. I didn't realize it was that long, but Dad filled me in on the details later. I stayed in bed and had visits from doctors, who all tried to persuade me to talk.

I don't know why they wanted me to open my mouth and form a sentence. I had nothing to say to anyone. I can't remember a single shade from those dark days. Color deserted me the moment Mum stopped breathing. Or maybe I stopped looking and listening.

It was terrible, yet it felt right at the same time. Things had to be disjointed and wrong and out of place. They couldn't carry on as they had before; the whole world had collapsed and there would never be cobalt blue again.

I stopped talking and Dad left the Royal Marines; we both gave up things. I remember the empty palette of silence.

Were there any colors as Mum's coffin was lowered into the ground? The muffled brown tones of sobs? Green, wailing clouds? Slate gray muttered condolences from Dad's soldier friends? I imagine their rifles firing petrol black shapes into the air, the way they do at military funerals in America.

I'll never know what shades paid their last respects to Mum. I can never paint that final picture.

Weeks blurred into grayish white whispers. The first colors I remember again were so bright, so alive I thought my retinas were on fire. Nan managed to get me up and out of the house. I have no idea how. She took me to the park around the corner from our old house because Dad needed some "space." The park had plenty of space if he'd bothered to look—a large adventure playground on the right-hand side of the field as you walked off the street.

I know it was a turquoise day—Saturday—because lots of kids and their parents were in the playground.

Whitish gray noise punctuated with sudden dots of bright red and yellow.

I caught my breath. It felt shocking to see color again, to realize it hadn't disappeared completely from the world, along with Mum. Children laughed and shouted as if nothing had actually happened.

"Go on, Jasper," Nan said, coughing puffs of flaky blancmange pinks and violets. "Have a play. It'll do you good. Why don't you run on over to those little boys with the ball?"

She pointed into the distance, but I didn't follow the direction of her finger. I watched the light pink, almost translucent ribbons of high-speed trains speeding past. The railway line was behind a fence close to the playground, my favorite spot when I visited the park with Mum. She let me stand at the fence for hours and never tried to persuade me to get on the swing or seesaws, which always made me feel nauseous.

I caught flashes of people in the trains, a blur of fuzzy features. How could they be traveling on a day like this? It felt disrespectful to Mum that their journeys continued after her death. They hadn't even noticed that only one person stood watching their train at the fence, not two as usual.

I looked around to tell Nan I wanted to go home, but I couldn't find her. A group of five women huddled to my right and three to my left. Three stood separately, studying their phones. I didn't recognize any of them.

"Nan!" I yelled. "Where are you?"

The aquamarine screams from my voice curled up like a dragon, rising above the playground, ready to strike at anyone. *Everyone.* Tears poured down my face as I spun around and around.

"Help! Help me! Where are you?"

The ground lurched up towards me and punched me hard in the face. I felt something warm and sticky on my cheek.

I heard a rasping lilac pinkish cough and bluish footsteps with black, wavering outlines. A woman wheezed raspberry mousse zigzags as she knelt down beside me.

"I'm here, Jasper. It's Nan. Did you trip over?"

I grabbed her arm and clung on tight, afraid that if I didn't, she would vanish in a puff of lilac smoke.

"Don't go. Don't go. Don't leave me. Don't ever leave me."

"I'm not going to leave you," she said. "I promise."

She did leave me. That wasn't her fault. She didn't mean to break her promise. She died two weeks later. I didn't go to that funeral either. Dad wouldn't let me because I'd been rocking too much and flapping my arms, which was embarrassing.

I never saw coughs of light, delicate lilac and blancmange pink or raspberry mousse zigzags ever again. That made me sadder still. They were straightforward colors that always tried their best. I loved them and they loved me back, without ever wanting difficult favors in return.

17

WEDNESDAY
(TOOTHPASTE WHITE)

Evening

Thanks for coming round to say hi, John. Goodbye.

John is a sharp rusty-nail-colored word. I've tried to shut out the tint of Bee Larkham's hurtful mistake by hiding deep beneath my duvet, but it's time to finally be honest with myself. Bee didn't invite me inside her house the first time we met. She couldn't even remember my name.

Now I've re-created all the correct colors, I can't bear to look at the painting again. It's embarrassing. My mistakes are too painful to view, even in private, when no one can laugh at me.

I climb out of bed and turn the picture around to face the wall. I check my notebooks and find my original diary entry from that day.

It's as I feared.

I didn't record Bee Larkham's blunder in my notebook on January 18. It only contains the date and time of my visit, which lasted five minutes and eighteen seconds, and no other details.

I don't recall when it happened, but at some point I allowed myself to preserve only sky blue from our initial meeting. It bled into all the other colors and ruthlessly overpowered them. I didn't attempt to stop it because the hue was so similar to Mum's. I'd never have let another shade do that.

The color of Bee Larkham's voice painted over the scene at the doorstep, covering up the uncomfortable truth—that this encounter was far more significant for me than it ever was for her.

I don't have time to wallow in my wounded pride or whatever it is that's left a horrid metallic taste in my mouth. I apologize to my paints for cursing them.

I must repaint more scenes while they're bubbling away in my mind. Dad won't check on me. It's 10:03 P.M. He's gone to bed early. I can't see the colors of the TV; he might be looking at a book. It's probably the same book he was pretending to read a month ago: a Jack Reacher thriller by Lee Child. Except he wasn't reading a novel by his favorite author when I walked into his bedroom. He put his *real* book behind the cover of Lee Child's.

Understanding Your Child's Autism and Other Learning Difficulties.

I expect he's studying it right now. Trying to get a grip on why I'm difficult. Why I'm different from other teenage boys.

Why I'm so hard to love.

I bet the book doesn't mention anything about my colors. They're not as difficult to love as me, except when they're making constant demands for attention.

I dab my brush twice in the pot of water and breathe shallowly through my nose as my tummy mouth wakes up. I'm going to restrict myself to painting two more pictures from the day of my first conversation with Bee Larkham.

I'm being selective. I have to be.

I don't want to repeat myself. Bee Larkham played loud Martian music again on the evening of January 18. I've already recorded the colors from the previous night and doubt I can improve upon the picture.

There are other more important details to recall, other stories to tell. It will take time to reveal their true colors.

Thirty to forty pictures—that's how many I'd have to paint if I wanted to capture the dramatic colors featuring Bee Larkham's Martian music from this date onwards. If I did force myself to paint all these canvases, I'd have to add dark brown, irregular rectangular shapes with bluish gray rings to the bottom left-hand corner of every single one.

That would be the knocking on her front door, usually from a man, late at night, when the music had reached its brightest peaks. Often, the man visited Bee Larkham's house and went back inside David Gilbert's house. Sometimes the man returned to Ollie Watkins's house, other times the man walked from Bee Larkham's to David Gilbert's and then to Ollie Watkins's house. That made it hard to keep track of their identities when they kept swapping houses.

Other times, more people on the street paid Bee Larkham visits late at night when she played loud music. They didn't go back into David Gilbert's or Ollie Watkins's houses. I wrote their addresses in my notebooks in case I ever needed to show them to the police: mainly numbers 13, 17, and 25. Ted, who has been made redundant from his IT job, lives alone at number 13. He's bald, wears black, rectangular glasses, and is easy to identify. Karen is a journalist and usually has a sparkly silver phone stuck to her ear. She's next door at 17; and Magda, Izaak, and their baby son, Jakub, live at 25.

Izaak has a tattoo of a cross on his right hand, below his thumb, but it's impossible to check for that from my window. The police shouldn't rely on my records: different men could have come out of number 25 to complain about the music. Magda and Izaak had lots of visitors who wanted to see their baby back then.

I need delicate light blues and dark, sludgy browns to re-create the next scene. They cut through the darkness that night, sluicing color up my blank canvas.

I have to make this painting stand out, because it was different from the pattern that developed over the next few months. Bee Larkham argued with a stranger and it wasn't to do with her Martian music. The row happened *before* she turned the music up to full blast on her iPod, *not after* like all the other times that followed.

This picture has to be a mottled lapis-lazuli-colored word.

It must be *unique*.

18

January 18, 9:02 P.M.
Out with the Old and in with the New on paper

I was painting voices in my bedroom—cobalt, cool and sky blue—to
see how they'd look during an imaginary conversation.

The answer? They fitted perfectly together, speaking with one
united voice.

They were friends. Great Friends.

Bang, bang, bang.

Murky clouds of dark chocolate.

I put down my brush and scooted to the window, almost ripping
the curtains off the rail as I pulled them back. It was fifteen minutes
before the next recital of Martian music began, according to my notebook.

A man stood at Bee Larkham's front door. He was of average height,
which to me meant he wasn't any taller or smaller than other men I'd
seen on the street before. His clothes weren't grabby for attention either. He didn't have a dog with him.

I'd written: *Probably not David Gilbert, but he could have left Yellow
French Fries at home.*

The blond woman wore a long periwinkle blue dress. This had to be
Bee Larkham because she was the only woman I'd seen at this address.
She liked loud music and hated unpacking. She said I was unusual, in
a good way.

I opened the window to listen. I caught snatches of vivid blue, but
they trailed off before I could understand their meaning. The man

turned and pointed at the skip, which made the woman's shoulders rise up and down.

"I don't care! I don't care!"

Those were the only sky blue words I managed to catch, tossed up into the night. I wondered what Bee Larkham didn't care about or who or why. My best guess? The skip color. She didn't care about the nasty yellow because it was doing its job, getting rid of everything that upset her in the house.

Out with the Old and in with the New.

I felt sorry for Bee Larkham because I was sure she didn't have any choice about skip colors. If she had, I was positive she'd have chosen a shade of blue, the same as me. I was certain of one thing: Bee Larkham was under attack for something that wasn't her fault.

I wanted to alert the police, even though Dad had confiscated my *Encyclopedia of Birds* for two days after my 999 call about potential skip thieves. Before I could look for my mobile, the argument was over. It couldn't have been serious because they'd already made up. As the man hurried back down the path and on to the street, the woman— Bee Larkham—shouted after him: "I'm glad! I'm so glad!"

Maybe the man had told a joke. I didn't know how he felt because I couldn't tell if he was happy or sad. He stopped and stared at the skip before stalking off. I was relieved he was gone, but disappointed too. I was unable to identify him by the house he entered on our street.

I jotted in my notebook he was *probably a stranger, someone who didn't belong on our street.* He was another man who wanted to welcome her to the neighborhood.

Bee Larkham reappeared a few minutes later, while I made notes at the window. She walked down her path, carrying a box containing more things to throw out, which couldn't wait until morning. When she reached the skip, she turned the box upside-down, smashing the contents—crockery, I think, judging by the colors.

Repetitive bursts of brilliant white and shiny, bright silver tubes.

Later that night, 3:03 A.M.
The Devil on paper

Hours later, long after the glittering, attractive shades of Bee Larkham's Martian music had finally faded away, I was woken up by different, more guttural shades.

Rough, scratchy browns layered with raspy oranges.

At first, I thought it was foxes. They run wild around here at night, in the day too. They're no longer afraid of humans. They've calculated their chances of survival as being high, based on the fact that most humans don't have the urge to kill or maim.

Skulk, a fried-egg-shaped and glossy red-tulip-colored word. That's the collective noun for foxes.

I listened to the sounds for a few minutes before climbing out of bed. Without turning on the light I made my way to the window and grabbed hold of my binoculars. I didn't need a torch or Dad's night vision goggles (bought discounted on eBay because he couldn't take supplies when he left the Royal Marines) to guide me. They were exactly where I'd left them on the windowsill.

The unpleasant brown and orange colors came from the skip. I couldn't see properly because the lamppost outside Bee Larkham's house had flickered for months before dying. The next working lamppost was fifteen meters away and not nearly strong enough.

Squinting through my binoculars, I couldn't identify the creature at first. It wasn't a skulk. It was too big to be a vixen or a male fox—a tod—or their cubs. Toad-like, the thing squatted over the cardboard boxes, ripping them open and searching inside.

A monster. I was too afraid to move as the creature shifted. Slowly, it turned around, still hunched over. It looked straight up at me, through me, inside me, ripping me apart with its gaze.

I fell backwards, dropping the binoculars on the carpet.

My body felt cold and clammy, my arms hung uselessly by my sides. Even if I could move them, I wouldn't have tried to reach for my mobile. I knew dialing 999 was pointless.

I was certain I'd seen the devil in Bee Larkham's skip; and it had seen me. The devil wanted to hurt me because I was the only person on the street who'd spotted it.

But I remember an important detail that was never in my original picture, the light lilac blue colors and textures I'd left out.

Even though I was terrified. *Because* I was terrified, I had to make sure the devil hadn't climbed out of the skip and found its way to Bee Larkham's front door or my own.

I had to be brave. I had to protect my new neighbor from evil forces on our street. I stumbled back to my bedroom window.

Bang, bang, bang.

Hyacinth and bluebell tubular shapes.

Before I had time to change my mind, I hammered on my window to scare away the monster. It slipped over the side of the skip and scuttled towards the alley, which drew a dividing line between Bee Larkham's and David Gilbert's houses.

A car drove past, and yellow beams picked out two legs—human, not goat—in jeans. Before he was gobbled up by darkness, I saw the man's hands. They didn't hold anything.

His left, gloved hand was clenched into a tight, tight fist.

19

WEDNESDAY
(TOOTHPASTE WHITE)

Later That Evening

I jump back into bed and wrap the duvet tightly around me. I was right to call the police that morning.

Dad had warned me about dealers. The operator should have listened to me. So should Dad.

A *man* had searched for something in Bee Larkham's skip, not the devil. He couldn't find what he was looking for among her old, unwanted belongings and the broken crockery.

He could come back.

I don't want him to look for me.

He mustn't ever find me.

I hide my face under the pillow but can still see the hues from the skip. *The colors from Bee Larkham's kitchen.*

I can't escape from these shades.

I need to sleep.

I want to close my eyes and never see icicles again.

I'm falling down Alice in Wonderland's rabbit hole, scrabbling about to get a footing.

Eat me.

Drink me.

Now I'm swimming through the Pool of Tears. Other animals and birds have been swept up in the tears, along with me. At least I'm not alone.

Tortoises. Elephants. Kangaroos.

Parakeets.

Twelve parakeets are in the water too, but they're not trying to get to dry land like the others. They're already dead.

A giant dancing china lady stands motionless on the banks, blood dripping down her immaculate, glossy white gown. She watches as four and twenty blackbirds float past. They don't belong here. Neither does she.

My tummy mouth itches. I want to pull it open and let the birds fly out. I can't.

I'm back in the kitchen at 20 Vincent Gardens.

Dazzling crystal whites.

I hate you!

You're killing me!

Stop, I'm begging you!

I'm lying on top of Bee Larkham. Her eyes are shut. I stagger to my feet. She's lying on her back on the kitchen floor. She doesn't get up. She doesn't open her eyes.

Blood's spattered on the tiles and down her noncobalt-blue dress.

Blood drips down my hand. It's all over my sweatshirt.

Glittering silver icicles stab my tummy.

I'm sorry.

Bee doesn't try to stop me this time. She's done fighting. She's given up. She knows it's all over.

Her eyes stay closed as I pick up the knife again from the floor. She doesn't want to watch. Neither do the parakeets. They turn their heads away. The Dancing China Lady doesn't flinch. She's shrunk back to normal size and can't peel her eyes away from the weapon.

Glint, glint, glint.

I wake up sweating, unable to move, unable to shake off the hues from my dream.

I open my mouth and yell silently for Mum.

Those kinds of screams never produce any colors.

20

THURSDAY (APPLE GREEN)

Morning

Crisp apple green days are usually worth getting up for, because I have double art before lunch. Today's different. Dad's keeping me off school. It's 8:46 A.M. and I'm lying in bed, staring at the fifty-two stars studded on the ceiling. Dad tried to re-create my bedroom back in Plymouth, the one Mum decorated when I was little, before we kept moving in and out of grotty rented houses across the country.

You can't hold on to the past.

I'd wanted to tell Bee Larkham that Important Fact the first day we spoke, but I couldn't risk upsetting her with the truth. I left it far too late with Bee. I need to teach that lesson to Dad before he makes another blunder, which will get us into even more trouble.

It's not his fault the stars are in the wrong places. I remember where they should go in the map in my head, *where they were in Plymouth,* but I can't return them to their real home. Someone else lives there now. They can't ever go back. If I attempt to chip them off, they'll stubbornly peel off the paint and leave the ceiling pockmarked and ugly. It'd end up feeling unloved because I'd never stare up at it again.

Leave it alone. That's the best course of action.

That's what I think about repositioning the stars, but also about the other stuff. I was determined to do the right thing last night after I'd painted the real picture of my first meeting with Bee Larkham. Now, my resolve wobbles like green Halloween jelly.

Probably because of *The Devil on paper* and my latest nightmare.

Do I truly want to go back over Bee Larkham's story? Isn't it better to do what Dad suggested and repaint the bad stuff with fresh, uncorrupted colors?

Forget everything.

I reach for the picture of Mum from beside the bed. I count across the heads and find her in the group, clutching a small boy as if she can't bear to let him go. *Me.*

Brave boy.

That's what she used to call me, even when I wasn't. Even when I cried because I didn't like the colors and spiky shapes of trucks rumbling past as we walked down the street.

I don't feel brave now. I can't get warm however many blankets I carry from my den to the bed. I feel the touch of the icicles.

I'm scared of the man who climbed out of Bee Larkham's skip. He didn't find what he was looking for that night, which means he could come back. He saw my face. He knows where I live.

I'm scared of Dark Blue Baseball Cap Man, who banged on Bee Larkham's front door. He saw me too.

I'm scared of dogs: Lucas Drury's Reddish Orange Triangles and David Gilbert's Yellow French Fries.

Most of all, I'm scared of letting Mum down. She'd want me to carry on, I'm sure.

When I was nine, she told me I had to be courageous, more courageous than I'd ever been before in my life.

It's important to tell the truth, even when it scares you.

She said the doctors couldn't make her cancer better. I had every right to be angry, but it wasn't the doctors' fault, or hers, or Dad's or mine. It wasn't anyone's fault.

She was angry too. And frightened. That was her truth. Also this:

You won't go through this alone, I promise.

Daddy is here for you and I will always love you.

You will always be my brave, beautiful boy.

Nothing will ever change that.

Believe me, Jasper.

That's what I'm going to do. I'm going to listen to Mum's honest cobalt blue and ignore Dad's misleading muddy ocher. I'm going to paint all day and night, all week, until I remember correctly, until absolutely every brushstroke is in its proper place. It could leave unsightly marks, like a ceiling without stars, but it's the right thing to do.

Before I begin, I check behind the curtains. The police car that was parked outside Bee Larkham's house has spawned another.

One, two, three, four.

That's how many police officers are knocking on doors along the street. I know they're not going to find out anything useful because the neighbors don't know what's gone on. Karen next door is always busy reporting on other people's stories, Ted at number 13 is probably out job hunting, and number 25's Magda and Izaak push a fire engine red pram around at strange times of the day and night. Dad says the only thing they ever talk about is Jakub and how badly he sleeps.

David Gilbert, of course, knows everything.

Then, my heart leaps. It feels like it's trying to burst alien-like out of my chest. I tear open the curtains. Parakeets cling to *all* the feeders in Bee Larkham's front garden. The man from number 18—Custard Yellow—listened to me.

He bought seed after he left me with the policewoman and filled all six feeders. He's a good man; he doesn't care about David Gilbert's reaction. He wants to do the right thing. *Like me.*

"The police are back."

The muddy ocher voice by the door makes me catch my breath. I spin around, almost falling over.

"I'm sorry." The man—Dad—walks towards me, wearing blue jeans and a blue shirt. "I didn't mean to make you jump. Are you watching them?"

I don't want to speak to him. I force the words out. "Yes. I'm watching the parakeets. The young haven't left yet. Maybe a few more days until they're fledged."

"I meant the police, but never mind. There are loads of parakeets today, right? I don't think any could have died. Not as many as you say."

"Twelve," I mutter back. "Exactly twelve, not more or less."

"How can you possibly know that?"

I don't reply. There's no point. Dad can't rewind time and bring all the parakeets back from the dead. He can't paint over these facts. I won't let him.

"The police still haven't heard from Bee," he continues. "That means someone else topped up the feeders this morning. It couldn't have been David, and I doubt it's Ollie. He hates their racket and won't want to get on the wrong side of David."

That's another lie because Ollie Watkins is a bird lover, like me. He's lost his mum too. It could be a trick. Dad could be trying to get me to admit I have an accomplice. If I confirm Ollie Watkins is feeding the parakeets, he'll make him stop.

"I didn't do it," I stress.

"I know that, Jasper." He steps back from the window. "Careful. The police think we're watching them."

A woman in uniform raises her hand.

I don't move. "We *are* watching them," I point out. "We're not using binoculars this time because that would be considered rude by other people on the street. No one likes a spy."

"Come away from there. They'll wonder what we're up to."

"It's too late," I say. "I think they already know what we're up to."

The woman in uniform crosses the road and walks towards our house. I grip the windowsill as my legs shake and my heart pounds bruised damson shapes.

"She's coming, Dad. She's going to arrest me for what I did to Bee Larkham. The police have figured it out. They've solved the crime."

"No one's going to arrest you, and for the last time, stop worrying about Bee." Dad's voice is spiky and hard. "The police still don't know anything about Friday night. You just need to do exactly as I say. Stay up here and don't come down. I'll sort this out."

He bounds down the stairs and must have reached the door before the policewoman knocked because I don't see any dark brown shapes. I tiptoe to the top of the landing.

"Hi! Can I help you?"

"Is it OK if I come inside, Mr. Wishart?" *Tinned tuna color.*

"I'm waiting for an important call, to be perfectly honest. I'm working from home today."

That's another lie, I'm sure. Not about working from home. I mean the telephone call. His voice has darkened because the falsehood's catching in his throat, but the policewoman won't notice. She doesn't realize what the colors look like when he lies, the way I do.

"It'll only be for a few minutes."

"Of course. Come in. Sorry. I apologize for the mess. The cleaner hasn't been this week."

That's because the cleaner doesn't exist unless you count Dad wearing bright yellow rubber gloves and halfheartedly scrubbing the toilet basin every fortnight.

I hear dark orange footsteps in the hallway. As they enter the sitting room, I creep down the stairs, careful to avoid the fifth, creaking, brownish pink step. The door is ajar and there's a pop of maroon as someone sits in the leather armchair. Dad, probably. It's his favorite seat. He'll have raced the policewoman to sit there first.

"What do you do, Mr. Wishart, if you don't mind me asking?" the policewoman asks. "Workwise?"

"You can call me Ed," he replies. "I work for a business software company now, designing apps."

"That sounds exciting."

"Hardly. It's things like data systems and survey apps, which are incredibly dull, but I work regular hours, most of the time anyway, when we're not bidding for new contracts. I get to spend more time with Jasper. That's important, you know, with his problems. Anyway, I'm sure you don't want to hear all about this. How can I help?"

"It's about your neighbor Bee Larkham," the woman says. "How well do you know her?"

Dad thinks for a few seconds. He's learnt this technique from the Royal Marines and TV shows like *Criminal Minds*.

It's important to stop and think before blurting out something by accident. Don't give in to interrogation techniques.

"To be honest, I don't know her all that well," he says finally. "I mean, only as well as other people on the street. Enough to say hello and goodbye to."

"Your son is a regular visitor to her house? Isn't that right?" There's a rustle of paper. The policewoman must be consulting her notebook the way I do, to make sure she hasn't made any mistakes. "He takes music lessons with her?"

"No, it's nothing as formal as that. He likes listening to music. They both do. He used to pop around after school to watch the parakeets from her bedroom window." He stops. "Wow, that sounds bad when I say it out loud. Jasper said it was the best view. I didn't think to question it. It sounded innocent. Jasper is an innocent."

More silence.

"Obviously, I've put a stop to all that now, considering the allegations," he says. "I've told him not to go anywhere near Bee's house, even to feed the parakeets."

Dad's doing all the talking, which breaks the rules.

Don't try to fill silences.

"I mean, you have to understand, I'd never have let him go over there, let alone up to her bedroom, if I suspected any funny business."

The policewoman speaks finally. "Do you suspect funny business went on at Twenty Vincent Gardens now?"

"I honestly don't know what to think. I mean the allegations from that boy's dad are shocking. I find them hard to believe, but why would he lie about something as serious as that?"

There's another short silence.

"Can I ask why you find what's alleged to have happened between Bee Larkham and a minor hard to believe?"

That's cornered Dad. He mutters something. His words come out in a jumble, so he starts again.

"I mean, she never struck me as predatory. You know, a pedophile. She seemed, well, normal. She didn't seem interested in Jasper. Well not in that way, anyway. They were friends."

"You didn't think it odd that a woman in her early twenties wanted to be friends with someone your son's age?"

The chair creaks darker maroon circles.

"Look, I've told you. I didn't suspect anything. I had no idea about the notes and the presents you say Jasper delivered for her. Bee and

Jasper both love music. They love the parakeets that nest in her tree. They have that in common too. That's what drew them together."

Also Lucas Drury.

"Is there anything else? I should be getting on. I'm expecting my work call any minute." Color bursts from the chair again as Dad fidgets.

"Just a few more questions, Mr. Wishart, if I may? Does Miss Larkham have any family that she could be visiting?"

"I don't think she has any family left. Her late mother lived on this street for donkey's years, but they were estranged. David at number twenty-two might know more about other possible relations or Ollie at number eighteen. His mum passed away recently and she was best friends with Pauline Larkham, apparently."

"What about her friends or boyfriends? Is there anyone else who could help us track down her current whereabouts?"

Only Dad holds the secret to Bee Larkham's whereabouts, but he's unlikely to give up the location of her body.

"I wouldn't know, sorry," Dad says. "Again, David Gilbert's your best bet. He's lived here for years and is always the first to know what's happening on this street. He's into everyone's business, if you get my drift."

"You have no idea where Miss Larkham could be?"

Dad doesn't miss a single beat.

"None. Whatsoever." He takes a breath. "I haven't seen her for days."

Even I can tell he's made a mistake. He should have ended the sentence after "whatsoever." He shouldn't have panicked and carried on, because he's invited another question from the policewoman.

"When was the last time you saw her?"

"Let me see." Dad's flustered. His chair's squeaking dark brownish plum. "She's usually around at weekends because she plays her music loudly and upsets the neighbors. I don't think I remember hearing anything this weekend. Have you asked David or Ollie over the road?"

He's playing for time again, but the policewoman's noticed he hasn't answered her question properly.

"I'll ask them, thanks. When was the last time *you* saw Miss Larkham?"

I suck in my breath. It all comes down to this. Is Dad finally going to tell the truth or not?

"Me? That would probably have been last Friday. Yes, definitely Friday. Friday was the last time."

"And where was that?"

"How do you mean?"

"Where did you see Miss Larkham? Here? Elsewhere?"

"Oh, I see. Here. On this street. Well, at her house. The front door of her house, anyway. I didn't go inside."

"What time was that?"

"It'd have been about nine thirty in the evening, I guess. I don't know exactly."

My hands grip the banister tightly.

"What was the purpose of your visit?"

Dad shifts in his seat again, making the colors dance noisily. "I wanted to talk to her about Jasper."

"So you did have some concerns about Miss Larkham's behavior towards your son?"

"No, not anything like that. She'd upset Jasper. They'd had a falling-out over something. I wanted to discuss it with her. Patch up any misunderstandings that might have happened."

I bite my lip, hard.

"Was anyone else with her?"

"No. I think she was alone, but I can't be sure. Like I said, I didn't go inside."

"And how did she seem to you?"

"Distressed, maybe? Agitated about the tiff with Jasper, but we straightened things out. We didn't talk for more than a couple of minutes, if that. I thought everything was sorted. Back to normal. She had her music on full blast for hours after that, probably until about one A.M."

"Was the—" The policewoman's voice stops. There's a bubble-gum pink crackle from her radio. "Copy that." The radio crackles again. "I have to go, Mr. Wishart. Perhaps we can pick this up again? And if you see Miss Larkham in the meantime, please let her know that we need to speak to her urgently. She should come into the station with her solicitor when she gets back."

"Of course. I'm not sure what else I can say that will be of help, but I'm working from home all this week as my son's not well."

They discuss this briefly. I only manage to catch the words *school* and *hospital* and *social worker*.

"Thank you for your time."

I dart back up the stairs as the footsteps clatter into the hall. The front door opens and shuts, chestnut circles.

"You can come down now," Dad says. "She's gone."

I think the colors from the landing have given me away, but he can't see them, of course.

"I know you're there, Jasper. There's no use pretending."

I take forty-five seconds to walk down the stairs. "You didn't tell the policewoman *absolutely* everything," I point out.

"I told her enough. I told her all she needed to know about Friday night, without getting us both into trouble."

I stand at the bottom of the stairs, gripping the banister. "Don't you think she needed to know about the baby in Bee Larkham's tummy?"

"W-what? What do you mean?"

I can't look at him, not after all the deliberate inaccuracies in his story.

Will Dad be caught? Will the policewoman check back, the way I'm comparing my paintings and notebooks against each other for misleading paint strokes and rogue colors?

There's no use pretending.

"We need to talk, Jasper. Before this goes any further. Before you—"

"Don't you have to wait for an important call from work?" I interrupt.

I know the answer. I'm testing him.

"I only said that to get rid of the police officer," he says, falling into my trap. "No one's trying to get hold of me. Not today, anyway."

Gotcha!

I spotted eight more lies in his story to the policewoman. There could be more, but I stopped counting.

Trying to keep track of all Dad's falsehoods is tricky. I'm not *that* clever.

* * *

In my head, I've painted over all the lies Dad told the policewoman with a large, soft brush. I don't want to think about them again, or the ones he told me in the kitchen after she'd left.

He refuses to believe what Lucas Drury told me in the science lab: the note Bee Larkham forced me to deliver to his house last week revealed she was pregnant. She wanted to meet up to discuss what to do.

I knew nothing, Jasper. I promise you.

Now we're in a Western-style standoff.

Bang, bang.

You're dead.

Likes the pheasants. And the foxes. And the parakeets.

I stare out of the window. Three bird feeders are empty already and the rest have less than a third left. The parakeets have enjoyed a feast. Will Custard Yellow remember to refill the feeders later today?

The parakeets are costing me a fortune. It doesn't matter how many times I refill the feeders during the day, I guarantee they'll be empty by evening. They're always hungry.

That's what Bee Larkham used to say. Well, at least that's what I think I remember, but my memory could be playing tricks on me the way it did about our first meeting and the devil in the skip.

I used to be a reliable painter.

That's not true anymore, even though I always use acrylics, which give me the shades and textures I can't get from watercolors.

My brush frequently deceives me.

I have to stick to the facts and paint them in all their painful, embarrassing, hurtful, smarting, squirmish colors.

I must accurately record my second meeting with Bee Larkham—the day she decided to dramatically change all the colors on our street.

It was a Tuesday, the bottle green day I agreed to become her accomplice.

21

January 19, 3:18 P.M.
Award-Winning Sky Blue on paper

Our first introduction had taken place straight after school, so I figured that was the time she expected me the following day. I didn't want to be late because second impressions are important too.

I broke into a run, but as I cleared the school gates, I bumped into someone. They stepped directly into my path.

"Sorry," I mumbled. "My fault."

A hand grasped my wrist.

I pulled away, not looking up. In my peripheral vision, I caught a glimpse of navy, not the black blazer I expected.

It was a woman with long red hair wearing shades of blue.

"I apologize." I bellowed loudly in case the person hadn't heard the first time. "Please let go."

The hand dropped. This had to be a mum picking up a Year 7.

Mum would have done that for me in the first few terms.

"You're the boy with the binoculars," a sky blue voice said.

I knew that color, Bee Larkham's voice. This time I did look up. I was wrong. This woman's voice was the exact shade of sky blue, but her hair was bright cherry red, not blond. It wasn't my new neighbor.

She wore a dark navy coat and had forgotten to do up some buttons on her light cornflower blue top. It flapped open. I glanced away. I didn't know who this stranger with the alien skin was or who'd told her about my binoculars, but news had traveled worryingly fast from my street to school and back.

"I'm sorry," I repeated again. "I have to go. I'm late for an important meeting."

"It's John, isn't it? No, but it's something beginning with J. Let me see." The woman paused. "Jasper! You're the boy from my street who loves parakeets as much as I do."

What?

The word formed in a cartoon-like cool blue bubble outside my body and drifted away, over the school gates.

"It's Bee. Bee Larkham. Don't you remember? You came over yesterday to say hello. I live opposite you. I'm your new neighbor in Vincent Gardens."

"Of course. Sorry." I looked down at the lumps of white chewing gum stuck on the pavement. This was Bee Larkham, but she didn't look like Bee Larkham. This woman had bright cherry red hair, not blond. She was wearing silver acorns, not swallows, in her ears. All my markers were off.

"You don't recognize me, do you?" she asked.

I didn't want to lie, not to Bee Larkham. Was this her? I honestly couldn't tell. I had to trust her voice.

Sky blue.

"You look different," I pointed out, "but sound the same."

"It's the hair. I dyed it this morning. I wanted a change from the past. Do you like it?"

"No. I don't like cherry red. You looked better blond."

"God, you're honest, aren't you? Tell it like it is, why don't you?"

I couldn't tell if she was upset or not, so I could only repeat the truth. "You're not yourself. You don't have red hair. It should be blond. Blond is your real color."

"Well, it's not naturally blond. It's mousy brown, but maybe you're right. My mum always hated red hair. I thought I'd try it, although I'm not sure this is the shade I was going for." She fiddled with the ends. "It's not permanent. I can wash it out."

"That's good. You'll look like Bee Larkham and be pretty again."

The Bee Larkham impersonator made a dark blue hollow-tube noise, which sounded like a cross between a snort and a laugh. "I'm going to ask you a favor, Jasper, since you've been so mean to me and you can't say no. Not now you've hurt my feelings."

I bit my lip, hard, trying to imagine what I'd said that could have wounded her.

"I'm giving out these flyers about my music lessons," she said. "Can you help me hand them out?"

I moved my head up and down. We were supposed to have our meeting at her house, but I didn't mind she'd changed the venue at the last minute. This way, I wouldn't arrive sweaty and hot.

I'd accidentally bumped into her, fortunately; otherwise I'd have turned up at her empty house. I'd have been there and she'd have been here, outside my school.

She handed me a pile of duck-egg blue paper, with words printed in big letters:

MUSIC LESSONS WITH GLOBAL
AWARD-WINNING MUSICIAN
Free taster sessions in piano, guitar, and electric guitar.
All instruments tutored. Singers welcome!

"What global awards have you won?" I asked.

I didn't look at her or anyone else as I stretched out my hand, gripping the paper. I concentrated hard to make sure I did the job correctly, to impress Bee Larkham and make her realize how helpful I could be. That way she might think of me if she needed more favors.

I can't be sure who took my flyers. I don't know if Lucas Drury grabbed one from her or me as he walked out of school that day. Maybe he was already drawn to Bee Larkham. Or maybe it was his brother, Lee. I guess it doesn't matter which of us was responsible, we're both culpable. Lee Drury began electric guitar lessons shortly afterwards.

"Oh, I got all kinds of big awards in Australia before I went into teaching," she replied. "I was in a few bands, playing keyboards and guitar. Sometimes singing. People loved me, you know?"

"What bands?" I asked. "What were their names?"

"You wouldn't have heard of them over here." She stopped talking as she gave out another flyer. "I'm only giving music lessons to get some cash while I renovate the house and sort myself out. Getting back into the music industry, that's my priority, you know? I'll need money for rewiring and fixing the roof. Mum's house is a wreck. I can't put it on the market like this. I'll lose too much money, which I need for demo tapes and videos. I have to put up with living here for the time being."

I didn't know anything about the music industry, but I thought she wouldn't have any trouble getting back into it. I believed in her already, even when I hadn't actually heard her sing a note.

"Thank you, thank you." Bee Larkham repeated the words as she dished out each flyer. She was doing a far better job than me, so I tried to speed up, but papers kept sticking together. I didn't want to hand out two or three at once.

In my peripheral vision, I saw a group of tall Blazers walk out of school. They took flyers from Bee Larkham's hand, not mine. *Fortunately.*

"Wow," she said, after they walked away. "Boys didn't look like that when I was in the sixth form. Is there something in the tap water around here?"

"I've no idea what's in the water." Why didn't I know the answer to her question? I drank tap water all the time, yet Bee Larkham had only recently arrived back in this country and already realized it was poisonous. I figured it would be safer to drink bottled water in future.

"Watch out! You're dropping some," she cried.

A couple of pieces of paper had slipped from my fingers and were snatched up by the wind.

"I'm sorry. I'm so sorry." I tried to snatch them back, but she caught my arm.

"No. It's OK. Look, look!" She tossed her paper up into the air to join mine. "They're free!"

We both laughed as they danced together in the wind, as one, as if nothing could ever separate them. *Like our colors.* I don't remember ever seeing them fall to the ground.

"You got me thinking after we talked yesterday," she said, staring up at the sky. "I've bought some bird feeders and seed to attract parakeets to my oak tree. The man in the pet shop says there's a large communal roost site nearby. I want to bring some color to this street, but I'm going to need your help. Are you with me on this, Jasper?"

"Yes, yes, yes!" I cried. "I love bright colors and parakeets more than anything else in the world. I'll do anything you want, Bee Larkham. Anything."

22

January 22, 7:02 A.M.
Pandemonium on canvas

Three days later, the colors Bee Larkham and me had desperately
wanted to bring to Vincent Gardens finally arrived.

Happy fuchsia pink and sapphire showers with golden droplets.

Cornflower and sapphire blues transformed to cobalt, into violet,
and back again, with flashes of golden, glowing yellow.

I grabbed my binoculars and threw the window open. The sight
made me scream bright blue clouds.

The parakeet had returned and wasn't alone. It had brought rein-
forcements, a *pandemonium*.

The birds clung to the six feeders in Bee Larkham's front garden.
I'd helped her hang them up in the oak tree after we walked home
together from school.

More and more parakeets arrived.

I counted twenty.

*Hundreds of tiny golden droplets exploded in a joyous fountain from
the shimmering blues, pinks, and purples.*

It was like being a VIP guest at the world's best fireworks display,
except I wasn't the only spectator.

The upstairs window of the house next to Bee Larkham's banged
open and a man appeared. I didn't recognize his cabbage green pajamas, but I knew that David Gilbert lived alone at number 22.

"Shoo! Get out of here!" He yelled prickly tomato red words at the
parakeets—brighter, more brittle tones than his usual dull grainy red.

No matter. The birds didn't care; they didn't fly away.

Instead, more parakeets arrived in a chorus of brilliant ultramarine with dustings of lilac and electric violet.

The window at number 22 slammed shut and curtains swished across the glass. As I jotted details in my notebook, another window in the street opened. This time it belonged to the house I liked most— number 20.

A woman with long hair, wearing a white T-shirt, waved at me. This had to be global award-winning music teacher Bee Larkham, even though her hair color wasn't red. She must have dyed it blond again.

I waved back. "They came, Bee Larkham!" I shouted croakily. "The feeders worked!"

Because of you, I wanted to add, but my voice had cracked to a delicate eggshell blue. The parakeets had come because of Bee Larkham's magnificent welcome, because of her bird feeders.

"We did it!" she shouted. *Bright sky blue.*

"Who are you speaking to?"

I didn't turn around. I recognized the color of Dad's voice, and no other man could have been in our house at this time. "It's Bee. Bee Larkham."

I hadn't told him I'd paid a visit to her house and she'd called him handsome or that I'd helped her hand out flyers outside my school and hang up bird feeders in her front garden. He wasn't part of our friendship. I didn't want him to be.

"Who?" He walked across the room to the window, wearing light gray Calvin Klein boxer shorts. His chest hairs curled up in embarrassment. Mine would have too, if I had any. "Oh. The new neighbor. I meant to tell you, David says she's Mrs. Larkham's wayward daughter. A total basket case, apparently, ever since she was a kid. They'd been estranged for years. She never visited her mum in the old folks' home and didn't even turn up to the funeral. She only came back because she inherited the house."

Estranged was a gray gravel-chip word and not pleasant to look at for long.

"Maybe she stayed away because she knew she wasn't loved," I said. "She realized her mum didn't want her and thought she got in the way."

"If you say so. I doubt she'll stay around long. She'll probably get the house ready to sell and move on as soon as possible. She's like a fish out of water on this street."

Dad was wrong about this on many levels. Bee Larkham had never mentioned fish and she'd bought bird feeders to attract the parakeets. That meant she was setting up home. She was staying.

Bee Larkham waved again. She leaned so far out of the window, I was afraid she might fall.

Dad sucked in his tummy as he waved back. "Maybe we should get around to introducing ourselves. I think she'd like that, you know, to feel welcome on this street."

I ignored him and watched the parakeets. Dad was wrong again; Bee Larkham already felt welcome. She didn't need to meet him now we'd become such Great Friends.

Later that morning, 8:29 A.M.
Pandemonium in Grave Danger on canvas

"Something has to be done about this situation before it gets out of hand." Scratchy red words bubbled angrily over the canvas of colors that erupted joyfully from Bee Larkham's oak tree.

The feeders had been empty since 7:31 A.M., but the parakeets continued their serenade, high up in the branches. I was enjoying the preschool recital, standing next to Dad on the pavement, until a man approached with a dog barking yellow French fries. His cords were a familiar cherry color.

"Shhh," I said, pointing up to the tree. "Don't disturb them, David Gilbert."

"Is he joking?" the man with the dull grainy red voice asked. "*I'm* the one who needs to be quiet?"

"He loves birds, particularly parakeets," Dad replied. "I can't drag him away."

I heard the grayish black geometric shape of footsteps. A man wearing a black duffel coat walked towards us, smoking a cigarette. I turned back to look at the tree, afraid I might miss something.

"What do you think of all this, Ollie?" Dad's muddy ocher voice asked. "Are you a fan of our street's new visitors or not?"

I didn't pay attention to the low mutterings or cigarette smoke because five parakeets fluttered from one branch to another, screeching glimmering violet-blue shades.

"I'll tell you what I think," the dull grainy red voice said. "Those buggers woke me up. I want to blow them out of that tree with my shotgun."

David Gilbert.

I closed my eyes and tried to block out the shotgun's toxic oil-spillage shade. It easily overpowered the amethyst blues of the parakeets. It merged with the rancid seaweed swearword, producing something far more dangerous.

Something that could wipe out all the wildlife on our street.

"Come on, David, it's not that bad," Dad said.

I couldn't speak. I couldn't defend the birds. I couldn't move.

This was the first time I let them down badly, but it wasn't the last.

I focused on important details about the Death Threat, which I could write down later in my notebook and produce as evidence for the police. I checked my watch and shut my eyes again. The time was 8:29 A.M. The potential murderer was David Gilbert at number 22.

There were three reliable witnesses: me, Dad, and Smoking Black Duffel Coat Man. I hadn't seen the color of this man's voice, but Dad had called him Ollie. This would probably make him Ollie Watkins, from number 18, but I'd have to check with Dad later to make sure my notebook records were truly accurate.

Bee Larkham hadn't heard the threat. She'd been shielded from the ugly colors, but they quickly darkened to an even nastier shade that I couldn't protect her from.

Murky brown unstructured shapes.

Bang, bang, bang.

My eyes flew open. Cherry Cords was no longer on the pavement. He stood outside Bee Larkham's house, knocking loudly on the front door. His dog barked yellow French fries next to him.

This time I acted, because my friend, as well as the parakeets, was in danger from David Gilbert. I ran after him.

"Come back, Son! We need to stay out of this. It's not our fight. You're going to be late for school!"

Dad followed, trying to catch my arm, but I shook him off. He was wrong, yet again. I had to protect my friend. This was *my* fight. She was *my* friend. They were *our* parakeets. We'd brought them to this street. We were in this together.

It took Bee Larkham forty-five seconds to open her door. She was wearing her cobalt blue dressing gown again.

"Wow. I have an early morning welcoming committee." She stared at the man on her doorstep, at me, followed by Dad. Last, she looked past us as she fastened her dressing gown tightly. Smoking Black Duffel Coat Man had stayed behind on the pavement—he must have wanted to keep out of the argument. Bee's mouth didn't turn up at the ends. It didn't even twitch.

"I want to talk to you about the parakeets, Beatrice," David Gilbert said.

"Her name is Bee, with an *e* not an *a*." My voice cracked. "And you should leave, David Gilbert."

I must have spoken too quietly because he didn't correct himself. He didn't leave.

I tried to speak again, but my light, cool blue words were wiped out by scratchy red shards of glass.

"You have *six* feeders, hanging from that tree." He pointed over his shoulder. "They're encouraging the birds to infest our street, which is something we certainly don't want."

A smooth, dusky blue sigh escaped from Bee Larkham's lips. "That's the point, David, to encourage the birds *to visit the street*. They're beautiful, don't you think? Such vivid colors; so exotic. It reminds me of home, of Australia. They make me feel homesick."

"That's all very well, but they're *incredibly* noisy. Over here, they're treated as pests, like foxes. If you encourage them with your feeders they'll end up staying. These sorts of birds develop habits rapidly. Believe me, I know. They wreck habitats and drive out other birds."

"Well, I certainly hope they do stay on this street," she said. "I think it could do with brightening up. They'll inject color into everyone's lives. Shake everything up around here."

Dad looked down at me as I applauded. Those were my views exactly; we spoke with one blue voice. We had stood up to David Gilbert, something no one else on this street dared to do.

"You're not going to take all the feeders down when I've alerted you to a potentially serious problem?" David Gilbert asked. "When the parakeets woke up half the street this morning with their racket?"

"No. I am not. This is nature, David. Who am I to interfere with the circle of life? The parakeets are free to come and go in my front garden as they please. I can't control them any more than you can."

"You are *interfering* with nature by encouraging the birds. Six feeders is totally overboard." His voice became a darker shade of blood red. "Not only are the birds a problem on a noise level, they could ruin people's gardens. They'll strip all the flower buds off the trees come spring."

Bee Larkham folded her arms in a tight knot and didn't reply.

"I take it from your silence, Beatrice, you're not going to be reasonable about this? Or about the music you've played at top volume ever since you moved in? Or the car you've left, leaking oil, directly outside Mrs. Watkins's house? It's an inconvenience for Ollie. He has to park much further down the street now." He pointed at Smoking Black Duffel Coat Man, who hadn't moved from the pavement.

"I'm sorry you're upset, but I must get on with chucking out the crap my mum collected over the years," she said loudly. "It all has to go. Even the precious ornaments you old people seem to like so much. I don't want to keep any of them."

She waved, I think at me, so I waved back vigorously, to signal I was 100 percent behind her.

I was her ally in a hostile environment despite her bad language.

As she closed the door, David Gilbert stuck his foot out. The door bounced back sharp chestnut as it hit his shoe.

"What do you think you're doing?" she asked.

"You don't seem to understand the way it works on this street, Beatrice," he said. "We look after each other. We treat our neighbors well, the way your mother used to. We don't deliberately go out of our way to upset the balance."

"Good. You and your friend here can lead by example and not upset me again. I've had enough of the pair of you already and I've not been back a week."

"I'm sorry—" Dad started.

"Please remove your foot, David," Bee Larkham said quietly. "Before I do something I doubt I'll regret."

"Of course, but let me tell you something I *doubt* you know," David Gilbert said, stepping back from the doorway. "Parakeets have officially been declared a pest by Natural England. That allows a landowner or an authorized person to shoot them if they cause a specific problem."

"Seriously? Are you threatening me? Is that what you're doing?"

"I'm threatening the parakeets," David Gilbert said. "Remember that, Beatrice."

"Leave me the hell alone! All of you!" She slammed the door shut, shiny conker-colored rectangles.

I silently screamed as I stamped my feet hard on the ground over and over again. I'd never felt the urge more strongly to kick someone than I did at that moment, standing next to David Gilbert.

"Was that necessary, David?" my dad asked. "They're just birds. They're not worth having a massive fall-out about."

David Gilbert took a step closer.

"Yes, I believe it was necessary. Beatrice Larkham needs to know the ground rules. She has to understand there will be serious repercussions unless she starts toeing the line on my street."

23

THURSDAY (APPLE GREEN)

Afternoon

I check from my window—Bee Larkham's long gone, but the battle line remains. It hasn't faded from people's shoes walking over it every day or been washed away by rain. It didn't disappear the day she died. It remains bright and strong in hue because David Gilbert hasn't gone anywhere. He's carrying on as normal, as if nothing's changed.

The line knows different. It became permanently etched on the pavement outside our house the day of his first threat, defiantly stretching across the road in a bright sky blue color, not caring what the other neighbors thought or said. It encircled Bee Larkham's front garden and disappeared down the alleyway at the back of her house.

Methodically, I go back through my bird notebooks and stack them next to the canvases I've completed—*Pandemonium* and *Pandemonium in Grave Danger*.

They're both facing the wall; the parakeets must be protected from David Gilbert's evil colors.

A line's drawn in my notebooks too, dividing the bird sightings before this date and after. From the day of David Gilbert's threats onwards, I didn't just record the sightings of parakeets, coal tits, pigeons, goldfinches, and chaffinches on our street.

I started a detailed log of David Gilbert's movements, the comings and goings of the man at number 22. I also jotted down descriptions of everyone who walked up Bee Larkham's front path in case they posed a danger to the parakeets, music pupils included. That was necessary, because wasn't there a chance that David Gilbert was devious? He could try to get other people on his side, the way Dad said he'd asked all the neighbors to sign his petition to get speed bumps installed on this street.

To be especially careful, I noted the movements of other neighbors too—particularly Cindy at number 24, a lunchtime supervisor at a local primary school who has two daughters. I'd seen Cherry Cords knock on her door several times, which meant they could be in cahoots.

I had to build up a case, which I could present to the police after I'd gathered enough evidence because they hadn't taken my first 999 call about the death threat seriously.

This was hugely time-consuming but totally necessary.

I had to collect evidence of criminal wrongdoing.

Evidence of a serious, imminent threat to the parakeets.

Evidence the police couldn't ignore.

I check my notebook from January 22 again, flicking forwards and back, and it confirms what I already know. My recording system had a fatal flaw: too many glaring holes.

I'd made a record of David Gilbert's first threat to kill the parakeets but failed to accurately record what he said to Bee Larkham on her doorstep minutes later. I'd tried to be truthful, but I remember ripping out the page in my notebook and tearing it into tiny bits later that evening. The terrible words had hurt my eyes too much.

That was a mistake, along with all the other gaps in my account, the incriminating empty pages that followed.

I know it's no excuse, but I couldn't guard the oak tree twenty-four hours a day. I had to go to school. I had to sleep. I had to eat. I couldn't stand all day and night at my window, with my binoculars, however much I wanted to.

Lives were lost during one of those blank spaces, when I didn't spot the danger. I wasn't around to prevent the attack.

My failure led to a dozen dead parakeets.

I can't fill in those gaps on white paper, the way I've repainted the disturbing scenes from our street.

It's not because I've blanked it out or can't remember but because I don't know exactly when the massacre happened.

Another mystery for me to solve, and I know I won't like what I finally discover.

Soft buttery yellow. Dad's creeping up the stairs to check on me. I can't bear to talk to him. To look at him, to see the color of his lies about Bee Larkham and Mum.

I spring forward and wedge a chair under the door handle.

Tap, tap, tap. *Small dots of caramel.*

I ignore the colors and shapes as the handle jangles impatiently.

"Jasper? Son? Can you let me in?"

I line up my brushes and rearrange my paints, ready for the next scene. I don't want to be interrupted. I don't want my memories to be colored in for me by Dad. They're mine, not his. *Like my binoculars.* He can't borrow them. He could damage them, make them useless.

"I want to apologize for what I said downstairs," he says loudly. There's a blob of khaki brown as he gently butts his head against the door. "We should talk about Bee. About the baby you think she's having too, if that's what you want to do. I was wrong to stop you from talking about her. I know that now." The door makes another light brown blob. "I'm trying to get my head around what's happened."

Is he?

I don't believe him. *I hate him. He lies. All the time.*

I watch the door. The handle's stopped moving, but I know he's still there. The floorboard creaks dusky pink. I want his color to fade into the background and disappear completely.

"I'm sorry for earlier, Jasper. Honestly, I am. I wish I could take back the things I said."

I'm sorry for earlier.

That's what Dad said the first time *he* met Bee Larkham.

I close my eyes and can already see the painting I must attempt next. Dad's voice: *soft, blunt shapes and light, muddy ocher.*

I'll make it dance around the paper with Bee's sky blue. The colors will circle each other suspiciously at first before they merge as if they belong together.

Which they don't.

I have to work hard to keep them apart. I don't want their colors to bleed into each other. I can't bear to see that happen. I don't want to look at the hue they produce.

"Go away!" I shout at the door. "I'm tired. Go away and leave me alone. I hate you both."

"Jasper!"

We can both lie. "I just want to sleep. I need to sleep. I'm going back to bed."

"OK, OK. That will do you good," Dad says. "But I can't let you lock yourself in. I can't let you hurt yourself again. I'll go away now and check up on you in fifteen minutes. I'm going to time it on my stopwatch. If the door's not unlocked when I come back up, Jasper, I'm going to kick it down, whether you're asleep or not. Do you understand?"

I look at my watch. It's 1:30 P.M. I'm going to time *him* on my watch, which he fixed. He's deceiving me yet again. He'll be back in ten minutes, not fifteen, but that's long enough to attempt another troubling painting.

I must re-create the unsightly color that's produced when muddy ocher is introduced to sky blue.

24

January 22
Dirty Sap Circles on paper

The threat to harm the parakeets lingered over me at school, long after the 999 call I'd made in the toilets.

My geography teacher, Mr. Packham, was upset because I'd kicked chairs and refused to sit down. He didn't understand I couldn't put my mobile away. I had to hold it and wait for a detective to ring me back. I needed to know what the police planned to do about David Gilbert.

Mr. Packham tried to take the phone off me and I screamed electric aquamarine clouds at him. He took me to the head teacher's office, instead of Learning Support. I sat on the dull navy chair beside the door for three minutes and twelve seconds. When Mrs. Moore told me to come in, she already knew the story. She'd rung my dad at work and he'd spoken to the police. They had his details on file from my other calls to the unhelpful 999 operators.

Your dad says not to worry about the parakeets. The police have logged your call. You mustn't get upset about this. It's not a problem.

What does logged *mean? Are the police actually doing something? Are they investigating David Gilbert? Will they arrest him and arrange patrols of our street to protect the parakeets while I'm at school? What are they actually doing?*

Mrs. Moore didn't know, which I stressed made her totally useless. After that, I had to work in the learning support room all day and didn't even leave to go to the canteen at lunchtime.

A teaching assistant brought a tray and sat next to me. Her jaw made a dark pink clicking sound as she chewed on a sandwich, which made me grind my nails into the palm of my hand.

The day stretched on, without any detective arriving to talk to me. *Bad news.*

I feared the police had closed the case before they'd even opened it, because it involved parakeets, not human beings, who were their first priority. I knew this was a huge mistake.

I told another teaching assistant who came to supervise me, but he wasn't interested. He told me to stop talking and get on with my work. After that, I gave up. I pretended I was working.

I pretended I was normal.

Deep down inside, I didn't believe my head teacher. I didn't believe Dad. I worried about Bee Larkham and the parakeets all day.

Two dozen parakeets fluttered around Bee Larkham's oak tree when I got back from school. Bee had also draped strings of peanuts from the branches of the smaller Chinese red birch. I raced upstairs to my bedroom and stood on guard with my binoculars at the window, but I didn't catch a glimpse of David Gilbert and his shotgun. Maybe I was wrong; the police hadn't ignored my call. They'd patrolled the street while I was away and protected the pandemonium of parakeets.

I'd scared David Gilbert away.

Despite this, Dad was worried about our new neighbor when he came home from work. He said we should double-check she was doing OK after the argument with David. I pointed out this was unnecessary as the police knew all about the bird killer at 22 Vincent Gardens.

My tummy growled budgerigar green colors, signaling it was close to teatime. They clashed with a bunch of wilting purple tulips Dad had picked up from the corner shop on the way home.

"Let's pop round now in case we miss her," he insisted. "She could go out for the evening."

He clutched the flowers in his right hand, the way he'd held my binoculars the night we watched her dance. Tightly. Like he didn't want to ever let go.

"She doesn't go out in the evenings," I argued. "She stays home and listens to her Martian music or plays the piano. Other times she covers her eyes with her hands and rocks on the floor while she holds a steel blue book. I've seen her from my window."

"Look. We're doing it, and when we get back we're going to have a chat about respecting other people's privacy. Are you coming or not?" He whipped his baseball cap off the coat rack in the hall.

I followed him over the road to her front door. I didn't want him to ruin things between Bee Larkham and me. The timing was also wrong: almost 6:00 P.M., when I should eat supper.

Dad paused, staring up at her roof.

"What is it?" I hoped he'd had second thoughts and would go home and cook my chicken pie, our usual Friday night tea.

"I saw a parakeet. It crawled into the eave space. There goes another."

"Wow."

I peered up, hoping for a glimpse of green tail feathers or a beak, just as Bee Larkham opened the door.

"Hello again, Jasper." *Sky blue.*

I looked down and counted seven cardboard boxes in the hallway. "Do you have any binoculars to watch the parakeets up there?" I pointed.

"Er, not to hand. Why? Did you forget yours?"

"Yes. I'll remember next time."

I checked her hair: blond, not red. Her earrings were little silver swallows. "One swallow's upside down."

"Is it?" She stared up at the roof. "With the parakeet?"

I snorted cool blue bubbles. "You're funny. Swallows and parakeets would never roost together. They're totally different species."

Dad cut in with muddy ocher before I could explain about her earring. "I didn't have a chance to introduce myself properly this morning. I'm Jasper's dad, Ed. We live over there." He pointed over his shoulder.

"I know where you live," she replied. "I've already had a chat with Jasper about the parakeets and binoculars. You know, watching *everything* from his bedroom window."

Dad took off his cap and looked down at me. He raked a hand through his hair. "I didn't know. Sorry. We've talked about the binoculars, but Jasper does love to watch birds."

"And what about you? Do you love birds?"

Dad coughed clouds of rust-tinged ocher. "Some birds. Some I like a lot."

"Listen to you! Anyone would think you're flirting with me, Eddie."

"I wouldn't think that," I replied before Dad said something silly. "He wanted to give you his name, which is Ed, not Eddie. That's all. Now we're leaving because it's almost six P.M., which is my teatime."

Dad chuckled. "These are for you." He handed her the tulips. "Apologies—I couldn't get anything better. They were the only nondead flowers in the local shop. Look, I'm sorry for earlier. I had no idea David would lose the plot like that about the parakeets. He means well but can be a tad OCD at times."

"That's the understatement of the year," she said. "I'm back two minutes and he's been around virtually every single day to complain about something or other, and now the parakeets. Does he actually have a gun? Should I be worried about him?"

"Yes," I cut in. "You should be extremely worried. David Gilbert enjoys shooting pheasants and partridges, which makes him a murderer. We can't let him shoot the parakeets."

"Of course not," she replied. "I won't let that happen. I promise I'll guard them with my life, Jasper."

I gave her my best smile as a present because I believed her. I thought she'd do absolutely anything to protect the parakeets, the same way I would.

"Did you realize, they're in your eaves?" Dad asked, looking up. "The parakeets, I mean. That could cause more trouble if, say, they unwisely decide to set up home in David's eaves."

"No way!" She stepped out.

"Yep!" Dad's muddy ocher mingled into her sky blue. I shivered at their dirty sap circles.

They stood side by side, looking up. Her and Dad. Me on the opposing side. Her arm almost brushed Dad's. She wasn't wearing blue today, which was disappointing. Her top made a deep V-shape, and her arms were folded beneath it, pushing up alien skin, which erupted into mounds from the fabric.

"Your clothes are too small for you," I said. "They look silly that tight. You need to buy a size bigger."

"Jasper!" Dad stepped back. "That's rude. Apologize to Miss Larkham right now."

Out of the corner of my eye, I noticed Bee hitch up her top. "Whoops. Too much cleavage. Sorry. This is the PG version. Call me Bee, by the way. Is that better?"

I didn't know why I felt cross when I should be happy. The parakeets liked Bee Larkham so much they'd looked for routes into her house. If they found their way into her eaves, maybe they'd come into ours too.

Maybe they'd persuade Bee Larkham to stay.

"I'm hungry," I said. "I want to go home. It's three minutes past teatime."

"I'm sorry." Dad turned towards Bee. "I'm afraid he doesn't have a filter. He usually says the first thing that comes into his head."

"Don't worry," she replied. "I'm not easily offended. He's already advised me to change the color of my hair." I felt her gaze shift to me. "You were right about that, Jasper. I wasn't being myself. Blond suits me far more than red."

I hopped from one foot to the other while Dad laughed soft carrot-cake-colored circles.

"I should get a move on and cook his tea before he gets even grumpier. Let me know if you ever need anything. Give me a knock. I'm around most nights."

"Thanks. I might take you up on that offer with some of the heavy lifting. You know, furniture and boxes I need to move."

"Of course. Any time." Dad walked away but hesitated. "By the way, let me know if Jasper becomes a nuisance and I'll have words. He has a tendency to get fixated on things. On people. He becomes attached too quickly, particularly to women. You see, his mum . . ." He stopped talking. "Anyway, I apologize in advance if he gets too much."

I'd never hated Dad more than I did at that moment. I wanted to explain to Bee he wasn't telling the whole truth. I had interests and hobbies, that's all. That didn't make me a nuisance.

"Jasper could never be a nuisance to me," she said, without hesitation. "He's already been massively helpful. I don't know what I'd have done without him earlier this week."

Bee Larkham explained to Dad about the flyers—instinctively realizing he was trying to make me look bad. She believed *me*, not him. She'd shifted her position and stood by my side now.

"In fact I could do with another favor, if you don't mind, Jasper? Wait one minute." She raced back into the house and returned with a handful of flyers.

"Is it OK if Jasper hands these out at school next week?"

Dad's shoulders moved up and down as he looked at the flyers. "You're a musician?" he said softly, his voice the color of warm, buttery toast again. "I'm seriously impressed."

"I'm running free taster sessions. I thought Jasper could pass them out among his friends."

I was flattered she thought I had lots of friends; there were at least thirty flyers, which massively overestimated my popularity. Still, my heart sank.

"Will you come with me?" I glanced up hopefully, but her gaze was fixed on Dad.

"I can't, I'm afraid. I have to get the house straight before the classes. There's more to do than I first thought. The house has been neglected for so long. That's what happens when an old person's lived here, I guess."

"Oh."

I couldn't say no to her, but I'd hated giving out the flyers last time. I hadn't wanted to draw attention to myself. It's hard to be invisible if you're trying to get people to notice what's in your hand. The best part about helping Bee Larkham was throwing the pieces of paper up into the air and watching them fly.

"I'll think of a treat if you manage to get anyone to come along," she said.

"What kind of treat?"

"Well, you love birds, don't you? How about a chance to watch the parakeets from the front bedroom window? That way you can see them up close. You can bring your binoculars if you want."

"Can I come any time I want?"

"Well . . ."

"Now you've done it," Dad said, laughing. "I can see myself having to drag him out of your bedroom."

"Ha! You're already picturing yourself in my bedroom, are you? Cheeky bugger."

I jumped. I didn't want Bee Larkham to use dog-diarrhea-colored words, which were beneath someone like her.

Uncouth. That's a hollow red word with a greenish tail, which Mum used to describe people who swore. She felt the same about bad words as me. She hated their colors too.

I looked up from Bee Larkham and across to Dad. She was laughing and tying her hair into a knot around her middle finger the way she'd done with the removal men. His cheeks were chili-sauce red, which I guessed meant he was embarrassed by his mistake.

She'd invited *me* to watch the parakeets from her bedroom window, not *him.*

He'd got horribly confused and messed up, which was why I hadn't wanted him to come over in the first place.

"No, well. That came out badly. What I meant to say was—"

"You know, a surprise visitor's always a welcome visitor," she said, interrupting his dark ocher tones.

"I'll remember that." Dad's left eye closed and opened again.

Bee Larkham laughed larger bubbles of soft sky blue. "I'm the perfect hostess. I rarely turn anyone away."

The dirty sap circles make me shiver as I check my watch. I've got exactly six minutes and thirty seconds to complete the next picture before Dad kicks open my bedroom door with sharp splinters of glistening orange.

I need to paint exactly what happened the following week, without leaving out any awkward shade.

Looking out of the window, I grasp my paintbrush tightly. I'm unable to let it go even though I'm worried about where its accusatory strokes will take me next.

Our street is empty.

The police cars have disappeared, the officers have given up looking for clues. Why haven't they checked the alleyway that runs behind the houses on the opposite side of the street? Or have they?

Have they missed the trail of bread crumbs that leads to Bee Larkham's back door?

Dad couldn't have left her body in the house.

Decomposing bodies smell and attract flies; he'd have known that from his TV crime shows. He must have carried lifeless Bee Larkham out the back door and through the alleyway on Friday night—the same route I used to flee her house.

Dad would have realized the front door was too risky.

He knew where Bee Larkham kept her back door key because I'd told him about the secret hiding place after he found me in my den with the knife.

25

January 27, 4:30 P.M.
Blue Teal and Fir Tree Green on canvas

"Is it that time already?" Bee Larkham opened her front door five days later and breathed out bright sky blue bubbles. Her feet were bare, her blond hair loose around her shoulders, the way I liked it. I counted seven cardboard boxes in the hallway again.

"It's four thirty P.M. exactly," I said, checking my watch. "You haven't moved the boxes yet. That's how many were there before."

"What? Yes, I'm slow. Mum had packed these before she went into the home. I've dumped a few in the skip already. There's so much old crap to go through, I keep putting it off. I can't face it without getting pissed first. Too many sad memories, you know?"

I tried to turn up the corners of my lips to form a smile as I stepped inside. She had to stop using vile-colored words.

"Can we go to your bedroom, please?"

She giggled shimmering light sky blue circular blobs, opening the door wider. "You're not one to beat around the bush, are you? How can I refuse that kind of offer from a lovely gentleman like you?"

I took off my shoes and placed them neatly next to the sealed-up boxes. I waited for her to go up first. That's what Dad said I should do.

Don't get excited and run up the stairs before she says you can go into the bedroom. Do exactly as she tells you, otherwise she might not invite you back.

"Let me show you where to set up," she said. "I'll need to be quick because my music lessons are about to start. The first student will arrive soon. You'll need to be quiet, OK?"

I moved my head up and down to demonstrate I understood.

Bee Larkham climbed the threadbare red stairs and disappeared into a room off the landing, second left. I followed, holding my breath. The carpet was stained and smelly, probably teeming with germs. Maybe mites.

"It's my mum's old room, but I'm using it now," she said.

The room was as empty as the sitting room, cold too. The music had forced out most of the furniture onto the van or the skip outside. The windows were open, and the walls were a melting snowman white with gray gritty bits, except in two small areas, where I could clearly see the shapes of two crosses imprinted in sharp, pristine white.

"My mum's porcelain crucifixes of Jesus were first to go on the skip," she said, following my gaze. "It doesn't matter how hard I scrub the wallpaper, I can't get rid of the marks."

"The devil was looking for the crucifixes," I said, remembering the thing I'd seen in her skip.

"Who?"

I shook my head. Mentioning the devil was a mistake; it might scare her away. I didn't want her to sell the house and leave. She had to stay with the parakeets and me. "Nobody. Nothing."

"Excuse the mess." She picked up a black dustbin liner, spewing out clothes that were shades of gray and brown. "I need to take Mum's old clothes to a charity shop tomorrow. I'll probably try to pick up a new wardrobe too. Her old one was falling apart and the doors wouldn't shut properly. I don't want anything expensive. Just something to dress the room for showings."

The room was currently dressed with a chest of drawers next to the window, four bin bags, a dustpan and brush, a can of furniture polish, and three cardboard boxes. The heads of china ladies poked out of the largest box.

"You don't have a bed," I said, pointing at the blow-up mattress on the floor. I liked her sleeping bag. *Midnight blue.*

"The mattress was ruined. I got rid of it. Mine too. I couldn't face the thought of sleeping in my old bedroom. I've cleared it out and cleansed it with crystals. Everything's in the skip apart from some of my old journals I'd forgotten I'd kept."

"It would make you too sad to sleep in your old bedroom," I said, shivering. "It would remind you of being a kid, like me. I keep journals about birds because they make me happy. Thinking about your dead mum and her crucifixes makes you sad."

Bee Larkham sniffed whitish blue streaks.

"No. That's where you're wrong, Jasper. That old witch makes me mad as hell, even now. I'd have thrown her stuff on a huge bonfire in the back garden if I hadn't thought it'd bring the neighbors round again. I might still do it. It could make me feel better. You know, show that I'm not afraid anymore. I'm strong."

I fiddled with my binoculars. *Estranged.* That's the word Dad had used to describe Bee Larkham's relationship with her mum. I hadn't understood what the word meant. Now I did.

It meant hating someone who was dead and buried so much you wanted to burn their belongings and destroy their stuff. You wanted to obliterate them until nothing was left except for a pile of ashes.

Mrs. Larkham must have been a terrible person for Bee to say such mean things about her. I guessed her mum's voice was a horrible chrome, orangey brown color. It couldn't have been sky blue like Bee's or cobalt blue like Mum's. The *old witch* would probably have hated the parakeets too, the way David Gilbert did.

I walked to the window because I didn't want her to see the frown marks forking between my eyes. She must have had valid reasons for hating her mum. I blinked away the cobalt blue color that drifted into my head. I wanted to protect it from the pumpkin hue of *estranged.*

"You can close the window if you like. It's freezing in here. I've been trying to air the room."

I didn't mind the cold because I had my anorak on. The coat rack downstairs didn't have a spare peg, not one that didn't look rusty, and I couldn't leave the anorak on the germy carpet.

"The parakeets! It's a perfect view!" I leaned on the windowsill, the crease marks melting away from my face like butter in a frying pan. Mrs. Larkham, the old witch who died in a home, was pushed far from my mind. Three parakeets sat on a branch tantalizingly close to the window. If I reached out and they didn't fly away, I'd almost be able to touch them. They were *that* close.

"I know. I love them." The parakeets fluttered higher up the tree as she joined me at the window. "They're the first thing I see in the morning, Jasper. They make me feel happy. They help me forget all the bad stuff, you know? It melts away."

Like butter in a frying pan.

"That's how I feel too," I said. "When I paint the parakeets. When I paint *you*."

"Wow. You're painting me now, are you? You'll have to show me."

"I will. Next time I come around to see the parakeets I'll bring all my paintings to show you."

"There's going to be a next time, is there?" Bee asked. "Because I don't remember inviting you, Jasper."

I bit my lip, hard. Until I tasted copper. Had I misunderstood her, the way Dad had about coming up to her bedroom? Hadn't she invited me to show her the paintings? Or in my excitement had I misheard her?

"Ignore me. I'm being a cow. Sorry. Of course, you can come back. You were a great success with the flyers. I've had lots of inquiries from your friends' parents."

I have no idea who picked up the flyers. I'd left them scattered about school so I didn't have to hand them out personally. I was about to tell her the truth—I'd prefer to find another way of being useful to her—when the doorbell rang.

Silvery blue lines.

"Shoot, that's him."

I flinched. "David Gilbert? With his shotgun?"

Bee snorted dark blue pebbles. "It'd better not be him again. I need a stick to beat that man off. His mate too."

"I don't have any sticks." Scanning the room for a weapon, I scooped up an ornament from the cardboard box.

"Again, another bad joke, sorry. It's my first music pupil. Keep it down up here, OK? More kids will arrive after him. I'll be an hour or so, I reckon."

I stood on guard at the top of the landing, holding the cold china figurine in my outstretched left hand, in case she was wrong and David Gilbert had turned up.

"Hello! Welcome!" Bee's voice rang out from downstairs. "Come in! Come in! You're very welcome. We're going to have fun."

I didn't see the music pupil who mumbled grayish white colors. I wasn't interested. I walked back into the bedroom and planned to put the ornament where I'd found it, until I looked more closely.

The china lady held out her ice blue skirts for me to admire. She didn't want to return to the box. She longed to be looked at. Her friends squeezed their heads and shoulders out from crumpled newspaper, attempting to break free and join her.

I placed the Dancing China Lady on the chest of drawers and pushed the box closer to the window so her friends could watch the parakeets too.

I lost track of time in Bee Larkham's bedroom, sucked down a rabbit hole into a new, colorful world, and didn't want to return to my old life, where the hues were less vibrant. Less real.

I feverishly scribbled notes about the parakeets, their numbers, movements, and songs. I didn't want to forget a single thing. I had to paint them later, each colored sound I remembered.

Their choruses were accompanied with the muddled sapphire blue of the piano; the guitar's white-silver shapes with cyan cores, and the sparkling amethyst and golden pointed shapes of the electric guitar. More parakeets arrived for the recital.

By the time Dad texted red and yellow bubbles on my phone, I realized the musical instruments downstairs had stopped. It was dark outside, but the parakeets continued to throw out colors from the branches.

Are you still at Bee's? Time for tea.

It couldn't be. I checked my watch: 7:00 P.M., past teatime and way later than I'd been invited to stay. The music lessons had finished an hour and thirty minutes ago, according to Bee Larkham's calculations, and she'd be wondering what had happened to me.

Bright silver and green tubes suddenly lit up and transformed into cat's-eye marbles—Martian music, not live musical instruments.

I took one last look—I was close enough to the tree to see two parakeets disappear into a hole. I waited a few seconds to see if they came out again.

My phone beeped more red and yellow bubbles.

Come home now Jasper.

I mouthed goodbye to the parakeets at the window and ran downstairs, excited that Bee Larkham wanted to share her Martian music while I described what I'd seen and heard over the last two and a half hours.

The hall was slippery, and I skidded in my socks into the sitting room. A woman lay sprawled over a beanbag, her long blond hair flowing onto the bare floorboards. A boy sat next to her on a cushion, holding a guitar.

"You certainly know how to make an entrance, Jasper!" The woman's voice was sky blue. *Bee Larkham.*

The boy on the floor giggled fir-tree green dots. "Sick!"

Another boy propped up the wall as if he were afraid it could collapse. I hadn't noticed him at first. I thought Bee was with one boy, not two. Above this boy's head was the mark I'd seen on the wall in the bedroom, the imprint of a cross.

She stretched out her hand to the boy by the wall even though I stood closer. "Give me a hand up, will you?"

The boy slouched over and reached down. He tried to pull her up, but she lost her balance and they both fell back onto the beanbag.

"Ooh! You're squashing me!"

"Sorry!" *Stunning blue teal.* "You're not helping!"

Bee Larkham didn't sound like she was in pain. She was laughing, along with the boy—a mixture of sky blue and blue teal. I didn't join in; the color combination had left me breathless.

"Have you met Lucas before, Jasper?" she asked, as he tried to stand up again. "He's come to pick up his brother, who, by the way, is an incredibly gifted natural musician."

The smaller boy on the floor grunted a darker fir green color, which meant I didn't think he was particularly happy to hear this.

"We got sidetracked listening to my music," she continued. "It sucks you in, you know? It makes you want to live in the moment and forget about everything else."

I did know. That's how I felt when I listened to Martian music. When I watched the parakeets. When I spent time with Bee Larkham.

"I saw twenty-one parakeets in your tree," I said. "Because you put out trays of apple, as well as the five peanut strings and six bird feeders, thank you."

"Not twenty or twenty-two?" she asked.

"Definitely twenty-one. I counted them one by one. Then I counted them again to be sure."

I couldn't have confirmed my news loudly enough, because she didn't respond. The boy on the cushion giggled greenish gray circles.

"I think they could be here to stay," I added. "They like it here. In your tree. On our street. With you."

If the parakeets wanted to stay, would she?

Bee Larkham nodded at the two other boys in the room. "They both go to the same school as you, Jasper. Did you know that? This is Lee and Lucas Drury."

"Twenty-one parakeets," I repeated. *"Which are here to stay."*

I didn't know that for certain, but I had hope, that tomato-ketchup-colored word. That's why I didn't answer her question—it was too trivial in comparison to my huge news.

The boys looked the same to me. They wore my school's uniform and must be pupils, but I didn't recognize their names. I doubted they liked the parakeets or even the Martian music as much as me. They couldn't possibly appreciate the colors the way I did, in all their Technicolor glory.

"Dad wants me to go home for tea," I said. "I don't have to. I can tell you all about the parakeets. I've made lots of notes." I held up my notebook and binoculars.

The boy sitting on the floor sniggered dark fir-tree green again.

I wanted her to insist I *must* stay and listen to the music with them, while I explained each colored sound, every movement of the para-keets. Instead, she giggled the lightest of sky blues and played with her hair, wrapping and unwrapping it around her index finger.

"Of course, Jasper. You should go home."

"But I—"

"You were so quiet upstairs I'd forgotten you were there," she con-tinued, talking over the color of my voice. "Can you let yourself out? I'm gasping for a glass of wine after all that teaching. It's thirsty work. Does anyone else want a beer?"

Bee Larkham didn't look at me again. She was watching one of the boys, the taller one. Maybe she was afraid he would run off with a guitar.

I moved my head again, holding my binoculars tightly as I walked out. The back of my neck tingled uncomfortably at the tinkle of green-ish blue laughter as I fumbled with my shoelaces in the hallway.

I'd done something to offend Bee Larkham, but I wasn't sure what. I sensed a shift. The color of my voice had subtly changed and she didn't like the tone as much. Not as much as the other boy's blue teal anyway. My voice wasn't beautiful enough for her.

How could I compete with blue teal? I had to work harder to make her like cool blue.

As I closed the front door behind me, I realized I'd forgotten to thank her for letting me watch the parakeets.

I'd been rude. Unforgivably rude.

Dad had made me promise to say thank you and I'd even rehearsed the speech in my head, but the unexpected visitors—the boys who were allowed to stay late to listen to Martian music and drink beer—had put me off.

I vowed to make it up to Bee Larkham. I'd polish up a new, even better thank-you than the one I'd practiced. I'd paint her voice over and over again to reveal its full beauty to her; the color only I could see. I'd also paint the best possible pictures of the sounds of the last few hours: the piano, the acoustic and electric guitars, and the parakeets.

I'd surprise Bee Larkham by presenting all my pictures and canvases to her. She'd accept my apology and invite me back to watch the parakeets again. We'd observe the birds together, side by side, because the other boys—particularly the one with the attractive-colored voice—would be gone.

We'd be alone in her bedroom with the china ladies, and this time my dad wouldn't interrupt us.

26

THURSDAY (APPLE GREEN)

Still That Afternoon

I manage to knock the chair away and jump into bed, seconds before Dad turns my door handle. My paintings—the originals from Lucas Drury's first visit to Bee Larkham's house and the ones I've painted again from that evening (the sound of the parakeets in the oak tree with the musical instruments in the background)—are spread out on the carpet. I didn't have a chance to compare them for differences and place them in the right order before filing.

It's 1:43 P.M.

Dad's two minutes early.

He doesn't close the door behind him as I'd expected. Instead, he steps inside. I hear a delicate lime green rustle close to the window. He's picked up a painting.

What is he doing?

This tests my powers of concentration far more than if he'd stared hard at my face for signs of life.

I want to throw back the duvet and shout: *Get your hands off my painting. You don't own Bee Larkham. You never did! She's not yours!*

Instead, I stay perfectly still. My eyelashes don't even tremble as he lingers over one painting in particular. I don't know for sure, but I suspect it's his first meeting with Bee: *Dirty Sap Circles on paper.*

What does he see when he looks at it now? Does it bring back happy memories or sad ones? I had trouble deciphering the picture. He must see it clearly, the secret language they both used, which I couldn't decode when I stood next to them on the doorstep.

I hear muffled brown with white flecks.

I want to sit up and check what he's doing, but I dig my fingernails into my skin to stop myself. I hear another, deeper-colored choking noise. I squint with one eye half-open. Tears roll down his face.

He's crying for Bee Larkham. He's sorry she's dead and doesn't have a proper grave.

He regrets what happened on Friday night.

Me too!

The words are a high-pitched aquamarine scream in my head. Nothing comes out of my mouth.

There's another leaf green rustle as the painting returns to the carpet. The door clicks shut. Dad's gone.

I remain on high alert in case he's lingering on the landing, waiting to catch me out.

I stay in bed for four minutes and fifteen seconds, until I see light brown woody circles. The front door opens and shuts.

Seriously? He's leaving me on my own?

I jump out of bed and peek from behind the curtains. Dad's in his usual running gear uniform: white T-shirt, navy jogging bottoms, and baseball cap. He makes it to the gate before turning around. I duck down as he looks up.

I count to sixty before I check again. This time he's at the end of the street. Now he's gone.

He fell for my deception and thinks I'm fast asleep. He has no idea how far from the truth he is. I don't have time to sleep because I need to correct all the terrible mistakes we've both made.

I'd planned to carry on painting, but this changes everything. I never expected him to leave the house.

Before he changes his mind and comes back, I investigate his room. It's a mess as usual; he hasn't bothered to straighten the duvet that's been unwashed for three and a half weeks. There's a half-drunk cup of gray tea on his bedside table and a chipped plate with a crust of stale toast. I'd clean up, if it weren't for the fact it'd alert Dad to the fact I'm nosing about.

I'm looking for the clothes he wore on Friday night. He must have got blood on himself too.

Has he washed his clothes? Or destroyed them? Or did he dump them with Bee Larkham's body?

I hold my breath and limit myself to twenty seconds prodding the laundry basket—it's radioactive.

Next I search the back of the wardrobe, behind his ex-military rucksack, the one he takes to Richmond Park. It helps him pretend he continued in the Royal Marines and eventually joined the SAS, instead of being forced to drop out of the regiment's selection course because Mum was poorly.

His walking boots are caked with mud. I don't remember him using them for our bird-spotting walks in Richmond Park. He usually wears trainers. When did he last wear these boots? We haven't been camping after the last disaster. He could have worn them on Friday night. It had rained and would have been muddy; he'd have left size-12 footprints in the alley at the back of Bee Larkham's house.

I want to linger, but there's other stuff to do while he's out. I run downstairs and find the note he's left for me on the kitchen table. It's written in scrawling red pen. He never expects me to find it.

If you do come downstairs, I've gone for a quick run to clear my head. Back soon. Left cheese sandwich in fridge. Take painkiller in saucer for tum.
Don't answer the door. Don't pick up the phone. Don't call the police.

I pop the pill in my mouth and wash it down with a swig of water from my Best Son mug.

EAT ME.

DRINK ME.

I'm back in *Alice in Wonderland*, like in my horrible dream, and I'm alone again.

Has Dad done this before? Does he often sneak out of the house when he thinks I'm asleep or hiding in my den?

I'd always assumed he was in the study, testing apps on his laptop, or watching TV downstairs while I covered myself in blankets and clutched Mum's cardigan, rubbing the buttons.

What if he doesn't stay with me all the time?

What if he seizes the opportunity to leave the house when he thinks I'll never find out?

This throws out my time line yet again. Dad could have moved Bee Larkham's body over the weekend, instead of on Friday night, when he knew I was in my den. He could have taken longer cleaning up and found the perfect burial spot much further away than I'd anticipated, somewhere muddy where he'd need to use his walking boots and camouflage clothes.

He could have driven for hours, with Bee Larkham's body in the boot of his car, and made it home before I crawled out of my den.

What else has Dad done when he thinks I'm out of the picture?

Where has he hidden the murder weapon?

I'll get rid of the knife and your clothes, he said. *You won't have to see them ever again.*

I knock into a chair as I cross the kitchen.

Clumsy clots.

I right the upturned chair and put it back in its exact place. I can't leave any clues behind, no disturbed furniture or muddy footprints on my return. I mustn't leave a trace that I'm attempting to track Dad's movements, that I'm searching his number one hiding place.

I let myself out the back door and stop, my back pressed against the wall. My heart's pounding reddish damson beats. I watch the bluish green of a thrush call out to me, encouraging me to press on.

I sprint across the lawn; the grass is long and unloved with dirty yellow patches. Out of the corner of my eye, I see the tiny cross marking the baby parakeet's grave. I can't bear to look at it directly.

I jangle the door to the shed, *dark bottle green,* and close it behind me. I head straight for the broken lawn mower and heave it to one side, disturbing dusty old leaves and a large, desiccated spider.

His cigarette stash is intact, but I can't see the knife or my jeans, sweatshirt, or anorak.

I kick an old bucket and spade and rearrange the garden hose. After three minutes and twenty-three seconds searching, I give up.

Nothing.

Dad hasn't just shifted the body; he's removed anything that links me to the scene of the crime.

He must have realized I was onto this hiding place and found a safer one. Maybe he figured it out during one of his secret runs when he thought I was asleep, or when I was curled up, sobbing for Mum in my den.

What else has Dad covered up? What story is he trying to tell on my behalf?

I stare at the back gate. I can't stop now. Can I?

Did he remember to shut Bee Larkham's back door and lock it? Is her key returned to its hiding place?

Before I talk myself out of this, I run back up the lawn. The gate swings open, *petrol green*. I check the street's clear before pegging it to the alleyway. I'm out of sight within thirty seconds. Rusty Chrome Orange's spies will have missed me if they happened to look away at the vital moment. I can't hear the yellow French fries of David Gilbert's dog. I've got away with it.

I pick my way over junk; weeds sprout through an old washbasin and a broken watering can. I'd stumbled over them as I ran away on Friday night. It couldn't have been easy for Dad either, carrying Bee Larkham's body in the dark.

I scour the ground, but I can't see any spots of blood or fragments of torn clothing, clues that Dad or I left behind. Maybe he picked his way through here again in daylight to check we were safe.

I hesitate after turning the corner. I've reached Bee Larkham's back gate. Do I want to go further? Do I want to retrace my steps from Friday night?

I have to. I've come this far. I can't go back now. Not until I know more. I want to remember. I need to fill in the gaps in my notebooks and paintings.

The gaps in my memory.

My heart's pumping brighter electric red as my hand reaches out and pushes open the gate. It's bust and doesn't open or shut properly, like some of the panels in the fence.

Bee planned to fix up the back garden but never got round to it.

It's as overgrown as ours. I keep my eyes down so I don't have to look at the accusing windows. In my peripheral vision, I can see the back door's shut. I don't remember opening or closing it on Friday night.

I only remember running away.

I find the small ornamental stone flamingo and flip it backwards. I shift it around, until I'm absolutely sure.

There's nothing there either.

Bee Larkham's spare key has vanished too. Dad forgot to put it back where it belonged after his cleanup operation. If the police search our house and find her key in a jar or pot, it's a mistake that could land us both in jail.

I'm about to retreat when I see petrol green-black darts.

Someone's jangling the latch at the back gate.

It's probably the police.

They're looking for evidence about what happened to Bee Larkham too. They've finally followed the trail of bread crumbs.

I mustn't be caught here. How do I get out? I can't escape. My arms aren't strong enough to haul me over the fence. It's too high anyway. I don't want to squeeze through the hole in the paneling into next door's garden; I might get splinters.

No choice.

I dive among the recycling bins in the lean-to. Flies buzz around the bags, which should have been put out on the street for garbage collection on Monday morning.

Bee didn't stick to her usual start-of-the-week routine.

Another clue Rusty Chrome Orange and the other officers should have spotted, along with the empty bird feeders.

White trainers *tap tap* bluish black past me and stop at the back door. The legs are blue jeans. I glance up. This isn't a police officer. A man wearing a dark blue baseball cap stands by the door, his hands on the glass. He's staring inside the house, searching for Bee Larkham. If he glances down he'll see me. I can't move.

I hold my breath as he bends over and picks up a brick with his left hand.

He *has* seen me. He's going to club me to death for my horrible crime. I open my mouth, about to scream, when I see greenish ice cubes with sharp edges. The man drops the brick, which makes a dull blackboard thud on the ground.

I watch as his arm disappears through the broken glass. His hand jangles the handle inside.

"Shit."

His hand reappears and flies up to his mouth. He sucks the skin as blood drips down his arm and spatters onto the ground. A droplet lands on his white trainer.

I'm going to throw up.

The blood spattered on Bee Larkham's kitchen floor when we fought over the knife.

Drip, drip, drip.

Dark Blue Baseball Cap Man's arm dives into the broken glass again, and this time he steps back, swinging open the door.

He's broken into Bee Larkham's house.

I should stop him. I can't breathe. I close my eyes. If Dad hasn't moved the body, if he couldn't get through the alleyway, the burglar will discover it. He'll find Bee Larkham lying on her back in the kitchen, blood spattered down her noncobalt-blue dress.

That's where I left her after she fell backwards, trying to get away from my slashing knife. Actually that fact's wrong too. It wasn't my knife. I used Bee Larkham's knife, the knife she used to cut the pie she'd baked for my tea.

"Hey! You! What are you doing back here?" It's a dull red voice with grainy scratches. David Gilbert. A dog barks yellow French fries.

I've been trying to cover up what I did, because those were Dad's orders. I don't want to follow his orders anymore. I want it all to be over.

"Are you a friend of Beatrice's?"

I'm about to crawl out and confess to the bird killer when another male voice speaks. It's muddy dark brown.

"Fuck off, mate, and stay out of this." This color comes from beside me, where Dark Blue Baseball Cap Man stands.

Two men are in the garden. One, wearing cherry cords and a

flat brown cap, is by the gate. A dog's straining on the leash he's holding.

"I think you'll find this is my business since I'm head of the local Neighbourhood Watch," David Gilbert says. "Did you smash that glass?"

I don't know the identity of the man in the dark blue baseball cap. He's offered up a few clues: the baseball cap and the color of his voice, which are both vaguely familiar.

He's been here before. I recorded a Dark Blue Baseball Cap Man in my notebook. He shouted clouds of dirty brown with charcoal edges at Bee Larkham's front door when we got back from the police station on Tuesday. He saw me watching him at the window and walked towards our house but never knocked.

Dark Blue Baseball Cap Man steps away from the door. He steps away from *me*. "You like to keep an eye on what's going on around here, do you, mate?"

The mate—David Gilbert—also takes a step backwards as Dark Blue Baseball Cap Man approaches.

"Tell me this. Where the hell was a friggin' busybody like you when my sons were being abused by this pedo?"

"I—I don't know what you're talking about." David Gilbert's back is pressed up against the gate. His dog barks brighter, thornier yellow colors. "I don't know anything about Beatrice's business."

"Business? That's what you call it? Clear off and let me do what the police should have done days ago."

He stalks towards the house again.

"I wouldn't advise you to do that. I'm calling the police. Whatever you think Beatrice's done, you're trespassing on private property." David Gilbert fumbles in his pocket and drops his phone. It clatters short brown lines with purple shadows on the ground. As he reaches down to pick it up, he sees me.

"Jasper?" He stabs his finger at the phone and puts it to his ear.

Dark Blue Baseball Cap Man looks down. "Jasper Wishart? Is that you? Get the hell out of there!"

I try to burrow deeper into the bins as he clasps my shoulder. I manage to wriggle free, but he catches hold of my leg and pulls. I grab hold of the bin. It's slippery and I lose my grip.

"Are you doing that bitch's dirty work again?"

"Get off!" I yell. "Get off me!" I aim kicks at him, but he's too strong. As he drags me out, I scream bigger and bigger jagged clouds of aquamarine. I hear the dull redness of David Gilbert's voice in the background, telling him to stop.

"Not until you tell me where she is!" Dark Blue Baseball Cap Man yanks me towards his spitting face. It's red and sweaty. His eyes bulge and his breath smells of Bee Larkham's house party.

Beer and lies.

Up close, his baseball cap doesn't look dark blue. It's faded navy and has the initials NYY embroidered on the front.

I've seen it before.

"Tell me what she did to Lee. You know what's been going on. Did she molest him as well? Or only Lucas? Tell me. I have to know if she touched my youngest. He just turned twelve for fuck's sake. What else was she giving him for free, apart from the music lessons?"

I close my eyes to block out his face and the colors. This is Lucas Drury's dad. His baseball cap is distinctive; I definitely remember it. I can't forget it.

Bee Larkham had warned me about this man:

He's got a bad temper. Lucas is safer with me than at home. I can protect him and his brother as long as Lee continues with his music lessons. I'll teach him for free. That way both boys can keep coming here and stay out of their dad's way. You will help me do that, won't you, Jasper? Help me keep those poor boys safe from their abusive dad?

I feel like I'm falling, yet I don't hit the ground. Faded Navy Baseball Cap Man's hands hold me up.

"I can't do this. I'm too young. I can't do this. I can't do this."

"Stop it!" He shakes my shoulders hard. "I know this is a stupid act you and Lucas dreamt up to protect that pedo. It might fool the police, but it doesn't fool me. I know you're both trying to defend her. Why? Why would you help a perv like that? Is it because you're getting some on the side as well?"

"Let go! You're frightening him." *Dull grainy red.*

I open my eyes. Hands appear in front of my face. They're grappling with Faded Navy Baseball Cap Man. It must be David Gilbert because there are still only two men in Bee Larkham's back garden. The dog barks and barks.

"He should be frightened," Faded Navy Baseball Cap Man says. "Or he can be beaten into telling the truth. It's his choice. I'll get it out of him either way because the police are getting nowhere with him. I know that for a fact."

"I've called the police and they're on their way," David Gilbert says. "Now let go of Jasper before you make this any worse for yourself. Touching him like that is assault and you've already broken a window."

Faded Navy Baseball Cap Man's fist swings upwards. He's going to beat me into confessing, but that's what I've been trying to do ever since my First Account.

"No, mate, *this* is an assault," he says.

There's a purple bruised thud as his fist strikes a face. It's not mine. The other man—David Gilbert—lets out a cry of brittle red splinters and falls to the ground. The dog whimpers, pale, uncooked frozen fries, and cowers behind him.

"I told you to keep the hell out of this. This is *my* business. They're *my* sons." Faded Navy Baseball Cap Man turns to face me again.

"Does she have a laptop or a computer in there?" He jerks his head at the house. "Or an iPad? Something that will tell me where the hell she's hiding?"

He shakes me hard again, but my lips have frozen and can't form words. I can't tell him the truth: I have no idea where she is because Dad never admitted what he did with the body on Friday night or possibly over the weekend.

As he lets go, I slide to the ground next to David Gilbert, the bird killer. Blood's gushing from his cheek and he's gasping for breath. He catches hold of my arm as the other man darts into the house.

"The police will be here any minute," he says. "They'll deal with him. Until they get here, keep next to me. I won't let him hurt you. I promise."

I hear the thin pastel yellow and soft pink zigzags of police sirens in the distance.

"That's the police now." He stands up unsteadily. "We need to get back onto the street. We'll both be safer there."

He sways, holding the side of his face. The other hand reaches down to help me up. *Too late.* Faded Navy Baseball Cap Man shoots out of the house, an iPad tucked under his arm. As he moves, a tiny, sharp silver splinter flies out from beneath his trainer and strikes the ground. It bounces and lands near me.

I know you.

"She's done a runner, hasn't she? She cleaned up before she left. I can smell the disinfectant in the kitchen. Where did she go? I bet she told you, didn't she? Her little bitch?" He holds up the iPad. "Or did she email you? What's her password?"

I hear blue marbled sobs. They're coming from my mouth as I pick up the object that Lucas Drury's dad accidentally kicked out of the house.

"Get away from him. You can't do this." David Gilbert stands in his path, but Faded Navy Baseball Cap Man pushes him to one side.

"Oh yes, I can. The police are doing fuck all to find Bee Larkham. I'm going to do it for them and I'm going to beat the crap out of her when I find her."

The police siren is zigzags of bright electric yellow and pink.

"Where is that bitch?"

He's going to force his face into mine again. He'll hit me, the way he smashed David Gilbert's cheek and turned it into a red, purply mush. He'll beat me into the ground and I'll never be able to get up again. I crush the object into my hand until I feel it pierce skin.

"You can't find her!" I cry. "You'll never find her."

"You little shit!" He lunges at me. "Where is she? Tell me! Tell me what she did to my Lee!"

I hear the black torpedo shapes of footsteps, the petrol green of the gate swinging open. Two policemen run towards us.

"Tell me!" Faded Navy Baseball Cap Man shrieks, as he's wrestled to the ground. "Tell me! I have a right to know!"

I try to block out the color of his shouts. I can't. They're stabbing my hands, which are clamped to my ears, and penetrating my eardrums.

"Don't any of you get it?" I shout. "Why won't any of you ever listen to me?"

I open my fist and throw her favorite swallow earring high up into the air.

"Bee Larkham's dead and so is her baby," I yell. "Stop pretending to everyone they're coming back! They're not! They can't!"

27

THURSDAY (APPLE GREEN)

Still That Afternoon

When will Dad get home from his run?

I pull the blanket tighter around my shoulders as I sit in the back of the police car parked outside our house. I was allowed to keep the door open after I explained I was worried about being trapped inside.

Two policemen handcuffed Lucas Drury's dad and led him off to a different car six minutes and two seconds ago, at 2:14 P.M. precisely. The ambulance has also left with David Gilbert inside, lying on a stretcher, with a large pad taped to his cheek.

The policewoman said he couldn't bring the dog with him to hospital. She tap-tapped the owl knocker on the door of 18 Vincent Gardens and asked the man who lives there temporarily—Ollie Watkins—to look after *Monty*. Up until today, I didn't know the dog's name was Monty. I still don't like its color.

The door of 18 Vincent Gardens opens again and a man in a black duffel coat walks out with a large dog on a lead. He talks to a police officer before crossing the road. He's not wearing black suede shoes or spotty red and black socks, but he's come from Mrs. Watkins's house and walks towards me.

"Jasper, it's Ollie," he says, as he approaches the car door. *Custard yellow.* "Ollie Watkins from number eighteen. Are you OK? I'm so sorry about what's happened. It's awful. Just awful."

He didn't need to confirm his identity. I'd seen the house number and recognized his voice color. I wish he hadn't crossed the road to speak to me. "I hate dogs. Their colors are awful."

"Really? Sorry. I rather like black Labradors. I'll keep him away from you."

He yanks the lead. Stubborn Yellow French Fries won't budge. Custard Yellow turns away and watches the police officers across the street.

"Yet more drama on our street," he says. "And Bee Larkham is slap bang in the middle of it again, surprise, surprise. She's always enjoyed being the center of attention, ever since she was a kid. That's what Mum and David used to say about her. I don't remember her much back then. I was away at boarding school and then Cambridge. Our paths didn't cross much."

I don't care.

He pulls the lead again. Yellow French Fries sits down. I drape the blanket over my head. I want to shut everything out, the way I do in my den.

"I wonder what the police are looking for in Bee's house," the custard yellow voice says. "They've been inside for ages and she's clearly not there. Like you said, she hasn't come back to refill the bird feeders."

He changes the subject to what I want to do when I'm grown up. Now it's something about how he studied economics at a college belonging to Christ before a career in a city and a transfer to a bank in Switzerland, where his fiancée lives. I've stopped listening.

I jump as I feel a hand on my shoulder through the blanket. It's hot and heavy. I don't like it.

"Do you want to wait for your dad in my mum's house? You'll be more comfortable there." It's the same color as Ollie Watkins's voice. He hasn't walked away yet.

I count my teeth with my tongue, one by one.

"OK," he continues. "I think you want to be left alone. Knock on my door if you change your mind. Hopefully your dad will be back soon."

"Did you remember to buy more seed for the parakeets?" I ask from beneath the blanket. "You have to keep feeding the birds or they will leave."

"Yes, Jasper. I promise I'll do that for you. Promises are very important to me. I always keep mine."

"I try to keep mine, but don't always manage to," I admit. "Other people are the same. They break promises all the time and don't ever say they're sorry."

"That's a shame, Jasper. I'll top up the feeders now. You can watch and check I'm doing it right, if you like."

Through the weave of the blanket, I see him walk back across the road. There's a snatch of yellow French fries as he opens his front door and leads the dog inside. It doesn't want to go with him.

Is Monty ashamed it did nothing to protect its owner, David Gilbert, when Lucas Drury's dad attacked him? Or doesn't the dog realize that a crime was committed under its nose?

I rip the blanket off as the front door to Bee Larkham's house swings open. A woman with blond hair appears.

It can't be. It's impossible.

I let my breath out in small, misty blue blobs.

She's wearing a uniform. It's a police officer, not Bee Larkham. She shakes her hand at a policeman in the street. He goes inside too, and they shut the door behind them.

It's funny. Even though I know what happened to Bee Larkham, I still expect to see her walk out of her front door and say hello to me before feeding the parakeets.

A tiny part of me can't believe she's dead. Most mornings when I wake up, I feel the same way about Mum.

Today, I remember Bee Larkham standing on her doorstep. Talking to me. Discussing her favorite shade of blue teal.

I painted the picture three months ago.

It's in box number twelve (haughty, dull gold), hidden at the back of my wardrobe, where Dad won't look.

28

January 28, 5:03 P.M.
Sky Blue Saving Blue Teal on paper

"There's no need to apologize for yesterday," Bee Larkham said when she finally stopped playing aquamarine polka dots on the piano and opened her front door.

I'd arrived to show her fourteen new paintings of the colors of the parakeets from her bedroom window. I'd stayed up until 2:14 A.M. to finish them, picking the highest, most colorful notes of their squabbles. I'd wanted to get them exactly right, because I was sure that would make her like my cool blue again after my rudeness.

"I knew you were grateful for watching the parakeets," she continued. "It's the least I could do anyway, considering what a help you've been to me already. You're by far the nicest person on this street. Not that it's much of a contest."

My mouth widened into a broad slit. I thought she was the nicest person I'd ever met, apart from Mum, of course. *That* was no contest.

"Why don't you come inside for a minute?" she said. "I hoped you'd pay me a visit today. I wanted to ask another small favor."

Uh-oh.

"I don't have to give out more flyers, do I?"

"No, it's not that. I think I've given out enough. Why don't we have a drink in the kitchen?"

"I don't drink beer," I said, remembering the night before. "I'm not allowed." To be honest, I didn't think I'd like it much even if Dad let me try alcohol.

Bee pushed her hair back from her shoulders to show me the silver swallows in her ears. "I was actually thinking more along the lines of a can of Coke or something like that?"

I didn't want to admit I wasn't allowed fizzy cans either. I kept quiet. She led me past a single cardboard box into the kitchen, which had a large wooden table and chairs and a dresser stacked with cookbooks. I checked the walls, but I couldn't see any marks of the cross. It was totally Jesus-free, probably because he'd been driven out by the smell of grease and old food.

"My mum was big into buying cookbooks and not actually making anything from them. She liked looking at the pictures. I guess she couldn't do much with her cruddy oven." She stopped by the dresser and ran her finger over the books. "I love to cook and couldn't bring myself to get rid of them. Well, not yet anyway. I need to go through them all and see which ones are worth keeping."

"My mum loved to cook too," I said. "She used to make cakes for me all the time. My favorites were her raisin scones."

"Lucky boy." Her hand dropped from the shelf. She walked to the fridge and grabbed a can of Coke.

I knew I wasn't lucky, because I never ate homemade cakes or scones anymore. Just shop-bought stuff. Mum's baking was a long time ago. Dad never kept her tins or pans; he said there was no point. He didn't know how to bake cakes—Dad claimed that was women's stuff. I told him that was stupid, but he still threw the cake tins away.

I didn't want to think about Mum's cooking or the sparky yellow color she used to make as she banged the oven door shut.

"This is you, Bee Larkham," I said, handing her my prized painting as we sat down at the table.

Bee stared at the piece of paper, sipping from her can. She looked back at me. Her face was blank and I couldn't read it.

"Don't you like it?" I asked.

"I love the colors, but . . . Don't be offended by this, Jasper, but it looks nothing like me. I can't even see my features. You know, a mouth and lips. Did you forget to add them in?"

"I don't paint faces or objects," I told her. "Only voices and other sounds. This is a painting of your beautiful voice. It's a perfect shade of sky blue."

"My voice is sky blue? You see that?"

I moved my head up and down to signal *yes.* "I see the color of sounds and music. I can see the color of a person's voice, like yours, *sky blue,* and focus in on the colors of the words in a sentence. So *voice* is peach sorbet, for example."

"Wow!"

I wanted to show her what else I could do. "I see the colors of letters and the days of the week. So today, Thursday, is apple green. My numbers have colors and personalities too. I like dusky pink and friendly number six."

"Wow! That's so cool. And the other pictures?"

She spent fourteen minutes gazing at all my paintings and asking questions about what colors I saw for the parakeets and the high notes and crescendos of her piano playing. I told her my favorite color was Mum's cobalt blue, but hers was a close second.

"This has been a treat for me," she said, standing up. "I had no idea you were so talented, Jasper. You've got a real gift. Can I keep these two?" She held up my favorite parakeet canvases. Their colors were the deepest, the most meaningful. She could see that too.

My throat closed up. I moved my head up and down.

"Thank you, Jasper. It means a lot to me." She walked over to the dresser and pulled out a white envelope. "Now about that favor I mentioned. I need you to deliver this to Lucas Drury at school tomorrow. It's urgent."

"W-what?"

Lucas was the tall boy with the attractive-colored voice who'd held up the wall in the sitting room last night.

"Do you like the color of the parakeets better than his blue teal?" I asked, holding up my painting.

"This isn't anything to worry about." Bee's sky blue voice was clipped and pointy. It ignored my question. "All you have to do is find Lucas at school tomorrow and hand him this envelope. It's nothing major. Anyone could do it, but I've chosen you, Jasper."

I didn't want to admit this wasn't simple for someone like me. It was the hardest thing in the world, because I'd never be able to find Lucas Drury. It'd be impossible.

"Can't I do another favor for you?" I asked. "Like hand out the flyers outside school?"

I hated that too, but it wouldn't be as difficult as Bee Larkham's latest task: locating one boy among hundreds.

Tears welled up in her eyes because I'd upset her with my stupidity. Maybe she'd guessed my inability to recognize faces or someone on the street had told her about my ineptness.

"I'm sorry," I said. "I know it's my fault. I can't help it. Please don't cry. I'd do anything to stop you from crying."

"Deliver this note for me." She pressed the envelope firmly into my hand. I looked down at it. The words *Lucas Drury* were printed on the front in blue ink, along with *Form: Claythorne.*

I felt a pang of jealousy, a wishy-washy pickled onion word. She already knew the name of his class but had never asked about mine.

"Dorset," I clarified.

"What?"

My class.

"Didn't you ask Lucas for his telephone number?" I pressed. "That would be the correct thing to do. You could ring the number and ask his brother to book another music lesson with you. It's a big school. I may miss Lucas tomorrow or not be able to find him."

"It's not about lessons. It's important his dad doesn't know I've sent the letter. I wouldn't ask you unless I was desperate, Jasper, but Lucas says his dad confiscated his mobile and vets his emails. I've no way of reaching him without going through his dad first."

Her body shook and she wrapped her arms around herself.

"Why do you need to?" I continued. "Why do you need to talk to Lucas Drury?"

I hoped he wouldn't come back. He'd get in the way of Bee and me watching the parakeets together.

She took a deep breath. "Can I trust you, Jasper?"

"I'm a trustworthy person," I confirmed, "but I often get confused. Dad always says that. I have to concentrate. Try harder than normal kids because things are more difficult for someone like me."

"Well, it's like this, Jasper. I'm worried about Lucas—Lee too—after things the boys let slip last night. I think their dad has a temper, like my mum had." She brushed the tears out of her right eye. "I know how bad it can be growing up in a house like that. I want Lucas to feel safe and understand I'm here if he ever wants to talk."

Her shoulders shook as she cried harder. "I want to help those poor boys because no one ever helped me when I was growing up. I never had anyone I could turn to, someone who would support me without wanting something in return. Promise me you'll find Lucas and give him the note in person?"

My fingers curled around the envelope. "I won't let you down, Bee Larkham. I'd never want to do that. I'll always help you if you're in trouble. You can count on me. I promise."

I didn't exactly break my promise to Bee Larkham, but I didn't exactly keep it either. I couldn't face attempting to hunt down Lucas Drury between lessons. I had no hope of finding him or his brother without somehow persuading the school office to read out their names on the Tannoy to ask them to pick up the note, which of course I couldn't do.

I couldn't tell Bee about my problems with faces either. How could I? She'd change her opinion of me; I'd become less useful. She'd think I was a freak, like Dad did.

Instead, I left for school earlier than usual the next morning. I found Lucas's form room, Claythorne, unlocked and left the envelope on Mr. Luther's desk. He'd give Lucas the letter at registration. He'd be able to find him a lot easier than I could. It was *almost* like giving Lucas the note in person.

Lucas must have received it because a woman who looked like Bee Larkham stood at the front window of 20 Vincent Gardens when I came home from school later that afternoon. She waved and blew a kiss—a thank-you for successfully completing her first mission.

She must have guessed I'd helped her.

I hadn't let her down by my inability to distinguish Lucas Drury from other boys.

Well, not yet anyway. I'm getting ahead of the colors. That happened later.

29

THURSDAY (APPLE GREEN)

Still That Afternoon

"What's happened, Son?" The man's panting a shade of dark ocher. It's Dad, but his voice sounds different when he's been running. "What are you doing in a police car?" His T-shirt sticks to his chest and sweat drips down his face as he grips the door. "What have you done now?"

He tries to help me out, but I shrug him off, walk over to our front wall, and sit down. I close my eyes as he follows me because I don't want to remember his face. I put the blanket back over my head to screen out the sunlight too.

"The swallow tried to escape but couldn't. The bird wanted to get away from Lucas Drury's dad. He's a violent man. He may have been to Bee Larkham's house before. I remember his color. He's smashed the glass in her back door."

"What? He's been here today? At Bee's house?"

Beneath the blanket, I see a small red dot in my palm. It's where I squeezed the earring tightly, a painful reminder Bee Larkham's still with me. She won't leave. Her ghost's watching the police officers open and shut her front door. She's trying to find out what's going on.

She wants to know if I'm telling the truth about what I did.

Whether I'm going to make things right and let her rest in peace.

A car pulls up and the door opens and shuts in an oval of brownish gray.

"Oh Jesus," Dad says. "That's all we need."

I squeeze my fingers over my eyes. The Second Coming arrives with large black rectangles. *Footsteps.*

"Hello again," Dad's muddy ocher voice says. "Can you please tell me what the hell's going on? What's this about Lucas Drury's dad?"

"Jasper's had a fright," a rusty chrome orange voice replies. "Perhaps we could go inside, Mr. Wishart? We should talk in private."

Rusty Chrome Orange.

Richard Chamberlain, *like the actor,* is back.

That's all we need.

"What? Yes. Come this way. You'll have to excuse me." Dad stops talking and starts again. "I need a shower. I've been for a run. I only slipped out for twenty minutes or so."

"Yes, I was told you weren't around in the last half hour. Jasper became involved in a serious incident."

"What happened? I didn't leave him for long. Hardly any time at all." Dad's talking in short bursts. "He was asleep in bed. I needed some air. It's been one hell of a week. I'm sure you can imagine."

"Let's do this inside, shall we?"

Dad's hands press through the blanket, steering me away from Bee Larkham's house towards ours, guiding me further and further away from the truth. His fingers dig into my shoulders, controlling me.

Say nothing.

Don't tell the police what you did to Bee Larkham.

Don't tell the police about the knife.

I can't tell Rusty Chrome Orange where it's hidden because Dad hasn't confided in me. He doesn't trust me enough. He thinks I could betray him.

His hands push me through the front door and to the foot of the stairs. "Go back to bed, Jasper. I'll come up and see you in a minute when I'm done down here."

"I understand he's shaken up and wants to rest," Rusty Chrome Orange says, "but I'll need to speak to Jasper later. We need to clear up a few things. Let's talk in here, shall we, Mr. Wishart?"

"Go upstairs," Dad orders.

I climb the stairs, counting to fifty, and sit down on the top step, underneath the blanket. I hear the sitting room door close, but it does little to block out the sounds and colors.

Rusty Chrome Orange tells Dad about Lucas Drury's dad being arrested for assaulting David Gilbert, shaking me, breaking into Bee Larkham's house, and threatening to kill a police officer. I didn't hear *that*, so it must have happened when he was put in the police car.

"Jasper was a witness to the initial assault because he was hiding in Miss Larkham's back garden, according to your neighbor Mr. Gilbert. Do you have any idea what he was doing there?"

Dad mutters darkish orange ribbons.

"He made some startling claims in the presence of police officers," Rusty Chrome Orange continues. "He claims Miss Larkham is, in fact, dead, not away somewhere as we'd believed initially. He also claims she's pregnant. Have you heard him suggest this before?"

The chair squeaks deep plum as Dad shuffles.

"This morning, Jasper said that Bee was pregnant. Lucas Drury told him at school yesterday, a conversation that made him go haywire. That's why he left school without permission. It's why he was in such a state when he dialed 999 to report Ollie being kidnapped."

I shuffle down the stairs to hear Rusty Chrome Orange better.

"You didn't think this could be relevant to our investigation into the relationship between Miss Larkham and Lucas Drury? You didn't think to report an alleged pregnancy with a minor?"

"Today was the first I'd heard about it from Jasper," Dad says. "I didn't believe it. Didn't want to believe it, anyway. I thought Jasper had misunderstood what Lucas told him. Often, he doesn't have a good grasp on what people say to him."

"I see. And his allegation that Miss Larkham is dead? He repeated the statement over and over again to the officers. He said that was why she couldn't be found, because she died on Friday night."

"Jasper gets terribly confused. He's been upset by your investigation and the fact that Bee's left the parakeets unfed. I've tried to reassure him, but as you say, he seems to have got it into his head that she's dead, which is absurd. She obviously did a runner when she realized she was in hot water with you lot about Lucas."

"That's what we believed," Rusty Chrome Orange says. "It seemed to make the most sense, but we're beginning to think we should look at this from a different angle."

"How do you mean?"

"Miss Larkham has now been officially reported missing. She failed to turn up to a hen weekend on Saturday. She'd timed her return from Australia to coincide with it. Her friends have repeatedly tried to contact her and the messages have gone straight to voice mail. Incidentally, we found her mobile inside the house along with her handbag and purse."

"I had no idea," Dad says. "No idea at all."

"There have been no sightings of Miss Larkham since Friday, despite her details being circulated to police forces nationwide. She hasn't attempted to book a train or get a flight to leave the country. She hasn't touched her bank account since last week."

"You think something has actually happened to Bee?" Dad asks. "Something bad?"

"At this stage it's a missing person's inquiry, which we're running alongside our initial investigation into her alleged relationship with a minor."

"Jesus. This isn't going to go away, is it?"

No, it's not, Dad.

"It gets worse and worse," Dad continues. "Is it possible she's topped herself? You know, taken the easy way out before she's arrested for the kiddie stuff? Not that it's an easy way out, to kill yourself, of course. You know what I mean."

"We don't know what's happened to her," Rusty Chrome Orange admits. "I'm curious about the statements your son has made. We have a recording of him making the 999 call yesterday, alleging a murder had taken place on this street, as well as a kidnapping."

"It wasn't a kidnapping, you know that already. As I said, Jasper got confused. He was upset after the pregnancy rumor. I'm sure he's got mixed up about the other thing too. There hasn't been a murder on this street. Not to my knowledge anyway."

"I've reviewed the tapes from our first interview. Jasper specifically referred to a murder. I remember he was clear about that fact."

"He meant the parakeets," Dad insists. "He's obsessed with the parakeets and afraid David Gilbert wants to harm them. He was distraught after a baby parakeet died and believes another dozen have been killed."

"So you say. We're back to the dead parakeets."

"You don't believe me? Is that what this is all about?"

"Not at all," Rusty Chrome Orange replies. "I'm wondering whether Jasper knows what he's talking about and it's *us* who have misunderstood *him*, not the other way around. Do you think that's a possibility? That we're the ones who've got the wrong end of the stick?"

"To be blunt, no I don't. I've learnt to take what Jasper says with a pinch of salt. You have to with a child like this. It's not easy."

"I'm sure. But your son is observant. He likes to watch people, doesn't he? Is there any possibility he could have seen something over the weekend that led him to believe Miss Larkham is dead?"

"Jasper was ill in bed all weekend," Dad stresses. "I stayed with him the whole time. He couldn't have visited Bee. He couldn't have seen anything important because he didn't leave the house. I can vouch for that."

"I meant through his binoculars, watching at the bedroom window. He spends a lot of time doing that, doesn't he? That's what your neighbors say. I've checked outside—he has a direct line of sight into Miss Larkham's bedroom from his. Has he mentioned seeing anything that's distressed him?"

"Jasper wasn't well enough to use his binoculars this weekend." The muddy ocher is clipped into tight edges.

There's silence again before Rusty Chrome Orange changes the subject abruptly. "Yes, of course. Remind me again, how did Jasper get those knife wounds to his stomach?"

"I've been over this with the other police officer at the hospital," Dad says. "I let him out of my sight for a short time and he hurt himself in the kitchen. It was a silly mistake."

"You didn't think to take him to a doctor? He required stitches yet you delayed treatment, according to the hospital notes."

Dad sighs button shapes of light ocher.

"Look, I'll be honest with you. I made a mistake. I should have taken him to a doctor, but I knew how bad it looked. It would mean Social Services getting involved again and questioning how I could have let something like this happen."

"Like today? That surprises me, Mr. Wishart. Why did you leave Jasper alone when there's a risk he could hurt himself again? When you know Social Services are already involved after the knife incident, when they've been involved with you previously."

"That was years ago," Dad points out. "My wife died and I'd come out of the Royal Marines. Both were major life changes. I was on my own. I had no extended family to help out. I was depressed and we moved about a lot, but I've turned it around. I'm no longer on medication. I have a good job. Jasper has a stable life now. We've put down roots here. We're happy."

Rusty Chrome Orange speaks again. "You said yourself that Jasper's distressed about what's happening and you left him unsupervised."

"As I told you before, I thought he was asleep. I wanted some headspace. I needed to run. It helps me think. I never dreamt he'd wake up and go over to Bee's house. I'd warned him . . ."

"What did you warn him?"

"Not to go over to her house again and not to feed the parakeets. I thought I'd got through to him, but obviously not. He didn't listen or fully understand."

"I see."

There's a pistachio-colored rustling sound.

"Do you know what's inside this plastic bag?" Rusty Chrome Orange asks.

"Err. It looks like an earring. A bird earring."

"My colleagues believe it belongs to Miss Larkham. Jasper was concealing it in his hand when the police officers arrived. He tried to throw it away and became agitated when it was retrieved."

"I have no idea how he got hold of it," Dad says. "He loves birds. Maybe he found it somewhere. Or Bee gave it to him."

"You haven't seen Jasper with it before?"

Dad's silent. I don't know what head gesture he makes.

"If you look carefully at the earring, up against the light," Rusty Chrome Orange says. "Yes, exactly like that. Can you see a dark brown stain?"

"Erm, I guess."

"We're testing it for blood. We're also getting a forensic team to carry out a thorough examination of her house, particularly the kitchen, where there's a strong smell of disinfectant. There are other things that concern us."

"Why are you telling me this?" Dad asks.

"If there's something you think we should know about Jasper, now is the time to tell us," Rusty Chrome Orange says. "Before this goes any further. Before it gets even more serious."

"There's nothing. I don't know anything about what's happened to Bee, if anything has, and neither does Jasper. This has nothing to do with either of us."

"I'd like to talk to Jasper, if I may, to hear that from him."

"That's not going to happen," Dad replies. "I can't let you upset him again. He's in a fragile state. You said yourself he's had a fright. Talking to you again could tip him over the edge. He needs time to himself in his den upstairs. That's his coping mechanism, along with painting."

"Very well, but we may need to insist upon talking to him soon. Depending upon what our forensic teams come up with inside Miss Larkham's house."

"You'll have to go through my solicitor first," Dad says. "Because that's the only way you'll have access to Jasper and myself from now on."

"Of course. We can go through formal channels if that's the way you wish to proceed."

"It is."

"I do have to warn you this matter has gone beyond me. Social Services must be informed about today. Jasper was witness to a serious crime and assaulted after being left home alone."

"That's not illegal at his age," Dad shouts. "We're talking about twenty minutes or so, probably less. I had no idea Lucas Drury's dad was going to turn up and go psycho. How could I? I'm not a psychic."

"Calm down, Mr. Wishart."

"I wish you'd all leave us the hell alone. I'm doing the best I can. I'm a single dad, a widower, with a son who has profound learning difficulties. Can't you see I'm trying?"

"I can. This is purely procedural. It's not personal."

Dad gets up from the leather chair with a dark purple sound.

"What I don't understand is why you're gunning for me instead of Lucas Drury's dad," he says. "He's attacked David and threatened my son. Isn't it possible he's hurt Bee too? He's got motive, considering what you think she's got up to with Lucas. Couldn't he have found out she's pregnant with his son's baby and attacked her?"

"We're keeping an open mind about Mr. Drury," Rusty Chrome Orange replies. "Colleagues will interview him today with a view to pressing burglary and assault charges as well as making threats to kill. We'll be taking things from there regarding our missing person's inquiry."

"Good," Dad says. "Hopefully that will clear everything up and we can all move on."

The door creaks open, *light coffee brown,* but I don't attempt to hide. The colors stop at the foot of the stairs. I see two blurry figures through the blanket.

"Goodbye, Jasper," Rusty Chrome Orange says. "We may see each other again soon."

"I know," I say. "I'm glad you've found her."

"Do you mean Miss Larkham? We haven't found her. Not yet. She's missing."

"Her swallow is a female bird and deserved to be found," I clarify. "She'd be lonely without the other one. They have to make a pair. They belong together. They're Bee Larkham's favorite earrings."

"Do you know where the other earring is?" Rusty Chrome Orange asks.

I shrink beneath the blanket because I can see it vividly, even when I shut my eyes. It was in Bee Larkham's ear when she lay dead on the floor in her kitchen. I think the Dancing China Lady saw it too.

Dad lingers in the hallway, after the door bangs shut, *dark brown rectangles.* He must be counting Rusty Chrome Orange's blackish footsteps too, calculating when it's safe to talk. Is Rusty Chrome Orange out of potential eavesdropping distance?

"This is getting serious for both of us," he says eventually. "You do realize that, Jasper? If they find traces of blood in the house . . . *Your* blood."

"My clothes and the knife aren't in the shed."

"Of course they're not there," he says. "I told you I'd sort everything and I did. There's nothing to worry about where all that's concerned. It's taken care of."

"I *am* worried," I point out. "You forgot to put the key back. That was a big mistake. You'd shout at me if I did something as dumb as that."

"I have no idea what you're talking about. What key?"

"Bee Larkham's back door key. It's not beneath the flamingo statue in her garden, where it's usually kept. I checked before Lucas Drury's dad arrived and attacked David Gilbert."

"I haven't touched Bee's key."

"Yes you did. You used it on Friday night to get into her house but didn't put it back where you found it. That was a mistake."

I count fifteen teeth with my tongue during the silence.

"Listen to me, Jasper. I promise you, I haven't touched Bee's key. I went there on Friday night, like I said I would, but didn't go around the back. I went to her front door."

He must be lying. Or could I have forgotten to return it in my panic?

"I went in and out the back door," I shout, not caring if Rusty Chrome Orange is listening on the other side of the door. "Which means I must have used the key because it's always locked. I always remember to put the key back. I didn't forget, even when the baby parakeet died. Where's the key now?"

"I don't know. Maybe Bee moved it?"

"That's impossible. She couldn't have."

"Or, I don't know . . ."

"Or what?"

"That leaves only one other option if you definitely returned it."

I tap my foot impatiently, making gray-brown bubbles.

"Someone else knew where Bee's key was kept," he says finally. "They took it after you ran out of her back garden on Friday night."

I'm systematically going through my old paintings because I'm determined to keep my promise to be a trustworthy artist.

I mustn't attempt to wash over the truth with different colors when I revisit fresh scenes.

I find the canvas from the day I first discovered Bee Larkham's key and place it on the carpet, close to my bed. I gaze at it with one eye shut, the way I'm taught to in art class at school.

Use your critical eye.

That's my left eye. It helps me put things into perspective and reassess my paintings.

This isn't my best by far. I mixed the sounds of the parakeets with people's voices, using impasto gel to build up the correct textures. I also made irritating watermarks and smears in the bottom right-hand corner. It's obvious I was anxious when I painted it.

Very anxious.

Worse than that, this picture is highly misleading.

It's missing something.

I don't mean the whereabouts of the key's hiding place in Bee Larkham's back garden, because I never paint what I see—only what I hear. That's what counts.

But this painting was definitely trying to conceal something—a hue that wasn't ready to fight its way through the other shades to the surface.

Not yet, anyway.

I mix my colors and start again.

30

February 6, 10:04 a.m.
Sky Blue with Muddy Ocher, Cool Blue, and Sapphire on canvas

"Do you think I could borrow Jasper for a few minutes, Eddie?"

A blond woman, wearing an unfamiliar dove gray dress, stood outside our front door on Saturday morning (turquoise). I inspected her ears (studded with swallows). She had a sky blue voice. This was Bee Larkham.

She was talking to Dad but looking at me. She must have missed me; although we'd waved at each other from our bedroom windows, we hadn't talked properly face-to-face for eight days. I'd knocked three times to tell her the amazing news: parakeets were nesting in her tree.

My timings were always wrong. I'd waited until the silverish cyan of guitars or royal blue piano lessons had finished and the boy or girl had left the house, but Bee Larkham was either on the telephone or Skyping a friend in Australia and couldn't break off.

"You can bring your binoculars with you if you want, Jasper. In fact you *must* bring your binoculars. I insist. I've got a massive surprise for you."

"Of course, Bee," Dad said. "If you're absolutely sure he won't be too much of a nuisance?"

"Not at all."

I hopped from one foot to the other; ready to go. I had my binoculars around my neck as I'd been watching the parakeets from my bedroom window.

"Now, before I forget, are you free this Friday night?" she asked, looking at Dad. "I'm inviting the neighbors around for some getting-to-know-you drinks. Do you fancy coming? No worries if you already have plans. I know it's short notice."

"I'd love to come," he said. "I never have plans on Friday nights."

"Oh dear. Listen to you! I thought a good-looking guy like you would be out on the town with a different date every night."

"I wish! Dates tend to lose interest when I tell them I'm a single dad with a child who—"

He forgot the end of his sentence and stopped talking abruptly.

"That's their loss, not yours," Bee said. "You shouldn't waste your time on women who aren't interested in children."

"Thanks, I'm sure you're right."

"Are we going to your house or not—for the surprise?" I asked. "Because I thought that was the plan."

"Yes, Jasper, sorry," Bee said, laughing. "Us grown-ups sometimes forget what we're supposed to be doing. Don't we, Eddie?"

"See you Friday night, if not before," he replied. "I look forward to it."

"Me too, Eddie. It's going to be a great night. I can't wait to get to know everyone on the street better."

Dad closed the door behind us. We walked across the road, looking both ways, because around four thousand pedestrians a year are killed after being hit by cars.

"Can I come too?" I asked.

"Where?"

Bee had forgotten already. She had a terrible memory.

"To the neighbors' party?" I prompted.

"Of course you can, if your dad lets you, but it's not *really* for the neighbors. I'm inviting loads of old friends who I haven't seen for years. I'm only inviting the neighbors to get them off my back."

"Why are they on your back?"

"You tell me, Jasper."

"I don't know that particular fact," I pointed out.

Bee sighed wisps of almost translucent sky blue. "My mum's dead and the days of me being kicked around are long gone. I don't have to put up with it again. I don't have to keep quiet. I can make a noise. I'll throw a party if I want to."

My worries had ballooned by the time we reached her front door;

she hadn't explained who was doing the kicking. David Gilbert was my number one suspect.

"Damnit. I'm locked out. We'll have to go around the back. Sorry, Jasper."

I followed her down the alleyway, picking my way over the rubbish. The grass was long and wet, leaving the hems of my jeans brushing damply against my ankles.

"Here we go." She used her right shoulder to shove open a gate leading to an overgrown back garden. "Home, sweet home."

She headed to a stone flamingo by the back door. After moving it with her foot, she bent down and pulled out a key. "My mum's old secret hiding place." She put the key in the lock. "The solicitor took it when he locked up the house. He said a burglar could find it and loot the place. I told him *whatever*. There's nothing worth stealing in here."

I wasn't interested in the key or Mrs. Larkham's solicitor.

"Dad's name is Ed, not Eddie. He says if someone kicks me at school I should kick back. Telling a teacher would make me a nark."

"What? Er, OK. Come and look at this." She took hold of my hand and led me through the kitchen. I removed my shoes and followed her upstairs. Lemons were underfoot. They made my socks wet, but that was better than the old, bad carpet smell.

"What do you think, Jasper?"

Her mum's bedroom had changed since I was last up here. A new wardrobe had arrived while I was at school and a large bed and dusky blue duvet replaced the mattress on the floor. Above it, where the wallpaper had been imprinted with shapes of crosses, hung my parakeet canvases.

"I wanted to cover up the horrible marks with your masterpieces," Bee explained. "Now I have parakeets inside my bedroom as well as outside. What more could a girl ask for?"

I was so happy I didn't attempt to stop my arms from flapping.

"They move exactly like that." Bee laughed spheres of sky blue. She flapped her arms too. "The birds are everywhere—inside, outside, in my garden, David's garden. They don't have boundaries like we do. You can't stop them from doing what comes naturally. They want to be happy."

It took a huge effort to place my arms by the sides of my body too. I followed her to the window. The Dancing China Lady was no longer alone on the chest of drawers. Thirteen friends joined her, pirouetting, playing with hoops and parasols, petting animals, and curtsying.

Dotted among the ladies were glittery purple and black stones. I wanted to touch them but was too afraid of knocking over the ornaments. I figured they must be precious to Bee Larkham because they hadn't ended up on the skip, unlike the sealed cardboard box I'd spotted among the junk on the way over here. Bee hadn't cared enough to look inside before chucking it out.

"Do you believe in love at first sight, Jasper? Even if other people think you're wrong?"

"The parakeets aren't wrong," I replied. "There's nothing wrong about them. They feel exactly right."

I'd fallen in love with the parakeets from day one. I couldn't begin to describe the feelings I had when I saw and heard them. I could only paint them. My colors didn't always do justice to the birds. They couldn't, not completely. Even the best painter in the world couldn't capture their sounds.

"It does feel exactly right. Everyone deserves to be happy, Jasper, even us." She put an arm around my shoulder. "You know, you're like the little brother I never had, the little brother I wish I'd had when I was growing up in this house."

"This one looks like your little sister," I said, picking up the dancing lady I'd used as a potential weapon against David Gilbert. She was the centerpiece of the window display, placed in front of the others with the best view of the parakeets. I was glad she hadn't returned to the box. "She's pretty. Like you."

"Ha!" Her arm dropped back to her side. "That little minx is causing me more trouble than the bloody parakeets!"

I winced. I loathed the greenish bronze color of *minx*. It mingled uncomfortably with the orange puke swearword. I didn't like how close they both were to the parakeets at the end of the sentence. I put down the ornament, careful not to chip it.

"Make sure you can see her properly from the window," Bee said, laughing. She pushed the ornament even closer to the edge of the chest of drawers. "There, that's better. It's a perfect view, right?"

"I'll check when I get home," I promised. I didn't think I'd have a problem seeing the ladies from my bedroom window using binoculars.

We watched, side by side, as a parakeet flew into the hole with twigs in its beak.

"Look, Jasper! I think they're nesting. That's the surprise I wanted to show you. They want to stay on this street, something I'd never thought anyone or anything would ever want to do."

I'd realized this fact days ago and had slept little since because I had to paint more and more pictures of their sounds. I'd guessed some were nesting in the eaves too.

I didn't know how to pretend to look surprised at Bee Larkham's news, so I widened my mouth as far as possible into a broad smile as she continued speaking.

"I think the parakeets are here for good. David said they're going to start breeding. He made it sound like the worst thing in the world, which of course it isn't. How can he possibly object to the start of new life? That's what this street needs. Hope."

I moved my head up and down and clapped my hands. That's what I had too: a tomato-ketchup-colored word, because maybe Bee Larkham would want to stay with her parakeet family on this street too.

"I knew you'd be excited," she said. "I'm sorry I couldn't talk to you, you know, when you called around before. The music lessons are using up a lot of my time. That and doing up the house. It's exhausting."

I couldn't take my eyes or my mind off the parakeets. "They're not scared of David Gilbert and his shotgun even though he's a bird killer and an incredibly dangerous man. I told the police those Important Facts when I dialed 999."

Bee wrapped hair around her finger. "You've reported David Gilbert to the police?"

She laughed bright blue when I confirmed this was correct.

"Good for you, Jasper. Maybe I should call the police too." She walked over to her bed and picked up a small, white padded envelope.

I hadn't noticed it when I walked in. "Something's come up and I urgently need you to give this to Lucas at school tomorrow."

I closed my eyes. I had thought the last letter was a one-off. That had stressed me out enough—finding Lucas's classroom before morning registration and hoping the form teacher would hand it to him without opening it first.

Hoping I hadn't let down Bee Larkham.

"Please, Jasper. It's important you give it to him. I told you I can't ring or email him because of his dad. I want to give him an emergency mobile phone so he can call me if there's a problem at home."

"He could speak to the police," I said. "If he dials 999."

"Yes, he could do that too. You want to help him, don't you, Jasper? He really appreciated the other note you delivered. I think it made him realize he has our support."

So Lucas Drury did get the letter. That still didn't mean I wanted to try again.

"Look, I know it's a pain for you having to look for Lucas between lessons. How about we make a deal?"

"A deal?"

"You deliver this for me and you can come round after school for an hour every day this week to look at the parakeets."

Every day this week.

"If I'm not at home or I'm busy with a lesson, you can use the key under the statue to let yourself in," she continued. "You saw where I put it, right? What do you think? You'd be helping Lucas *and* keeping watch over the parakeets. Because, you know, I think you're right about David. He was around here again yesterday, threatening the parakeets with his shotgun. I'm worried about them, Jasper. Terribly worried."

Immediately, I agreed to help and took the envelope. Bee Larkham was the only person on this street, apart from me, who realized the parakeets were in huge danger. I had to help save them from David Gilbert while Bee Larkham got to work on another rescue mission.

"Are you going to save Lucas and Lee Drury from their dad?" I asked.

"Absolutely," Bee replied. "I think Lucas needs me now more than ever."

31

February 8, 9:13 A.M.
Finding Blue Teal Ruined by Aluminum Giggles on paper

I accidentally turned up late on Monday morning to save Lucas Drury because I couldn't find a clean shirt. I had to scoop one from the bottom of the laundry basket and iron it out with my fists before I left for school. Superheroes never had this kind of problem.

I'd arrived at Lucas's classroom after registration—not before, as I'd planned—and the pupils were already at their desks. A man stared at me as I burst in. He sat at a computer, facing the desks, which meant he must be the teacher. *Mr. Luther.*

"Well, what is it? Cat got your tongue?"

Aluminum giggles.

"I have a letter," I said finally. "For Lucas Drury."

"Well, give it to him before I read out these sports listings."

I stayed put.

"What are you waiting for? Hurry up. I don't have all day."

I couldn't move. I gripped the envelope tighter. "It's for Lucas Drury," I said loudly. "From music teacher Bee Larkham. She wants to see you."

"Is that the new supply teacher?" the man at the desk asked. "Come here, Lucas. You're wanted."

More steel-colored titters, elongated globules with pink rims.

"Coming!" A boy in the third seat from the back slouched towards me. He had tousled blond hair, which didn't help. He appeared identical to the classmate who sat in front of him. The boy didn't look at me as he maneuvered around the desks. "I'll be right back, sir."

I followed him outside the classroom. He was going to be disappointed. Bee Larkham wasn't here. She was probably at home, emptying out cupboards and cleaning up.

Before I could explain, he grabbed the lapels of my blazer and shoved me against the wall.

"Don't come to my classroom again, Binocular Boy," he hissed. "Don't talk to me in school. *Ever.* Unless I say it's OK. Do you understand?"

I didn't understand why he was reluctant to let Bee Larkham and me save him, but I moved my head up and down anyway. Maybe he was afraid. I didn't think he was grateful. I could have been wrong.

"Leave any messages for me in the drawers under the periodic table poster in science lab three C," he said. "No one ever looks there. That's how we're going to communicate from now on. Understand?"

I shifted my head into the correct positions.

"Good." He let go of me and ripped open the envelope.

The corners of his mouth widened; he must have changed his mind about wanting to be saved. He fished out the phone and read the words on a small, dusky blue piece of notepaper.

"Tell Bee we're on for Saturday," he said. "Now beat it before someone sees me talking to you, dweeb."

32

THURSDAY (APPLE GREEN)

Later That Afternoon

Dad's disturbing my work, obscuring the vital shades.

He's downstairs, shouting putrid rotten-plum words into the telephone. It can't be the police because Rusty Chrome Orange has left already. It's not a work call either; he'd probably be fired if he swore at his boss like that. I creep further down the stairs, careful to avoid the squeaky, brownish pink step.

"I don't need another bloody social worker. You were no help before, were you? When I actually needed you. Well, we're doing OK now, thanks for asking. I'm coping fine. It was a freak accident that could have happened to anyone's sodding son."

He needs a clip around the ear and his mouth washed out with soap.

That's what Nan used to say whenever he swore in front of her.

I retreat to the safety of my bedroom. I have to prepare my next canvas and pick out the right tubes of acrylic.

A few minutes later, I hear dark primrose yellow as Dad runs up the stairs. He stops at my door but doesn't knock.

Paler, fluffy-yellow-chick footsteps head to the bathroom.

The shower's switched on.

Blurry dark gray and shiny clear lines.

I saw the same indistinct hues the night of Bee Larkham's party, but I'm not going to paint them now.

Instead, I must mix the color of multiple, interwoven threats.

<h1 style="text-align:center">33</h1>

Glittering Neon Tubes Harassed by Scratchy Red on canvas

Dad spent exactly fourteen minutes in the shower before the party. He came out of the bathroom humming and smelling of sharp citrus fruits. He said making an effort for ladies was important, because they appreciate *small gestures.* That's why he put on his best blue shirt.

"I don't think you'll enjoy tonight," he said, fastening the buttons in the bedroom mirror. "It'll be boring for a kid with grown-ups standing around, talking and drinking. You could stay at home and I'll keep coming across the road to check on you."

"Can I use your night vision goggles?" I asked.

"What? At home?"

"At the party. Bee said tonight wasn't for you. It's not for any of the neighbors. She's only doing it because people are on her back."

"That's what she told you?"

"She said I could stay up in her bedroom and keep watch on the oak tree. I need to protect the parakeets."

"I guess you can borrow them," he said, sighing. "If you must."

I confirmed I had to. It was imperative. Bee Larkham had told me about David Gilbert's multiple death threats. I had to stay on guard all evening because he could use the party invitation to launch a covert attack. He'd be in camouflage behind enemy lines.

"Did Bee really say that about the party?" Dad asked as we walked out of the house.

"She doesn't want to be kicked around by anyone," I replied. "She won't be quiet. She wants to make a lot of noise."

"Anything else?"

Quite a lot, actually—none of which I'd tell him.

After I'd relayed Lucas's message on Monday evening, she'd given me a hug and I'd watched the parakeets from her bedroom window for fifteen minutes and twenty-three seconds longer than we'd agreed. She'd also explained the qualities of the stones placed among the china ladies: amethyst to cleanse the room of negative energies and black tourmaline for protection.

"Bee Larkham says she's looking forward to tomorrow night a lot more than this dull party," I said finally.

"Why? Has she got a boyfriend? Does she have a pre–Valentine's Day date?"

"Oh no. Nothing like that." Dad had got completely the wrong idea as usual, but I couldn't tell him anything about Lucas Drury.

I knew Bee Larkham wouldn't like that. He was our secret.

David Gilbert had set up camp in Bee Larkham's sitting room. I suspected she'd only invited him to pump him for information about his plans for the parakeets. He was on his third glass of red wine and hadn't discussed shooting them. That's what Dad said when he flicked on the light in the bedroom at 9:43 P.M. I asked him to turn it off again because it affected the night vision goggles, but he couldn't see where he was going.

Even though the light was on, he had trouble walking in a straight line and bumped into the drawers by the window.

"Careful," I said, pointing to the ornaments. Bee Larkham had placed my chair by the window to give the best view of the oak tree. "Bee wants me to see the china ladies from the window. She likes them a lot."

"I can see that," he said. "It's quite a collection—if you like that sort of thing."

"Are you going to dance, like the china ladies?"

"What?"

"To the music downstairs," I replied. *Sparkling electric green and violet.* "It's loud, the way Bee likes it."

"You could say that," Dad murmured. "Can you feel the floor vibrating?"

"I've taken off my shoes." The neon colors sent pleasurable shivers along the soles of my feet.

"I've no idea who most of the people are, to be honest. I'll go back down if you're sure you're OK?"

I didn't need Dad. He was distracting me on my watch.

"I want to catch Ollie," he continued. "He's called in to speak to David. He's in a terrible state. This music probably doesn't help. It's hard being a carer at the end, particularly at his age."

I examined the night vision goggles, willing him to leave.

"Jasper? Did you hear what I said?"

"It's hard at the end. You can dance downstairs, like the china ladies. I don't mind. Bee likes dancing as much as her ornaments."

He sighed mists of light brown ocher. "I'll come and get you soon."

The door clicked wheat-colored blobs behind him. I didn't put my goggles down when it opened again four minutes later. The light never flickered on, but footsteps painted dark yellow stripes over the floorboards. The colors stopped near the china ladies and crystals.

"Sorry. Thought this was the bathroom." *A low, scratchy red voice with a fine Sahara mist.*

"You're wrong. Please leave."

I didn't bother turning around because the stripy steps retreated. They didn't go to the bathroom either. I never saw the color of the toilet flush from across the hallway. The person must have gone back downstairs to join the party.

I could smell cigarette smoke. It had traveled up the stairs, along with the neon green tubes. It didn't want to leave me alone in Bee Larkham's bedroom; the vapors thought I wanted company and clung to the peeling, unloved wallpaper.

Mum never smoked and she still died of lung cancer.

Life's unfair, Nan had said. *Terrible things can happen to the best people.*

She was right, as usual. Every single day I wish she wasn't.

*   *   *

Dad never came to get me; I had to find him among dozens of strangers. It was 11:43 P.M. My eyelids hurt, but I didn't want to take a nap on Bee Larkham's bed. That would be rude.

I hadn't seen the parakeets all night, obviously, but keeping guard was important. The birds were safe in their nests, far away from David Gilbert. No one had walked up to the oak tree, although five people had walked straight past it, down the path. They entered doors up and down the street: 25, 24, 17, and 13. I figured the party was close to ending; the music wouldn't pump out electric neon colors for much longer.

A man I didn't recognize lunged towards me in the hallway.

"Sorry," I said automatically.

He smelt of cigarettes and beer. He said "hello, you" and "goodbye" and I repeated the words back in the same order as he lurched out the front door, in case we knew each other. I doubted it. He had scuffed white trainers and a scratchy reddish voice.

I called for Dad in the kitchen. Two men turned around from a group of six, but nobody walked towards me. I figured he wasn't there. The sitting room, which created all the musical colors, was a better bet.

A woman with long blond hair danced in the center of the room, holding a glass of yellow liquid. She wore a short black dress, which wasn't much help—females dressed in black were dotted around the room. I studied the dancer's silver swallow earrings. This had to be Bee Larkham unless she'd loaned her jewelry to someone else. A woman with short red hair and a green dress shimmied around her, holding her hand.

The room smelled of smoke and had spawned a large royal blue sofa and chairs. It must have been another delivery when I was at school because I hadn't noticed the colors of the truck's arrival. Men and women sprawled over the furniture and held up the walls with their backs, but they didn't look at me. They stared at the dancing women and sucked on cancer-causing cigarettes.

"Bee Larkham," I shouted above the music, towards the woman who was most likely my neighbor and friend. "Have you seen my dad?"

"Eddie's there." The blond dancing woman pointed, laughing. "You walked straight past him, sleepyhead!"

I followed the direction of her finger. A man with a blue shirt slumped over the sofa, a can of beer balancing in the crotch of his jeans.

"Jasper!" He tried to stand up but fell back down onto the cushions again. His shirt looked like the one Dad had spent three minutes admiring in the mirror before we left the house, except this one had a wet patch where liquid had spilt down it.

"Someone's worse for wear." A deep, murky claret voice chuckled. It came from the man who sat opposite, holding a glass of wine. His dark navy sweater had diamond patterns.

"I should take Jasper home," the man on the sofa said. His voice was muddy ocher. "It's late. Are you ready to go, Son?"

I rolled the strap around his night vision goggles the way Dad liked, as a thank-you for helping confirm his identity without embarrassing me.

"He looks beat. I should be going home too, Ed. I've stayed longer than I meant to. I'll walk out with you both, if I may." Diamond Sweater Man stood up unsteadily. "Whoops. I think I might have had a few too many. The alcohol's certainly been flowing tonight."

"You can hold on to me if you want," Dad said. "I think I'm sober. *Relatively.*"

"What? You can't leave yet. The party's only just getting started!" Bee turned around and around, spilling her wine. "Don't be a party pooper, Eddie."

"I'm sorry, I must. Jasper needs to go to bed."

"Oh, what a shame. I was hoping you'd stay on for a nightcap."

"I'd like that. I'd like that a lot, but you know . . ."

"Don't worry, Bee Larkham," I said. "I don't think it's necessary for anyone to stay on. The parakeets will be safe tonight. I've been on guard the whole time. David Gilbert hasn't been anywhere near their nests all evening."

"Ha! That's because I can't sssee the little blighters at night," the man next to me said, slurring scraps of claret gravel. "Wait till morning and I can get a better view. I won't miss. I'm an excellent sssshlot."

I took a step backwards. *No way.* The diamond sweater man Dad had offered to help up from his chair was none other than bird killer David Gilbert. He'd managed to dodge my identification system; he wasn't wearing cherry cords and didn't have Yellow French Fries with him. His voice had tricked me by transforming from dull grainy red to murky claret, probably because he'd been drinking. More confusing still, I'd spoken to someone with a similar-colored voice in the hallway.

Bee was wrong—inviting him here wouldn't help us. It was a big mistake. He'd used it as an opportunity to gain reconnaissance info on the parakeets.

"David's joking," Dad said. "Take no notice of him, Jasper. He doesn't mean it."

I dug my fingernails into the palm of my hand, but that couldn't stop me from rocking on my heels.

"I meant every word," he argued. "He can tell the police that if he wants. *Again.*"

"Please don't do this, David," Dad said. "You're winding him up."

"Yes, simmer down!" Bee called out. "It's a party. Remember, David? We're trying to enjoy ourselves."

"Are we? I'm not sure what tonight is about." David Gilbert slammed down his glass of wine, making it spill, and lurched towards Bee. "I'm sorry. I've said it before and I'll say it again, those birds are a bloody nuisance—particularly first thing. You have to do something about them *now*. They'll start coming here even earlier for food once it gets lighter in the mornings."

"I love the sound of them," Bee replied, "which means I don't have to do anything at all."

"It's unfair to your neighbors, particularly to Ollie's mum in the time she has left," he continued. "The same goes for your music and DIY at all hours. Ollie says he has to bang on your wall because the constant noise is torturing her in her final weeks. Can't you see what you're doing to that young man and his poor mother?"

"I can see you're interfering in things that have nothing to do with you," she said. "This is my house. I'll do whatever I want."

"It's your mother's house, Beatrice. I've visited many, many times ever since you were knee high. Pauline was a good friend of mine, as well as Lily Watkins. I know she'd be mortified at the way you're behaving, what you're doing to Lily."

"You were never *my* friend," Bee shouted. "Never. Not when I was a kid. Not now. Eddie was right. It's time for you to go. You've outstayed your welcome yet again."

She swore a rotten-sprout word at him.

I clenched my fists tight. David Gilbert didn't move. He'd threatened the parakeets again and wouldn't listen to Bee Larkham or my dad.

"You heard Bee Larkham!" I yelled. "Go home, David Gilbert, and don't come back. Cigarettes cause one hundred thousand deaths in the United Kingdom each year. I hope you die of cancer. I hope you die soon. That will be my birthday wish this year. I hate you!"

"Jasper! That's enough. We're leaving."

Dad grabbed my arm and pulled.

I screamed large aquamarine clouds with jagged surfaces at him, but he wouldn't let go. I hurled his goggles, making a reddish brown sound with black nodules on the floorboards.

"No!" Dad cried.

The vivid greens and purples disappeared as the music stopped. Bee wasn't dancing. She put her glass down next to the iPod and walked towards us. Reaching down, she picked up the goggles and handed them to Dad.

"Thank you for sticking up for me, Jasper. No one's ever done that for me before, they've never fought in my corner." She turned to face David Gilbert. "Get out of my house, you stinking hypocrite."

Bee Larkham reached out towards Dad and me. Did she want to touch me? Hug me? Commiserate with me?

I didn't wait to find out. I fled her house to escape from the clutches of David Gilbert.

Dad followed me across the road and into our house. He didn't say anything until I came out of the bathroom after brushing my teeth and changing into pajamas.

"You can't say things like that to people. About them dying of cancer. Even if you don't like them. You can't. OK? You'll need to apologize to David tomorrow. I'll have to take you over there. You can't tell people you hope they die."

He'd repeated himself. I wasn't sorry. I truly hoped David Gilbert died of cancer. *There.* Now I'd repeated myself, and I hadn't drunk any beer, unlike him.

"Will Ollie Watkins apologize for banging on Bee Larkham's wall?" I asked. "Because that's rude. I bet Bee banged back. That's what I'd do if someone pounded on my wall."

"You're changing the subject. That's something completely different. Ollie's mum is dying of cancer and they both want some peace and quiet in their last few months or weeks together."

"That's what I want too. Peace and quiet. Please go."

I shut my bedroom door and leaned against it, because I didn't want Dad to follow me inside and start repeating himself again. I had to set my alarm clock as usual even though tomorrow was Saturday.

David Gilbert planned to kill the parakeets in the morning, probably as they gathered on the feeders. I'd dial 999 again, before he had a chance to leave his house with his shotgun. The police had to catch him in the act. This time they'd believe me and stop him, mid-ambush.

I wrapped the duvet around me. My mind whirred, keeping me awake, but my eyelids were heavy. I saw the color of the TV downstairs and the silvery white sound of beer bottles clinking as Dad opened the fridge. Their colors were in the background because yellow, blue, and green flashing tubes continued to thump out of Bee Larkham's house.

As I fell asleep, I thought I saw something else beneath the music: *light brown circles.*

I had to be wrong. It couldn't have been the front door opening and shutting because the TV continued to hum black lines with rough gray strands.

Dad wouldn't leave me alone at night. I used to have nightmares about waking up in our old house in Plymouth and discovering I was by myself. Mum said that would never happen.

Leaving me on my own would be all shades of wrong.

34

FRIDAY (INDIGO BLUE)

Morning

The spacemen arrived over the road at 8:02 P.M. last night. They wore white suits that covered their entire bodies from head to foot as they entered 20 Vincent Gardens. They stayed until midnight and left behind two police officers in a car.

Eight hours and forty-two minutes later, the people in space suits returned to Bee Larkham's house and Shona, a social worker, turned up at ours. The two arrivals can't be a coincidence; their colors are virtually the same hues.

Shona had a croaky gray voice, because she had a sore throat. I explained her colors would be totally different if she hadn't been ill because voices can change dramatically like that. We debated what color it could be and I chose green. I couldn't tell for sure what shade, maybe fern or racing car.

"Can I let you in on a little secret?" she whispered. "I'd like to be bright scarlet. It's my favorite color."

"Now you're being silly," I replied. "Whispers can't be bright scarlet. They are only ever white or gray moving lines that conceal the real color."

Next I told her she needed to wear gloves if she wanted to look at my tummy and should probably wear a mouth mask to stop me from becoming infected with her germs. Shona apologized and said she didn't have one. She coughed a lot and fired questions at me about GP checkups and how often Dad left me alone in the house.

I said "once," because that was the truth for yesterday.

We discussed the hole in my tummy. At first, Shona wanted me to play with a doll and reenact how I hurt myself, but she gave up because I couldn't stop laughing.

I'm thirteen, not three.

I stuck to the lines Dad had given me before she arrived. I did a good job, I think. I didn't deviate from the script.

I was playing with a knife in the kitchen, our kitchen, when it slipped and cut me. I didn't tell Dad to begin with because I didn't want to get him into trouble. I covered it up and pretended nothing had happened. Dad's told me hundreds of times not to play with knives.

That wasn't a total lie as Dad *has* told me not to play with knives, and Shona seemed pleased about only receiving 75 percent of the truth. I think that was all she had time for. She was due to visit another boy whose family had "complex issues." She left ten minutes ago after promising to visit me again soon.

Dad's stood at the window in the sitting room ever since. He must want to make sure she's truly gone.

"Forensics are taking forever in Bee's house," he says eventually. "They must be going soon, surely?"

I walk out of the room, up to my bedroom, without replying. I need to examine my parakeet paintings while I still have a chance. The spacemen won't leave 20 Vincent Gardens until they find what they're looking for: evidence of my wrongdoing.

They're not dumb like Rusty Chrome Orange.

They're going to find it soon. We both know that.

It's simply a matter of time.

35

February 13, 8:22 A.M.
Parakeets Disturbed on paper

Fourteen parakeets flew from the feeders in the oak tree with screeches of disapproval at the splintering bright green sounds.

It was the morning after the party, and a woman with long blond hair hurled empty wine and beer bottles into the skip outside number 20. I'd stopped painting and walked over the road. I said "good morning" to the parakeets under my breath as I approached.

"How's your dad this morning, Jasper?" she asked, reaching down into her sack. "He seemed to enjoy my party."

"He's in bed, Bee Larkham. He has a headache."

"That figures." She laughed sky blue ribbons.

"I reported David Gilbert to the police at six fifty-two A.M. I'm not sure they're doing anything about him. They haven't turned up yet."

"The police are never there when you really need them," she replied quietly. "They're never much use, but good on you for trying."

"What are we going to do?" I asked.

"You can start by helping me clear up, if you don't mind. I need to get everything straight before tonight."

I'd meant about David Gilbert, but never mind. Maybe she wanted to discuss him inside the house, where we had more privacy.

"You want to straighten things in the house before Lucas Drury comes round," I stated.

"Yes, before that." Bee hurled another bottle into the skip. She didn't speak for one minute and eleven seconds because she was concentrating on her aim.

"Jasper, you do know you mustn't tell anyone about Lucas? Not at school or anyone on this street. Not even your dad. Particularly not your dad."

"OK. But Dad would probably understand why you want to save Lucas. He was in the Royal Marines and saved lots of people's lives before he had to leave."

"He probably killed a lot of people too."

I hadn't thought about that before. I didn't want to. Death frightened me. So did Dad sometimes.

"Sorry. I shouldn't have said that. I'm being a cow this morning. I don't feel myself after that row with David. Have you had breakfast?"

"Not yet. Dad's not up."

"Come inside," she said. "I'll look after you. We'll play happy families and pretend we're mum and son. You'd like that, wouldn't you, Jasper?"

I moved my head up and down into the pattern of an affirmative gesture.

"Good. We'll talk about David and the parakeets and I can show you the new crystals I bought. Like this one." She whipped out a long silver chain from beneath her top. Attached to the end was a black tubular stone. "Obsidian is one of the strongest protection stones in the world, Jasper." She took a step closer towards me. "Which means neither of us has anything to be frightened of anymore."

Bee Larkham's cereal wasn't the same as my usual one, so I pretended I wasn't hungry because I didn't want to hurt her feelings. She gave me a bin bag and gloves, and I walked around downstairs, helping pick up cans and cigarette butts. When that was done, I headed straight for the bedroom, which was my favorite place in the house.

Bee hadn't had time to make her bed. The duvet was pulled back, and beneath the pillow, the ears of a white rabbit poked out from the corner of a steel blue notebook. I didn't touch it because that was private. I kept my notebooks close to my bed too and didn't like Dad looking in them.

Beside the bed was a small, clear stone and plastic sweet wrappers.

I threw the rubbish into the bin bag too and spotted an empty beer can in the corner, but the sound of the parakeets drew me to the window.

Why oh why hadn't I brought my binoculars with me? I vowed to carry them around with me at all times.

Dark mahogany brown, elongated shapes.

Someone was knocking on the front door. I couldn't see who had turned up when I looked directly down, even when I pressed my body against the glass. Bee stopped the vacuum cleaner's gray and white spirals and opened the door.

Two parakeets climbed out of the hole and fluttered up to their friends, higher in the tree.

I didn't hear what was being said downstairs at first. The angry birds screeched icy green and yellow glass at each other, distracting me.

Bee's voice rang out, luminous sky blue with white points: "No!"

Was David Gilbert back? I reached for the mobile in my pocket. *Not there.* I'd left it at home. I raced to the top of the landing, fists clenched. I didn't pick up one of the china ladies this time because I knew how much they meant to Bee.

"I'm not going to change my mind," she said. "The answer's no."

A voice—whitish with almost translucent, quivering lines and a pale red hue—murmured softly: "Please."

David Gilbert must have wanted Bee to accept his apology about last night because it's rude to upset your hostess. I didn't hear what else he said, but it distressed her even more.

"I don't want your flowers! Like that makes it all OK?"

I was proud of Bee, the way she stood up to the dangerous bird killer. She didn't seem to need my help.

The man muttered another set of white, wavering lines with pale reddish edges.

"Stop coming here," she said. "Or I'll call the police. I'll tell them everything. I'll give them my diary. I mean it. It's a record of everything that's happened."

I had no idea she was keeping a log of David Gilbert's movements too.

I clapped loudly as she slammed the front door.

Dark brown with black running through.

Bee ran up the stairs, straight past me and into the bedroom, without saying a word. I followed as she flung open the window and leaned out. She didn't want me to see her crying.

"Don't worry, Bee Larkham," I said. "The police will listen to you if you report him. It'll help our case against him if you give them your diary. They'll take more notice of your records than my notebooks because I'm just a kid and they don't believe me."

Bee turned around. She picked up one of the china ladies from the chest of drawers. The woman clutched a parasol tightly. "What case are you talking about, Jasper?"

"David Gilbert's threats to kill the parakeets," I prompted.

"Oh, that."

Her grip must have accidentally loosened as she leaned out of the window again. I heard hundreds of small, silver-white tubes as the figurine smashed on the ground below.

"I'm sorry," I said.

"Don't be," she replied. "You're not the person who's going to be very, very sorry."

Later that evening I tried to mend the ornament. I'd scooped up as many pieces as I could from the front garden. I'd wanted to return her so Bee Larkham would place her back in the window, but I couldn't find all the fragments of the parasol and gown. They'd smashed to dust.

I was far too embarrassed by my messy glue and the lady's cracked face and ruined dress and parasol to give her back. I put her under my bed because I didn't want to upset Bee Larkham. I wanted to protect her from the truth:

Some things are too fragile for this earth. They can never be fixed.

36

FRIDAY (INDIGO BLUE)

Still That Morning

I spread out my parakeet paintings on the carpet and compare them alongside my notebooks. A pattern emerges, which I'd never noticed before. Whenever I delivered one of Bee Larkham's envelopes to the science drawer, I spent an hour after school in her bedroom, which later produced three paintings and sometimes as many as five or six.

I was lucky Bee had continued to write notes when she could text Lucas on the mobile I'd delivered. She told me she liked communicating the old-fashioned way. It was more personal. Also, Lucas desperately needed stuff that had to be put into envelopes: money, Xbox games, and even cigarettes to cheer him up.

Saving Lucas Drury only to kill him with cancer-causing cigarettes seemed like a dumb plan to me. I went along with it because I had calculated the first baby parakeets would be born around February 27. Weeks after that, I might get my first glimpse of them, probably sometime at the end of March.

I *had* to paint the colors of their first chirps.

I'd stopped worrying about taking the notes and small packages due to our routine. I delivered an envelope from Bee Larkham to Lucas Drury on Monday at lunchtime and checked on Wednesday morning for anything to bring back from Lucas Drury to Bee Larkham. Nine times out of ten there wasn't, but I liked to be thorough.

This regular schedule helped me paint better pictures because I saw the colors of the adult parakeets' shrieks up close from Bee Larkham's bedroom; they surpassed the more muted tones I experienced across the street.

For some reason, I haven't recorded in my notebooks all the details about my bird-watching visits—the questions Dad asked me whenever I returned from Bee's house, such as

How is Bee? *Not ill.*
What is she up to these days? *Don't understand the question.*
Does she ever mention me? *No.*

These are the other nonparakeet things I remember now about the visits to her bedroom:

a. Sweet wrappers
   Orchid purple-, silver-, and sapphire-colored ones were by the side of the bed.
b. The steel blue notebook with the white rabbit on the cover
   It was always nearby—on the table, on the floor, or hiding, half-covered by a pillow.
c. Lucas Drury's library card
   I found it on the bedside table. Bee Larkham must have borrowed it because she was too busy to register for her own.
d. The china ladies
   As my parakeet painting collection grew, the number of china ladies shrank. The parakeets and the ornaments couldn't live alongside each other. They didn't get along.

Later, I realized Bee Larkham was becoming clumsier and clumsier. She knocked the china ladies out of her bedroom window one by one. Whenever I found a broken ornament in her front garden, I didn't attempt to mend it. I collected all the pieces and threw them away before she had to see the disfigured faces again.

I think she was glad I helped her get rid of the evidence.

Bee never asked me what I did with the headless bodies. She didn't miss them. She didn't miss them at all.

37

March 12, 2:23 P.M.
Parakeets Feeding Babies on canvas

The parakeets had flown back and forth from the feeders and into the hole in the tree and the eaves for weeks, but I hadn't managed to catch a glimpse of what I knew to be true: babies must be inside the nests.

Possibly one or two per family. That meant up to six nestlings could be concealed inside Bee Larkham's tree and eaves.

The adult parakeets had refused to be intimidated by David Gilbert and stayed to breed, the way Bee Larkham had bravely stood up to him. She said she wasn't bothered he'd applied to the council for a noise abatement order against her. She'd sworn a mushy-tangerine-colored word at him when he called round.

Bee was watching from the window with me and took photos on her mobile of two adult parakeets peering out of the hole and one of a single parakeet preening itself and cleaning its feet.

"Lucas lost the phone I gave him, silly boy," she said. "I'll have to take the risk and tag these piccies to him on Facebook as he's busy with football tournaments this weekend. He'll love them. They're so cute!"

"Have you almost finished saving him?" I asked.

I was afraid of the answer—scared Bee might no longer need me to deliver her messages. She could stop my bird-watching time from her bedroom window at a crucial period. I'd estimated the eldest nestlings were only two weeks old, far too young to peek out of the hole.

I needed longer.

"I honestly don't know," Bee said. "It's total madness, but I can't seem to stop myself, you know?"

Yes, I did.

A small part of me—5 percent—wished she would stop, because I didn't like her talking about Lucas Drury. I didn't trust him either. Why was he being distracted by football tournaments instead of concentrating on being saved by Bee Larkham? My remaining 95 percent wanted this arrangement to continue. At least until I'd seen the color of the baby parakeets' first chirps and they'd learned to fly.

"You shouldn't stop," I told her. "Neither of us should stop what we're doing. We should stick to the original plan, whatever happens."

That evening, 8:45 P.M.
Crushed-Moth and Tangerine Circles on paper

Some people don't think it's important to stick to plans. They tear them up and scatter the pieces around for others to pick up like litter because they're selfish and don't worry about the consequences.

They also skulk about outside houses in the dark, with baseball caps pulled down low to cover their faces.

I broke off from watching the eaves with my binoculars and trained them on the person who stood by the wall outside Bee Larkham's house. He wasn't dressed like David Gilbert and didn't have a dog with him, but he stared up at the oak tree. This made him suspicious and quite possibly a threat to the parakeets.

I logged the sighting in my notebook and dated it.

Bee Larkham's house was shrouded in darkness, apart from the upstairs bedroom window. A light was on, the curtains closed. The person—a he—fiddled with something in his pocket. Was he reaching for a weapon? I grabbed my mobile and ran downstairs while Dad chatted to someone on the phone in the bath. By the time I reached the front door, the figure had already entered the alleyway.

I ran out of the house.

Was it David Gilbert in disguise? Could he have completed a reconnaissance mission to spy on the parakeets and was he now reentering his house via the alley and back garden to throw me off his scent?

As I turned the corner, I gasped cool blue spirals. Bee Larkham's gate was open. I moved quickly through the alley, climbing over scattered junk. A figure was already bending over the flamingo statue by the back door as I stumbled through the gate. The person stood up again, holding the hidden key.

"Put that back," I said loudly. "It doesn't belong to you."

My fingers had punched 999 into my mobile. I was ready to press call.

The figure in the dark blue baseball cap spun round. "Jeez. You scared the shit out of me, Jasper."

He knew me and had a blue teal voice. I'd only met one person recently with that color voice: *Lucas Drury.*

But he wasn't supposed to be here. He was at a football tournament. That's what Bee had said earlier when we discussed his weekend plans.

"Are you spying on me, Jasper? With your binoculars?"

"No, Lucas Drury," I replied, gripping the strap tighter.

"You didn't see me here, right?" He unlocked the back door and put the key in his pocket.

My guess about his identity was correct because he didn't provide another name, but it still didn't feel right. Maybe his football tournament had been canceled at the last minute. Or he'd let the organizers down and hadn't turned up. That struck me as the kind of thing Lucas Drury would do. He wouldn't mind changing other people's plans without asking permission.

I walked closer. His baseball cap was actually faded navy, with the initials NYY in deeper indigo, which almost totally blended in with the cotton.

"New York Yankees," I said.

"What?"

"Your baseball cap. You should put it back."

Lucas Drury pulled it down lower over his face. "It's my dad's. I borrowed it."

"I meant the key," I clarified. "It belongs beneath the flamingo statue. You should put it back."

"Er, OK. Thanks." He bent down and shifted the statue. "Now beat it, Jasper."

"Do you have a meeting with Bee?" I asked.

"What? Not exactly. It's a surprise visit, but she won't turn me away. She said I can use her spare key any time I want." He breathed in cloudy dark teal mist as he opened the door. "Forget I said that, Jasper. You mustn't talk about this at school, OK? Or anywhere else. This is private stuff between me and Bee."

I moved my head up and down. I hoped Bee Larkham would come to the door and *we* could talk. I'd ask her why she'd told Lucas Drury about the key's hiding place.

I thought that was our secret, one of the things that made our friendship special. I didn't want to share that bond with Lucas Drury, but I couldn't get in the way of Bee Larkham's rescue mission.

"I won't tell anyone about your surprise visit, Lucas Drury," I confirmed.

His left eye opened and closed as he walked inside. He didn't call out to Bee as he shut the door and slipped away into the dark house.

I returned home and kept watch over the oak tree with my binoculars until after midnight. No one came out of 20 Vincent Gardens or the alleyway. Bee Larkham's special operation to save Lucas Drury went on long into the night, accompanied by crushed-moth and tangerine circles from the music playing in the bedroom.

I thought those colors were bad enough, but worse was to come twelve days later.

I would see a dreadful shade and shape that obliterated most of the brushstrokes that came before and afterwards, almost destroying me.

Short lines of black with blood orange shadows.

38

The Death on paper

Dad had taken me into town after school to buy trainers and we'd had tea at a new pizzeria. He'd spent four days preparing me for this expedition, showing me photographs of the restaurant and the shoe shop on Google Maps to avoid any unwelcome surprises.

When we pulled up in the car outside our house, Dad's mobile rang and he had to take the work call. He ran into the house, but I lingered behind.

Immediately, I sensed the colors were wrong, terribly wrong. The parakeets shrieked and squawked for help. I ran across the road, forgetting to check first. A car hooted deep red deformed stars. I ignored it. The birds swooped from the tree to the ground and back again, screeching and howling brighter, more painful shades.

I saw the tiny bundle of green feathers as I drew close.

"No!" I screamed sharp, acrid blue.

A cacophony of horrid, vulgar colors echoed through the street.

Garish blue greens glazed with an icy yellow mist.

I picked up the baby parakeet and cradled it in my hands.

The bird was cold, tiny droplets of blood sprinkled on its soft chest. It had fallen from its nest and died before I could help it.

Sobbing, I banged on the front door. Bee Larkham had to hear the bad news from me, not someone else. She was definitely inside. Playful ribbons of salmon and sugar-mouse pink music grew bolder in color from behind the bedroom window curtains.

The pretty, entwining ropes of color had distracted her; otherwise she'd have opened the door. I ran around the back, through the alley and into her garden, cradling the baby parakeet. The spare key was where it belonged, beneath the flamingo statue.

I unlocked the door and ran into the house, up the stairs. I could hear a rhythmic noise fighting against the musical pink ribbons, overpowering it with short lines of black with blood orange shadows.

A creaking sound like Bee was jumping on her bed, the way I do every Sunday morning before football.

"Bee!" I screamed. "Bee Larkham, come quick! It's an emergency."

I flung open the bedroom door, and that's when time stood still and things changed forever.

A naked blond woman was on the bed. She was bouncing on top of a body, which was also naked. I didn't look at the face. I saw too much alien flesh. Shiny purple sweet wrappers lay sprinkled over the duvet.

"Shit!" a blue teal voice exclaimed.

The woman fell sideways, almost toppling off the bed. "Get your clothes on, Lucas! Quick!" *Sky blue.*

I ran downstairs and out the back door, tossing the key into its hiding place. Luckily no cars passed by because I sprinted across the road, carrying the dead baby bird, the howls of parakeets in my ears.

I don't remember much more about that evening, for example, how many china ladies had watched naked Bee Larkham and naked Lucas Drury. I don't remember how Dad got me to calm down—probably by letting me rub the buttons on Mum's cardigan in my den and spin on the chair in the kitchen.

There are three facts I do remember:

1. I buried the baby parakeet in our back garden. Nothing fancy. I didn't feel well enough to decorate the grave or make a cross yet. Dad told me to put a stone on top because a cat or fox would try to dig it up.
2. Bee Larkham called round later that evening. She didn't come inside our house. This time she was wearing clothes. I saw a woman in a long ice blue skirt through the banisters and heard Dad call her Bee.

I never told Dad I'd seen her naked because I thought he might be cross. I did tell him I never wanted to watch the parakeets from her bedroom window again.

They had an argument, but I only heard snatches. Bee said, *You were only ever a one-night stand.* Dad called her out on that lie. He thought *it meant more than that.* They argued again. I was glad he'd taken a stand against her. She deserved it.

I distinctly remember this third fact because I repeated it over and over to myself in bed that night:

3. *I hated bouncy, alien-flesh Bee Larkham.*

Dad hated her too. He called her a *silly little tart* when he slammed the door shut, *brown rectangles with charcoal shading.*

For once we agreed about something.

39

FRIDAY (INDIGO BLUE)

Afternoon

The icicles have come for me again. They're trying to pull me down the rabbit hole towards the Mad Hatter.

He's inside Bee Larkham's kitchen along with white-suited spacemen. They shouldn't have visited this street. They'll be killed.

Twelve of them.

I need to stop the massacre. I can't. I have to escape from the house, but the front door's locked.

I run to the back door because I've found the secret key. I still can't escape. The Mad Hatter won't let me. He blocks my way. He's wearing a dark blue baseball cap.

"Wake up, Jasper. This is urgent."

A hand stretches into my den. It's reaching towards my shoulder. I open my mouth, ready to scream clouds of aquamarine.

"It's me. It's Dad. I need you to come out of there. Something's happened and we have to talk."

He backs away from the den because he knows I don't like to be crowded. As I crawl out, he walks over to the window and leans against the sill.

"You need to sit down, Jasper. I've got something distressing to tell you."

"I've been lying down because I was tired after checking through my parakeet paintings," I point out. "That means I don't need to sit down again, thank you."

"Fine." Dad sighs smooth, muddy ocher circles.

I wait for him to start speaking again.

"D.C. Chamberlain rang while you were asleep. He has news, which you're going to find disturbing."

"Did the spacemen find spots of my blood in the kitchen and leading out the back door?" I ask. "I guess they may have found traces in the alley as well."

Dad rubs his face, the way he does when he's smothering himself with shaving foam. "D.C. Chamberlain didn't mention the forensics side of things, but he said the investigation into Bee's disappearance is moving at a fast pace. The team's working overtime."

"How fast is fast?" I query. "Did he specify the velocity?"

"We're getting sidetracked when you need to focus on what I'm trying to tell you. The point is a dog walker found something unpleasant in the woodland not far from here this morning. D.C. Chamberlain wanted us to hear it from him first, because it could be on the local news tonight."

"What news? ITV London or Capital FM?"

"Both probably. The dog walker found a body, Jasper, early this morning. He found a woman's body."

"He found Bee Larkham's body," I confirm.

This doesn't come as a particular shock to me since Dad must have moved it somewhere, otherwise the people in space suits across the road would have found it by now.

"D.C. Chamberlain said they don't know that for certain. They haven't identified it yet. It's not one hundred percent definite, but there's a slim chance . . . It might be . . . What I'm trying to say, Jasper, is we should prepare ourselves for the worst possible scenario—the police might have found Bee's body."

"Why don't *you* know for sure it's her?" I ask. "When you carried her body out of twenty Vincent Gardens, drove it to the woodland, and left it there for the dog walker to find?"

"Jasper! Stop it!"

"I found your walking boots in the bottom of your wardrobe, which means the woods were muddy. You left her body in the mud because you didn't want me to get into trouble with the police. Now you're involved and we'll both go to prison."

"Shut up!" He grabs my arms and squeezes tight. Too tight. "I need time to think before we speak to D.C. Chamberlain again. I have to decide what we're going to tell him."

"Get off me!" I yell.

I kick him hard in the shins. He lets go and I'm as fast as a parakeet. I swoop out of the room, onto the landing. I'm running down the stairs. He's David Gilbert, chasing me, trying to hunt me down. I'm the baby parakeet soaring to safety. I've already spotted the trap: the chain across the front door that will stop me from flying the nest.

"Come back!"

I don't. I change direction. I grab Dad's mobile from the table in the hall and skid into the bathroom, slamming the door shut. He hammers dark brown circles. He can't get in. I've locked it.

"I'm sorry, Jasper! I'm sorry. Please believe me. I shouldn't have grabbed you like that. Or shouted at you."

I dial 999. Dad's changed his password to stop me from using his phone, but I don't need it for emergency calls.

I'm connected to the operator.

"Please help me. My dad's trying to kill me. Hurry!"

"Jasper!" Dad bangs harder on the door. "Don't! Open up now! I didn't mean to hurt you. Open up or I'll have to break down the door."

This time, the operator doesn't waste time asking me dumb personal questions. They must have this information on file.

"We're on our way, love," the woman says. "Don't open the door until a police officer tells you it's safe. Hang tight. They won't be long."

My legs won't hold me up any longer. I slump to the floor. Bee Larkham had warned me about Dad.

She said he'd killed people.

I think she was right.

He's proved time and time again he can't be trusted.

He tells lies *all the time.*

He duped me into thinking he shared my interest in the baby parakeets and that he'd protect them and me from harm.

I don't believe a word he says.

I'm going to tell the police every single thing he's done.

40

March 31, 8:01 A.M.
Baby Parakeets on paper

My first glimpse of a baby parakeet should have been thrilling, but its colors were far too muted, dusted with the lightest of pastels and unconfident, tiny circular shapes.

Dad and me watched two tiny green faces poking out of the hole in Bee Larkham's oak tree.

"Nature's amazing," he said. "It blows my mind. It's such a pity David doesn't appreciate how lucky we are on this street. But you mustn't worry about him, Jasper. I'll never let David harm the baby parakeets, I promise."

"Shush," I replied. "I can't hear them properly."

"Sorry."

I was too. Even when I opened my window and half-hung out, I was too far away to hear properly.

If I returned to Bee Larkham's bedroom, everything would be different.

That couldn't happen. I didn't want to think about *short lines of black with blood orange shadows.*

Seeing those colors had made me sick and kept me off school for days. I had trouble blocking them out. Dad hadn't seen them. He wouldn't understand.

I had stayed in my den and pulled the forget-me-not blue blanket tightly shut when I wasn't watching the baby parakeets.

I tried to forget, but however many blankets I piled up at the entrance, the repulsive shades and tints from Bee Larkham's bedroom managed to drift inside.

April 2, 11:01 A.M.

Electric Blue Dots and Speckles of Soft Yellow on canvas

The day of Mrs. Watkins's funeral, those appalling tones and textures finally disappeared along with the coffin.

"Is the body inside?" I asked Dad.

We watched the black hearse pull up opposite 18 Vincent Gardens from our sitting room window on Saturday (Turquoise) morning. I shuddered when I saw the light marshmallow pink and white flowers. I've never much liked sweets that maliciously jam my teeth together. I watched Bee Larkham's oak tree instead, hoping for another glimpse of the baby parakeets.

"Yes, Son. Mrs. Watkins was taken to a funeral parlor after the doctor pronounced her dead a week ago on Friday."

The day after the baby parakeet died.

"She's been there ever since?" I shivered. "On her own?"

"Well, her body was there. She wouldn't have known anything about it because she . . ." He forgot what he was trying to say and started again. "Her soul wasn't in her body. It had left and gone to heaven."

"Where Mum's soul is?"

"Yes, exactly."

"That sounds nice if you want to believe it. I don't believe Mum's in heaven because I don't believe in God."

"Well, that's your choice, Son."

I hadn't expressed myself well. I meant to say I refused to believe in God.

A man wearing a black suit walked out of 22 Vincent Gardens. He joined another man wearing a black suit who came out of number 18. They stopped and talked on the pavement across the road.

"I should go and pay my respects to Ollie," Dad said. "Since I couldn't make it to the funeral."

"Because of me."

"Funerals aren't the place for children and there's no one to leave you with. Unless you've changed your mind about spending time with Bee?"

I hadn't spoken to her since *short lines of black with blood orange shadows.*

I hadn't seen her either, except from a safe distance. She'd waved at me from her bedroom window. I didn't wave back. She mistakenly thought I was looking at her, but I only wanted to see the baby parakeets' colors.

The mention of Bee Larkham's name pushed the bedroom's hues from my mind, and all I could see was sky blue.

"Have *you* spoken to her?" I asked.

"Bee? Yes. Yesterday, actually."

"What was she doing?" I quizzed Dad as I followed him to the front door. "What was she up to? Did she ask about me?" I bit my tongue. I'd repeated *exactly* the same questions Dad asked *me* about Bee Larkham after her party for the neighbors that wasn't really for the neighbors.

"Let me see, she was saying goodbye to a music pupil. It was a bit awkward at first after our quarrel, but she apologized for not being there for you when the baby parakeet died and for getting het up with me that night. She said it was a big misunderstanding. She hasn't been herself lately and she's sorry for upsetting us both. I think she meant it. We agreed to draw a line under everything."

I stared at the battle line, which stretched across the street. It still existed because David Gilbert wasn't in the coffin. Mrs. Watkins had died of cancer. It was possible my wish the night of the party had gone haywire and struck the wrong person by accident, making me a murderer.

"Bee Larkham was most probably giving an electric green and exploding purple guitar lesson to Lee Drury."

"I've no idea," Dad admitted, stepping into the road first. "The lesson was over when I got there."

As we reached the two men on the opposite pavement, the bedroom window at 20 Vincent Gardens swung open and Saint-Saëns, *Carnival of the Animals,* streamed out. I recognized the colors of the pianos and strings: "Introduction and Royal March of the Lion."

Dad had magically summoned Bee Larkham, and she'd responded

with the loudest, most vibrant colors she could conjure up. Two dancing china ladies watched the display from her bedroom window.

"Disrespectful," one of the men muttered in soft gray lines.

I couldn't tell the two men apart in their black suits and the muted
colors of their hushed voices.

He was wrong anyway, whoever he was.

I knew straightaway this music was meant for me—Bee Larkham's
way of saying sorry because she knew how much I loved these colors,
the parakeets too. They shrieked with joy and joined in with the choruses. A baby poked its head out of the hole in the tree.

Light cornflower blue with speckles of soft yellow.

Another baby parakeet appeared in a gap in the eaves.

Trembling forget-me-not blobs and light desert-sand speckles.

I didn't need to hear Bee speak.

I'd seen the true color of the baby parakeets for the first time.

I recognized Bee's remorse in the music's electric blue dots and
wood-paneling red-browns. She was begging forgiveness because she'd
missed me. I hadn't visited her house over the last nine days. I hadn't
delivered any notes to Lucas Drury. I hadn't seen a shade that came
close to sky blue.

"I've changed my mind," I told Dad. "You can go to the funeral. I
want to go to Bee Larkham's house. I want to see the color of the baby
parakeets up close in her bedroom."

"Are you sure? Because if you're happy with that, I can nip back in
and change into something more suitable."

"Something black," I said, "which is a sign of respect to the dead."

The front door opened and a woman stepped out in a dazzling
cerulean blue, long dress. Her obsidian pendant swung from her
neck.

"Good God," Dad muttered. "Bee couldn't have known."

"Oh yes, she did." The man in black had a dull grainy red voice. This
had to be David Gilbert. "I put a note through her door, telling her the
time the hearse was arriving."

"Bee likes notes, so I'm sure she read it," I said. "She says they're
more personal than emails or texts."

She waved at me, but the vividness of the blue and the music's shimmering hues had glued my arms to my body. It erased the palette of colors I'd seen in her bedroom, expunging Lucas Drury's shades. They mingled pleasurably with the sapphire blues and fuchsias of the parakeets.

I focused on the musical colors twisting and dancing in front of me. The whitish gray murmur of voices remained in the background.

Ignore her.

What is she playing at?

She's deliberately goading you.

Let's go.

A car door slammed shut. *Dark brown oval shape and shimmering black and gray lines.*

"Jasper? Jasper! Did you hear me?"

I dragged myself away from the colors of the music and focused on the muddy ocher voice.

"I said I'm not sure this is such a good idea after all. Maybe I should stay home with you?"

"No, Dad. You should go and bury Mrs. Watkins with the men in black. I don't like their colors. I prefer sky blue. I want sky blue and the color of the baby parakeets. I have to paint their genuine colors. I owe them that."

"First of all, I want to say how sorry I am about the death of the baby parakeet," Bee Larkham said, as she led me into her sitting room. "I've been thinking about it a lot. It's made me sad, terribly sad we couldn't grieve together, which is totally my fault. I was wrong to ask you to leave when I was busy. I apologize, Jasper."

Had she? I didn't remember her speaking to me, only to Lucas Drury. He had to get his clothes on. Quickly.

Because I'd seen his alien flesh. Hers too.

"The music lessons and house DIY use up so much of my energy," she continued. "I'm rushed off my feet, but I should have made time for you when you needed me."

I was glad she'd mentioned music. She'd painted a new scene in her head, with shades I didn't recognize. Yet I much preferred this picture to the one from her bedroom. I accepted it unquestioningly, grateful the old colors were gone. They'd been a terrible mistake, which she was sorry about.

"I buried the baby parakeet in our back garden and recited a poem because I don't accept there's a God who lets good people die," I said. "Or parakeets. Would you like to see the grave?"

"That's thoughtful of you, Jasper. Yes, I'd like to pay my respects. Perhaps I can recite something too. Your dad's left, hasn't he? Is it safe to go over there now?"

I walked to the window. The poppy red car, usually parked directly outside our house, had gone. Dad was on his way to the crematorium, following the men in black.

"Safe," I repeated, glancing at her reflection in the glass before looking up at the tree. I caught a snatch of powder blue color from the baby parakeets. "Your dress is cerulean blue."

"I knew you'd like this shade. Wait here, while I grab my things."

I'd hoped she'd invite me upstairs to see the baby parakeets, but we hadn't got back to normal yet. She went up by herself and came back down again, carrying the white rabbit notebook. She slipped it into her handbag as she slung it over her shoulder.

"Let's do this, Jasper." Bee held out her hand, and I took it. She didn't mention the unmentionable ever again.

Neither did I.

Bee cried *a lot* when she saw the tiny cross. I'd told her the baby parakeet was almost four weeks old. She said it was unspeakably sad for something so small to suffer; it was wrong for the young to be hurt.

Where were its parents? Why didn't they protect it?

I put my arms around her waist to comfort her after she placed a jasper healing stone on the grave.

"Thank you," she said, rubbing her necklace. "This is an emotional day for me. I thought I could go through with all of this, being back here, but I'm not sure I'm strong enough. It's too hard. I think I've made a terrible mistake."

This was the only time she acknowledged that what had happened between her and Lucas Drury was wrong. It was enough for me. I was glad she regretted it.

She pulled the notebook out of her handbag and leafed through the pages while I stared at the white rabbit on the cover.

"I hope you don't mind, Jasper, but I'm not going to recite a poem. I want to read from a book I used to love and was made to hate as a kid. It's from *Alice in Wonderland* by Lewis Carroll."

"Dad read it to me when I was small," I said. "I didn't like it either. The White Rabbit was worryingly late and I was scared of the Mad Hatter."

"Me too. He talked in riddles, and riddles can be hard to understand. Most people have trouble with them." She brushed away tears from her cheek. "Anyway, I wrote down this quotation from *Alice in Wonderland*. I used to read it over and over again. Are you ready?"

I confirmed I was.

She took hold of my hand. "Remember, this story is about what it was like being Alice. This is her story, no one else's. They're her words."

She began:

First, however, she waited for a few minutes to see if she was going to shrink any further: she felt a little nervous about this; "for it might end, you know," said Alice to herself, "in my going out altogether, like a candle. I wonder what I should be like then?" And she tried to fancy what the flame of a candle looks like after the candle is blown out, for she could not remember ever having seen such a thing.

I couldn't remember Alice in Wonderland saying this. It didn't sound significant to me. I wouldn't have written it down. "I don't like it. I think Alice is sad."

"She *is* sad," Bee replied, "but she tries hard to get back to normal, and that's what counts. Remember, she had to do it on her own. That's tough for any child."

"I try hard to be normal too," I admitted. "It doesn't always work for me either."

Bee Larkham cheered up after we went inside and I showed her the baby parakeet paintings in my bedroom. She was particularly interested in my records of the movements of people on our street. I pulled out all my boxes from the bottom of the wardrobe and showed her the most recent notebooks.

Leafing through them one by one, she eventually looked up.

"Well done, Jasper. These are incredibly detailed about the times of my music lessons. Did you name any of my pupils? Or any of my visitors, like, say, Lucas or his brother, Lee?"

"No," I replied. "I'm not interested in them. I've named David Gilbert, when I'm sure it's him, when he's walked back inside number twenty-two. That's one hundred percent verified."

"Great stuff. This should help our case against David. You know, his threats and the shotgun. If we ever need to go to the police again."

I moved my head up and down. "Your journal will help our case too."

"This?" Bee's hand dipped into her bag and pulled out the steel blue book, which contained her favorite *Alice in Wonderland* excerpt. I stared at the white rabbit on the cover again. I wasn't sure I could trust him. If it hadn't been for the rabbit, Alice would never have crawled down the hole and got into all that trouble.

"Yes, I think you could be right. It's all here in black and white. Everything that's happened." Bee touched her forehead. "Jasper. Can I beg a huge favor?"

"Yeeess. I think so. Because we're friends again."

"Can you fetch me a glass of water? I'm feeling nauseous and light-headed. I've been throwing up all morning and can't keep anything down. I have no idea what's wrong with me today."

"Nausea can be caused by many things, such as gastroenteritis or food poisoning. Maybe you ate some uncooked meat or fish that was out of date." I watched Bee Larkham's face take on a faint tone of Key lime pie. "Sometimes it's other things, like a tapeworm, an ulcer, an eating disorder, or a pregnancy."

Bee Larkham's face changed to the color of curdled cream.

"Jasper," she said faintly, "I really could use that glass of water."

I was glad to be useful again. I poured her a drink in the kitchen, using the bottled water from the fridge I'd asked Dad to buy after her warning about tap water.

"Thank you," she said, when I returned to the bedroom. She'd put her notebook away and was perched on the edge of the bed. "It's deliciously cold, the way I like it." She placed the glass down and walked over to the window, holding her handbag. She looked more like herself again, although her cheeks were raspberry ripple. "So this is what my tree looks like from over here. I've often wondered."

"Yes."

"You can see the baby parakeets fairly well from here, but it's a much better view from my bedroom window. I'm lucky. I can see the babies so close, I don't need to use binoculars."

"I've missed seeing the parakeets from over there," I admitted. "I've missed seeing you, Bee Larkham."

"Me too. This whole situation has made us both sad. Why don't we both try hard not to be unhappy again?"

She turned around and walked across the room. "Come back to me, Jasper. Come back to the parakeets. They've missed you too."

Her hand dipped into the handbag again. She pulled out a violet-blue envelope.

I stepped backwards; neither of us said a word.

She never mentioned Lucas Drury. She didn't need to. His name was written in black ink on the envelope.

I didn't tell Bee Larkham I'd figured out the sparkly sweet wrappers contained condoms. I'd found one in Dad's bedside drawer and made a water bomb while he was at work.

As I pondered what to do next, I caught a flash of color, a muted cry from a parakeet across the road.

One step towards her—that's all it took.

Hand trembling, I reached out and took the envelope—a tiny gesture that had life-changing consequences for both of us.

Straightaway, we shifted back to our old routine as if nothing had ever happened. As if I'd fallen down Alice in Wonderland's rabbit hole and never told anyone what I'd seen when I finally returned home.

Our little secret.

That's how badly I wanted to paint the colorful sounds of the young parakeets.

41

FRIDAY (INDIGO BLUE)

Evening

Spin, spin, spin.

That's what I long to do, but I'm not in the kitchen at home. I'm in a strange house belonging to emergency foster carers. There's only one chair in this bedroom, and it won't turn around and around. It's *static*.

Definition: motionless, changeless.

The curtains are creamish white with rainbows, which are all wrong. Real rainbows don't have those hues. I should tell *them*, but I don't want to go downstairs. They're called Mary and Stuart. I put my hands over my ears when I first arrived because I didn't want to see their colors.

Dad was arrested for shouting at the police officers and pushing one. *That's assault.* I wasn't given much time to pack: ten minutes to throw some clothes and personal belongings like a comb, toothbrush, and underwear into the old black rucksack the policewoman found in my wardrobe.

I don't care about that stuff.

What about all my paints and paintings and boxes of notebooks?

You can't take everything. Choose what's most important to you.

I hated doing it.

But I had to defend the youngest parakeets, every single one.

I told the policewoman that leaving a bird behind before it had fledged would be a terrible crime.

Mary's voice is skin tone and Stuart's slate gray. Eventually, I had to hear their words. I had to see their colors. They're not bad shades.

They say I can come and go as I please. I can get food from the fridge or the cupboard in the kitchen if I'm hungry. I can go to the toilet. I can watch TV in the sitting room. They'll move to another room if that makes me feel more comfortable.

I'm not comfortable in any room in this house.

I have Mum's cardigan. I rub the buttons, harder and harder.

My new social worker, Maggie, with the shiny light apricot voice, won't let me return home to dismantle my den. I didn't have time to do it earlier. I wanted to construct it again here from scratch, but she said the foster care was probably only for one night, two at the most, *until things calm down at home* and the police sort out *important stuff* with Dad.

This room isn't as big as my bedroom at home. There isn't enough space to arrange all my baby parakeet paintings on the stained, light green carpet.

Down the side of the bed, some kid called Seb has carved his name into the paint. I don't know him. I don't want to meet him.

I have a handful of paint tubes, the ones I grabbed before my ten minutes were up. I brought all the baby parakeet paintings but was forced to leave the rest behind. I'm worried about them. They're all alone in my bedroom.

They'll wonder where I am. They could be scared.

The boxes of notebooks won't like me being AWOL either. They hate being out of order. I know they're mixed up. I remember now—a pesky white rabbit's hopped into one of the boxes. Rusty Chrome Orange discovered Bee's steel blue notebook during my First Account at the police station. I don't know how it got there or why it's visiting.

I do know my paintings and notebooks will miss me the way I miss Mum.

Cobalt blue.

The way I missed Bee Larkham when I didn't see her even though I didn't want to and never realized that was what I was doing. I wanted her back, whatever pictures she created.

Because I loved her colors; she made me feel closer to Mum.

I don't want to paint here, because I don't know the boy who slept in this bed before me.

Seb.

Maybe his dad tried to kill him too. Except Dad told the police he wasn't doing that.

It was a misunderstanding. *My* misunderstanding.

Dad was trying to help me, not kill me.

I rub the buttons on Mum's cardigan over and over again.

Rub, rub, rub.

I want to crawl into my den and never come out.

Skin Tone knocks on the door. "Please can I come in, Jasper?"

"No! I can't do this! I'm too young!"

"Please, Jasper. Can we talk? I'd like to get to know you better."

I tear the books off the shelf and drag the furniture to the door, jamming it under the handle. A barricade.

Ignoring her pleading skin-tone shades, I pull the duvet over my head. The bookshelf is all out of order and hurts my eyes.

I felt just as bad after finishing my three most recent paintings. The shades had stabbed my eyes and made them water after I finished the last strokes. I left them behind in my wardrobe, but I try to remember what happened next.

Nothing was right about the afternoon of Tuesday, April 5.

This was the bottle green day the schedule became disjointed because Lucas Drury and Bee Larkham wouldn't stick to it. Why didn't they realize a schedule only works if everyone does the right thing at the allotted time? If they don't, it causes chaos.

The parakeets sensed this shift before me. The shades of their cries became deeper.

Everything started to implode.

Implode: *a bright yellowish green, unripe banana word.*

Meaning: *to collapse inwards in a sudden and violent way.*

I hug Mum's cardigan closer.

Rub, rub, rub.

42

April 5, 1:32 P.M.
Blue Teal Mist Paints over Sky Blue on paper

Bee Larkham's letter was *still* in the science lab drawer where I'd left it on Monday afternoon. It was now a day later and Lucas Drury hadn't collected it even though Bee said it contained a twenty-pound note and three cigarettes.

She'd quizzed me after school last night. "Are you sure you delivered it?"

"Yes, I'm sure. Maybe he's ill."

"Did Lucas seem ill when you gave him the letter?"

Tricky: *a cucumber-green-colored word.*

"Erm. No." That was 75 percent of the truth because I hadn't seen him, so he didn't seem ill to me. Neither of us had told her how we exchanged letters at school and now wasn't a good time to confess about the science lab system.

"Can you take another letter tomorrow?" she'd asked. "It's urgent."

"That's not how our schedule works. I deliver on Mondays, not Tuesdays. The days are scarlet, not bottle green."

"I know, but this is important. I'm worried about Lucas. I'm scared about what's happening with his dad. Remember, I said he's violent?"

I didn't say anything.

I knew things must be bad at home if Lucas Drury couldn't come to the usual place and collect his letters. That's why she wanted to talk to him. It wasn't about the other thing, the thing in her bedroom with the sparkly wrappers, because she was sorry about that. It was a horrible mistake, which she regretted. That's why we never talked about it. She wanted to forget the colors, the way I did.

"Can I watch the young parakeets from your window when I get home?" I'd asked. "I want to find out if the colors of their sounds have changed."

"Take this last letter and you won't have to earn your time watching the babies from my window. You can visit for forty-five minutes three times a week, I promise, without any strings attached. Actually, make it four times."

I'd ignored her comment about strings attaching themselves to me because that was downright silly. Ditto the parakeets. Technically, they were no longer babies. In just under two weeks, some would fledge.

Anyway, that's how I found myself in the deserted science lab during a Bottle Green Tuesday lunchtime, placing another letter on top of the one that Lucas Drury was unable to collect on Scarlet Monday because things had gotten so bad at home.

"Stop it!" a bluish green voice shouted.

I almost wet myself. I hadn't heard anyone come into the lab. I spun around. A boy in school uniform walked towards me.

"I'm stopping. I'm leaving."

"No, I meant stop with the letters, Jasper. I knew she wouldn't get the message—I knew she'd send you back here again. I don't want you to deliver Bee's letters anymore. You both have to stop." *Blue teal.*

"Lucas Drury."

"Yes, Jasper?"

"But that's the agreed schedule. I deliver Bee Larkham's letters to you and I always check to see if there's anything to take back. She hasn't told me the schedule's changing again."

"That's because she can't accept it's over." Lucas snatched the letters from the drawer and dropped them in the bin. "She must be *made* to understand."

"I don't understand what you're talking about," I said. "She didn't get the message. Neither did I."

"Jasper, Jasper, Jasper." Lucas pummeled his temple with his fists. "You're doing my head in."

I apologized.

"I don't know what to do. Bee Larkham hasn't told me what to do."

"Can't you think for yourself for once?" Lucas yelled. "You don't need Bee Larkham."

He grabbed my neck and squeezed tight, pinning me against the wall. My head slammed, *dull brown,* into a poster of the periodic table. Cerise stars buzzed furiously inside my ears as I struggled for breath. Lucas was wrong. I did need her, the parakeets too. She fed and protected them from David Gilbert.

"C-c-can't breathe." My hands scrabbled with his. "Sorry."

He let go. "Sorry! I'm sorry, Jasper. I shouldn't have done that. It's just . . . You have to get on with your own life because she'll only drag you down with her. I see that now. I thought this was about me, but it's not. It's all about Bee and her problems."

"I can't see anything," I said hoarsely. "I don't know what to do about the letters. She didn't tell me what to do."

Lucas sighed wispy blue teal mist as he stepped backwards. "OK. If it helps get you off my back, tell Bee one last message from me. Tell her I meant what I said before. It's over. I can't do this. I'm too young."

"You'll need to write the message down and I can deliver it to her," I said, coughing. "That's the deal. I give her the envelope and I'm allowed to watch the parakeets for forty-five minutes after school. It's fifteen minutes less than before but still worthwhile."

"No, Jasper. I'm done with these stupid notes. I'm done with all of this. I want out. It's too much. Give her this."

He shoved an object into my hand.

"It's your lost mobile phone," I said. "You found it."

"Give it her back. I don't want her presents. I don't want her money. I don't want anything from her. I want to be left alone."

"You don't want to be saved," I clarified.

"Yes, that's right. There's a girl I like in my year and I don't want Bee to ruin things for me with her. She's my age, Jasper. It feels right. It feels *normal.* Bee needs to find someone her own age."

"What age should I tell her is correct?" My forehead crinkled.

Lucas ran a hand through his hair, checking it was in place.

"Repeat this message after me, Jasper: *I can't do this. I'm too young.*"

I close my eyes and obey.

"I can't do this. I'm too young."

"That's right. Now again and again until you remember it. Until it won't leave your head and it's all you can think about."

"I can't do this. I'm too young. I can't do this. I'm too young. I can't do this. I'm too young. I can't do this. I'm too young."

I repeated the message to Bee Larkham, word for word after school. Tears streaked down her face.

"Why can't I have what everyone else has, Jasper? Why shouldn't I finally find happiness, wherever it might be? Why? Tell me that, Jasper? What is it that makes me so unlovable?"

I crept away home. I couldn't watch her cry.

I was too ashamed to admit I didn't know the answers to her questions. I never got to see the parakeets from her bedroom window. It wasn't a good day to ask.

I was afraid, terribly afraid, she might say: "No, Jasper. Never again."

43

April 6, 5:13 P.M.
Sky Blue Paints over Cool Blue on paper

You must come over this evening. I'm sorry I didn't let you stay longer yesterday.

Bee Larkham had knocked on my front door at 7:51 A.M. and invited me back after school. She said she felt guilty for diverting from our agreed schedule and would let me have additional time tonight.

"Bee! Look at that one!"

Now we stood at the bedroom window, watching the young parakeets fluttering and chirping among the safety of the branches. *Cornflower blue with spots of violet and light pink.*

"There's another!" I cried, as a small parakeet fluttered from the eaves and crash-landed into the oak tree with a haze of lilac blue. "He doesn't want to be left behind!"

"No one ever does, Jasper. But you can help stop that from happening." *Sky blue ribbons.*

Bee Larkham walked over to the bed and sat down. I stared at the chest of drawers, trying to figure out what she meant.

Only one ornament remained, the final Dancing China Lady. I felt sorry for her; she looked lonely without her fragile companions. They'd all deserted her. They couldn't have been true friends.

Suddenly, I realized that was me—Jasper Wishart—a china ornament in human form, dressed in jeans and a green sweatshirt.

Fragile.

Waiting to be smashed into tiny pieces that couldn't be put back together again. No one would try to mend me.

I'd be on my own when the fledged parakeets had left the nests. Their parents would leave them soon and they'd move on to join a communal roost.

Could Bee see that too? Was she trying to warn me?

"I am your friend, aren't I, Jasper?" Bee said, before I could ask for clarification. "Please just do this one last favor for me. Take one last letter to Lucas. Tell him it's an emergency and I have to see him. I have to talk to him."

Bee was getting mixed up again when she should have been concentrating on how we were going to make sure the birds kept coming back to the tree once they'd left the nests.

I'd already delivered her *one last letter* to the science lab at school yesterday. There couldn't be another one. That was the agreement. The schedule had been torn up. *Null and void.*

"I don't want to do it again," I replied. "And neither does Lucas. He said it's over. He doesn't want to be saved by you. He doesn't want to hear from you again or have any more presents. There's a girl he likes in his year. He doesn't want you to ruin things with her. It feels right. *It feels normal.*"

"Yes, you told me that at length, which was *really, really* helpful, but I know if I can get through to him, I can make him change his mind. He'll understand what I'm going through. Please, Jasper. I have to see him this evening. Or tomorrow night. I wouldn't ask you if this wasn't urgent."

"No, thank you. I've delivered your one last letter yesterday as per the agreement and Lucas put it in the bin, with the other one. We are still friends, thank you."

Bee stood up. "I think you should go home, Jasper. Straightaway." The sky blue had hardened into dark steel.

I checked my watch. "I've only been here for twenty-three minutes. We agreed forty-five minutes."

"Everything's changed," Bee said. "I don't think we can have an agreement after the way you've behaved today."

"What do you mean? You said we were still friends. We are, aren't we? I did as I was told. I delivered your one last letter. You said if I did that I could visit three times a week for forty-five minutes. Actually, make that four."

"I hate what I've become." She covered her face with her hands. "What he's turned me into."

"I don't understand."

She looked up. "This is simple, Jasper. Do this for me tonight or I won't let you watch the parakeets from my bedroom window ever again. I'll stop feeding them unless you do exactly as I say."

April 6, 6:02 P.M.
Reddish Orange Triangular Shapes on paper

I loathed these colors and shapes even more than I hated the yellow French fries of David Gilbert's dog.

I saw other colors and shapes too: the amethyst and jade pointed sounds of the electric guitar. *Familiar golden lightning bolts.* They came from the address Bee Larkham gave me.

17 Glynbourne Road.

Lucas Drury's house.

I walked down the path and stood outside the front door, hand raised to knock. The letter couldn't wait until school. I had to deliver it that night; otherwise the parakeets wouldn't get any seed for tea, breakfast tomorrow, or lunch.

We'd studied Google Maps together and I'd practiced the journey in my head without making a mistake; it wasn't far to walk and I'd be back long before Dad returned from work.

Twenty minutes at the most.

Because Bee Larkham was my friend, we'd run through all the possible things that could happen to help make me feel better about visiting a stranger's house on my own.

If his dad opened the door:

Pretend you're a friend and ask if Lucas is around to hang out.

If Lucas wasn't in:

Don't leave the letter. Ask what time he'll be back and say you'll pop back later because that's what friends do.

I rang the doorbell. The wavering silver-blue lines erupted into reddish orange triangles. *A dog barking.*

In my picture, the color obliterated the vivid purple and greens of the electric guitar. The beautiful notes had been savaged to death.

"Get that, will you, Son?" a man's murky dark brown voice shouted. "I'm on the phone."

We'd talked a lot about Lucas's dad.

Don't make him angry. He's got a terrible temper.

Bee hadn't prepared me for this.

I hadn't signed up for *this*: a dog.

The red triangles stretch into pointed deep orange darts.

"For the love of God, shut up, Duke! Get the door! I'm still on hold." *Dirty brown spikes with gray edges.*

I was about to leave but hesitated for a fraction of a second too long. The door opened. I screamed, stumbled backwards, and fell as a dog leapt out. Propped up on my elbows, I watched the arch of its jump in slow motion, knowing it was about to land on top of me. Abruptly, it pulled back and yelped dark red, threatening shapes.

"Yes?" A boy wearing the same uniform as me stood next to the dog, a German shepherd, I think. His hand jerked again. "Quiet, Duke." He looked at me. "Jasper? From Vincent Gardens? You watch people from your bedroom window with binoculars."

"Yes, thank you." Lucas Drury had confirmed he knew me. That was enough for me.

I didn't pay much attention to this voice. Ruddy red and dark orange triangles drowned out most of the rival color. I scrambled to my feet and shoved the envelope at him. One word was written on it: *Lucas.*

I recited what Bee had told me to say. "It's an emergency. She has to see you tonight. Tomorrow at the latest. It's important. Use the back door key. Don't tell anyone. Particularly not your dad."

"Er, what?" the boy said.

A man in a faded navy blue baseball cap joined him at the door. Jeans. White trainers, possibly. I watched the dog's pointy red triangles, unable to tear my gaze away.

"Who is it?"

"No one important. Some freak from school."

I turned and fled in case he dropped the lead and the dog ran after me.

"By the way, Binocular Boy," he shouted, *darkish green with a tiny dab of mossy blue*. "Is this note supposed to be for Lucas or me?"

Oh no, oh no, oh no, oh no.

I didn't reply.

I carried on running until I reached the park. I stayed on the swings for forty-three minutes, playing the conversation over and over again in my head.

Is this note for Lucas or me?

I ran over the colors in my head—Lucas Drury was blue teal and Lee Drury, fir tree green.

The color of the boy I'd spoken to had been overwhelmed by the shades of the dog, but I remembered more green in his pitch than blue.

I hadn't spoken to Lucas.

I'd given Bee Larkham's note to another boy who looked like him, wore the same uniform, lived at his house, and had a similar-colored voice.

Lee Drury. Who'd stood next to a man with a murky dark brown voice. *His dad.*

It was another twenty-one minutes before I could walk home. Once I reached my street, I ran as fast as I could.

If I were at home, painting this scene all over again in my bedroom, I'd add a smattering of light grayish violet dots to my picture. This was the sound of someone tapping on glass.

Bee Larkham stood at her front downstairs window as I pounded the pavement with black disc shapes. I pretended I didn't hear her banging. I couldn't speak to her. I couldn't tell her I'd delivered her note to the wrong brother.

She'd never let me watch the parakeets from her bedroom window again.

The next day at school, Lucas Drury hissed white hollow tubes at me in the corridor. He accused me of putting a cat among some pigeons. His dad had read Bee Larkham's note and hit a roof.

Lucas said we were both safe for now because his dad didn't know the letter had come from Bee. She hadn't signed it with her name, as usual: only initials. I mustn't tell anyone that she'd given me the note. I had to pass a message from him to Bee Larkham tonight:

Don't try to contact me or we'll all get into huge trouble.

I moved my head up and down, because it meant Lucas Drury would let go of my blazer and disappear back into the waves of anonymous faces in the corridor.

I didn't admit the truth—I couldn't possibly tell Bee Larkham what had happened.

I had to protect the parakeets. That was the most important thing. My original plan.

That's all I ever wanted to do.

I remember that fact above every single terrible thing that happened next.

44

SATURDAY (TURQUOISE)

Morning

I'd pulled down the bookshelf barricade and was already dressed when Maggie, the new social worker, arrived to take me to the police station. I hadn't gone to bed. I hadn't slept. I hadn't painted. I hadn't talked to Skin Tone or Slate Gray or apologized about the damaged books. I hadn't eaten breakfast because I didn't like the color of the cereal packet, but Maggie said we could stop off and buy a snack on the way.

She brought me to *that* room again, the one with the dog-eared Harry Potter book, *Top Gear* annual, and evil one-armed clown. They welcomed me back like a long-lost friend when I walked in, but I told them I didn't like being here and wanted to go home to check on my notebooks, which were out of order.

It was day forty-nine.

Some of the young parakeets were due to abandon their nests today. I had to say goodbye before they left.

The room looks the same, including the vomit stains on the sofa, *my* vomit stains. Maggie had warned the detectives about the tricky mirror, which played mind games with me last time. They're not taking any chances. They've got rid of it. The camera's in the same place as last time.

Watching me. Trying to catch me out.

Rusty Chrome Orange has returned today, *unfortunately*. Maggie said his boss is in charge of the murder investigation. She thought it was important I talked to someone I already had a connection with, someone who is specially trained in how to talk to children and young people.

The Boss was wrong.

I have no connection with Rusty Chrome Orange. He can talk, but I guess he missed the training session about how to listen.

There's also a solicitor and an Appropriate Adult because I don't want to see Dad. Not yet. He wouldn't be allowed in here anyway. Another detective is interviewing him about our row.

He'll also be quizzed about what happened to Bee Larkham, Maggie said.

In TV crime shows, they don't allow suspects to be interviewed together because they can change their stories and try to make them the same. I've decided to stick to mine. I don't know what story Dad's telling.

The Appropriate Adult will speak up for me, Rusty Chrome Orange said. She's here to look after my interests because Dad couldn't be present.

I've never met this woman before in my life and have no clue how she could look after my interests. She doesn't know what they are. She probably doesn't know a single fact about parakeets or paintings or colors. I wanted Maggie because I like her color, but she had another appointment.

"I want you to be clear about what's happening, Jasper," Rusty Chrome Orange says. "I want to make sure you understand why you're here today."

"OK." I rub the button in my pocket.

It's a relief to finally confess. Without Dad here to stop me, I can tell Richard Chamberlain—*like the actor*—everything. Well, tell him *again.* I'll have to take it slowly, because there's nothing bright about him, apart from the color of his rusty chrome orange voice.

"That's good, Jasper," Rusty Chrome Orange says.

I rub the button faster. *Harder.* His voice is grating, scratching down my spine and igniting tiny balls of fury in my head.

"Perhaps you can explain to me why you think you're here today?"

Maggie the social worker had sat me down and explained some Important Facts before we came to the police station. She thought I was going to cry and put a box of tissues on Skin Tone's coffee table. I didn't need them because I already knew 99 percent of what she told me.

I knew Bee Larkham had been murdered.

I'd guessed the body in the woods was hers.

I didn't know her body had been stuffed inside the hen suitcase. That was the remaining 1 percent.

I take a deep breath.

"Because you've found the body of my neighbor Bee Larkham. A dog walker discovered the suitcase in the woodland not far from Vincent Gardens at around eight forty-five A.M. yesterday. You want to ask me questions about the murder of Bee Larkham."

"Very good." Rusty Chrome Orange's head bobs up and down. It reminds me of an old TV commercial with a nodding dog. I love that dog. I don't love Rusty Chrome Orange. It's not "very good" that Bee Larkham was murdered. Shouldn't he be reprimanded for saying something as dumb as that? Her murder is probably the polar opposite of "very good."

"Now I want you to think carefully before you answer the next question, Jasper." I count five seconds. "Can you tell me the last time you saw Bee Larkham?"

Another simple question. "I saw her the day she died. A week ago on Friday."

"That's interesting, Jasper. *And* helpful."

I try to button a circular blob-shaped sigh, but it escapes from my mouth. It's neither interesting nor helpful. It's the truth. It's what I told him during our First Account if he'd bothered to listen.

Ice blue crystals with glittery edges and jagged silver icicles.

"Can you explain to all of us what you mean when you say that was the day Bee Larkham died?" Rusty Chrome Orange continues.

Seriously? Wasn't I clear enough?

"Friday, April eighth," I stress, "was the day Bee Larkham was murdered."

My solicitor scribbles in his pad. Why is he writing down what I've said when he can play back the camera footage? Is he afraid it's not working?

Rusty Chrome Orange leans forward. "That's the part I'd like you to explain to me, Jasper. How can you be sure that was the day Bee Larkham was murdered?"

I take a deep breath, deeper than the time I jumped fully clothed into that lake when Dad and me went camping in Cumbria. I knew it'd be cold, but nothing prepared me for how the icy depths turned my legs to stone, dragging me down to the bottom.

Dad jumped in to save me. He's not here today. He can't save me again because he's trying to save himself. Other detectives are comparing his story against mine, looking for chinks in our stories.

"Because I murdered Bee Larkham."

Five words. I'd expected them to provoke a torrent of questions from Rusty Chrome Orange, but the room remains silent. Perhaps he still doesn't get it. He can't connect the dots.

"I murdered Bee Larkham on Friday, April eighth."

I rearrange the words into another sentence to help Rusty Chrome Orange understand. I'm building the story, brushstroke by brushstroke.

"I'm sorry," I add. "I had no idea I was going to stab Bee Larkham to death when I went round to her house for tea or that my dad would clean up all the blood and hide her body in the hen suitcase from the hallway and take it to the woodland near our house."

"I think now's a good time for my client to take a break," my solicitor says. His voice is a comforting coffee with generous splashes of milk.

Now? I've only just begun my confession and it's going to take forever at this rate.

"I'm good," I say. "Well, not exactly good."

Obviously, I can't be good when I've killed Bee Larkham. I can never be good again. I can only ever be bad. It's what I deserve. If I believed in hell, I'd be going straight there without passing Go.

"We need to take a break, Jasper," the solicitor says. "You and I need to talk before you say anything else to this detective."

I'm about to say I want to keep going, but Rusty Chrome Orange's color blots out my voice.

"Of course. Jasper Wishart has requested the interview is stopped. This interview is adjourned at ten fifteen A.M."

"I didn't request the interview was adjourned." I'm mumbling from behind my hands. "The solicitor did."

"That's noted, thank you, Jasper," Rusty Chrome Orange says. "It's not a problem. We can start the interview again when you feel ready. Do you want something to eat or drink? We have cans of Coke and chocolate bars in the vending machine if you'd like a snack?"

"Thanks, but Dad says caffeine and chocolate make me hyper."

"Well, let us know if you change your mind."

I've changed my mind already.

Dad discovering I've had a can of Coke and a Mars bar is probably the least of my problems now I've confessed to murder. It might also be the last chance to have anything like that because I doubt there are vending machines in young offenders' institutions or wherever it is they plan to lock me up.

It's too late anyway. Rusty Chrome Orange has walked out. The door clicks shut into a woody, textured circle. Only me, my solicitor, and the Appropriate Adult are left in the room. She hasn't said a word. She definitely doesn't know my interests.

I feel completely alone. I can't stop shivering. I've jumped back into the freezing cold lake again. This time no one wants to help pull me out. I'm at the bottom of the lake.

No one can find me. No one will bother to look.

45

Interview: Saturday, April 16, 10:30 A.M.

The solicitor was right. I *had* needed a short break from Rusty Chrome Orange. His colors cluttered up my head and made strange, unwelcome shapes. My solicitor's name is Leo, which makes me think of a lion, a watermelon pink word.

Leo has a milky-coffee voice and doesn't look like a lion, which is disappointing. On the plus side, he has an easy-to-memorize black goatee beard and red glasses. Leo bought me a can of Coke and a Kit Kat because the vending machine was out of Mars bars. I'd warned him I might flap my arms like a parakeet, but he said I could flap as much as I wanted, which was nice of him. To be fair, he hasn't seen what I look like when I do that.

He was far more interested in talking about my rights and discussing what I wanted to tell the police. I told him what I'd done. I said this was something I wanted to get off my chest. That's the phrase my teaching assistant uses when I turn up for our meetings at school.

Is there anything you want to get off your chest?

I found it odd the first time she said it, but now we have a good laugh. It became "our thing" after I told her it reminded me of the creature that bursts out of the man's chest in the film *Alien*.

Rusty Chrome Orange has finished explaining I've been formally arrested and cautioned over the murder of Bee Larkham. I have certain rights now, like the right to not say anything. I can remain utterly silent.

"Do you understand what I've explained to you?" Rusty Chrome Orange asks.

I move my head up and down. I don't have to say anything. He just explained that.

He tells me he would prefer me to say the word *yes* out loud if I can, but the camera will record my nod.

I don't say anything. I move my head again.

"Can we continue?" he asks.

Leo confirms that we can, his voice deepening into coffee with creamy full-fat milk.

"We are resuming our interview at ten thirty A.M.," Rusty Chrome Orange says. "Please will everyone present state their names for the record?"

We go through the list. Leo speaks for me because I don't want to. There's another addition, Sarah Harper. She's also a detective constable like Rusty Chrome Orange, but her voice is a more tolerable color.

Dull light green.

I wouldn't want to paint it but can put up with it for now.

Rusty Chrome Orange asks me to confirm that no police officer has questioned me about this investigation during the break while the camera was switched off. After Leo says this is correct, Rusty Chrome Orange starts at the right place for once, from where we left off.

"I would like to read out what you stated during our last interview. You said: 'I murdered Bee Larkham on Friday, April eighth.' Do you remember saying that?"

I do. I try not to giggle because this is serious. I'm imagining an alien bursting out of Rusty Chrome Orange's chest.

"Can you please answer yes or no, Jasper?"

"Yes."

I start to rock. I can't help it. No one tells me off or asks me to stop. Maybe they haven't noticed.

"Will I be taken straight to prison? I want to see my dad before I leave. Can I see him now?"

"We're only asking questions at the moment," he replies. "That's all that's happening. You're not being taken to prison. You don't have to worry about that."

"I am worried about what will happen to Dad if I go to prison. I don't think he'll be OK."

"Your dad's fine," Dull Light Green says. "We'll ask you a few more questions and you can take another break."

She hasn't answered whether I can see Dad or not. I guess that means no. Maybe once I've confessed properly they'll let me.

"Perhaps we can rewind to that day," she suggests. "To the day you claim you murdered Bee Larkham."

I often don't understand the way people speak. Well, most of the time, really. People don't say what they mean or mean what they say. They talk in code, which I can't decipher. But I'm not stupid. The way she says that makes me think maybe she doesn't believe my story.

Now I want to block her colors out as well as Rusty Chrome Orange's.

You claim you murdered Bee Larkham.

I imagine her other statements, as we get deeper and deeper into the interview.

You claim a lot of things, don't you, Jasper?

What else are you going to claim today?

Why should we believe anything someone like you claims?

I accepted the color of her voice when she stated her name for the record. I don't like it now. I can't trust it, the way I can't trust Rusty Chrome Orange's color. I can't rely on my first instincts where voices are concerned. I'm the culprit who can't be trusted.

I rest my head on my hands. Dull light green and milky-coffee colors merge into one curdled mess with rusty chrome orange. It's going to explode in my head like a deadly rocket, blasting through my gray matter and destroying all the cells in its path.

"My client has indicated he wishes to cooperate fully," Milky Coffee says, "but this is a lot for him to cope with, as I'm sure you can both understand. I think it's best if I speak on his behalf at this stage."

Neither of the detectives says anything. I wonder if they're moving their heads from left to right or up and down. Either way, I have to admire Leo's skill, cutting straight through their grating colors. I wouldn't be able to do it alone.

I've lost my concentration, my thread that can pull the whole story together.

"Jasper is prepared to give a full written statement about how he accidentally killed Bee Larkham with a knife during a fight in her kitchen on the evening of April eighth. He fled her house, with the knife and his parakeet paintings, and stayed in his den until his dad got back home from work."

"A knife?" Rusty Chrome Orange says, like an echo.

"Yes, a knife," Milky Coffee confirms. "As I understand it, Bee Larkham kept a long-bladed knife in her kitchen drawer. She used it to cut a pie that day."

I sit up and look at Leo. He's doing a good job of dealing with Rusty Chrome Orange, despite the fact he has to repeat words and sentences as if he's dealing with a deaf person. He's also missing out bits and skipping ahead and back again, but that's my fault.

I'm not sure I've told him *everything* 100 percent correctly.

"Jasper says that Bee Larkham had baked the pie specially for him that evening," Leo continues.

Rusty Chrome Orange's and Dull Light Green's mouths widen at the edges as they look at me.

"That was nice of Miss Larkham," says Rusty Chrome Orange. "To bake you a pie."

I scream and scream harshly chiseled aquamarine with icy, pointed spires at Rusty Chrome Orange because he's the stupidest man I've ever met.

The pie wasn't nice. It wasn't nice at all.

It was a weapon, far more vicious and calculating than the knife I used to kill Bee Larkham.

46

I don't need a paintbrush. I'm painting the colors in my head while Leo talks to the detectives.

The day of Bee Larkham's murder should have been a breathtaking indigo because it was a Friday, but all I could see was sky blue. The color of Bee Larkham's voice.

I'd been avoiding her since Wednesday evening. I'd bolted out of the house and had my key ready after school so I could unlock the front door and hide inside. I kept my curtains closed, checking on the feeders through the gap in the fabric. My plan had worked. Bee Larkham continued to feed the parakeets because she hadn't discovered my catastrophic mistake yet.

Lucas hadn't told her. He didn't want anything to do with her. I'd written his message in my notebook—warning her not to get in touch—but hadn't passed it on. I couldn't. I couldn't sleep properly either, not since I'd delivered the note.

My timing was off from the moment I woke up on Friday, April 8. My alarm didn't go off. Neither did Dad's.

We both ran about like mad things.

"See you tonight," Dad yelled.

"Tonight," I confirmed, banging the door shut. *A large rusty brown expanding rectangle.* I ran down the path.

"Wait, Jasper. It's me. It's your friend, Bee Larkham." There were frosted edges around her sky blue voice.

She'd been waiting for me to pull the gate shut. Her silver swallows flew in opposite directions and her eyes were scratchy red. I didn't want to stop and talk to her, because she could make me tell her about the mistake I'd made.

"I have to go, Bee Larkham. I'm late. Like the White Rabbit in your favorite story."

"I hate my story. I told you that before. That's not my ending."

I blinked. I didn't see her lips move because I was looking at the pavement. I must have imagined it because I thought I remembered her saying this was her *favorite* story as a child. Before she outgrew it and stopped liking it.

I looked at her when she spoke this time, to make sure I didn't make another dumb mistake.

"Did you deliver the note I gave you on Wednesday evening?" she asked.

"Yes. I delivered it to seventeen Glynbourne Road. You have to carry on feeding the parakeets. Like we agreed."

"And you definitely gave it to Lucas?"

"I need to go now. I kept to the new agreement. Goodbye."

"Hold on, Jasper. We have to talk about this. It's important."

"I delivered the note to his house. OK? He took it."

That wasn't a 100 percent lie, because a "he" had taken the note. It just wasn't the right "he."

"He never came to me on Wednesday night or last night. Did you see him open the envelope? Did he actually read it?"

"I don't know. I didn't wait. I didn't go inside the house." I tried to walk around her, but she moved position.

"I should have told you to wait for an answer," Bee said. "That was my mistake."

"No," I replied. "The big reddish orange triangular dog jumped. From the door. At me. That was the mistake."

Bee ignored my bombshell revelation. "Something must have happened with his dad. That's probably it, because he wouldn't ignore me like this, not when I've told him my news."

"Lucas doesn't want you to save him. He said you drag people down with you."

Bee stared at me. I couldn't tell if she were angry or sad.

"Come see me after school. Please?"

"No. I hate dogs. I can't go back to Lucas's house. You can't make me go back there. That wasn't the agreement. I kept to the agreement."

She pulled out a lock of hair from behind her ear and twirled it around her finger. Funny marks had sprung up on her wrists, like red stripes on a stick of rock.

"I feel terrible about how badly I've treated you, Jasper. I want to make it up to you. Please let me make it up to you? I'm thinking big treats, lots of time all next week, watching the parakeets. That should give you plenty to paint at home."

Why didn't I run before I found myself sucked back in?

"I've missed seeing your paintings," she continued. "I'm guessing you've been hard at work because your bedroom curtains have stayed closed. You've been painting the parakeets, haven't you? Will you bring your pictures round after school? We can look at them together after you've watched the parakeets from my window."

A man approached us and muttered *Hello, Beatrice*. She didn't say anything; she couldn't have recognized him either. He spoke softly in whitish gray blurry lines. I counted ten steps as he passed by. On the eleventh, he glanced over his shoulder. Maybe he hoped Bee had finally recognized him, but she was looking at me. This time she held her black obsidian pendant instead of her hair.

"I want to see your paintings of the parakeets. They're such a joy to look at. They help me forget the bad stuff."

Bee had said that before, in her bedroom. I still hadn't worked out what she meant. She turned around and looked down the road, but she couldn't have spotted anything bad. It was empty apart from a man, probably the man who'd walked by and said hello. He turned right at the bottom of the street.

"That's all you want to do?" I asked. "You want to talk about my parakeet paintings? Not about Lucas Drury?"

"Well, not only that, Jasper."

I stepped to one side. "I'm not going back to that house. To that big dog. With all the horrible-colored barking."

Bee ran a hand through her hair. I stared at her wrist because I didn't want to look at her smudged mascara and tearstained cheeks.

"Red crisscross lines."

"Never mind your colors," she said. "I'm worried about the parakeets."

"You're feeding them because I did exactly as I was told," I pointed out. "I delivered the note to Lucas Drury's house. We both kept our sides of the agreement."

"I know, but David's threatening me again. He's already trying to get a noise abatement order against me. He's going back to the council to complain about the parakeets unless I stop feeding them. I might have to stop feeding them, Jasper."

"You can't stop feeding them," I protested.

"That's what I told David," she said. "He's frightening me, Jasper. Really frightening me. He's not like normal people. He *enjoys* killing. If he doesn't shoot the birds himself, he'll find someone else to do it. He says the council's pest control officers can gain access to private land to destroy parakeets if they become a nuisance. They have those sorts of powers."

I pulled my mobile out of my anorak pocket.

"No, no, I don't think we can call 999 yet. I thought we could come up with a plan together, about how to fight him. I know you've got lots of notes. The police will have to listen to the two of us if we pool our evidence together. We could see exactly what we have on him, *a pattern of incriminating actions*."

"Yes, Bee Larkham," I said, without hesitating. "We must do that. I'll come round after school with my notes."

"And your paintings of the parakeets. Don't forget those. I'd love to see them. I need cheering up and they always make me feel so happy."

"Don't worry, Bee Larkham. I won't forget."

"Good." She clapped her hands together. "How about six P.M.? Why don't you stay for tea? That way we won't have to rush. Do you like pizza?"

"Tonight I eat chicken pie, not pizza. That's what I always have on Friday night. Dad's working late and he's left the box in the fridge. I have to cook it in the oven at one hundred and eighty degrees Celsius for thirty minutes."

"In that case, I'm going to bake you the best home-made chicken pie you've ever eaten," Bee said. "I've already found a recipe in one of my mum's old cookbooks. You're going to love it."

47

Interview: Saturday, April 16, 11:01 A.M.

"I want you to take this slowly," Rusty Chrome Orange says. "From the time you entered Bee Larkham's house on the evening of Friday, April 8. There's no need to rush. We can take this at your own pace."

Leo explains that I don't want anyone to look at me while I talk. They agree. I can't find the right words even when they move seats. Rusty Chrome Orange suggests I try another way.

He tells me to paint a picture in my head—a good idea, but it's tough because I'm afraid of the colors. I know they want to harm me.

Remember, one brushstroke after another. That's all I have to do: tell this section of the story one stroke, one splash of color at a time.

"You came, Jasper!" A blond woman stood in the doorway of 20 Vincent Gardens. Her hair tumbled around her shoulders, damp and curling at the edges. I smelt coconut, which was unfamiliar, but she had silver swallows in her ears and a long, black pendant hung from her neck.

Obsidian: the strongest protection stone in the world.

"I wasn't sure you'd definitely turn up."

Sky blue. Definitely Bee Larkham. Her voice was such a distinctive color I couldn't get her confused with anyone else.

"You always keep your word," she continued. "That's what I love about you, Jasper. You never let me down. You always want to do the right thing."

I clutched my portfolio tighter to my tummy. Over my shoulder was a bag of notebooks, containing a record of David Gilbert's threats. I looked down at the mat, which had lumps of mud caked in the bristles.

A large, black suitcase stood next to it, ready to leave.

"Come in, come in."

Coconut wafted into my nostrils again as the door closed. She took my anorak and hung it on the coat rack.

"What do you think?" She twirled around. Her long blue dress fanned out as she pirouetted.

"I've been thinking about what you said this morning. You need to install CCTV cameras outside your house because I can't be on guard from my bedroom window all the time. I have to go to school and sleep. That way we could catch David Gilbert trespassing in your front garden."

"No, I mean about my dress. I wore it especially for you because I know how you love the color. It's cobalt blue. Your favorite."

"It's not cobalt blue."

"I'm sure it is, Jasper. The lady in the shop told me."

"She was wrong. It's too dark to be cobalt blue."

Bee laughed sky blue with dark gray peaks, higher and pointier than before. If I were painting the picture, I'd reflect that in the brushstrokes.

"If you say so, Jasper. I mean, you're the expert in colors and paints, not me! Anyway, I wanted you to know I was thinking about you when I bought it yesterday. The shop lady *claimed* this was cobalt blue and I took her word for it. Silly me. That was your mum's color, wasn't it? Cobalt blue?"

"Mum was always cobalt blue."

"And what color am I?"

"You're sky blue. I've told you that before, Bee Larkham. You should put up a fence around the oak tree to protect the parakeets. We could also ring the RSPB instead of the police. I found the telephone number on the Internet."

Bee clapped her hands together. "Of course! Sky blue. Silly me! That means your mum and me are practically the same color. That almost makes us sisters. Well, family anyway. Family's important, Jasper. Don't you think? It's something I never had and always wanted."

Mum never had any sisters. She was an only child. Plus, cobalt blue's made using cobalt oxide and salts of alumina. It was first used as a color name in English in 1777.

"In 1818, John Varley the watercolorist suggested substituting cobalt blue for ultramarine when painting skies," I said.

"Hmmm." Misty clouds almost obscured her sky blue.

Bee flicked her hair over to one side. *More coconut.*

"Why don't you come into the kitchen and sit down while I finish getting ready? I've been busy packing sparkly clothes for my friend's hen weekend. I couldn't decide what to take. In the end, I piled so much into the suitcase I had to sit on it to get the zip fastened. Anyway, time got away from me."

"It's six P.M.," I said. "The time we agreed I should come over to talk about our plans for David Gilbert and to look at my parakeet paintings."

"Yes, but you're the only boy I know who turns up on time. Most boys I know are late. Lucas was always late. Don't you remember how he was always late?"

I didn't remember that fact. I didn't know him well enough to say whether that was true or false. "He was at school today," I volunteered. "I don't know if he was late or not for lessons. He's older than me and we're not in the same classes."

I followed her into the kitchen. It didn't look or smell the same as usual. Plates and bowls and other utensils were stacked in the sink, unwashed. Dirty pots and pans were piled on every surface, including the table, where I'd planned to lay out my paintings. It had three brown apple cores and a spillage of sugar from a large white packet. Bee had also forgotten to throw out an empty milk carton.

"You saw him?"

"Who?" I wanted Bee to fly around the kitchen, tidying up, the way Snow White did with all those woodland animals: the squirrels, rabbits, and mice.

"Lucas."

We were back to Bee Larkham's favorite subject other than parakeets, the parakeets we were supposed to be looking at if she'd wiped down her table. This was my fault. She'd invited me here to talk about David Gilbert and I'd brought up Lucas Drury's name by accident. That was me, not her. Why had I done that?

"Mr. Paulson, the deputy head teacher, read out Lucas Drury's name during assembly and a boy collected the award for his class," I clarified. "They were recycling winners this week. The boy, Lucas Drury, wasn't late, by the way. It only took him twenty-nine seconds to get up onstage. That was quick. Some kids can take one minute and seventeen seconds to pick up their prizes."

Bee fiddled with her dress. I didn't think it fitted her properly. It didn't match her necklace either.

"Maybe Lucas likes to keep me waiting. Like on Wednesday night, when he didn't turn up. I cooked him a late supper and waited for two hours, Jasper. Can you imagine? Who lets a lady wait for that long when she's cooked a lovely dinner?"

"A person who doesn't own a watch?" I suggested.

"Not someone like you, Jasper." Bee crouched down and peered inside the oven. "I don't have a timer. We'll both need to keep an eye on my pie." She pulled on large blue-and-white striped gloves and opened the door, breathing in deeply.

"Aaah." She closed her eyes.

I received a waft of something delicious too. *Chicken pie.*

"You'd never keep me waiting like that, would you, Jasper? You're a gentleman. A real gentleman."

"I have a watch. That means I'm always on time."

"That's another thing I like about you, Jasper." She banged the oven door shut. *Yellow sparks.* "Timekeeping is a rare quality in boys, and good manners. They're both completely underrated nowadays, but women like gentlemen."

She ignored the mess and opened the fridge instead. My palms itched. Why wasn't she tidying up? She pulled out a bottle of wine and held it in both hands. "I need a drink. You have no idea how much I want a glass of wine, Jasper, but I can't."

"I don't mind," I said. "You should drink if you're thirsty."

Bee put the bottle back in the fridge. "Thanks, but I'm being good. I have to be good. Which is hard for me. Because being bad is a lot more fun, don't you think?" She let out a streaky blue gale of laughter.

I opened my portfolio, unsure what to say or do.

I wanted to display all eight pictures for us both to study. That was the original plan, after we'd discussed David Gilbert, but the table was sticky and cluttered. As well as spilt sugar, she'd forgotten to clean up after breakfast. Two cornflakes stuck to the wood. I slumped into a chair and picked at a cereal scab with my nail. It had dried hard and sharp.

"*Ow!*" It stuck beneath the nail, piercing my skin.

Bee Larkham didn't say anything as I sucked my finger. She hummed a pink ballet-pump tune in my direction, one I didn't recognize.

"I'm glad you brought up about Lucas being at school today," she said finally. "I've been worried about him. You too. I haven't seen either of you since I asked you to deliver my note. It made me wonder what went wrong."

I shifted in my seat. I didn't want to talk about the reddish orange dog barking and the dirty brown with gray edges of Lucas's dad shouting again.

"I have to go." I stood up, knocking over the chair with a radiation of dull brown circles.

"I'm sorry, Jasper. Sit back down."

"I want to take my paintings and notebooks home. You said you wanted to look at them, but you haven't asked about them once. You're asking about Lucas. That's all you're interested in when you should be interested in protecting our parakeets."

"That's not true," Bee said. "I didn't mean to upset you, Jasper. I'm upset. Like you."

I stared at the blood pooling underneath my fingernail. The cornflake was sharp, like a tiny knife. How could something tiny cause so much pain?

"I can't let you spread your lovely paintings out on my messy table. Sit down again while I make a space for you."

I hesitated. The way I had when she caught me on the street.

Leave or stay.

Stay or leave.

I wanted to leave, but Bee scurried around like Snow White, without the animal helpers, tidying the table. She flung the empty milk carton in the bin, scooped up the apple cores and spilt sugar, and threw armfuls of newspapers into a recycling basket.

"Wait, wait, I'm not done yet. I'm such a slob. It's been a difficult week. I've let things drift. Don't even look at all the washing up I have to do. The dishwasher broke and I got behind."

She soaked a blue sponge under the tap. *Light blue-gray lines.*

The water spattered onto the white tiles.

Drip, drip, drip.

Darker thimble shapes.

Bee was in danger of slipping in the spilt water and hurting herself. Accidents were most likely to happen in the home and resulted in around six thousand deaths a year.

Before I had time to warn her, she sloshed water over the table, splashing one of the paintings in my lap. I shoved my seat backwards and stood up, grabbing hold of the chair to stop it toppling over again and making more shapes.

"Sorry, sorry. I want it to be perfect for your paintings. The table has to be completely clean to showcase your work. I don't know what I was thinking, not clearing up before you arrived."

I stared at my painting. A small wet spot grew in size. It made the adult parakeet sapphire blue sound run into an offspring's lighter tone. It changed the tempo of their voices, making them both off-key.

"My picture's ruined."

"It's not ruined, Jasper," Bee said.

She was wrong, the way she'd been wrong about things before. I didn't like her voice. It had sharp edges and pointy shapes.

"Ruined isn't a spot of water on a painting. It's barely even noticeable. Ruined is when your life's going down the toilet and there's nothing you can do to stop it. Ruined is losing the love of your life and not knowing how to get him back."

I closed my eyes and felt myself rocking. I didn't want the parakeets' songs to be ruined, not when they sang them so beautifully.

Not fair. I'd be letting the birds down if the painting didn't capture their colors perfectly.

"The parakeets are the love of my life," I pointed out. "Now they are, anyway. Before that was Mum. She'd have loved the parakeets too. She wouldn't have wanted to lose them. I don't want to lose them to David Gilbert. I want to stop David Gilbert before he hurts them."

"And we're back to the parakeets," Bee said. "Which I'm, like, totally glad about?" She sighed, *rolling bluish white mist.*

It didn't sound like a longing sigh, a longing to see their voices and music, the longing I felt when I saw and heard them. I sensed for the first time she felt differently. Even when she spoke the same words as me, they had a strange, unfriendly tint.

"Honestly, I'm glad to be talking about the parakeets again. Yippee! We can run through your interesting conspiracy theories about David Gilbert too now, if you want."

"Yes, that's what I want."

She polished the table surface with a towel that was encrusted with dried, old food.

"Look, all shiny and new! Now let me take a look at your pictures."

I pointed to a puddle. "It's wet there."

"Sorry." She rubbed harder. "Forgive me, when my life's in such a mess, for not getting everything absolutely perfect for you, the way you like it."

The words in the sentence tried to be kind. It sounded like Bee was making an effort, *a proper effort.* But the corners of her mouth hadn't moved and edges had crept into her colors. I'd only recognized a smile—a teeth-showing smile—when I first arrived.

"Do you still want to see my paintings?" I had to check. I didn't know what she wanted, what she was thinking. We didn't have a connection. I'd broken it somehow after I'd walked into her messy kitchen and her smile went away.

"Please, do." She picked up the hems of her dress and curtsied. "I'd be thrilled if you'd do me this honor. I can't think of anything else. The suspense is killing me."

I honestly didn't want to kill Bee Larkham. I took my time, arranging the pictures on her table. They had to be in the right order, in sequence with the notebooks, but Bee Larkham tapped her foot on the floor, making teddy-bear-colored circles, which was distracting.

"Do you want to see them chronologically, in date order? Or by theme? For example, ordered by singing, feeding, pruning, fighting, peeping out of the hole, or on the branches. Or maybe—"

"The truth is," she interrupted. "I've been trying to understand why Lucas didn't turn up to meet me after he read my note. That got me thinking. What if this isn't Lucas's fault? What if this is *your* fault?"

My tummy contracted at the sharp words.

"This is the sunset collection," I continued. "And these are their songs at sunrise."

"Lovely. Your paintings are lovely, Jasper. As usual. And I know you heard me." Her voice was low, as if she were afraid of eavesdroppers. "Some people on this street, like David Gilbert, think you're dumb. They tell me you're dumb because you're not like normal kids, but I know you're not. I know you heard me, Jasper."

I carried on arranging my work, laying out the paintings of the parakeets feeding and fighting, singing and chatting.

"Did you make a mistake when you delivered my note, Jasper? Did you deliver it to the wrong house on Wednesday? Did you give it to someone other than Lucas? Tell me what went wrong!"

"Reddish orange triangles and dirty brown spikes with gray edges!"

"Answer me properly, Jasper. In English. I don't understand your color talk. Did you make a mistake? I'll forgive you, if you admit you made a mistake. Everyone makes mistakes. I make them all the time."

My face was wet with tears. I couldn't bear to look at her. I continued to look at my paintings.

Sunset, sunrise, feeding.

"Jasper?"

"I thought it was Lucas," I said. "I gave it to the boy in uniform who opened the door."

"Now this is important." She talked slowly; the way Dad did when he was annoyed or when he wanted me to calm down. "Take your time before you answer, Jasper. Is there any possibility, any possibility at all that you might have given the note to his brother, Lee?"

I didn't need to take my time.

"It's possible. I don't know. I didn't ask his name. I'm sorry. The triangular reddish orange barking dog confused me. I had to get away. Fast."

Bee shook her head. "That's not so bad. Not as bad as I feared. At least you got the right address. The letter's somewhere in the house."

"It's burning."

"Something was burning in Lucas's house? Was that what threw you?"

"No. Inside your oven."

"Damnit. My pie!" She flew across the kitchen and flung open the oven door. "Phew. I thought I'd ruined it." Clutching the dirty towel, she yanked out the pie and threw it onto the work surface.

Bang. *Red sparks.*

"Hot, hot, hot!" She blew on her fingers and stuck them under the tap. *Blurring gray lines.*

"I should go home. Dad will be wondering where I am."

"That's not likely, is it?" Bee spoke without looking back. It sounded like a question, but she didn't wait for a reply. "I doubt he's missed you at all because he's not home from work yet, is he?"

Under the table, I checked my watch. She was right.

"Did you even tell him you were coming to see me tonight?" she asked. "Does he know where you are?"

I continued to study my watch.

"Don't worry, Jasper. I'm sure your dad won't mind. He likes me. He always has, ever since the party. Maybe even at first sight. I saw you both watching me from your bedroom window the night I moved back to this godforsaken street."

I wasn't sure Dad did like Bee because he'd called her a silly little tart, but I didn't want to upset her again. She thought a God who didn't exist had forsaken her. I hadn't.

"I'm sorry about your fingers. And about Lucas not turning up to meet you. And about how I gave your important note to the wrong brother. I'm sorry, sorry, sorry."

The angular greenish blue word trilled on my lips.

"Don't be, Jasper. I'm a lot happier now I know what happened. Lucas never got my note. His brother must have forgotten to give it to him. You know what young kids are like, right? They're unreliable. They screw things up, *important things*."

I counted my teeth with my tongue because I'd forgotten to put Mum's button in my pocket.

"Where are my manners, Jasper? You must be starving. Let's have some pie."

"I'm not that—"

"Please don't say you're not hungry, Jasper, because that would be rude after I've gone to all this trouble to cook you a special pie. I've even made my own pastry instead of buying it."

I didn't want to be rude, but she'd been rude first. She hadn't looked at my paintings. Not properly. She hadn't asked to see my notebooks or brainstormed more ideas about how to tackle David Gilbert. She only wanted to talk about Lucas Drury and why he hadn't turned up to meet her. I hesitated again as she pulled out a knife from the drawer.

"How about a nice big slice?" She didn't wait for my answer and slammed the metal through the dark brown pastry, with one long laceration.

I couldn't take my eyes off the knife. It flashed bright steel beneath the pendant light overhead. In a fraction of a second, I could see my distorted reflection in the metal.

Then I was gone, as if I'd never been in Bee Larkham's kitchen. Never even existed.

48

Interview: Saturday, April 16, 11:23 A.M.

"You're doing well, Jasper. Can we go back to talking about the knife?" Rusty Chrome Orange asks. "The knife that Bee Larkham used to cut the pie?"

I close my eyes again and feel the paintbrush in my hand. It's trying to defend me.

But it's no good.

Everyone knows a paintbrush can't win in a fight against a knife.

"What do you think of my chicken pie, Jasper?"

The pastry was flaky, the way I usually liked it, but overcooked on top. I'd scraped off the burnt bits when Bee Larkham wasn't looking, but I could still taste copper. It wasn't the same as my usual Friday-night chicken pie that came inside cardboard packaging.

"I think it tastes almost OK." An unidentifiable piece of dark meat had bobbed up through the sauce. I prodded it with my fork.

"Almost OK? You're a hard person to please, Jasper."

"The sauce is lumpy and tastes of pennies and the pastry is over-cooked and bitter," I muttered. "Apart from that, it's OK."

"Wow. Thanks for the compliment. I'm overwhelmed." She took a bite, closing her eyes. "Mmmm. Delicious. It's funny how a good, home-cooked meal can make you feel better, something you've cooked from scratch and know where all the ingredients have come from."

I never knew this fact for sure. Dad and me never cooked anything from scratch. It usually came out of a packet from the freezer or fridge and had to be reheated in the microwave or oven. Dad's specialty was lasagne ready meal.

"Now I'm feeling less light-headed I can look at your parakeet pictures properly. Pass them over, Jasper. I'm sorry I didn't pay enough attention earlier."

I repeatedly stressed how worried I was about her getting greasy pie marks on my paintings, but she insisted she'd be careful. She looked at each one—ranging from ten to fifteen seconds per painting—and placed them in a neat pile on the chair next to her.

The last one had the spot of water in the corner. Bee didn't mention it. This one was her favorite, for some bizarre reason. She couldn't tell it was ruined, the way I could.

"I want this one for my collection. Would you give me your wonderful painting? I'd like it right there." She pointed to the white wall behind me, bare apart from a rusty nail. "It's where my mum used to hang a dreadful sea scene that I always hated."

"Are you sure?" I asked. "I've done far better paintings, like the one at the start of the pile. This one's damaged."

"No, I feel something when I look at this one, more than I feel about the others," she replied. "Don't get me wrong—they're all fab. It's just this painting is like me, imperfect but still beautiful. That's right, isn't it, Jasper? You see all my flaws yet you like me, don't you? You like me a lot."

"I love the color of your voice and your music," I admitted. "You're beautiful and you love parakeets. You want to protect them from David Gilbert. You're my friend."

"Thank you. You're a sweet boy. I'm sorry I was snappy with you earlier. I was going wild with worry. I think you're perfect too. You're an amazing painter, Jasper, and all-round human being." She burst out laughing. "Listen to us having a luvvie-fest!"

She reached out her hand and waited. I passed her my plate, trying to avoid looking at the red stripes on her wrist. I'd finished my pie and she probably wanted to do the washing up.

"No. I wanted to hold your hand, Jasper. Can I? I know many

autistic children hate being touched and hate loud music, but your dad said you're different. You're not like other autistic children. You have other problems though. Lots of them, he said, which makes life difficult."

When had Dad talked about me? What else had he said about me?

She waited until I stretched my left hand out, our fingers almost touching. My hand wobbled and I wanted to hide it beneath the table. I wasn't sure what she wanted to do with it.

"Closer," she said. "I know you can do it."

I shifted in my seat, my fingertips brushing hers. Suddenly, she grasped my hand tightly. "How are we going to fix this problem you've caused, Jasper?"

I tried to pull away, but she held on. "I wouldn't ask you again, unless I was desperate, and I am. You don't know what it's been like for me these past few days. I've been going out of my head with worry."

"I'm sorry," I muttered. "I told you already I'm sorry. I see but don't see faces. Remember what I said about the big dog that barks reddish orange triangles? I can't go back there."

I attempted to wrestle my hand back, but she hung on.

"Get off me!"

"Calm down, Jasper, and stop shouting." She released her grip. "It's not nice. It's not what nice boys do."

I rubbed my wrist. I wanted to stand up but felt too dizzy. Her words had sealed me to my seat, as if she'd pasted my chair with glue. She wouldn't release me. I was stuck, like Alice in Wonderland, and couldn't get back up through the rabbit hole to safety.

"I'm too young. I don't want to deliver your letters. I don't want to talk to Lucas. I hate him."

"That's not true, Jasper. You don't hate him. *Hate*'s a strong word for a little boy like you to use."

"*Hate*'s a smoky green word," I corrected. "And I'm not little. I'm five foot, which makes me just under average height for my age."

Her gaze burrowed into my forehead. I wanted to throw something to make her stop. All I could see in front of me was the pie dish.

Creamy sauce oozed out, making my tummy lurch. I shifted my gaze and stared at the knife instead.

"Look at my paintings, but not at me. I don't like it."

"Sorry, Jasper. I'm not looking at you, I promise. I need you to do this one last thing for me. I need you to give Lucas another note early tomorrow morning at home before his dad wakes up. I'll write it for you now."

"I won't, I won't! I'm not playing this game. I'm going home." I stood up and almost fell over. The room swam around me, knocking me off balance. If I fell, I doubted Bee Larkham would catch me.

"No, Jasper, you're not. You're not going anywhere yet. I've tried to be nice. I've looked at your paintings. I'll even hang one on my wall. I've let you drone on about your David Gilbert obsession. If you refuse to do this for me, I'll . . ." Her voice trailed off.

I could feel her watching me when she'd promised she wouldn't.

I stared at the knife. It shone brightly under the light.

Glint, glint, glint.

I couldn't take my eyes off the utensil even though its colors clashed. The knife was flashing silver, but the word was deep purple with a red, shifting core.

Bee leaned forward. I could see her features grotesquely distorted in the blade. Even when I shifted in my seat, she was still there, reflected in the sharp edges.

"You do know about me and your dad, don't you?"

"Dad called you a silly little tart." He was wrong, dead wrong about that. Tarts conjured up images of succulent strawberries or sweet, cinnamon apples dusted with icing sugar, but I had a nasty, sour taste in my mouth.

"Did he? That's the way he liked me the night of the party. The night we had sex, upstairs in my mum's old bedroom, while you were asleep across the road."

Sex: a bubble-gum pink word with a naughty lilac tint.

I slammed my hands on my ears and closed my eyes.

"It wasn't the best sex, if I'm being perfectly honest. I thought it'd help get Lucas out of my head. I was wrong. I thought about Lucas *the whole time.* Your dad was drunk and feeling sorry for himself, sorry that you were his son. He said it was hard for him, having a son like you. He wished he could be single again."

The words drifted through my fingertips into my ears. I tried to filter them out, but they were like fine diesel particles in the air, which penetrate people's airways and nestle in their lungs, causing cancers.

"It meant nothing to me, but that night could change your life forever, Jasper. It could mean the difference between living with your dad here on this street and somewhere else, with strangers who don't understand your special needs. They won't understand how things have to be a certain way, how you need help recognizing faces. Because that's your particular problem, isn't it, Jasper? I get that now."

I felt my hands being ripped from my ears.

"I can say your dad raped me, Jasper. That he was drunk and forced himself on me that night. Social Services would take you away from him. They'd take you away from your precious parakeets and put you in a new home, far, far away from the birds."

I screamed jagged white clouds with aquamarine peaks.

"It would be my word against his," she continued, talking over me. "No one would believe you, if you repeat what I've said. The police wouldn't believe a word you said. You're what they call an unreliable witness."

My hands fought to come free, ripping at sky blue, grappling with something solid.

What was fighting me?

I fell to the floor, gripping something in my hand.

"Damnit. You've broken my necklace."

Fingers snatched the stone from my clenched fist.

"You have to do this one thing for me, Jasper. You owe me."

"No! No, no, no!"

I had to get my paintings. I had to save my parakeets and escape. I couldn't leave them alone in this house. Opening my eyes, I grabbed the chair leg and pulled myself up. Bee Larkham blocked my way. I couldn't get past her.

Instead, I lunged across the table towards the pie.

49

Interview: Saturday, April 16, 11:39 A.M.

"That was when you picked up the knife?" Rusty Chrome Orange asks. "The knife you used to stab Bee Larkham with?"

"Not yet. Too soon."

As usual, his timing stinks. I don't want to talk about it. My head hurts and I need to find another chair.

One that I can move around and around in.

Spin, spin, spin.

"You're doing really well, Jasper," Rusty Chrome Orange says. "We're nearly there. Now relax, close your eyes. I want to take you back there again."

I do as he instructs and I've returned to Bee Larkham's kitchen. I'm stretching across her table. Freeze-framed. Unable to edge forwards or backwards until Rusty Chrome Orange gives the order.

"Take your time," he says. "We can do this at your own pace with as many breaks as you want. There's no need to rush."

He's wrong as usual. There was a desperate need to rush.

I had to rescue my paintings and notebooks. This was all down to me. Dad couldn't save us. He wasn't back from work yet. He didn't know I was here.

It's hard for him having a son like you.

He wishes he could be single again.

Sex: a bubble-gum pink word with a naughty lilac tint.

The color of Bee Larkham's voice had seeped inside my head and I couldn't wash it out, however hard I tried. Sky blue paralyzed me, seeping into my blood. Before long, it would take over my body. I had to stop it.

The table was too broad. I couldn't reach over it completely to get my paintings. As I stretched, my armpit knocked the pie. The knife skidded off the dish, twirling on the table.

Round and round it spun, playing its own deadly game of Russian roulette.

Live, die, live, die, live, die.

Opposing words and colors:

Jade green, violent red, jade green, violent red.

Bee caught the knife, slamming her hand down hard. *Dart-shaped grainy wood colors.*

"Careful, Jasper. You could get hurt." She walked around the table. "Is this what you're after? Your precious parakeet paintings? Here, take them."

She tossed the pictures at me. They landed, scattered in different directions, on the table, on a chair. Some settled on her dirty, smeared floor.

"I'll still keep this one, though, Jasper." She held up the smudged canvas. "I'll hang it on my wall to remind me what a horrid, selfish little boy you are." She slammed the picture down on the dresser behind her, next to her broken necklace. The plates shuddered with anger.

My eardrums almost burst with hatred for Bee and Bee's hatred for me, which was far more powerful. It poured inside my ears, poisoning me. I felt it working its way deeper and deeper inside my body.

Sky blue.

Not cobalt blue.

Never cobalt blue.

I'd saved three paintings. Not enough. Not nearly enough. I had to get them all. *Four, five.* I reached for another. *Six.* I had to liberate my notebooks too.

No man left behind.

Wasn't that the mantra of the SAS? Dad's favorite topic.

Bee wasn't finished with me. Or my parakeets.

"Where are my manners? You've given me a present, Jasper. I should give you one in return."

I ducked down and rescued the painting that had landed under the table. I couldn't let her claim another picture.

"Don't. Want. Present." I can't be sure I said the words out loud as I stood up again, but I felt their colors nudging uncomfortably around my head. They tried their hardest to be noticed.

Bee turned and looked at her bookcase, next to the dresser. "Where is it?" She hummed under her breath. I recognized the trilling "Aviary" burnt pink sugar notes from *Carnival of the Animals*.

"Aha. Here." She pulled out a dusty burgundy book—exactly the same color as the word *final*.

"*Mrs. Beeton's Book of Household Management*. You wouldn't believe the unusual recipes in here, Jasper, particularly in a section on Australian cookery. I couldn't possibly throw it away. It's different. *Like you*."

I re-counted my paintings.

Seven. I had them all, except the damaged canvas Bee wouldn't give back, on the dresser. I couldn't save it.

I shoved my paintings into the case as she continued to flick through the book, licking her finger as she turned each page. My pictures weren't in the right order. No time to sort them. I stuffed my notebooks back in the bag and picked up the portfolio, hugging it to my chest. No time to fasten it.

"Take this recipe," she continued. "It's the pie I made today. I had to use four rashers of bacon, a few slices of beef, and three hard-boiled eggs for the pie, the pie you ate, Jasper, and thought was only *OK*."

Don't. Care.

I thought I'd said the words under my breath. I hadn't. They came out of my mouth in silvery ice blue bubbles that annoyed Bee Larkham.

"I think you will care, Jasper," she said.

I held on to the chair to get my balance. I had to maneuver around the table, get out of the kitchen, walk into the hall, open the front door, and *run*.

Not far, but could I make it?

"You'll care a lot more when I tell you what was in the pie you ate this evening. You see, I lied to you, Jasper. It wasn't chicken pie."

She thrust the book in front of me. "What do you think of this, Jasper? It's your favorite topic."

I didn't feel the portfolio fall from my grasp or the bag of notebooks slip off my shoulder.

Soft mint green rustles.

All my paintings had scattered, landing around the plates, the pie, and the knife on the table.

I heard small, rusty red-tinged thuds as my case and bag hit the floor. I couldn't pick them up.

My gaze was drawn back to the page again.

PARROT PIE

Ingredients: 1 dozen paraqueets, a few slices of beef (underdone cold beef is best for this purpose), 4 rashers of bacon, 3 hard-boiled eggs, minced parsley and lemon peel, pepper and salt, stock, puff paste.

Mode: Line a pie dish with the beef cut into slices, over them place 6 of the paraqueets, dredge with flour, fill up the spaces with the egg cut in slices and scatter over the seasoning. Next put the bacon, cut in small strips, then 6 paraqueets and fill up with the beef, seasoning all well. Pour in stock or water to nearly fill the dish, cover with puff paste, and bake for 1 hour.

Sufficient for 5 or 6 persons.

Seasonable at any time.

I couldn't scream because I was throwing up.

Pale red, curdled vomit.

More and more.

"Jasper!"

I stuck my fingers down my throat again and again. I had to get the pie out. It didn't work. The dead parakeets were trapped in my body. I had to cut them free. My paintings screamed ice-greenish yellows and freezing sapphires. I lunged across the table and grabbed the knife. I turned it towards my tummy.

"Stop it, Jasper! No!"

My voice returned. I didn't recognize the color.

"I hate you," I yelled. "You're killing me!"

I closed my eyes and felt the point of the knife pierce through material and find my tummy.

Soft, buttery skin.

Slash, slash, slash.

Bee screamed ice blue crystals.

A hand made a grab for me. I swatted it away. Silvery bluish icicles attacked again and again.

"I'm sorry!" the sky blue voice screamed. "Stop it, Jasper. I've gone too far. I was joking. I told a bad joke to punish you. I'm sorry. It's not true. It was chicken. *Just chicken.* I promise you. Forgive me."

I don't forgive you!

I screamed vivid turquoise and white jagged daggers back at her.

My head wanted to split in two like a juicy watermelon. I couldn't hear her blue crystals or icicles because I'd launched a counterattack, a thunderstorm of vivid, startling aquamarine.

Hot pincers seared through my tummy, but I could only see the color of my shouts, mixing with the screeches of the parakeets.

Greenish yellow with freezing sapphires.

Their distress calls soared from my paintings, accusing me, hating me. I'd failed to protect them. I'd eaten them.

Give the knife to me.

No. I have to get them out.

Bee's hands tried to grab the knife again.

I wouldn't let it go. I couldn't. Not while the parakeets were still inside me. I couldn't stop. I had to stop *her.*

"Give it to me!"

"No!"

I swiped the air, and this time the knife found her skin.

Pale blue jagged crystals.

Bee grabbed her right arm. Blood seeped through her fingers.

"Please, Jasper. I'm sorry. I didn't mean to hurt you. If I could take it back, I would. Forgive me!"

I slashed at my sweatshirt and discovered flesh again.

"No! You're not cobalt blue. You never were. You tricked me!"

"Jasper! Stop, I'm begging you!"

Her hand was in the way.

"You have to put the knife down before we both get badly hurt. You'll get us both into trouble."

She tried to wrench the knife from my hands. One of us tripped. I don't know whose fault that was. We both lurched; the kitchen had tilted like an unseaworthy boat. Bee Larkham stumbled backwards, holding my wrist. Her eyes were fixed on the knife.

We both fell.

The parakeets screeched at us to be careful.

Bee Larkham screamed.

Ice blue crystals with glittery edges and jagged silver icicles.

She fell first, me second, her head striking the floor with a dirty-charcoal-colored crack.

It happened in that order. I'm certain. Because that's the only explanation I have for how I ended up on top of Bee Larkham.

Four seconds later, I rolled sideways and saw more blood spattered on the tiles.

Spot, spot, spot.

It dripped out of my tummy and down my jeans. It splashed over Bee's cobalt-blue-that-wasn't-cobalt-blue dress, running down her right arm and from the palm of her left hand.

The parakeets' cries inside my head had transformed into blinding white. *All-consuming.* I picked up the knife again to save them.

Bee Larkham couldn't stop me this time. She didn't open her mouth or her eyes. She didn't move.

The ice blue crystals and silver icicles had disappeared, taking all their glittery, jagged edges with them.

I was alone with the knife and the howling, terrified parakeets.

50

Leo, my solicitor, keeps saying the words *accident* and *manslaughter* over and over again. I've counted the words eight times since I was told, well, advised to stop talking.

Strongly advised.

Rusty Chrome Orange and Dull Light Green agree this crucial scene—me holding the knife above Bee Larkham's motionless body—is a natural break in the story.

We have to find out how this ties in with what his dad claims happened, at what point he became involved. We're interested in what actions Ed Wishart took that night and what he told Jasper to do next.

My Appropriate Adult wants another break. She must be tired. Maybe she finds it hard to concentrate, like me.

There are too many things to remember all at once; too many that remain stubbornly missing. At least I can recall that small segment.

Then there's a big gap.

That's the part they should ask Dad: how he got Bee Larkham's body into the suitcase in the hallway and took it to the woods. I can't help them with that section of the story. I don't know what he did with the hen clothes that were in the suitcase either.

"What are you going to do with Bee Larkham's body now you've found it?" I ask. "Because no one's been able to tell me that right from the start."

The white and gray murmuring of voices melts away. Rusty chrome orange lingers, like an unwelcome smell: the aroma of burnt pastry.

Singed parakeet pie.

"You don't have to worry about that, Jasper," my solicitor says. "It doesn't concern you."

"It does. Concern me. Everyone deserves a proper burial: Mum, Nan, Mrs. Larkham, the baby parakeet, and Mrs. Watkins. Not the twelve parakeets. They didn't get a funeral."

I close my eyes and tick the bodies off in my head. I think I got the deaths in the right order, because that's important.

"The honest answer is we don't know yet," Dull Light Green says. "We're trying to find out if there are any extended family members. Miss Larkham's body is with the coroner while the postmortem examination is completed. Cause of death has to be established. It's taken a little longer to run all the tests, being a Saturday."

It's taken *us* most of the day, but I thought we'd finally established I killed Bee Larkham with her knife, the knife she used to slice open Mrs. Beeton's pie.

I don't want to go back and explain it all over again because they've misunderstood or misheard.

"Can I see my dad?" I ask.

Dull Light Green says she's sorry, but we have to be kept apart for the time being. That's police protocol.

"Are you still scared of your dad, Jasper?" Rusty Chrome Orange asks. "Yesterday you told police officers he'd killed people before and you thought he was trying to kill you."

I tell him I made a terrible mistake. Dad wasn't trying to kill me. I was confused. I was upset about Bee Larkham. I shouldn't have made up accusations about him and I'm sorry. I bet he's sorry he pushed the police officer too. He didn't mean it.

I'd pushed *him* to the breaking point as usual.

I don't tell him the rest. Richard Chamberlain—*like the actor*—doesn't get anything.

I'm scared *for* Dad, particularly now.

51

Interview: Saturday, April 16, 2:00 P.M.

"I know this is going to be difficult for you, Jasper. But before we move on to talk about what happened next, with your dad, we'd like to discuss Bee Larkham's chicken pie with you."

Wasn't Rusty Chrome Orange listening?

"The parakeet pie," I clarify for the record.

I've had another break for lunch, but avoided the sandwiches because prawns make me throw up. I'm trying to be helpful. It's an effort. I want to see Dad. I want to say sorry for dialing 999 and getting him involved.

"The recipe said to use twelve parakeets," I continue. "Mrs. Beeton's cookbook called them paraqueets."

"That was cruel of Bee," Rusty Chrome Orange says. "To make you think you'd eaten parakeets, your favorite birds. It must have made you incredibly angry and upset."

My tummy mouth opens and closes once for yes.

"Jasper?"

He didn't receive the secret signal through my shirt. Maybe the fabric's too thick. Or maybe his mind's on something else.

"Eating my parakeets made me angry."

I can't say anything too complicated. Keeping the sentence simple makes it easier for him to understand.

"You didn't actually eat them, Jasper," Rusty Chrome Orange says. "I want you to understand that. I'm sure of it. Bee Larkham made you think you'd eaten parakeets, to be cruel. She realized she couldn't manipulate you into taking any more messages to Lucas and was distressed after discovering she was pregnant. She wanted to hurt you. *Badly*. The way she'd been hurt."

Unfortunately, I don't believe a word he says.

"I hurt her too. With the knife. There was a lot of blood. I'm sorry."

I want to tell him how we'd studied George Orwell's *Animal Farm* in English class.

All animals are equal, but some animals are more equal than others.

It was the same with Bee and me. Rusty Chrome Orange has probably never heard of *Animal Farm* or Orwell's *1984*. He wouldn't understand what I want to tell him:

Bee Larkham and I were equally guilty, but I was probably more guilty than her.

"Let's leave the pie for the moment and discuss something that might make you more comfortable," Rusty Chrome Orange says. "I'd like to talk about your paintings, if I may. You're an amazing artist, Jasper. I wish my sons had an ounce of your talent. They spend all their time playing Minecraft, but *you* could be famous when you grow up."

"Minecraft," I repeat. I don't know what's more surprising, the fact that he has sons or that they're into playing one of the all-time best computer games.

"What color are they?" I ask.

"Their color?"

"The color of your sons' voices. Are they the same as yours?" *Please tell me they're not.*

"I don't know, sorry."

"OK."

"Your parakeet paintings are my favorites out of all your pictures. I think they're sensational. Truly wonderful abstract art."

Rusty Chrome Orange picks up a large plastic bag from beside the table and places it in front of him. I see a blur of color. These can't be my paintings. They're safe at home.

"I want you to know I asked your dad's permission to look at your parakeet paintings, Jasper," he says.

I stare harder. I see a blur of parakeets, struggling to breathe beneath the plastic.

They're suffocating.

"He gave us his permission to go into your bedroom and fetch them. Is it OK if we look at them together?"

"No!" *Piercing aquamarine with white edges.*

"We're just going to look at them," Rusty Chrome Orange says. "We understand they're very precious to you. We'll return them as soon as possible."

I refuse to look at him. I hate him.

Dad should never have allowed the police into my bedroom. My paintings are mixed up. My notebook boxes are out of order.

So are Rusty Chrome Orange's questions.

"Have you found the white rabbit yet?" I ask, because that creature's out of place too.

"We're just interested in the parakeet pictures for now," he replies. "Your dad explained how you only paint sounds, not actual objects. That's incredibly original, Jasper. Extraordinary. When did you start painting like that?"

Five, four, three, two, one. Three, five, four, one, two.

He won't answer my question; I won't answer his.

I count backwards and out of sequence, mixing up my number colors on a giant piece of white paper in my head. Now I'm painting cobalt blue over the rusty chrome orange.

"Do you want to try a new line of questioning?" my solicitor asks.

"OK, let's start with this, Jasper. Are these the parakeet paintings you took to Bee Larkham's house on the evening of April eighth?"

He pushes the plastic-imprisoned pictures towards me. "Some are on paper, some on canvas. You kept them separate from all your other parakeet paintings. You hid them in a black case—an art portfolio, I'm told—beneath the blankets in your den."

He's been inside my den?

I haven't dared look in detail at these paintings since that night—I just peeped inside the portfolio once to check all seven were accounted for. However, I remember the brushstrokes of each.

"I can see the dates on the back of the pictures," Rusty Chrome Orange says. "You painted them all the week Bee Larkham died. Perhaps you could look at them again? To check if these are the right paintings?"

I don't want to. I know without examining them they'll be all wrong, like everything else today. The sunrises will be mixed up with the sunsets, the fights with games of playful chasing. I'm not going to let him wind me up. I don't want him to win.

"I find these paintings surprising, Jasper, not only because you're painting the sounds of the parakeets. Do you want to hear what I find surprising?"

No. I start to paint again in my head, splodging delicate smoky blue over his words. I'm not interested in anything he has to say. Rusty Chrome Orange talks anyway.

He keeps repeating the word *surprising,* and now all I can see is the word's silvery yellow. *My* colors aren't strong enough to paint over its hue.

"I find it surprising you had the presence of mind to collect up all your paintings, the portfolio, and bag of notebooks, and take them home after you accidentally stabbed Miss Larkham to death."

Rusty chrome orange again, splashing through the silvers and yellows in my head. He's jumped ahead to me leaving the scene of the crime.

"Your solicitor claims you carried the knife *and* the paintings home after you stabbed Miss Larkham," he says. "Is that correct? Or did someone else help you?"

I try again. I streak cobalt blue across my mind. It's so beautiful. *Calming too.*

"Before we cautioned you earlier, Jasper, you told us that your dad cleaned up all the blood and moved the body," Dull Light Green says. "Was he with you at this point? Did he carry the paintings home?"

I cover my eyes and paint a new picture in my head: a parakeet shrieking, demanding that Bee Larkham's bird feeders are refilled. Will Custard Yellow hear? Has he remembered to feed them? He said he never broke a promise.

"Jasper was specific in our conversation earlier—*he* carried the knife and paintings home alone," Leo says. "He put the items in his den for safekeeping and waited for his dad to get home from work."

"That's what we need to talk more about, Leo," Rusty Chrome Orange says. "Where *exactly* was his dad while this was happening? When did he get home from work? When did he try to help his son? We need to drill down on the timings, who was where, when. Who did what."

Whitish gray blurry lines.

"Jasper?" *Milky coffee.*

I take my hands away from my face.

"D.C. Chamberlain wants to talk to you about what happened immediately after the fight with Miss Larkham," he says.

"OK."

I stare at the table because I don't want to look at Rusty Chrome Orange.

"You see, Jasper, the problem is this," he continues. "We don't understand how you managed to carry everything yourself without smearing bloody fingerprints on any of these paintings, the portfolio, or the bag of notebooks. You were bleeding from your stomach and also carrying the knife. Forensics tells us that none of your blood was found on the pictures or the bag. How is that possible if you left the house alone, as you claim?"

I have no words. I have no colors; there's no point pretending I do. I remember the spots of blood on the floor, the spatter down Bee Larkham and me. I don't know where else the blood ended up.

"Perhaps we could move on," Leo says.

"Of course," Rusty Chrome Orange says. "Did you take this painting to Miss Larkham's house that evening, along with the other seven?"

He pushes a photograph towards me, not a painting, but I recognize the distinctive swirls of paint.

I suck in my breath, bluish white pasta spirals. "Yes. Water splash."

"Thank you for confirming that, Jasper," he says. "You see, this painting is different to the others. It interests us most of all."

I don't get it. Why does everyone like this painting? Bee Larkham damaged it with a splash of water but still picked it as her favorite. That was the odd part—she loved it *because* it was flawed.

Like her.

I sigh. *Moving translucent lines with a hint of blue.*

"Do you know where we found this painting?"

No, I don't.

"It was hanging on the wall of Miss Larkham's kitchen," he says. "Did you see her put it there?"

I hesitate, then shake my head. No, I definitely did not see her put this on the wall.

It must be a lie. He's trying to trick me.

"A large smear of Miss Larkham's blood was discovered on the back of this canvas, along with *her* bloody fingerprints. Again, there was no trace of your blood on this picture."

"Do you understand what D.C. Chamberlain is saying to you?" my solicitor asks.

No. I move my head from side to side.

He's talking to Rusty Chrome Orange now. "You're confusing him. You need to get to the point instead of trying to lead him. Please ask him direct questions."

"Can you explain how this painting came to be hanging on Bee Larkham's wall, if you didn't see her put it there before you killed her?"

Impossible!

Of course I can't!

How can I possibly do that?

"I'm sorry if we're muddling you," Rusty Chrome Orange says. "What we're trying to clarify is how this canvas got on the kitchen wall."

I don't know. I don't know.

"Did *you* hang this picture on the wall after you stabbed Miss Larkham? Before you ran from her house?"

No, no, no.

"Did you see anyone else hang up this picture in the kitchen that night?" he continues. "Could it have been your dad? Was he with you in the kitchen when you killed Miss Larkham?"

I cover my eyes with my hands and rock.

I can't do this. I'm too young. I can't do this. I'm too young.

"Do you want to say anything in answer to these questions, Jasper?" Leo asks.

"Tell them I want my painting back," I shout, from beneath my hands. "It doesn't belong to Bee Larkham. Not now. Not ever. I didn't see Dad touch it and it couldn't have been Bee Larkham. Dead people can't hang up pictures. It's impossible. Everyone knows that!"

52

Interview: Saturday, April 16, 3:10 P.M.

I've had another break with my Appropriate Adult in tow. What's Dad telling the police? They still haven't let me see him. That's because he's been arrested in connection with the murder of Bee Larkham too. I want to tell him I'm sorry. I'm sorry about everything.

Leo says the detectives are still confused, mainly about how the parakeet paintings got home, who helped me, and who put the painting up on the wall. I need to explain this all over again in as much detail as possible.

I have to work hard to keep everything in the right order this time.

I start straightaway when we meet up again because I don't want to be told to take it slowly in this interview. I want to get it over and done with, because this is the part that incriminates Dad.

I close my eyes.

I begin.

Drip, drip, drip.

I'm standing again, holding the knife. Bee Larkham's on the kitchen floor. She's not moving.

I don't remember seeing my parakeet painting hanging on the wall. I see the pattern of blood on the floor. *Spot, spot, spot.*

I look at the knife. *Glint, glint, glint.* The parakeets don't want more cuts. They screech at me to escape.

I run away from dead Bee Larkham's house.

Over the road and into *my* house.

Stop! Reverse!

I've forgotten all my paintings and notebooks. I hesitate at the bottom of the stairs.

Too late to go back.

I'm the worst soldier in the world. I've left my parakeets behind enemy lines. I've eaten some and abandoned the others.

I can't go back, I can't go back, I can't go back.

I can't see the dead parakeet pie.

I can't see dead Bee Larkham.

Now I'm in my den, blanket pulled down. Entrance closed. I rub and rub and rub a button from Mum's cardigan. My tummy mouth screams at me: *You killed Bee Larkham!*

I try to yell to Dad, but nothing comes out of my real mouth. I can't see any colors in the house. It's quiet. He's not back from work.

The knife stays with me in the den, watching over me. My clothes are blood-spattered. I can't pull them off. My arms don't work. My mouth doesn't work. My legs don't work.

My tummy mouth hurts.

How did Bee kill the twelve parakeets? Did she borrow David Gilbert's shotgun and shoot them? Did she set a trap? Did they suffer?

When did she kill them? When I was at school? The night I delivered Lucas's message and she cried? On Thursday night because she'd guessed I'd failed her? Or this morning, when she realized I'd been lying all along?

The front door bangs shut: a rich brown, loosely rectangular shape.

"It's me! I'm home!" *Muddy Ocher.*

I don't know how long I've been alone in the house. I can't see the clock from inside my den. I can't move. I can't look down at the watch strapped to my wrist.

Dad bounds overripe banana colors up the stairs and steps into my bedroom. "Is everything OK in there, Jasper? Have you had your tea?"

Rub, rub, rub.

My tummy mouth screams for help. He doesn't hear. He's going to leave.

Come back!

"Call me if you need anything. I'm going to grab a quick bite to eat downstairs."

Rub, rub, rub.

Dad's gone.

No. I'm wrong.

The door clicks open again, *peanut shell brown*. He's back with a dusky pink creak outside my den.

"There's blood on the stairs, Jasper. There's blood on the carpet in here as well. What's happened? Are you hurt?"

The blanket's wrenched down. A hand stretches in. I scream ice blue jagged shapes at him.

"Ohmigod. What's happened? Jesus Christ. Where's all this blood come from?"

The hand pulls me out. I kick and scream more rough aquamarine crystals. I drop the knife.

"Jasper, Jesus. What have you done to yourself?"

I open my eyes. Now I'm the one on the floor and he's standing above me with the knife in his hand. He drops it as I lift up my sweatshirt.

"Oh God." He rips off his shirt and shoves it against my tummy. "I have to stop this bleeding." He presses harder. "Why, Jasper? Why did you do this to yourself? Was it because I had to work late? Are you punishing me? I'm sorry, Jasper. I couldn't help it. The meeting ran over."

He presses harder. Pointy, silver stars stab me all over.

"You're hurting me!"

"I'm sorry." His grip on the shirt loosens. "Let me see and I won't touch this time. I promise. I'll just look."

He stares at my tummy. "Thanks, Jasper. You're doing brilliantly. You're going to be all right. This looks superficial, but we're going to need to get you to a doctor to check you out."

"Bee said . . ."

"Bee said what?"

I stare down at the blood on my hands and sweatshirt. It's spattered over my jeans and anorak too. How will the stains ever wash out?

"Jasper? Does she know about this? How does she know?"

"I can't go to the doctor," I yell. "Bee says I'll get us both into trouble."

"She saw you do this and didn't call me? She didn't take you to A & E?"

I'm shaking and crying. Snot runs down my face.

Silence.

"Wait. Did she do this to you?"

"No!" I shout. "I stabbed her because she deserved it."

"Jasper!" He picks up the knife again. "Did you hurt Bee with this?"

"I'm too young. I can't do this. I'm too young. I can't do this. I'm too young."

"Oh God." He rushes over to the window. "The light's on in her front room. I can't see an ambulance parked outside. Maybe you didn't hurt her badly? What were you arguing about?"

I'm rocking forwards and backwards, forwards and backwards.

"Parakeets."

"Jesus. How badly did you hurt her, Jasper? Can you remember? Does she need to go to hospital as well?"

I close my eyes to keep out the color, but the red seeps behind my eyelids.

"Stop it, you're killing me!"

Dad drops the knife and sinks to the carpet, beside me. "It could be a mistake. You could have made a mistake. Couldn't you?"

I want to be sick. I retch repeatedly, but I can't bring anything up.

"I'll get you cleaned up and then I'll go over the road," he says. "I'll sort it, I promise. I'll sort Bee. I'll call the police and an ambulance when I know how bad it is."

"I'm sorry, I'm sorry, I'm sorry."

He pulls me to my feet and steers me to the bathroom.

"What about *that*?" I turn and point at the weapon on the carpet.

"Don't worry. I'll get rid of the knife and your clothes. You won't have to see them ever again."

He turns on the shower tap and doesn't wait for me to answer.

"This changes everything, Jasper. I can't take you to a doctor until I've checked on Bee. I can patch up your stomach with tape, and we need to stop any infection. We have antibiotics so we can manage it. I saw far worse in the Royal Marines, right? We'll come through this." He sits me down on the side of the bath and undresses me, slowly peeling off my clothes. "When I'm done, I'm going to give you some painkillers and half a sleeping tablet. When you wake up tomorrow morning, this nightmare will be over and I'll have sorted Bee Larkham. Do you understand?"

I do.

I tell him where to find Bee Larkham's back-door key.

I stop talking.

I sleep.

53

My solicitor and Rusty Chrome Orange are extremely interested in the "cocktail of drugs" Dad gave me: the antibiotics, painkillers, and sleeping tablet, which explain some of the gaps in my memory.

I don't have the answers to their questions. I'm not a doctor.

Why don't you ask my dad? You said he's under arrest. He's being questioned by other detectives. Don't you swap notes like in the movies? Don't you talk to each other?

I don't remember how many tablets I took. I don't remember swallowing them. I don't remember Dad helping me into the shower, putting on my pajamas, pulling out the blood-smeared blankets from the den, or putting me back inside with Mum's cardigan.

He must have done all those things, but a gray, swirling mist descended on that scene in the bathroom. I remember it drifting in and out of my brain, snatching memories from the furthest recesses. I tried to hang on to them, something in particular I needed to tell Dad.

Something to do with the parakeets. Something he had to do at Bee Larkham's house.

He had to save the parakeets.

From what? What must he do?

The mist ripped the thought from my mind.

The parakeets had disappeared. Dad too.

I was alone.

What do you remember next, Jasper? Close your eyes. You're not in this interview room. Imagine you're in your bedroom den again.

I obey Rusty Chrome Orange.

I'm back.

I'm sitting up and my den is spinning around me.

I've forgotten my parakeet paintings. I've forgotten my notebooks. I've left them in Bee Larkham's house.

That's what I needed to tell Dad. He was here. A moment or two ago. Maybe longer. I'm not sure. I don't know what time it is.

My paintings are alone in the kitchen. With Bee Larkham. Dad's sorting her. Because I did a bad thing. I hurt her. With a knife. The knife she used to cut open the parakeet pie.

"Dad?" My voice is a grayish blue croak. I crawl out of the den into the dark room. My eyes are blurry and can't focus on the clock. My watch isn't strapped to my wrist. I don't know where it is.

I'm on the landing. Dad's door is open. His bed is empty. It hasn't been slept in. That's because Dad's not asleep. He's over the road. That's the last thing I remember him saying.

I'll go over the road. I'll sort Bee.

I should help him. I have to get my paintings back. He won't remember them. Or my notebooks. He won't think they're important. He might be distracted by all the blood and not notice them.

I get down the stairs on my bottom. The chain's on the front door. The sitting room door's shut. The kitchen door's open. That's the one I go for. I hear a dark brown, rhythmic noise from the sitting room.

I hold on to the furniture and get to the back door without bumping into anything. I turn the handle. The door's unlocked. I'm outside. Rain slaps my face. Hard. It stings my skin through the pajamas.

I go through the back gate and follow the battle line across the road. It keeps me steady and on track. It guides me towards the alleyway, over the abandoned rubbish, and to the back gate. I'm in Bee Larkham's garden.

At the back door.

Something's out of place.

Now I'm in Bee Larkham's kitchen. Things have swapped around in here—my painting portfolio and notebook bag.

Other things too, but the mist's descended again and transformed into a darkish fog. Not enough light. There's also a strange smell, which makes stars dance on my tummy.

Bee Larkham's still lying on the floor.

She's not moving. I don't want to look at her.

Dad's already here.

He's sorting Bee Larkham. The way he said he would.

He's kneeling beside her. Blue jeans, dark blue baseball cap, and a blue shirt: the usual uniform.

"Is Bee Larkham dead?" I ask.

He jumps, steadies his hand on the floor, and looks around. He sucks in his breath, *white pasta spirals.*

"Did I kill her, Dad?" I ask again.

He doesn't look at me. He can't bear to look at me. The mist is pulling me away. I must try to focus.

"Tell me, Dad. Did I?"

His head jerks.

"Did I kill her?"

"Yes, Son." The whitishgray whisper pierces through the fog.

"I'm sorry, I'm sorry, I'm sorry. Help me, Dad!"

His arm rises. He points to the table. There's my bag of notebooks and fastened portfolio.

Dad's sorted everything. He's packed my paintings inside the case.

His arm moves again. This time it points to the door. He doesn't need to tell me what to do. I know I have to run. I know we can't speak about this again.

Dad has to carry on sorting Bee Larkham.

He said he would.

He's helping me.

I grab my portfolio and notebook bag, turn, and run.

54

Interview: Saturday, April 16, 4:10 P.M.

Back up! Reverse!

How did we end up in this strange, new location? Rusty Chrome Orange has made us perform a three-point turn in our interview. We've screeched off in our getaway vehicle—away from the knife and my parakeet paintings and Dad sorting Bee Larkham—to a totally new location.

It happened after he was called out of the room and came back in again seven minutes and forty-one seconds later. Now I can't keep up even though I've had another break. I'm not even trying.

My mind's locked on the scene in Bee Larkham's kitchen when I returned.

My portfolio and notebook bag were definitely on the table. The parakeet pie had vanished and something else had stolen its place, something that shouldn't have been there. It's hard to recall. My brain cells dance about wildly, mixing up the paints.

If only I'd looked to the right. I might have seen my parakeet picture on the wall, where Dad must have hung it after he sorted Bee Larkham.

Bee Larkham couldn't have put it there herself, because she was already dead. It must still be there, on her wall, calling out for help, begging to be rescued.

Rusty Chrome Orange says I can't have my other paintings back yet, because they're *police evidence*. He's already lost interest in my work and wants to discuss Bee Larkham's neck instead.

"I'm not sure I can help you," I say. "I'm not an otolaryngologist."

"What's that?" Rusty Chrome Orange asks.

"A head and neck surgeon."

Dumbo.

"We know that talking about your dad has upset you," Dull Light Green says. "We need you to focus if you can, Jasper. We'd like to move forwards, before we take another short break."

"Can I see my dad?"

"Let's cover this first, please," she says. "D.C. Chamberlain is asking if you ever touched Miss Larkham's head or neck."

I mull over the baffling question for a full thirteen seconds, before curiosity gets the better of me. "Why?"

"Please can you answer the question, Jasper?" Rusty Chrome Orange butts in. "You told us previously you broke Miss Larkham's pendant. Did you accidentally grab her neck when that happened?"

"Why can't you answer my question?" I hit back. "I asked it first. Your colors are rude and pushy. They should get in line and wait their turn. Why would I touch Bee Larkham's neck?"

Leo pushes a glass towards me. I push it back, sloshing water on the table. That was a mistake. It reminds me of Bee Larkham splashing water over her kitchen table with a sponge.

"She was messy," I say. "She didn't like to clean. She didn't do the washing up because the dishwasher was broken."

"Did it make you angry that her kitchen was messy when you like order and neatness?" Rusty Chrome Orange asks. "Did it make you want to touch her neck?"

"I don't like your neck!"

"You described how Miss Larkham fell after you fought over the knife," he says. "We're wondering if you put the knife down and squeezed her neck while she was lying on the kitchen floor. Before you went home and told your dad what had happened?"

The ticker tape of events in my head is stubbornly jumbled. I don't think I'm ever going to get it straight. We've jumped forwards and backwards so many times, it's impossible to straighten it out and fill in the missing gaps. How could I bear to touch Bee Larkham?

Rusty Chrome Orange speaks again. "Did you put your hands around Miss Larkham's neck to feel for a pulse before you ran home?"

"She was dead. I killed her."

"You didn't grab Miss Larkham around her neck and squeeze tight? Maybe by accident?"

"No!"

"Did you see your dad put his hands around her neck at any point?"

"I don't know what you're talking about!" I stand up and grab the glass of water. "I hate you!"

I hurl it across the table. Rusty Chrome Orange ducks just in time.

55

Interview: Saturday, April 16, 4:24 P.M.

I've apologized, of course. I had to. For throwing the glass at Rusty Chrome Orange, I mean. Not the missing his head part because I'm such a rotten shot. I'm like that in all ball games at school.

Assaulting a police officer is a serious offense, and I don't need that added to my list of crimes.

I'm sorry. My head was about to explode. Sometimes I lash out.

"I accept your apology," Rusty Chrome Orange says. "I know this is stressful for you. You'll feel better when you've had a sleep and recharged your batteries."

I'm not a car, dummy.

"I've already told you I did it. You can take me to prison now. I don't want to answer more questions. I want to go."

"You're not going to prison."

He hasn't forgiven me. He's making things more difficult for me now because I almost assaulted him with a glass of water.

"You're right—a juvenile detention center or a young offenders' institution," I clarify. "Whatever you want to call it."

"We're finished with you for now," he says. "We're arranging with Social Services to take you back to the temporary foster carers. If we need to speak to you again tomorrow, we'll let your social worker know and she'll bring you back here."

I don't move. I must have misheard. This can't be right. I killed Bee Larkham and almost assaulted a police officer.

I'm guilty.

"You're free to go with your solicitor, Jasper," Rusty Chrome Orange says. "Maggie, your social worker, will look after you."

"And Dad?"

"Your dad is still being interviewed. He'll stay with us awhile longer as we wait for forensic results."

I'm stuck to my chair, my hands folded around my body.

The police and my solicitor have got mixed up again. Rusty Chrome Orange probably tried to explain it to his boss while he was out of the interview room and got it all wrong.

As usual.

I wait for them to realize their mistake. There's no point standing up to be forced to sit down again straightaway.

"I don't understand," I say. "Ice blue crystals with glittery edges and jagged silver icicles."

"Listen to me, Jasper." Richard Chamberlain's rusty chrome orange is a more muted color than before. "We're letting you go because you're not responsible for the murder of Bee Larkham. We don't believe you killed her."

His words make no sense.

Dad said the nightmare would be over when I woke up the day after I stabbed her, but it wasn't. It went on and on.

"I did it!" I shout. "I told you I did it. I killed Bee Larkham. Don't blame Dad. He was trying to protect me."

I take a deep breath.

"I confessed to killing Bee Larkham with the knife and now I must be punished," I say firmly. "That's what's supposed to happen. That's the correct sequence of events. Why can't you see that?"

Rusty Chrome Orange and Dull Light Green look at each other.

"He needs to know everything," my solicitor says. "He may understand this better if you explain the full facts to him."

Rusty Chrome Orange's head moves up and down.

"We're letting you go, Jasper, because we've received the preliminary results of the postmortem examination. We already know how she died."

As I watch him, my hand automatically curls around an imaginary blade, the knife that Bee Larkham used to cut the parakeet pie. The knife I held. The knife I used to kill her.

Rusty Chrome Orange leans forward in his chair. "You were right about Miss Larkham being pregnant, Jasper. She was in the early stages. We're running a paternity test against Lucas Drury's and your dad's DNA to see who the father was."

My hand still holds the invisible knife.

"The postmortem has revealed historic repetitive knife marks on her wrist and thighs, which we suspect she made herself. Her right arm and left hand had superficial cuts, which we think you made that night. But they weren't life-threatening wounds. That wasn't why she died."

"I killed her," I repeat. "She was bleeding. She was dead on the floor in the kitchen. Dad told me I did it."

"No, Jasper," Rusty Chrome Orange says. "She was strangled to death, not stabbed. You didn't kill her, Jasper. We believe someone else murdered Bee Larkham."

56

DAD'S STORY

It's funny how two people can remember the exact same thing differently, like they've been guests at completely separate parties. They manage to cheat the lucky dip, grabbing the best parts to remember and ignoring the uncomfortable truths that brush against their fingers.

Pick me, photograph me, tell people about me.

Maybe I'm wrong. Maybe we don't actually see everything or we forget important stuff. No one's perfect. Least of all Dad and me. He says our boys' camping trip to Cumbria two years ago was a fantastic holiday.

I'd say a rude word, except I wouldn't want to see the color.

"It's going to be epic," Dad had said as we rolled our clothes on his bed. "An epic adventure for both of us."

Rolling was important because that's what soldiers did to make their clothes fit into rucksacks before they went off on special operations in Afghanistan and other war zones around the world.

Roll, roll, roll.

It felt like making pastry for an apple pie contest instead of getting ready for war. I moved T-shirts and sweatshirts up and down with my hands, but they didn't like those shapes and squirmed free. They wanted to make their own shapes in my Star Wars rucksack.

"You're not doing it right," Dad said. "Let me do it for you. It'll be quicker." He forced my clothes into long sausage shapes.

"They can go in here." He picked up the large backpack he'd bought from an Army and Navy surplus store. He'd shown it to me eight times already, checking the compartments and fiddling with the straps over and over again. He must have been worried something would fall out. That made me nervous too.

"You don't need to bring your Star Wars rucksack. It's not a proper one. This is the real thing."

I carried on packing my rucksack with sausage-roll clothes. It had a large zip that stretched over the top, like a mouth. Nothing could fall out. Nothing could escape.

"I know you like your rucksack, Jasper, but it's not necessary when I've got this big one."

I put another T-shirt inside.

"Look, yours is a toy one. It's not sturdy enough. It could break or get dirty. You wouldn't like that, would you? You'd get upset. I don't want you to get upset this weekend."

A toy rucksack?

I was outraged on behalf of the Dark Lord. There was absolutely nothing toylike about Darth Sidious.

"I have to bring it. I take it everywhere."

"I know you do, but I think it'd be good if you could get used to not taking it everywhere with you."

Dad had the oddest ideas sometimes. "Why. Would. I. Want. To. Do. That?"

He sat down on the bed. "Because things can't stay the same all the time, Jasper, however much you might want them to. We can make changes, like this weekend. We can be impulsive and go with the flow. We can decide to go camping last minute. We can take one large rucksack, instead of two. Not everything has to be regimented all the time."

Dad wasn't making any sense. He'd bought an ex-military rucksack because he missed that life. We were packing our clothes like soldiers. My chest tightened. I pulled out the photograph of the campsite he'd given me to help me get used to the idea. I stared at it. Dad had said we needed to spend time together to bond after Mum's death.

I couldn't understand why we *needed* to sit silently together in a wet field when we could not talk to each other at home.

"My rucksack's got lots of compartments too," I said. "I can put stones in them."

"You can put whatever stones you like in here. Look at all the pockets it's got." Dad opened his rucksack again. "It's like the one I used to have in the Royal Marines."

"Hmmm." I rubbed my hands together and sat down on the bed.

"What is it now, Jasper?"

I thought hard for thirty-seven seconds. "Darth Sidious died during the battle of Endor."

"Fine! Bring your bloody rucksack. Just stop rocking, will you?"

I clapped my hands over my ears to dilute the color of the swearword: *sticky earwax orange.*

"Let's try to make this weekend work," he said. "Please. I need this break. Do it as a favor for me, Jasper. Can you do that for me?"

Dad doesn't remember wanting to leave my Darth Sidious rucksack behind. He talks about how we worked together to put up the tent on the first night in pouring rain and later roasted marshmallows on another family's campfire because we didn't have any dry wood. He posted the photographs on Facebook.

"The site of our first adventure!!!" he wrote, with three exclamation marks. One wasn't enough.

I remember that camping trip differently.

I remember how we got lost on a hike in the rain.

I remember the tent leaked and we woke to find my rucksack in a pool of muddy water, soggy and ruined.

I remember Dad talking about how much money we'd saved on food after other families asked us to join them around their campfires for dinner.

"I feel for you," a woman had said on the first night. "It must be tough being a single dad."

His head bobbed up and down.

These are the other things imprinted in my mind:

- Not sleeping because the rain hammered purple inkblot shapes on our tent on the first night

- Sobbing over my wet and muddy rucksack the next morning
- Throwing my wrecked rucksack into the lake
- Taking a deep breath and jumping into the water to save it
- Dad jumping into the lake to save me, but not my rucksack

Only now do I remember another thing.

Remember isn't the right word, because I hadn't forgotten it. I couldn't possibly have known this Important Fact back then. I realize *now* how much Dad sounded like Bee Larkham when we argued over my Darth Sidious rucksack in his bedroom.

Do it as a favor for me, Jasper. Can you do that for me?

57

SUNDAY (APRICOT)

Morning

I'm back at the home of my *temporary foster carers*. My tummy hurts and I don't want to talk to Skin Tone or Slate Gray. I don't know them. I have to wait for Dad to come and collect me because he won't leave me alone in a strange house for another night, not when I have to go home and sort through my notebooks and paintings and say goodbye to the parakeets.

I still don't understand what Rusty Chrome Orange told me in the police station yesterday or the way Leo explained it afterwards.

I didn't kill Bee Larkham. Someone else did.

I repeat the words over and over again as I rub the buttons on Mum's cardigan, but they don't make any sense.

Dad was in her kitchen, clearing up the mess: the body and spots of blood. Other things too.

I asked him if I had killed Bee Larkham.

Yes, Son.

Has he forgotten he was there? Has he lied to protect me?

Could he have blocked out what he did, the way I can't recall absolutely everything?

I don't know what Dad remembers about the night Bee Larkham was murdered. He hasn't told me because he doesn't like talking about her.

I want to paint until Dad gets here. I gave a list of things to Maggie and she's fetched them from my bedroom. *My real bedroom.* I'll be back there tonight. Maggie saw parakeets in the oak tree in Bee

Larkham's front garden. She couldn't remember how many. She apologized for not counting them.

She says this is a temporary placement and Children's Services would need to get a court order to keep me here longer. Dad is cooperating fully with the police and has already provided a DNA sample so they won't need to do that unless he's charged with an offense.

She expects he'll be bailed later today. If that happens, he'll be allowed to come home with strict conditions, such as reporting regularly to the police station and handing over his passport.

I'm glad. I don't want to go to court. Dad shouldn't either. He didn't do anything wrong apart from try to help me.

Today, I'm going to be especially brave for both of us. We're the only ones left. Our family has just two members because Mum and Nan died and left us, not to go to heaven but somewhere else. I don't know where.

Dad and me.

Me and Dad.

For the first time, I will attempt to paint ice blue crystals with glittery edges and jagged silver icicles to help me recall every single detail about that night correctly. I don't have the right equipment to do it properly. I forgot my impasto gel, which I need to build up the textures of Bee Larkham's screams, and I only have one large canvas; it's all Maggie could carry with my other stuff.

I should have two canvases: one to paint Bee Larkham's colors as I hurt her with the knife and the other to show the colors when I returned to her kitchen to fetch my notebooks and paintings.

Two separate scenes.

Two pictures.

But I only have one canvas—one chance to get this painting right.

I prepare my paints in a line—ultramarine, cerulean, and cobalt blue as well as black. I forgot titanium white, which is bright, and have to settle for the duller zinc white. I fill my favorite pot with water, the one Maggie found in the bathroom at home.

When I can no longer put off the moment, I attempt to paint the color and shape of Bee Larkham's murder:

Ice blue crystals with glittery edges and jagged silver icicles.

I thought the original colors and shapes were correct, but Rusty Chrome Orange insists they're wrong.

I didn't kill Bee Larkham.

I'm not familiar with this strange, new picture I have to create. I haven't tried to paint it before.

I must paint my version of the truth, not anyone else's.

I dip my brush into water and white paint, scrubbing it onto the canvas. I flick cerulean blue in spatters on top and mix black and white together to make the color of the silvery jagged spikes. I dab it on with the brush because I can't use scraps of cardboard to mold the points and icicles into peaks without the impasto gel.

It's the best I can do:

This is Bee Larkham screaming as she fell.

Her body's lying on the kitchen floor, near the hallway door.

Her eyes are shut.

Blood's spattered on the tiles and down Bee's cobalt-blue-that-isn't-cobalt-blue dress. There's a puddle of pale red, curdled vomit.

The parakeet paintings are scattered over the table.

The parakeet pie is on the table.

The kitchen's a mess, pots and pans stacked in the sink.

The knife's in my hand.

I thought I'd finished my painting, but more colors and shapes drift into my brain.

Pale yellow spots. The kitchen clock was ticking. I add the dots to the top right-hand corner.

A strange shape came from Bee's mouth, curly white, with an inconsistent texture as she gasped for breath. I try to re-create it, but again, it's impossible to do it properly without impasto.

My paintbrush moves on; it doesn't want to linger too long on the dead.

It follows my orangey footsteps into the hallway. I saw the hen suitcase. It stood upright and closed, by the coat rack. I grabbed my anorak from the peg, threw it on, stuck the knife beneath it, and ran out of the house.

I add a dark brown shape, almost like an elongated broomstick, as the front door banged shut.

The picture's finished—an accurate depiction of what happened in Bee Larkham's kitchen. Why is that misleading me?

I want Dad to explain where I've made the crucial mistake, but he can't. He's still explaining things to the police.

I imagine he's telling the detectives he believed the colors in my original painting too. He thought I'd killed Bee Larkham and tried to cover up my crime to stop me from going to jail. He put her body in the suitcase in the hallway and drove it to the woodland.

The colors tricked us both.

I have to try again.

This time I will paint over my finished canvas with the new colors to create the scene I saw later that night.

I rub a button until I feel better about doing this.

I'm going back to Bee's kitchen to save my parakeet paintings and notebooks. I have to reenter through a new door this time.

The back door.

Instinctively, I dab grayish brown in the bottom left-hand corner— me shifting the flamingo statue to reveal Bee Larkham's spare key. The color bleeds into the white paint beneath and instantly looks wrong.

It doesn't belong there.

I conceal the colored blob with white brushstrokes because it *is* wrong.

When I arrived the second time, the back door was *already* open and the key was in the outside lock. Dad must have left it there.

Now I'm back in the kitchen.

I don't have to add the pale yellow spots of the ticking clock because they're already on my canvas.

My brush wavers.

I'm 75 to 80 percent sure I didn't see curly white shapes—the sounds coming from Bee Larkham's mouth when I returned.

The kitchen looked different, darker too, but I can't paint the confusing new details flooding my head because I only ever paint sounds, never objects.

The Dancing China Lady had arrived, and she definitely wasn't there before. My paintings had leapt back into their portfolio, next to the notebook bag on the table.

That night had an audience of two: Dad and me.

Dad wore a dark blue baseball cap and knelt beside the body of Bee Larkham. Maybe he was checking her neck for signs of life, the way Rusty Chrome Orange suggested I might have done.

I couldn't watch.

He sucked in his breath with white pasta spirals and spoke in whitish gray whispers, which I quickly add to the canvas.

I didn't see the suitcase this time because I grabbed my case from the table, along with the bag of notebooks, and fled through the back door. It was open. I didn't close it or return the key to the flamingo. I never looked back as I ran out of the garden and down the alley, rain lashing my face.

The colors come back quicker the further I get away from Bee Larkham's house.

A car beeped musky red blunt-pointed shapes in the distance. A fox ran across the road. Me in pursuit. We parted ways at the creaking petrol green gate.

I was back in my garden and then our house, in the kitchen; a half-drunk glass of orange juice on the counter where I'd left it earlier.

I mix a velvety dark chocolate color on my palette and streak lines onto the canvas. *A rhythmic pattern.*

The same brown noise I heard when I left the house.

I ran for my den. Up the stairs, *light, blurry pastel yellow.*

There are four more distinct colors I hadn't remembered until now.

Dark, overripened banana footsteps came up the stairs as I buried the portfolio under blankets in my den.

Silence. Except for the egg-yolk circles of my clock.

A few seconds later, another color and shape: *blurry dark gray and shiny clear lines, almost like TV static, but not quite.*

Dad was taking a shower.

I couldn't move from my den. I hugged Mum's cardigan.

Cobalt blue.

I wash the color of Mum's voice over the entire painting to make me feel better. Trying to create this picture today without the right equipment was a mistake. Everything about it feels wrong.

I don't trust the colors, not the ice whites or the spirally shapes or the whispers or Dad's TV static lines.

I can only trust Mum.

I can only ever trust cobalt blue.

Mum and me had different colors for days of the week, numbers, and music, but that didn't matter.

We had a shared language. One we could both understand. One that never let Dad in.

I miss Mum. I want her back.

She used to love doing jigsaws and crosswords and solving problems.

I need her to help solve my puzzle. I don't think I can do it by myself. I'm not clever enough. I don't have all the pieces and the ones I have make no sense. They're mixed up and I can't go home to sort through them.

Bee Larkham has the missing piece.

Or Dad.

Leo, my solicitor, said the police initially believed I was the last person to see Bee Larkham alive.

Now they think it was someone else.

I think that person must be Dad.

It's definitely Dad.

58

SUNDAY (APRICOT)

Afternoon

I didn't like Seb's bedroom, but now I'm too scared to leave. I'm terrified of returning home to an empty oak tree and eaves. Abandoned nests. The young parakeets could have joined a roost already, without waiting to say farewell.

I trace the curly *S* of his name as I lie on the strange boy's bed. We share that letter in our names.

S-E-B

J-A-S-P-E-R

S and also an *E*. Nothing else. I don't know Seb's hobbies or interests. I don't know where he is now.

I dig my nail into the *E*.

I can't let go.

I've packed up my paints and the rest of my stuff. My rucksack's waiting by the side of the bed. It's watching the door.

So am I.

I'm frightened of leaving this house with Dad.

Skin Tone and Slate Gray are talking with the social worker, Maggie, downstairs. They're all talking to Dad because the detectives have allowed him to leave the police station *for the time being*. He wasn't charged with assault or murdering Bee Larkham.

He's been given bail, as Maggie expected. He may get called back to the police station for further questioning. The detectives will let his solicitor know. Not Leo. A woman called Linda.

Maggie says Social Services have discussed my case long and hard.

They've taken into account the fact there are no other relatives I can stay with and that being with strangers is particularly traumatic for someone like me.

They're letting me return to Vincent Gardens under strict 24/7 supervision by her department.

Dad says he's innocent and it's time for us both to go home.

In the car, Dad explained the police had to let him go because there is *insufficient evidence to place him at the scene of the crime.*

Forensics found dozens of fingerprints in Bee Larkham's house. Some matched his because he was at her party, along with lots of other people.

That doesn't prove anything.

The police are trying to track down everyone who's visited the house, including all the music students. They're doing more door-to-door inquiries along the street and reexamining witness statements. They're continuing to look at DNA found on Bee's body and suitcase.

The initial results have ruled Dad out, which is *good news for both of us.*

You have to believe me. I had absolutely nothing to do with any of this.

I don't know what or who to believe.

I know nothing feels right on this street because

1. The bird feeders are empty. I can't see a single parakeet in the oak tree or eaves.
2. The Dancing China Lady hasn't managed to climb back up the stairs to her usual place in the window. She must have stayed behind in the kitchen.
3. Police ticker tape flutters around Bee Larkham's front door.
4. A man wearing a black hat wouldn't say hello to Dad as we got out of the car. He refused to reveal the color of his voice. Dad said the man was David Gilbert and he was deliberately snubbing him because of his arrest. David Gilbert probably thought he was guilty too.

Nothing feels right in my bedroom because

1. My den's been torn down and someone's tried to erect the blankets again. They've done it all wrong.
2. Mum's cardigan doesn't smell the same, even though I took it to Skin Tone and Slate Gray's house. It hadn't been left alone here.
3. My paintings look sad, like they don't want to see me again. I'm not sure I blame them.

Everything's *off* (a dark brownish black word). Light gray dust defiantly smears across my wardrobe, not caring about the streaks. When I look closer, I see the shapes of fingerprints. Behind the doors, it's as bad as I'd suspected. My boxes aren't in the right order.

"Someone's been in my wardrobe when I wasn't here," I shout. "They've opened up my boxes and messed around with my notebooks. I know they're not right."

Dad's sitting at the table, holding a hot drink, when I burst into the kitchen.

"I'm sorry, Jasper. I should have explained in the car. The police searched our house while we were gone. They took a few things away, but they're all itemized. I can show you the list if you want."

"They took my parakeet paintings and I want them back," I insist. "All of them. Water marks too."

"They're hanging on to those for the time being, along with some of your notebooks. All the others are back in their boxes upstairs."

"They're not right," I say. "They're out of order. They're all wrong."

I look across the kitchen. Gray marks stain the cutlery drawer too. More fingerprints.

"Don't worry about those." Dad puts down his cup. "The police were checking for fingerprints. I told them that's where I put the knife, Bee's knife, after, you know . . ."

Is that true? I was sure he'd hidden the knife somewhere secret beyond this house and garden, somewhere he knew I could never find it.

"*I'll get rid of the knife and your clothes*—those were your exact words," I point out.

"Yes, you're right. I did that. I threw all your bloodied clothes away, including your anorak. I knew you'd never wear them again. I put the knife away in the drawer because I wasn't sure what to do with it. I wanted to forget about it."

"You lied then," I say. "You're lying to me now."

"No, you misunderstood me, Jasper. You misunderstood absolutely everything about me and Bee, right from the start."

"You had sex with Bee Larkham. I understand that! I understand she wasn't Mum. She wasn't cobalt blue! She was never cobalt blue! She wasn't even close!"

I run out of the room and up the stairs. Dad doesn't try to stop me, not even when I go into his bedroom.

I find the book he's hidden beneath the Lee Child cover.

Understanding Your Child's Autism and Other Learning Difficulties.

I tear out the pages, one by one. "I am not a manual! I am not a manual!"

He stands in the doorway. He doesn't attempt to save his book. He doesn't contradict me.

"I didn't kill Bee Larkham!" I shout.

"I know that," he says quietly. "I never thought you had, Jasper. And you have to believe me when I say I didn't kill her either."

"I don't! I don't believe a word you say!"

59

MONDAY (SCARLET)

Morning

It's too scary to empty all the boxes in my wardrobe onto the floor at once. I couldn't do that. I have to search one box at a time for the missing white-rabbit notebook. I can narrow the hunt. Rusty Chrome Orange pulled it out from one of the boxes during my First Account on April 12. Then the creature disappeared again because it didn't want to be caught trespassing on someone else's property.

I start the search before Maggie arrives to talk to us both while I'm signed off school. She's going to visit us regularly from now on and take me back to the police station again tomorrow to see if I can remember anything else about the evening of April 8. I only have five minutes until she gets here, which isn't long enough. Rabbits are timid creatures. They won't come out of hiding if they're afraid.

I should tell Maggie that. If I forget, I can always call her. She's given me a special telephone number. I can ring her at any time of day or night if I'm frightened.

This is what Dad and me are going to do now Maggie's left after drinking a cup of tea and eating two custard creams.

We're each going to write lists of Important Facts for the next fifteen minutes and compare the two. When we swap, we're allowed to put up a hand to ask a question if we don't understand a fact or want to make a statement.

Dad's Important Facts
1. *I didn't kill Bee Larkham.*
2. *I wasn't in Bee Larkham's kitchen on Friday night.*
3. *I didn't empty her suitcase, put her body inside, and carry it to the woodland.*
4. *I spoke to Bee at about 9:30 p.m. on Friday night, at her front door. I'd knocked a few times during the evening, but she was playing music at full blast and probably didn't hear.*
5. *My boots were muddy from walking to work and taking a shortcut in the rain. My baseball cap is underneath the coats on the rack in the hall. It's where I left it after my run. You can check. It's faded black in color.*

I compare it to my list:

Jasper's Important Facts
1. *I didn't kill Bee Larkham.*
2. *Dad was wearing a dark blue baseball cap in Bee Larkham's kitchen on Friday night.*
3. *Dad confirmed I'd killed Bee Larkham.*
4. *Dad lied about what he did with the knife.*

My hand shoots up. "Are you telling the truth about number two on your list?"

"Yes, Son."

I can't breathe.

I drop the list and run upstairs. I shove the chair beneath my door handle. I'm not going to ring Maggie. She can't help me.

I have to dial 999 because this is an emergency.

I need to tell the police I definitely think Dad killed Bee Larkham. It had to be him.

He was there. In Bee Larkham's kitchen. Wearing a dark blue baseball cap. Touching her neck.

"Jasper! I promise you it's the truth. I wasn't there that night."

I've left my mobile downstairs.

I hammer on the window. No one hears me. They can't see my colors.

"I didn't do anything wrong," Dad repeats from behind the door. "You have to believe me, Jasper. I wasn't there. Honestly, I wasn't. The police believe me. They would never have let me take you home if they thought I was dangerous. They're reinterviewing Lucas Drury's dad. He's a suspect now. He's already been charged with assault, burglary, and making threats to kill. He denies everything, but D.C. Chamberlain thinks they'll get a confession out of him because the baby was Lucas's. Not mine. The police have confirmed that already from our DNA tests."

I don't know who I should believe.

Dad.

Lucas's dad.

Lucas.

I'm not coming out. The world outside my bedroom door is far too dangerous.

The young parakeets have realized that. Some have already fledged, but they remain close to their nest at night. I saw them roosting in the branches of the oak tree, their parents nearby.

They don't want to leave me alone. They know I'm not safe, here in my bedroom, living on this street.

60

MONDAY (SCARLET)

Afternoon

I've rebuilt my den and all my paints that came with me to the foster carers are back in their right places.

That makes me feel better.

I'm going to paint the night of Bee Larkham's murder properly this time—using two separate canvases. That way I can look at the two paintings side by side and work out where I made my mistakes.

I'm doing it correctly this time, using the appropriate paints and equipment, which I've laid out on the table: keys, combs, Dad's old credit card, and strips of cardboard as well as brushes and palette knives.

Using a large, soft brush I do a quick white wash over the canvas before dividing my impasto gel into three sections on my palette. I mix white paint, bright sky blue, and gray into each.

My blue is the exact shade I need, hard and metallic. *Unforgiving.*

I layer the blue mix onto my picture with a palette knife, building up large, sharp peaks with a piece of cardboard and my fingers. I flick sharp titanium white paint at the blue pinnacles and prod more into the pointed edges, with my fingers and a key.

I smear on the gray next, molding sharp icicles with the credit card and comb. My art teacher recommended experimenting at home with unusual tools, and these are the best for creating razor-sharp shapes.

I know these sounds are correct: Bee Larkham screaming as she fell backwards.

I fell next.

Bee lay on the floor, eyes shut, on her back.

Using more white gel mix, I make the twirling shape, which came from her mouth, and add the color of the clock.

I date the picture correctly on the back of the canvas:

April 8: *Ice Blue Crystals with Glittery Edges and Jagged Silver Icicles on canvas*

I place the painting by the window and begin my second, more troublesome picture, showing my return to Bee Larkham's house later that night.

I re-create the pale yellow of the clock's ticks. After that's completed, I hesitate like last time, but it's not because I doubt my tools or want to apologize to my canvas.

It's true the color of the clock is the same in this painting and the one under the windowsill, but I need to concentrate on the differences. The curly white noise that came from Bee Larkham's mouth is missing.

I'm 100 percent sure now.

Other things are different too.

I'd concentrated on trying to remember the colors of the sounds in the kitchen when I was at Skin Tone and Slate Gray's house, but those definitely weren't the important changes.

It was what I saw, not the colors I heard, that had altered the most.

Bee Larkham was lying on the floor with her eyes closed when I left her. But when I went back to the kitchen to rescue my paintings, her eyes were open.

She was staring right at me—definitely dead.

My hand shakes. Her eyes scared me that night. They terrify me now.

Every single aspect of this picture is wrong. Not just the eyes: *shut then and open now.*

Bee was wearing a black top and turquoise skirt, hitched up to her knees. *Alien flesh.* She'd changed clothes and position, lying on the floor on the other side of the table instead of by the hallway door.

Her left hand was bandaged.

The room was darker than before—the overhead pendant light wasn't switched on, just a smaller side lamp.

Looking back to that night, my eyes want to focus on the spatters of blood on the kitchen floor, but they've gone, together with the puddle of vomit.

They've taken the dirty plates and pots with them; all the washing up's vanished. The kitchen's clean and tidy. The parakeet pie's disappeared from the table and the Dancing China Lady has taken its place.

She's watching a man in a dark blue baseball cap lean over Bee Larkham's body.

Bee Larkham's eyes look like opaque stones.

I shudder again.

I remember smelling something strange and acrid: disinfectant. There's another scent too, which hurts my tummy. I've smelt it before.

My sealed art portfolio was on the clean table, my bag containing notebooks next to it.

Someone had tidied away the mess—they cleaned up the blood and vomit and washed the dishes. They gathered together my pictures.

I thought that person was Dad, the Dark Blue Baseball Cap Man, helping me out. But it doesn't explain why Bee looked different and why she was lying in a new position.

When I compare this picture with the canvas by the window, the differences terrify me.

They prove I didn't kill Bee Larkham. She must have got up from the floor after I'd left. She'd bandaged her hand and changed her clothes and mopped the floor with disinfectant. She'd collected my paintings and hung one on the wall, placing the others inside the portfolio.

I see what I couldn't see before.

This is the correct painting, the one I should have believed from the start. It's a genuine depiction of what happened.

I'm calling it

April 8: *The Truth on canvas*
The first painting—*Ice Blue Crystals with Glittery Edges and Jagged Silver Icicles*—misled me badly.
It's a fake.
I don't know the colors or shapes of Bee Larkham's murder.
I never did. I wasn't there when she died.

61

MONDAY (SCARLET)

Later That Afternoon

I've agreed to talk to Dad, but I'm not opening the door. We're sitting on opposite sides. He pushed his list under the gap at the bottom, because I said I wanted to discuss number 4.

"I told you I'd sort Bee and I did," Dad says. "I called on her while you were asleep and asked her what the hell had gone on. She'd bandaged her hand. She told me you'd lost your temper when she refused to go to the police about David's threats to the parakeets. You attacked her with the knife and slashed yourself to make it look as though she'd attacked you first. She said you were out of control and violent. She called you a menace."

"All wrong," I say, putting my paint-smeared hands on the door. "It's all wrong."

"I know, I'm sorry. I handled everything wrong. I should have taken you to a doctor that night. I shouldn't have listened to Bee. I should have talked to you about what happened afterwards, but I wanted it all to go away. I had no idea . . ."

He stops talking and starts again.

"Bee said that, as a favor to me, she wouldn't press assault charges," he continues. "She didn't want to talk to the police. She warned me if I took you to a doctor, Social Services and the police would become involved. The police would press charges against you, whether she cooperated or not. We both agreed to keep quiet, for your sake—we wouldn't tell anyone what had happened. Neither of us would ever talk about it again. That's why I told you to keep quiet, Jasper. It's the only reason, I promise."

Bee had painted the wrong picture, a false one with deceitful colors like the one I produced earlier. She'd presented it to Dad to hang on his bedroom wall and he'd accepted it unquestioningly over the colors of my painting.

He stood next to Bee Larkham, not me.

"She did a favor for you because you had sex together after the party," I say.

Silence.

"I won't deny it. But we're talking about a one-time thing. I regretted it later. I'm so sorry."

"Like you regret having me. It's hard for you having a son like me. Bee told me. You wish you were single again."

"No! That's not true. Look, I should have put a stop to your relationship with Bee long ago. I had no idea how she was manipulating you. Manipulating everyone on this street. She's in your head, Jasper, and you have to get her out of there. She told lies."

I can't.

"I wasn't trying to replace Mum, if that's what you think," Dad goes on. "It had nothing to do with Mum. I was lonely."

Me too.

"Will you come out now?"

"I have to paint. I have to find the white rabbit before I forget again." I hear the color of his sigh through the door.

"Let's talk more after that," he says. "Because there's something else I need you to understand, Jasper. I spoke to Bee at nine thirty on Friday night, but the neighbors also heard her loud music until after one. They've verified my account. David Gilbert called round to complain again about the noise. He had another argument with Bee. He was the last person to see Bee Larkham alive. Not me."

62

MONDAY (SCARLET)

Still That Afternoon

I don't have to go downstairs—Dad's left a cheese sandwich on a plate outside my bedroom door. I wait until the colors of his footsteps fade away before retrieving it. I shift my desk back into place, jamming a chair between the door handle and the bottom of the drawers.

If Dad tries to shoulder the door, it won't budge.

He won't do that, he says, because he doesn't want to kill me.

He didn't kill Bee Larkham.

He wasn't in Bee Larkham's kitchen on Friday night.

I could be imagining seeing someone because of the drugs Dad gave me. He never heard me leave the house.

Maybe I didn't return.

Maybe Dad was right. It *was* a horrible nightmare. I dreamt it all, a scene that didn't connect or make sense.

I've had a chat with Maggie on her special telephone number. She says it's good I'm talking to Dad.

I'm going to leave the paintings for now because they're too confusing. I begin the hunt for the white rabbit notebook again; it doesn't belong in this house. The animal lives over the road, but there's sticky tape across the door so it can't return. Maybe that's why the creature's visiting me.

I find it at the back of the wardrobe in the fourth box I open, wedged between old notebooks detailing my first few months living on this street.

I never put the rabbit in this box. *In any box.* The only possible way it could have got in here is if Bee Larkham left it behind when she was in my bedroom. But she hadn't left it lying about, waiting to be scooped up by accident. She must have deliberately placed it in the box.

Didn't she want it?

Had she left me a surprise present?

Or had she forgotten to make me promise to keep it safe?

I open the first page.

This diary belongs to Beatrice Larkham, aged nine and three months. If you find this diary, please return to 20 Vincent Gardens.

Bee—I can't call her Beatrice, like David Gilbert—had drawn pictures of rabbits on the inside cover. To be honest, they're terrible. Opposite is the reading from *Alice in Wonderland,* the one she'd recited at the grave of the baby parakeet. This handwriting looks different. Neater.

I flick ahead. It's boring stuff: what she ate, which girls she played with at school. *When* she was at school. She spent pages and pages sick at home, reading the Bible. I'm not sure what was wrong with her.

I skip to a turned-over corner. I straighten it out because creases look all wrong and if I don't, it'll bother me all day.

Thursday

Mummy says I've been a bad, cheeky girl. An untidy bedroom is a sin. Had to read the Bible together for two whole hours! No TV. Wish I could remember to be a good girl. It's hard being good.

Mummy and Mrs. Watkins are going to prayer meeting tomorrow night. I'm staying at home. Hopefully the babysitter won't make me read the Bible. It's boring. I can't tell Mummy that. She'll be angry again.

Friday

Looking forward to Mummy going out. Saw my babysitter on the way home from school and checked about the Bible. He said we could have a Mad Hatter's tea party like the one in my favorite book, Alice in Wonderland. Can't wait!!!!!!

I climb into my den and put the diary under a blanket. Bee Larkham's childhood was dull. If she hadn't been murdered, I'd tell her I don't think much of her gift. I'd give it back to her without saying thank you. I'd prefer to see the parakeets from her bedroom window. Surely she could have guessed this Important Fact?

I don't understand what I'm supposed to do with her dreary diary. *What was Bee Larkham trying to tell me?*

63

TUESDAY (BOTTLE GREEN)

Morning

Maggie will be here in ten minutes to drive me to the police station. To be on the safe side, I'm not shifting the desk or removing the chair from beneath my door handle until she arrives.

I'm reading Bee Larkham's diary from where I left off. It's not much of a diary; it doesn't accurately record her life. I flick backwards and forwards. There are too many gaps: pages torn out and entries violently scribbled over with black pen, ripping the paper.

Some of the pages I wish I hadn't read. I wish she hadn't written them. The Mad Hatter did terrible things to her the night of the tea party and the other nights he babysat while Mrs. Larkham went to prayer meetings. I wish I didn't know about it, but I can't squeeze the colors out of my head.

I wish I could go back in time and tell Mrs. Larkham to find a different babysitter.

I reread one of Bee Larkham's entries:

Why won't Mummy believe me? Why am I so bad? I hate the Mad Hatter. I hate him. I want him to stop coming here. I want him to stop making me cry. I'll ask God for help again. He has to help me.

Bee drew pictures of the March Hare, the Dormouse, and the Mad Hatter, who doesn't look right. He's not wearing a hat. He's a stick man, holding a cup.

The white rabbit jumps from page to page, throughout the diary, and lands at the back. There, it lies lifeless on the ground, all four legs sticking up in the air. Eight words are printed in capital letters beneath the dead animal:

GOD WON'T HELP ME. I WANT TO DIE.

"Bee Larkham wanted to die," I tell Rusty Chrome Orange in the interview room. "That's the truth. God did nothing. He never helps because he's nowhere to be found."

Maggie's with Leo and me. I told Rusty Chrome Orange I didn't need an Appropriate Adult because Leo and Maggie are pretty appropriate. He agreed and said *good point.*

"Is that something she told you?" Rusty Chrome Orange asks. "Did she discuss with you why she was self-harming?"

I'm not sure what that means.

"She hated the rabbit. I know that. She killed it at the end. She hated the Mad Hatter too."

"Do you know what rabbit he's talking about?" Rusty Chrome Orange asks Maggie.

"It's the first time he's mentioned it to me," she replies. "He usually only talks about the parakeets."

"They still haven't been fed," I point out. "The feeders were empty again this morning. We don't have any seed or apples. We haven't been shopping yet. Can the police feed them?"

"I'll certainly look into that for you, Jasper," Rusty Chrome Orange says.

"Ollie Watkins's mum died of cancer. I wonder if that's why he's forgotten to feed the parakeets." He's sad and lonely, like me.

"Don't worry," Maggie says. "We can buy seed on the way home."

After that, Rusty Chrome Orange explains Dad's story to me again, *his* version of events. Some of this Dad told me at home. Other parts he left out, like falling asleep in his favorite armchair after talking to a friend on his mobile and having *a few too many beers.*

That's where Dad told the police he slept on Friday night, after he visited Bee Larkham but didn't go inside her house. He stayed on the doorstep. It's why *if* I did get up in the night, I didn't see him in his bedroom.

Later, he thought he heard a noise, which woke him up. He had a shower to help his stiff neck and went to bed.

His story's verified. David Gilbert heard Bee playing loud music until 1:00 A.M. He knocked on her door and complained. She swore at him and he left. He's been interviewed by the police too and says he didn't kill her either.

Once we've got that sorted, we keep going over the same thing again and again—the scene in Bee Larkham's kitchen and the Dark Blue Baseball Cap Man. I brought along my paintings, but Rusty Chrome Orange hasn't looked at them. He has more and more questions.

Could you have dreamt going over to Bee Larkham's a second time?

Maybe.

Do you remember any other details that could be helpful?

The Dancing China Lady shouldn't have been in the kitchen.

Are you sure you saw the ornament? We found Bee's broken obsidian necklace in the kitchen, but not the porcelain figure.

I'm certain the Dancing China Lady was there. She saw everything.

Did you see the suitcase in the hallway when you returned? Had it changed position?

I didn't go into the hallway.

Did you go upstairs to check on the parakeets from the window?

No.

Are you sure you didn't see clothes on the bed in the front bedroom? Clothes we think Bee packed in her suitcase and someone else emptied out again that night?

I didn't go upstairs. I didn't see the sparkly hen clothes. I didn't see the parakeets.

Do you remember the colors of any sounds in the kitchen?

The clock.

What time was it?

Didn't check.

Do you recall any smells?

Disinfectant and something else. I can't remember what. I didn't like it. It hurt my tummy mouth.

Can you describe the man you saw bending over Bee's body?

Dark blue baseball cap. Blue jeans and blue shirt.

Did you get a good look at his face?

Yes, I saw his face.

Would you recognize him if you saw him again?

No. I can't describe his hair color. The baseball hat covered it, but I don't usually look for that sort of thing. I didn't recognize the shape of his head. Or his socks.

"Could it have been someone you know, other than your dad?" Rusty Chrome Orange asks. "Someone you've spoken to before? Did you recognize the color of his voice?"

No. He whispered whitish lines.

"Did you recognize the baseball cap?"

No. Dark navy, dark blue, and black are common colors for baseball caps. I can't use them as markers to remember faces. They're easy to mix up, the colors are too similar from a distance. Plus, only a single light was switched on in the kitchen.

"Could you estimate the age of the person you saw?"

No. I'm not good with ages. He was kneeling over Bee. I don't know how tall he was either.

"Could he have been a boy rather than a man?"

I don't know.

"Did you get the impression he knew you?"

He saw me, if that's what you mean. He definitely saw me. He didn't say my name. He whispered two words to me over Bee Larkham's dead body: "Yes, Son."

He knew Dad said that to me or made a lucky guess.

"Is there anything, anything at all you can remember which might help us find who did this to Bee Larkham?"

"Bee had wanted to die before," I reply. "Then I accidentally broke her protective necklace and she didn't have a choice. That was my fault. I'm sorry. I'm sorry about everything."

"That's OK, Jasper," Rusty Chrome Orange says. "Don't worry. It's not your fault."

I *am* worried.

I've seen a murderer but can't recall his face.

He's seen me too.

He probably remembers *my* face.

64

TUESDAY (BOTTLE GREEN)

Afternoon

Maggie agreed to stop off at the pet shop on the way home. The man with the moldy-damson voice said he was out of bird seed and wouldn't be restocked for another week. Her iPhone gave a list of other pet shops within ten miles, but she didn't have time to take me anywhere else. She has to visit another boy.

Dad comes out of the house as we pull up; he'd been waiting for me at the window. He walks over to Maggie's side of the car. They talk quietly while I wait on the pavement, staring at the oak tree.

She must have briefed him about the bird seed problem before she drove away.

"We'll buy seed today, I promise," Dad says.

"We could try Ollie Watkins. He may have seed. The parakeets shouldn't have to wait any longer."

"I doubt Ollie's got anything like that in his house," he replies. "Birds aren't his thing. He hates their noise as much as David."

He's wrong because Ollie Watkins fed the parakeets before. I don't understand why he's stopped. He's a bird lover, like me. I cross over the road, looking for cars both ways.

"Hold on, Jasper. Come back."

I walk up the path to his house, 18 Vincent Gardens, and knock on the door, *lighter brown radiating out from the dark.*

"I don't think this is a good idea," Dad says. "Let's go home. I promise we'll go out again and buy some."

The door opens.

"You haven't fed the parakeets," I tell the man in blue jeans and gray sweater. "You promised. A promise is a promise. That's what you said. You always keep your promises."

"Pardon?" *Grainy dark red, a dull shade.*

"David. Apologies." Dad steps forward. "Is Ollie in? Jasper has got it into his head he might have bird seed."

I stumble backwards. "You don't belong here, David Gilbert. You're out of order. You're not wearing the right clothes either."

Blue jeans instead of cherry cords.

"I didn't expect to see either of you," the man says. "I thought you were both at the police station."

"Neither of us has been charged with anything, David," Dad says, a rough, dark edge to his voice. "Because neither of us has done anything wrong."

"Dad's on bail," I clarify, as another man appears at the door. *He's wearing red jeans.* "We didn't kill Bee Larkham or hide her body. I didn't take the Dancing China Lady. That was someone else. It was the Dark Blue Baseball Cap Man."

The two men inside the house stand side by side. They're the same height and both have dome-shaped heads. I make myself compare their hair: both darkish. One has gray streaks.

Blue jeans/gray pullover.

Red jeans/black sweatshirt.

I can't tell the color of their socks. Their clothes are all wrong; they should swap. Instead, I focus on their voices.

"What's he talking about this time?" Dull Grainy Red asks. "Because it's usually the parakeets." This has to be David Gilbert; it's his voice color.

I pick the second man, wearing red jeans, to address.

"They need feeding," I tell him, because this must be Ollie Watkins—unless he's returned to his fiancée in Switzerland and someone else has moved into 18 Vincent Gardens.

"Come in." The man coughs scratchy custard yellow with strange-colored streaks. "Don't stand out there on ceremony."

"Well, if you're sure, Ollie," Dad says. "We won't stay long. I need to give Jasper his lunch."

The door opens wider and Dad steps inside. "Are you coming, Jasper? It's only for a few minutes. Lunch just needs pinging in the microwave."

I step inside and the door shuts behind me. I can't walk any further into the hall. I remember Bee's party. I remember my paintings. I don't want to be here. I want to feed the parakeets.

"Are you OK, Jasper?" The man standing beside me is wearing his usual uniform: blue shirt, blue jeans. *Dad*.

"It's only for a few minutes," I repeat. "No longer. It's lunchtime. Macaroni cheese."

We follow the two men into the kitchen. It feels wrong; everything's topsy-turvy.

David Gilbert's here, but Yellow French Fries isn't. Ollie Watkins lives here, but he didn't open the door and he's wearing red jeans with matching tones of hacking coughs instead of pure Custard Yellow.

The room we're led into is equally baffling. It's the same shape as Bee Larkham's kitchen, but the furniture has ended up in the wrong places. A dresser with animal ornaments and decorative plates is up against Bee's adjoining wall.

"Excuse the mess," the man in the red jeans says, pointing to a stack of boxes in the corner. "I reckon I'll have a few more trips to the charity shop and the house will be ready to go on the market. I'll book my flight back to Switzerland soon."

Ollie Watkins.

"It's definitely the end of an era," Dull Grainy Red says. "I'll be sorry to see you go, Ollie. It's so sad—your mother and Pauline both gone within nine months of each other. That often happens when a close friend dies, I believe. It badly affects the one left behind."

"And Bee," I pipe up. "Don't forget Bee Larkham died too. She was murdered in her kitchen, behind this dresser, on the other side of the wall. Strangled to death, not stabbed, as I'd originally believed."

Dad and the two men look at me. I walk up to the dresser and turn my back. One of the plates has a jade-colored edge, which is vying for attention with a larger, turquoise-rimmed plate.

"Is there any news on that front from the police?" Dull Grainy Red asks. "They've questioned me too, but they're not letting on what's happening behind the scenes."

"The dad of that boy is still in the picture," Dad's muddy ocher voice says quietly. "He's clearly got a history of violence. I think he's a likely candidate, if you get my drift, but the police aren't letting on much to me either."

"Let's hope the police charge him soon." *Custard yellow with deep scratches.*

"A terrible business." Dull Grainy Red again. "To think this happened on our quiet little street. I don't feel safe in my own home. Not after he went for me and Jasper like that in Bee's garden."

"Don't worry about him, David." *Dad's muddy ocher.* "They've got him for assaulting you and Jasper at the very least. He'll have his day in court. There's not a chance he'll be back here any time soon."

"Maybe it was someone else. It could have been a random attack by a total stranger." *Custard yellow* until the man coughs up dark shards of rhubarb.

"That's even worse! How will I be able to sleep thinking a random madman could break into my house?"

"Don't worry yourself, David. The police think it was probably someone she knew because there was no sign of forced entry. She let that person into the house on Friday, a late-night caller."

"No," I tell Muddy Ocher, without turning around. "She didn't let him in. The Dark Blue Baseball Cap Man used the spare key, from beneath the flamingo statue in the back garden. The back door was open. Mrs. Larkham kept the key hidden under the statue. The solicitor took it when she died and Bee put it back again because *there's nothing worth stealing in the house.* Now it's gone."

"That's not right, Jasper," Muddy Ocher says. "The police have the key. It was beneath the statue, like you said. They found it when they searched the garden. They showed it to me in an evidence bag on Saturday and asked if I'd seen it before."

"It was gone on Thursday afternoon, before David Gilbert turned up and told Lucas Drury's dad I was hiding among the recycling bins." I examine a plate, with ink blue patterns.

"No, Jasper. The key was there all along. You must have missed it when you looked."

Dad's wrong, not me.

"Was that why you came into the back garden, David Gilbert?" I ask. "You'd forgotten you'd taken the key and knew you'd made a mistake? You had to put it back, but you were interrupted."

"What? No. I heard raised voices as I was walking Monty. That's when I found you. I stopped that man from hurting you. Don't you remember?"

"Someone knew the key was there," I point out. "That's what Dad said. Someone realized they shouldn't have taken it. They put it back again after Bee's murder because they knew they'd made a mistake."

"That's impossible," Dad says. "Forensics arrived on Thursday evening, after Lucas Drury's dad broke into Bee's house. The police said the back gate was sealed to preserve any evidence. No one could have got in that way. The police would have noticed."

I think about that for a few seconds. I'd seen the police officers in the patrol car at the front of the house. The back gate is another missing part of the puzzle, I'm sure.

"Anyway, how would anyone know where to look for the key?" Dad asks. "It couldn't have been common knowledge that Bee hid it under the statue."

"Lucas Drury knew where the key was kept and liked Surprise Visits," I murmur. "He has a temper like his dad and didn't want Bee to ruin things with the new girl at school. He borrowed his dad's baseball cap. He doesn't put things back where they belong."

The colors talk over me, blotting out my cool blue.

"Come to think about it, that *is* where her mother kept the key," David Gilbert says. "Lily and I used it to water Pauline's plants whenever she was admitted to hospital. I told the solicitor where to find it when he locked up the house after her death, but the boy's right, Beatrice must have put it back. Has Jasper told the police the key was gone when he checked? It could be important."

"I'm not sure." *Muddy ocher.* "I wasn't present in any of the formal interviews. They're getting information out of him slowly, as he remembers it, piece by piece. They think he bottled up his memories of that night and got them mixed up in his head because of the shock of what he witnessed. New details come back to him each day, but it's going to take time to get the whole story in the right order."

I move along the dresser and pick up a brown china rabbit in a pink dress, which is joined at the hip with a friend in a blue dress. It has a name on the bottom, which I've read before. I check the next brown rabbit and the next. They have the same name. All eighteen rabbits wear light pastel clothes. Some play instruments or read books.

"Royal Doulton," I say. "Like the dancing china ladies."

As I turn around, Dull Grainy Red says: "I love Royal Doulton. It's the best china in the world. Lily had fine taste. She used to collect it. Pauline too."

"These rabbits are all brown," I reply, "but Bee hated the white rabbit. She killed it at the end of the story because it forced her to go down the rabbit hole and do those things. She hated it. It made her feel bad."

I move along the shelf and pick up a white-patterned cup from a saucer. A fine crack runs through the china, cutting an animal in half.

"This one's a hare, not a rabbit," Dull Grainy Red says. "You can tell by the length of the ears. They're much longer. I should know. I've shot a few hares and rabbits in my time. It looks like a March hare to me."

My hand trembles. Bird killer—and rabbit killer—David Gilbert stands directly behind me, looking at the delicate object in my hands. He wants to slaughter this hare, the way he wants to kill all living things. Except this hare isn't alive. It's already been broken. The teapot and three saucers too, but they've been glued back together again.

"The infamous Mad Hatter tea set," David Gilbert continues. "Do you remember this, Ollie? Beatrice smashed it during one of her tantrums. Such a bad child. Your mum cried for days. Pauline was beyond mortified, and I was distressed too. Lily used to let me borrow it whenever Clara, my little niece, came to visit. Sometimes Clara and Beatrice had Mad Hatter tea parties together in my kitchen when Pauline needed to go out, but that all ended after Bee ruined it."

"I only remember bits and pieces." *Custard yellow stripes.* "It was a long time ago. Bee smashed the tea set while I was back at Cambridge."

"Really? I thought I remembered Lily saying you helped glue it back together."

"I did. Mum rang me at uni and told me what Bee had done. I came home for the weekend to comfort her."

"Of course, you always were a good son to Lily, the polar opposite of Beatrice with Pauline. Shortly after her wrecking spree here, she broke some of her mum's prized china collection too—the angel figurines."

"I don't remember. I'd probably returned to Cambridge by then."

"Her behavior didn't improve with age. Did you know that after Pauline died, she smashed her precious lady figurines? I tried to reason with her, but she wouldn't listen, as ever. It was pure spite, especially since Pauline had promised them to your mum. I wouldn't have minded a few on my dresser too. I told her so, not that it did much good."

"Bee always did what she liked, whether it hurt someone else or not." Ollie Watkins's custard yellow voice coughs violently, making blobs of claret. "Sorry. I thought I'd shaken off this chest infection."

"You've got run-down with everything you've been through." *Dull grainy red.* "You need to look after yourself, Ollie. Get to the doctors and ask for some antibiotics. That should do it, along with quitting smoking, of course."

"Beatrice Larkham was aged nine and three months and she wanted to die," I say loudly. "She thought her mum was an old witch. She hated the Mad Hatter because he hurt her. He held a teacup and made her cry."

"Mum's collection is delicate. Please don't touch it." Hands take the cup from me. "It could break again and we wouldn't want that to happen, would we, Jasper?"

I look along the shelf and back at Red Jeans Man and Blue Jeans Man. They stand side by side.

Them against me.

They've swapped clothes. Their voices merge, talking as one as their colors shift.

There's a new battle line and it's no longer running down the street.

It's inside this kitchen. I take a step towards Dad because he doesn't realize we could be in danger: *a scorched orange word with harsh red undertones.*

"Everything is changing today, like it did in Bee's kitchen on the eighth of April. The Dancing China Lady wasn't there and then she turned up and everything was different."

"Sorry, you've lost me," Dull Grainy Red says. "I have absolutely no idea what you're talking about."

"Come on, Jasper. I think we should go." This is Dad's color.

"The parakeets haven't been fed," I remind him. "That's why we're here. We came to get the bird seed, not to have a Mad Hatter's tea party with people who were never Bee Larkham's friends."

"I'm afraid I'm all out of seed. I've been busy sorting out the house before I fly back to Switzerland. I'm sorry, Jasper."

"*You've* been feeding the parakeets, Ollie? You're as bad as Beatrice. What were you thinking? I could wring your neck."

"You're a killer, David Gilbert," I say quietly. "The rabbits and the parakeets know that too. You're guilty. I knew that all along, but no one listened to me."

"What did that boy say?" *Dull red. Definitely dull grainy red.*

"We're going now, Jasper," Dad says. "There are a few other pet shops we can try. We'll head out after lunch, I promise. Somewhere must stock bird seed unless the whole population of West London has decided to feed the wild parakeets."

"Heaven forbid," one of the men mutters shards of dark red.

"I think he's the Mad Hatter who made Bee Larkham cry," I say, as we walk out the front door.

"Who?" Dad asks. "David or Ollie?"

"I'm not one hundred percent sure."

I can't make up my mind because they've both confused me in different ways. I need to look at the white rabbit again and decide which one's the real culprit.

65

TUESDAY (BOTTLE GREEN)

Later That Afternoon

Dad hasn't kept his promise. Again. We can't go and buy bird seed together because of a work emergency. Something about a hard-disk failure and having to restore everything from backups and retest all over again.

I have no idea what he's talking about, but he said it was a total nightmare. If he didn't go into the office straightaway and get it sorted his boss would go nuts and he could lose his job. Dad laughed when I asked if his boss preferred cashew or Brazil nuts, so he couldn't have been all that worried.

Anyway, he made yet another promise: he'd buy bird seed on the way home.

I mustn't open the front door to anyone while he's out. Not even if I know the person's name. *Unless it's a police officer*, like Rusty Chrome Orange. Dad's taken his key; he'll let himself in.

I mustn't dial 999 either. Unless the house is burning down, which is unlikely after last year's rewiring and no appliances, like the iron or the deep-fat fryer, have been left on.

Dad wrote down Important Facts to help me remember them:

1. Don't worry about the house burning down. I shouldn't have said that. Everything in the house is fine.
2. Don't answer the front door to anyone, unless it's a police officer or a social worker.
3. There's not going to be an emergency. You won't need to dial 999.

4. Don't get me into trouble again by dialing 999!! I wouldn't leave you unless I absolutely had to.

We've estimated, using a route planner on Dad's laptop, he's likely to be away for seventy-four minutes. He could be back sooner, depending if anyone else from work turns up to help out.

There's nothing to worry about. *Nothing at all.*

Dad said he could ask one of the neighbors to come over, but I refused. I don't like babysitters or tea parties. I'm safer on my own.

I'm worried now he's gone.

I'm worried about the white rabbit and the Mad Hatter tea set that nine-year-old Bee Larkham broke.

I'm worried about Lucas Drury and his Surprise Visits that I had to keep secret. He borrowed his dad's baseball cap and forgot to put Bee's key back beneath the flamingo statue on the night of one Surprise Visit. He gripped me by the throat in the science lab and squeezed hard, making it difficult to breathe. Less than a week later—after Bee had been murdered—he looked like he'd fought a tornado and had a split lip and scratched hand. He blamed his dad for that.

But what if Bee had fought back when she was attacked?

I rearrange my pictures and paints on the table in my bedroom. I start afresh, slapping white onto the paper, but it's dry and chalky in texture. My strokes are scratchy and lack precision.

I can't paint properly, not when I'm thinking about the white rabbit. I dig Bee's diary out from beneath the blanket in the den. I flick forward, past her entry about the Mad Hatter's tea party.

She drew a picture on one of the pages—Alice, with the Mad Hatter, the March Hare, and the Dormouse. Underneath, she'd added a large teapot and cup and saucer. She must have gone wrong, like I had with the white paint. The whole page is crossed out again and again, using a black pen.

Mrs. Watkins agrees with Mummy that I'm a hateful girl who's telling lies about a good person. They're both praying for my soul. I'm not lying. I hate the Mad Hatter. He won't stop. I want him to leave me alone.

I close the diary. I'm frightened of David Gilbert at 22 Vincent Gardens. He goes into houses where he doesn't belong, like Mrs. Watkins's house, and knows where people hide their keys. He wears hats: a black one and a brown flat cap. He could have a baseball cap at home. Doesn't everyone?

He was friends with Bee's mum, Pauline Larkham, and Ollie's mum, Lily Watkins. He's connected to everyone, *to everything*.

I thought he hated Bee Larkham because she was noisy and liked parakeets, but he hated her long before that. Bee was a *bad child*. She smashed Mrs. Watkins's Mad Hatter tea set and destroyed Mrs. Larkham's Royal Doulton china ladies, one by one. Both women were his friends.

David Gilbert *loves* Royal Doulton. He admitted borrowing the Mad Hatter tea set for his niece and could have been nine-year-old Bee Larkham's babysitter. He also liked the china ladies.

Was he looking for ornaments in the skip outside Bee Larkham's house, the night I thought I'd seen the devil?

Maybe he wanted the last figurine—the Dancing China Lady—before Bee had a chance to smash it. Could he have tried to take it at her party? I remember the man with the scratchy reddish voice claiming he was looking for the toilet.

That was a lie—he'd made a beeline for the ornaments.

It's why the Dancing China Lady was in the kitchen the night Bee died. He'd stolen it from the bedroom and planned to escape through the back door.

Had Bee been downstairs instead of in bed? Maybe she'd slept on the sofa in the sitting room. That was when she surprised him, after he'd stolen the ornament and was about to leave. She heard a noise and woke up.

I must tell the police my new theory.

Is this an emergency? Should I dial 999? I think about it for two minutes and thirty seconds. I don't think Dad would necessarily describe this as an emergency because I'm seeing Rusty Chrome Orange again tomorrow. I can tell him this Important Fact Number One at the police station. If I ring now, it will get Dad into trouble all over again.

I check my watch. Dad's been gone for fourteen minutes. He could be back in an hour. Or sooner. I can tell *him* when he gets back. I take my paintbrush downstairs with me to get a glass of water because it might not like being left alone in my bedroom. The house makes soft-pink-colored creaks, like a tiny mouse is scurrying about.

I should also tell Rusty Chrome Orange about the key in the lock of Bee Larkham's back door. Lucas Drury knew where it was kept and so did David Gilbert. Maybe the dangerous bird killer was trying to put it back when Mr. Drury, wearing the baseball cap Lucas had borrowed, ruined his plan.

David Gilbert must have returned later, once the police had gone. Could he have nipped through the alley behind his house? I have no idea how the police sealed Bee's back gate, but possibly with tape that could have been easily peeled off?

Anyway, the key is Important Fact Number Two.

I should tell Rusty Chrome Orange something else too—I'm sure I did leave the house a second time. I wasn't dreaming. I saw the person wearing the dark blue baseball cap. Not Dad. Everyone believes that now, including me. It *could* have been David Gilbert in disguise.

He knows I don't recognize him. Dad told him at Bee's party I have problems with faces. He's heard Dad call me "Son." He could have copied his usual uniform of blue jeans and blue shirt. I make a note of Important Fact Number Three in my head, to tell Rusty Chrome Orange.

I run the water in the sink for twenty seconds because I like the bluish gray lines it makes, a different color to the shower. The kitchen clock says 2:02 P.M. Dad could be back in fifty-seven minutes. I walk past the sitting room door, which is open.

It was shut *that* night. I heard velvety dark chocolate lines.

Dad snoring.

Followed by the color of the shower.

That's Important Fact Numbers Four and Five.

My colors confirm Dad's story. He is telling the truth. He said he thought he heard a noise at around 3:15 A.M. He had a hot shower because his neck hurt from sleeping in the armchair that makes maroon creaks.

I wish he'd come back. I'd tell him I believe him. I don't think he was in Bee Larkham's kitchen. I definitely saw someone. I was definitely there. I remember the disinfectant smell and another unpleasant scent. It reminded me of Bee Larkham's party and being confused by David Gilbert and Ollie Watkins.

That's Important Fact Number Six.

I take the glass with me back upstairs. The bruised-apple step creaks. Before my foot can touch the next step, I hear a key in the lock of the front door.

Blackish dark green with a brittle consistency.

Blue shirt, blue jeans walks inside. He's not holding a bag.

"You're back too soon, Dad. You didn't buy the seed. You need to go out again."

Dad looks at the floor. Is he upset I've told him off? Angry? Annoyed? I can't tell.

"I'm sorry, and thank you very much for trying, but you need to try again. When you get back I'll tell you who I think murdered Bee Larkham and why. It's all in her diary."

He looks at the coat rack instead of me. He examines my school scarf, wrapping the end of it around his hand.

My mobile vibrates red and yellow bubbles in my pocket, which is odd, because the only person who ever calls or texts me is Dad.

I call up the message as I carry on walking up the stairs to my bedroom.

Called off job! Got bird seed. Back soon. Love Dad x

I drop the glass of water.

Help.

I type the word, but my mobile flies from my hand before I can press send. The man wearing blue jeans and a blue shirt has already dived up the stairs and grabbed my ankle. I kick free, but his hand clamps onto my other foot.

"Get off me, David Gilbert!" I scream.

"Where's Bee's diary?" he hisses white-gray jagged lines.

I kick him in the face. Hard. He curses under his breath, whitish globules. I scramble backwards; he's quicker. He's on top of me, crushing my chest.

"Where is it?" *Juddering, hard white lines.* He's whispering again.

"Can't. Hear. You."

"Where the hell is it?" He coughs violently, curdled red and yellow.

"In my den. In my bedroom."

The scarf is around my neck. Tightening again and again.

Can't breathe.

He drags me by the scarf to the banister.

His breath smells like Bee Larkham's party. Her kitchen. The kitchen of Mrs. Watkins's house.

Cigarette smoke.

His voice is more custard yellow than red.

Two men can't become one.

Wrong man.

He's changed his clothes to look like Dad.

The color of his voice changed too.

Can't breathe.

Choking.

Dad.

Want muddy ocher.

Mum.

Want cobalt blue more.

"It's you, Ollie Watkins," I gasp. "I know it."

His grip loosens. "You're wrong."

I wheeze as his hands slip from my neck.

"I'm not wrong," I say, coughing dark sapphire blue. "About the color of voices. Even when they trick me. I see through them. Eventually."

"Jasper, Jasper." His head moves from side to side. "What are you talking about this time?"

I take a large gulp of air. "Your chest infection and smoking changed the color of your voice. It went from custard yellow to scratchy red, which confused me, but you're the Mad Hatter. You were at the party. You had a reddish voice because you were ill. You went into Bee's bedroom to get the Dancing China Lady and you said goodbye to me in the hallway." I wheeze and start talking again. "You came back the day before Valentine's Day. You said sorry to Bee at her front door and tried to give her flowers. It was you. All along. You spoke in grayish white whispers over Bee's body in the kitchen."

Ollie Watkins hacks streaky yellow-red blobs.

"It's tragic when a child commits suicide, don't you think? You couldn't cope with the trauma of Bee's murder and the cloud of suspicion over your dad. He could still be charged, right? Why did he go running out of your house like that and tear away in his car? Very irresponsible to leave someone as vulnerable as you home alone. No one will question your death by hanging. Not with your problems. It's sad, but understandable."

My hand scrabbles at the scarf as he yanks harder. He tries to loop it around the railing. My other hand grasps the paintbrush. I swing it up and stab Ollie Watkins in the eye. He screams acrid yellow and dark red spots, the scarf loosens, and he falls backwards, down the stairs.

I run. Up to the landing. Into my bedroom. He's coming. Deep yellow, almost brown, footsteps pound up the stairs. *Behind me.*

I slam the door, grab the chair, and wedge it under the handle. It jams beneath the desk.

Bang, bang, bang!

He's already here, but the chair's firmly lodged in place.

Barricade assembled.

Will it hold? Will it hold?

Bang, bang!

The chair shakes, the door shakes. He hurls himself against it, again and again. *Red stars explode from the large brown rectangles.*

I run to the window and hammer on the glass, *shards of brittle lilac.*

"Help." I mouth the word over and over again. My throat's painful. I can't speak anymore. "Help."

I open the window as the parakeets flutter around the hole in Bee Larkham's oak tree.

Help.

The banging stops.

Footsteps run down the stairs. *Blurry lines of yellow.*

Now I see *sharp white points and bright ice green-blue tubes.*

He's smashing things in the kitchen. Throwing glass.

I flap my arms at a car. It drives past, *deep plum torpedo shape with a navy haze,* followed by a motorbike, *gray and black intermoving lines.* A man wearing a brown flat cap and jeans walks out of 22 Vincent Gardens with a dog. It barks yellow French fries. I wave at the man, who must be David Gilbert, but he drops his keys and bends down.

Bang, bang, bang at my bedroom door. *Fiercer red darts. Larger brown rectangles.*

"I'm sorry, Jasper. I lost my temper. I shouldn't have touched you. Give me Bee's diary and I'll leave. I won't hurt you. I promise."

Ollie Watkins is back. He doesn't keep his promises. He didn't feed the parakeets—he hates them as much as David Gilbert. He killed Bee Larkham by strangling her.

He's going to kill me and make Dad think I wanted to die. He'll take Bee Larkham's diary.

That's why he's here. He wants to destroy the evidence.

He knows I've read the diary. He's the Mad Hatter who hurt Bee. He stole the Dancing China Lady because he wanted it for his dead mum.

I hang further out the window. The street is deserted: not a single moving vehicle or person apart from David Gilbert, who is patting Yellow French Fries. Even the parakeets have stopped singing.

There's a new color. *Dark, spiraling pond green.*

I spin around. The door handle screw turns.

Ollie Watkins found a screwdriver in the kitchen drawer. He's taking off the handle.

The man and dog walk down the path of 22 Vincent Gardens.

Help me, help me, help me. I can't shout—my throat hurts too much.

The handle jangles violent shades of orange. It falls off, beneath the chair. The door shifts again.

I throw a book out of the window and my favorite paint pot. It smashes on the ground below. *Greenish ice tubes.* The man wearing the brown flat cap stops. He looks in my direction.

I throw my binoculars. I throw my notebooks. I throw everything I can find, transforming the colors into new, disturbing shades as they hit the ground.

He's walking again, towards our house. Towards me? The bedroom door makes large, spiny harsh orange shapes. They're thornier and brighter.

The door opens and slams repeatedly into the desk, pushing it aside. I see a foot.

I climb out of the window, half in, half out of my bedroom.

"No, Jasper! No!" The man drops the dog lead and breaks into a run. I look over my shoulder.

A leg's inside and now half a body. The barricade's falling into spiky, maniacal orange shards. Ollie Watkins is pushing his way through. He'll reach me in seconds.

I pull my other leg through the window, squatting on the window-sill.

"Stop! Stop!" The man in the flat cap's screaming bright scarlet.

He runs in front of a car.

It toots red-rose star blobs at him, startling the young parakeets in Bee Larkham's oak tree.

They rise in a wave of peacock blue, green, and violet squawks from the branches.

A glimmering stained-glass window.

They're all abandoning the street.

They can't stay any longer. The feeders are empty. They don't need their nests or the branches of the tree at nighttime, they've summoned up enough courage to join the roost.

They're leaving me alone with Bee Larkham's murderer, Ollie Watkins from 18 Vincent Gardens.

They're taking their beautiful colors with them.

Come back!

Wait for me!

I can't bear the ugly, spiny orange shapes in my bedroom.

I want the smooth, shimmering blues and curvy, golden droplets in the sky.

I stretch my arms out.

"Wait!" *Cool blue with spiky white peaks.*

My colors blend in perfectly with the birds.

I close my eyes, push off with my feet.

I fly.

Epilogue
THREE MONTHS LATER

"I came as soon as I heard the news on the radio. Is it true? Is it all over?" Dull grainy red questions rain down on Dad at the front door. "Did I misunderstand the journalist?"

"No, you heard right. It's come as a bolt from the blue for us—the police and his barrister too. Come in. I'll make us both a cup of tea."

"If you're sure it's no bother, Ed?" His voice darkens to claret but is still distinctively scratchy. "I know you have your hands full."

Dad wasn't carrying anything when he left the sitting room. He put his newspaper down next to me on the sofa, where I'm resting my leg. That's probably why he insists that making a hot drink isn't a problem.

I don't need to hear Dad say this man's name or see his cherry cords to know this is David Gilbert from number 22, the neighbor I thought was going to harm the parakeets, Bee Larkham, and quite possibly me—in that order.

I was wrong about him, the way I've been wrong about a lot of people.

David Gilbert ran in front of a car in a bid to save me from Ollie Watkins. After I jumped from the ledge, he looked after me until the ambulance arrived because it turns out I can't fly like a parakeet.

The male paramedic said I was unlucky because I'd struck a concrete post under the window and landed in a strange position, badly breaking my right leg and wrist. He didn't understand the opposite was true—I was extremely fortunate. My left painting hand wasn't hurt. It wasn't even scratched.

David Gilbert was more than our neighbor and stand-in first-aider that day. He became a Key Witness in the police inquiry.

Ollie Watkins couldn't flee our house because David Gilbert stayed with me in the front garden, blocking his escape route. The back door was locked and he couldn't find the key. Police officers discovered Ollie Watkins hiding inside my den when they knocked down our front door. He was arrested and charged with murdering Bee Larkham and attempting to murder me.

Dad had begun preparing me for the trial—he said we'd both have to tell our stories to a jury later this year. David Gilbert would also have to get ready to give evidence in court.

These Important Facts changed in a single telephone call from Rusty Chrome Orange earlier as we arrived home from my hospital appointment. He told Dad about a Crown court hearing in front of a judge to prepare for the trial.

The charges were read to Ollie Watkins, who burst into tears in the dock. His ex-fiancée cried too as he pleaded guilty to both counts to the surprise of everyone, including his own brief, who leapt up and asked for time alone with his client.

Rusty Chrome Orange told us it was quite a spectacle (an iridescent, mother-of-pearl word). The judge agreed he didn't like surprises and told everyone to get out of his court. Ollie Watkins and his defense barrister had a discussion in the cells beneath the court and returned fifteen minutes later.

The barrister then explained to the judge everything that Ollie Watkins did that night and on the day he attacked me.

He wanted to get it off his chest.

The judge moved straightaway to sentencing because, like me, he wasn't fond of delays. He gave Ollie Watkins the only possible punishment for murder and attempted murder: a life sentence. Rusty Chrome Orange said he was led away from the dock sobbing.

We expected Ollie to take his chance with the trial jury even though the evidence against him was overwhelming.

Dad agreed he was shocked too, but relieved I wouldn't have to go through the trauma of describing Ollie Watkins's terrible colors in court.

We can all move on. Try to put this behind us.

I wasn't surprised by Ollie Watkins's decision because I've learnt over the last six months that people often make plans and alter them unexpectedly. Sometimes they feel guilty about ripping up other people's Original Plans and other times they simply don't care.

Their minds change as well as their voice colors.

Dad's talking to David Gilbert in the kitchen—something about Overwhelming Evidence. The door's open six inches, but I can only hear snatches of color. I pick up my crutches and ease myself off the sofa. My leg's grumbling, but I tell it to be quiet. I move slowly towards the muted shades.

I stand outside the door despite the fact that No One Likes a Spy.

"D.C. Chamberlain claims the forensics had him bang to rights," Dad's muddy ocher voice says, above the silver and gleaming yellow bubbles of the boiling kettle. "There's no way he could have wriggled his way out of that kind of proof."

I'm not sure what else Ollie Watkins banged loudly or wriggled through apart from my bedroom door, but I know the police discovered the Dancing China Lady in a box in his dead mum's house along with a dark blue baseball cap. Dad told me this after his conversation with Rusty Chrome Orange.

"Apparently his DNA matched traces on Jasper's clothes, Bee's body and suitcase," Dad continues. "They found a strand of her hair in the boot of his car. The police also traced mud on the suitcase from Bee's back garden to a carpet inside number eighteen."

He tells David Gilbert how Ollie Watkins remembered to wipe the fingerprints off Bee Larkham's back door key, but police found a thread matching one of his sweaters stuck in the garden fence. He had squeezed through the gap to return the key after police sealed the gate to the alley. He'd realized his error and had to return it.

The hole in the fence was a vital clue I'd missed when I couldn't work out how the killer had returned to Bee Larkham's back garden.

Dad's forgotten to mention another crucial piece of evidence against Ollie Watkins—I could identify his voice from the attack. There was no mistaking his custard yellow, even with the streaks of red chest infection. His fingerprints were also on our spare key, the one he saw me take from beneath the flowerpot the day I ran out of school.

"I'm relieved your lad doesn't have to go to court. You too. You've both been through enough."

Dad mumbles dull ocher.

"I've had sleepless nights about giving evidence too, but I still wanted to look him in the eye, really look him in the eye," the dull grainy red voice says. "I need to understand why he did those terrible things to poor Beatrice."

Richard Chamberlain—*like the actor*—said the murder investigation team already knew this before Ollie Watkins pleaded guilty. They managed to piece together what went on from the pages of Bee's diary, my notebooks, and interviews with David Gilbert and me.

Ollie Watkins frequently babysat for Mrs. Larkham when he came home from uni and played the Mad Hatter's Tea Party with Bee Larkham before abusing her. Bee's mum and Ollie's mum never believed her when she told them. They sided with Ollie because he was such a good lad and Bee was a wicked, ungodly child. She punished them by smashing their china collections.

After Mrs. Larkham died, Bee tried to punish Mrs. Watkins all over again with loud music and by refusing to hand over the china ladies promised in her mum's will. Instead, she taunted Ollie Watkins by putting the ornaments in the window before smashing them one by one.

Dad finishes explaining these Important Facts to David Gilbert.

"I feel terrible, Ed." *Dull grainy red darts interspersed with dark cherries.* "I never knew what young Beatrice was going through. I wish I could have helped her back then, but I never suspected a thing." He stops as Dad's muddy ocher mingles into his words. "No, Ed, it's true. I should have been kinder to her. I made her life a misery when she returned, complaining about the music and the parakeets. I said some awful things to her on the night she died. I wish I could take it all back, but I can't."

"Don't upset yourself, David. You're not to blame. You mustn't beat yourself up about this."

Dad's right. David Gilbert never beat anyone up.

He's not guilty of any crimes even though I rang 999 many times and told the police he should be arrested.

It's all Ollie Watkins's fault.

He made Bee Larkham want to die as a child and killed her when she grew up because she repeatedly threatened to report him to the police and hand over her diary. Ollie Watkins had a lot to lose, Rusty Chrome Orange said—his highly paid banking job and fiancée in Switzerland, who has now dumped him.

Ollie Watkins's mum had told him where Bee kept her spare key. That's what his defense barrister told the court. He thought Bee was asleep when the loud music had stopped for a few hours and let himself in the back door around 3:00 A.M. to search for her diary, which described the bad stuff and her attempts to get help from Mrs. Larkham and Mrs. Watkins. Ollie was out of his mind with worry that detectives could try to build a case against him using her childhood entries; he didn't know lots of pages had been torn out and scribbled over. He couldn't find the diary because Bee had hidden it in the box in my wardrobe. He took the Dancing China Lady, before Bee disturbed him in the kitchen and they argued. She threatened to tell his fiancée and the police—anyone who'd listen—before he grabbed her by the throat. He killed her and emptied her suitcase upstairs so he could drag her body back to his house.

When he returned to the kitchen, he saw me in my pajamas and pretended to be Dad by calling me his son. He thought he'd got away with it but deliberately stopped me in the street after I ran out of school. He wanted to test my reaction to seeing his face again.

David Gilbert had inadvertently helped him by explaining I had problems recognizing people at Bee Larkham's party. He also told him that Dad always wears blue shirts and blue jeans to make it easier for me to identify him whenever we're in public. That's why he'd changed his clothes when he decided to attack me even though it was unintentional on the night he killed Bee.

Dad relayed these Important Facts after asking our neighbor if he took sugar in his tea. David Gilbert confirmed one spoonful and wanting to know everything even though he found it incredibly upsetting.

I used to think I'd never have anything in common with bird killer David Gilbert, but that's not 100 percent accurate. Every week he buys peanuts and seed for the parakeets and tops up Bee's bird feeders when my leg is too painful to walk across the road.

After Rusty Chrome Orange rang, I also told Dad I wanted to know absolutely everything too, even the sections with ugly-colored words that scare me and make me want to rub the buttons on Mum's cardigan in my den.

I had to learn the truth about Ollie Watkins—the man who disguised himself as a fellow bird lover and my friend. I owed Bee Larkham that much because she couldn't explain the full story herself. Someone had to do it for her.

Dad's repeating himself now, telling David Gilbert this isn't his fault. I'm not sure why he doesn't understand that Ollie Watkins has pleaded guilty. No one blames David Gilbert, not even me.

"You're very kind, Ed, but I can't stop thinking about how much I upset Bee, particularly about the parakeets. I can't apologize to her, but it's not too late for me to make things right . . ."

I lose my balance and the door creaks open. *Creamy chicken soup.*

"Jasper! Your dad and I were just discussing Bee Larkham."

"I know, David Gilbert. I was eavesdropping and accidentally pushed open the door before I could stop myself."

He and Dad laugh. Their voices mingle together and create a flattering ash mahogany. I haven't painted this voice combination before and long to start a new canvas in my bedroom.

I'm not sure why they both find my statement funny because I was telling the absolute truth. Then I remember what Dad told me the day I was admitted to hospital—that we should tell each other the truth from that day onwards without trying to dress it up in any way.

I'd burst out laughing despite the popping, silvery pain because I immediately pictured the word wrapped in a floral dress and topped with a silly, floppy hat.

Dad and David Gilbert are probably dressing up words in funny clothes in their heads too.

"I was just about to tell your dad how I want to do things differently on this street, starting from today," David Gilbert says. "That means I need to ask your advice about something, Jasper."

"You should stop shooting pheasants and partridges," I reply. "That's my advice."

"Thank you, Jasper. I'll remember that. It's about this. I'm finding it very confusing."

He passes me a brochure. "I picked this up in the pet shop when I was buying some seed earlier. Perhaps you can help? Can you tell me which is the best bird table? I'm thinking of putting one in my front garden so I can continue feeding the parakeets once number twenty is sold."

Dad speaks as I carefully study the pages. "That's a lovely idea, David, thank you."

"Well, we never know who might eventually move into Mrs. Larkham's house, do we? We want the right sort, hopefully a family with young children who enjoy the local wildlife as much as Jasper."

"Buy this one, please, David Gilbert." I point to a deluxe wild-bird station, which has four hanging feeders and two water baths. The brochure says it's designed to attract a wide variety of birds. "Bee Larkham would have approved of this purchase. She always wanted to bring as much color as possible to our street."

After lunch, Dad and me visited our old neighbor in the graveyard because we had plenty of news. As soon as I'd been discharged from hospital and could put weight on my foot again we came to keep her company. Back then, I told Bee Larkham that Lucas Drury's dad hadn't gone to jail for hitting David Gilbert and breaking into her house. Another judge had given him a suspended sentence.

But this part was new today—Rusty Chrome Orange says Lucas and Lee now live with their mum and her boyfriend. They'll go to a different school in September because they both need a Fresh Start.

I also told Bee about David Gilbert's bird-feeding station and the Wishart family camping trip next summer. We'll spend a whole year preparing for it and I can choose the tent and a new rucksack from an outdoor shop.

I kept back the most difficult news until last. I explained that the tears running down Ollie Watkins's face in court probably meant he was sorry for the awful things he did to both of us, particularly to her.

I left a parakeet feather on her grave, because I've forgiven her for the pie—chicken, not parakeet. Rusty Chrome Orange and Dad have told me that repeatedly and I finally believe them.

Bee Larkham was my friend, 95.7 percent of the time. She was good and bad and thousands of shades in between. I prefer to remember her sky blue and hold on to that color. It helps fade the other unpleasant hues, particularly today's custard yellow.

Dad and me will continue to visit her grave every week—as well as Mum's memorial bench in Richmond Park—because someone has to look after her. She doesn't have anyone else. There's a child's grave nearby. Whenever I see it, I think that could have been me, buried close to her, keeping her company full-time in this strange, quiet place.

Last time I talked to Bee Larkham, I saw a man putting flowers on the child's tombstone. Dad's corrected me about this—he claims it wasn't a single man, but two separate mourners who were both wearing similar, dark clothes. Rusty Chrome Orange says he's going to help us with my condition—he's putting Dad in touch with someone who can assess my problems recognizing people. He told Dad not to get his hopes up—there's no cure for face blindness or the different way I see the world.

That's good, because I don't want a cure for synesthesia. I'm not sick. I don't want to lose my colors. I can live with the other thing too—I have my ways of coping, like using head grids at school so I can memorize my classmates' identities.

Dad and me are back home, painting. It's not my usual style: we're using rollers to redecorate my bedroom. I'm sitting down, mixing the colors we've carefully picked together, while Dad stands on a ladder, chipping off the stars, which never wanted to come here.

This wasn't their home. They belonged in Plymouth.

While I was treated in hospital, Dad asked if I wanted to move again.

That way I wouldn't have to see Ollie Watkins's and Bee Larkham's houses every single day when I was discharged. I had a lot of time to think about his question because all I could do for hours was lie in bed and think about Bee Larkham, Ollie Watkins, Lucas Drury, David Gilbert, Dad, and what happened on this street.

I knew we couldn't leave. I had to tempt the parakeets back with peanuts and seed. Plus, I had to stay at 19 Vincent Gardens and change the colors Dad and me have started to create together.

We both know they're not perfect yet. They need more work, but that's OK.

This is where I belong, where Mum's voice found me even though she'd never visited, where a neighbor I hated, David Gilbert, ended up helping me and regretting not helping Bee Larkham first.

The radio's pulsating bronze specks and ginger-cat button shapes, but the shades of the parakeets outside the window are stronger, more vibrant. They want to see me, so I use my crutches to get to the window. I can't move fast, but they're patient because they sense I won't be like this forever. The doctor says my cast can come off next week and a physiotherapist will teach me exercises to strengthen my leg muscles.

I think the parakeets want to say goodbye to me properly this time. They've found the large roosting site nearby, which has hundreds of parakeets. Each day, they come back for food because I top up the feeders with help from Dad and David Gilbert.

The parakeets rise into the air from Bee Larkham's oak tree in one giant carpet of green feathers and a musical chorus of rippling flamingo pinks, purples, blues, and exploding golden droplets.

"Goodbye," I whisper.

They're the most beautiful colors *ever.*

"Is everything OK, Jasper?" Dad asks. "Are you too tired to carry on?"

My answer surprises me. "No. I want to carry on."

I hadn't thought I'd want to when the parakeets left me behind, the way Mum and Nan did. I thought I'd be too sad to keep going.

But I know the parakeets will be back for food. They'll nest in the hole in the oak tree and the eaves again early next year.

It's a dead cert, like number one is a whitish gray color and number eight is dark blue lace.

I can wait for the parakeets to return. Tomorrow doesn't scare me anymore.

We're decorating my bedroom the color it should be. We've created the exact shade together.

It's the only color it could be.

I press my hands against the wall by the window and feel the wet paint beneath my fingertips.

Today is the perfect color.

Today is cobalt blue.

Acknowledgments

I'm enormously grateful to a large number of people who helped me craft my novel. Big thanks firstly to my fantastic editor, Tara Parsons, who loved and championed my book in the United States from the beginning, and to the rest of the Touchstone team who made my journey to publication so enjoyable. Particular shout-outs go to Isabella Betita at Touchstone for all her patience and help and also to Michelle Brower at Aevitas Creative Management, who did an incredible job, spreading the word about *Bee Larkham* and gaining my US deal.

I feel immensely privileged to be edited in the United Kingdom by Martha Ashby at HarperCollins. Her insights and support have been phenomenal and much appreciated, as have the hard work of the sales and publicity teams, including Fliss Denham.

I constantly pinch myself at my luck in having the wonderful Jemima Forrester as my agent. You believed in me from day one, worked tirelessly on my behalf, and helped fulfil my ambition of becoming an adult fiction author. Thank you to the foreign rights team at David Higham Associates who have sold my book around the world, and also to Georgina Ruffhead.

I owe a particular debt to the generosity of the synesthesia community in the United States, the United Kingdom, and Germany. I couldn't have written this book without learning from your experiences. Interviewees include the inspirational Amythest Schaber (who also helped me understand face blindness and autism), Susanne Geisler, Alisha Brock, Victoria Schein, and Julia Nielson. I was assisted by James Wannerton from the UK Synaesthesia Association; Jamie Ward, professor of cognitive neuroscience at the University of Sussex; Dr. Mary Jane Spiller, senior lecturer in the school of psychology at the University of East London; Professor Sean Day, from Trident Technical College, South Carolina, and members of his world-famous Synesthesia List, particularly Sigourney Harrington.

For prosopagnosia, I received invaluable insights from Hazel Plastow of Face Blind UK and Robyn Steward, via the National Autistic Society. Thanks also to the society's head of campaigns and public engagement, Tom Purser, and media officer, Piers Wright, for guiding me.

I learnt about parakeets from the incredibly patient Birdman—you don't want to be named but I'm indebted to you—as well as Dr. Hazel Jackson, from the UK's University of Kent's Durrell Institute of Conservation and Ecology (DICE) and the Royal Society for the Protection of Birds's Dr. Kirsi Peck.

Artist Reshma Govindjee kindly let me mix acrylic paints with her and re-create the color of voices and screams on paper. For all things police related I was extremely lucky to be assisted by DC Karen Stephens from the Police Federation of England and Wales and the *Daily Mail*'s chief crime correspondent, Chris Greenwood, who also helped with court procedure. Thank you also to Tracey Puri for help with social work questions; lawyer Andrew Moxon for answering legal queries; the Royal College of Surgeons for all things bones related; and Dr. Helen Day, senior lecturer in English literature at the University of Central Lancashire, for sharing your vast knowledge of *Mrs. Beeton*.

As well as thanking the people named above, I should also add that any mistakes in my book are down to me. I have also used poetic licence in places.

Lindsay; Victoria; Richard; my mum and dad; and my husband, Darren, helped with early reads and edits. I had the support of other authors and friends, including Chris; Charlotta; Faye; Sarah; Jo; and my sister, Rachel. My former agent, Ajda Vucicevic, never doubted I could do this, along with old Bristol writing pals John and Caroline.

Finally, thank you to my family: my mum; dad; Rachel; my lovely sons, James and Luke; and Darren. My children forgive my "goldfish bowl" memory whenever I'm writing. My husband has read this book countless times and makes my life complete. I'm luckier than I can ever express to have such love and encouragement.

References

Books

Bate, Sarah. *Face Recognition and Its Disorders*. New York and Basing-stoke, Hampshire, UK: Palgrave Macmillan, 2013.

Cariello, Carrie. *What Color Is Monday?: How Autism Changed One Family for the Better*. Bedford, NH: Riddle Brook Publishing, 2013; London: Jessica Kingsley Publishers, 2015.

Cytowic, Richard E., and David M. Eagleman. *Wednesday Is Indigo Blue: Discovering the Brain of Synesthia*. Cambridge, MA: MIT Press, 2009.

Leatherdale, Lyndsay. *Prosopagnosia, Face Blindness Explained: Proso-pagnosia Types, Tests, Symptoms, Causes, Treatment, Research and Face Recognition All Covered*. IMB Publishing, 2013.

Mindick, Nancy L. *Understanding Facial Recognition Difficulties in Chil-dren: Prosopagnosia Management Strategies for Parents and Profes-sionals*. London and Philadelphia: Jessica Kingsley Publishers, 2011.

Students of Limpsfield Grange School and Vicky Martin. *M Is for Au-tism*. London and Philadelphia: Jessica Kingsley Publishers, 2015.

Ward, Jamie. *The Frog Who Croaked Blue: Synesthesia and the Mixing of the Senses*. New York and Hove, East Sussex, UK: Routledge, 2009.

Articles

Baron-Cohen, Simon, Donielle Johnson, Julian Asher, Sally Wheel-wright, Simon E. Fisher, Peter K. Gregersen, and Carrie Allison.

"Is Synaesthesia More Common in Autism?" *Molecular Autism* 4, November 2013: 40, https://doi.org/10.1186/2040-2392-4-40.

Moos, Anja, David Simmons, Julia Simner, and Rachel Smith. "Color and Texture Associations in Voice-Induced Synesthesia." *Frontiers in Psychology* 4, September 2013: 568, doi: https://doi.org/10.3389/fpsyg.2013.00568.

Whitchurch, Anna Kelman. "Synaesthesia in a Child of Three and a Half Years." *American Journal of Psychology* 33, 1922: 302–3. This little boy—Edgar Curtis—also featured in an edition of *Popular Science*: "To This Child Musical Sounds Have Color!" November 1922, p. 54.

Videos

The Autistic Me. Directed by Matthew Rudge. BBC documentary. 2009.

An Eyeful of Sound, an animated documentary about synaesthesia. Produced by Joshka Wessels. Directed by Samantha Moore. 2010, https://vimeo.com/11649675.

Philharmonia Orchestra. *Olivier Messiaen 1908–1992: Messiaen and Synaesthesia*. http://www.philharmonia.co.uk/explore/films/388/olivier_messiaen_1908-1992_messiaen_and_synaesthesia.

Amythest Schaber. Neurowonderful: Ask An Autistic, https://www.youtube.com/user/neurowonderful.

Professor Jamie Ward's synaesthesia films, Go Cognitive, http://www.gocognitive.net/interviews/jamie-ward-synesthesia.

Websites

Centre for Face Processing Disorders, Prosopagnosia Resarch at Bournemouth University, Prosopagnosia in Children, prosopagnosiaresearch.org/about/children

Face Blind UK: Living with Face Blindness, www.faceblind.org.uk

The National Autistic Society, www.autism.org.uk

Synesthesia, www.daysyn.com

UK Synaesthesia Association, www.uksynaesthesia.com

About the Author

Sarah J. Harris is an author and freelance education journalist who regularly writes for national British newspapers. She lives in London with her husband and two young children. *The Color of Bee Larkham's Murder* is her first adult novel.

THE
COLOR OF
BEE LARKHAM'S
MURDER

SARAH J. HARRIS

INTRODUCTION

Thirteen-year-old Jasper Wishart lives in a dazzling world of color that no one else can see. But recently Jasper has been haunted by the color of murder. Convinced he's done something terrible to his new neighbor, Bee Larkham, Jasper revisits the events of the last few months to paint the story of their relationship from the beginning. As he struggles to untangle the knot of untrustworthy memories and colors that will lead him to truth, it seems that there's someone out there determined to stop him—at any cost.

TOPICS AND QUESTIONS FOR DISCUSSION

1. Jasper believes that his father will never understand his synesthesia, how his life is a "thrilling kaleidoscope of colors" only he can see. Why do you think his father appears unsupportive of Jasper's unique ability? How does this affect their relationship, especially when compared with the connection Jasper shared with his mother?

2. Why do you think Jasper has such an attachment to the parakeets and to birds in general?

3. *The Color of Bee Larkham's Murder* presents an especially unusual mystery: the protagonist claims he is the one who murdered Bee Larkham—but this is neither explicitly confirmed nor denied until the end of the story. Did you believe his claim at the beginning of the book? Did your suspicions shift throughout? What other characters did you suspect and why?

4. How does the out-of-order sequence of the book affect the reading experience? Do you think the story would have been weakened if it had been told chronologically?

5. "Good and bad aren't stamped on pupil's foreheads to help me sift through their identical uniforms." How does Jasper distinguish good from bad in the people he meets? Talk about the qualities that Jasper considers likable and comfortable versus unlikable.

6. Jasper associated his mother with cobalt blue and Bee Larkham with sky blue. Why do you think Jasper might have initially associated Bee Larkham with the same color as his mother (albeit a different shade)?

7. "I'm a reluctant witness, a reluctant helper—the roles I'm used to playing," Jasper thinks. Do you agree? How might the accuracy of this claim change throughout the book? Can you relate to Jasper's feelings in your own life?

8. Discuss the passage from *Alice in Wonderland* that Bee reads at the grave of the baby parakeet: *"First, however, she waited for a few minutes to see if she was going to shrink any further: she felt a little nervous about this; 'for it might end, you know,' said Alice to herself, 'in my going out altogether, like a candle. I wonder what I should be like then?' And she tried to fancy what the flame of a candle looks like after the candle is blown out, for she could not remember ever having seen such a thing."* Jasper thinks: "I couldn't remember Alice in Wonderland saying this. It didn't sound significant to me," but it clearly carries great emotional weight for Bee. What do you think it meant to her? How else might it relate to the events of the book?

9. "'The police wouldn't believe a word you said. You're what they call an unreliable witness,'" Bee Larkham tells Jasper. Do you agree? How might his face blindness and synesthesia affect this—for better or for worse?

10. Jasper thinks: "Bee Larkham and I were equally guilty, but I was probably more guilty than her." Do you believe this is accurate? Also consider discussing the *Animal Farm* quote Jasper cites

above in relation to the book: "All animals are equal but some animals are more equal than others."

11. Near the end of the book, Jasper remembers a "boys' camping trip to Cumbria two years ago" with his father, who calls it a "fantastic holiday," but Jasper remembers it very differently. What does this tell you about their relationship? Is there an experience in your life that you remember differently from someone you shared it with?

12. "I realize *now* how much Dad sounded like Bee Larkham when we argued over my Darth Sidious rucksack in his bedroom. 'Do it as a favor for me, Jasper. Can you do that for me?'" Why do you think Jasper makes this connection? How do these requests differ in nature?

13. Why do you think Bee planted her diary in Jasper's room?

14. Did your opinion of Bee change after learning about her history? Is so, discuss how.

ENHANCE YOUR
BOOK CLUB

1. Jasper is not alone in his affection for the color blue. Maggie Nelson's *Bluets* is all about the color blue, including history, color theory, observations from various philosophers and writers, and Nelson's own relationship with the color. Consider reading this book and discussing it with your book club.

2. Look up the work of Chuck Close, an artist who, like Jasper, suffers from face blindness. Close paints portraits to help him cope with his affliction. What do you notice?

3. There's no shortage of artistic synesthetes, including Billy Joel, Pharrell Williams, Duke Ellington, Vladimir Nabokov, David Hockney, and more. Look up the work of these individuals and research others. What do you notice?

4. A quote from *Alice's Adventures in Wonderland* by Lewis Carroll is the epigraph and the book is featured prominently in the plot. Consider reading *Alice* with your book club and discussing why you think Harris chose to include it. See if you can find more parallels in it to *The Color of Bee Larkham's Murder* other than the ones explicitly mentioned. Be sure to also research Lewis

Carroll; he was posthumously accused of being a pedophile due to his close relationships with young children—most notably with Alice Liddell, who inspired his most famous character.

5. Crime TV shows are frequently referenced throughout the book and serve as models of what Jasper expects to happen in the murder investigation. Watch an episode or two of shows such as *CSI* and examine the archetypes and roles they portray. How do they compare with the events of Harris's book, and how do they affect our perceptions of crime and punishment?

A CONVERSATION WITH SARAH J. HARRIS

Can you talk about what inspired you to write a story about a person with synesthesia and face blindness? What kind of research did you conduct in order to write the character of Jasper so vividly?

I've been interested in synesthesia and face blindness for many years, after coming across the conditions during my work as an education journalist. The central idea for the book eventually came to me in a dream: a scared young boy running across a suburban street at night, terrified by the colors he had just witnessed, the colors of murder. I carried out extensive research into synesthesia and face blindness to help me write the book—interviewing experts in the UK and people with both conditions across the world. I had assistance from many synesthetes in the United States and remain a member of Sean Day's world-famous Synesthesia List (http://www.daysyn.com/Synesthesia-List.html). I'm also a member of the International Association of Synaesthetes, Artists, and Scientists.

How did you choose the colors that Jasper sees for each word, number, or other element of his life—the "yellow French fries" of David Gilbert's dog, the "toothpaste white" of *Wednesday*, the "bubble-gum pink with a naughty lilac tint" of *sex* and of course, the "sky blue" of *Bee Larkham*?

I interviewed synesthetes about their colors for a wide variety of sounds—such as voices, footsteps, doors closing, and birds singing—

and everyone had distinct colors for the sounds. I decided to develop my own color code and make sure it was consistent, so if footsteps outdoors were dark charcoal–colored one day, they wouldn't be bright violet the next. I kept huge grids, detailing the colors of every sound I used in the book by theme—for example, voice colors, street sounds, parakeet songs, etc.—to help keep track of them. I also tried to imagine the colors from a child's perspective and think of words he would be most likely to use, such as in relation to foods and everyday items. To me, *Wednesday* seemed as fresh as white toothpaste, *hope* was as bright as tomato ketchup, and *sex* was a sweet bubble-gum pink. I imagined the barks of David Gilbert's dog to be unpleasant to Jasper's ears—sharp splinters of a yellow color he disliked but again, in relation to food. I knew that Bee Larkham's voice must be a beautiful shade of blue that was similar to his mum's cobalt blue.

This is your first story for adults, but you chose a child as a protagonist. Why did you make this decision? What was the experience like writing for an adult audience rather than a YA one?
After my dream, I knew this story had to belong to Jasper. I remembered his terror as he ran across the street, and it felt far worse that a child had experienced this trauma than an adult. I could also see Jasper very clearly in my head, standing at a window and watching birds through binoculars, and struggling with his face blindness daily at school.

When the idea initially came to me about Jasper's character, I didn't know whether I would be writing another YA novel or an adult one. As I wrote, it became clear to me that this was an adult book due to the themes I wanted to develop further. It also meant that I could write a longer book than I would do for YA, and use stronger language in places, which was in keeping with some of my characters. I was writing out of contract at the time, so I found the whole experience very liberating. I could write whatever I wanted and Jasper's story was the only one I ever wanted to tell.

Similarly, what helps you tap into the world of childhood to render such believable characters and settings? While Jasper has an unusual

gift, many of his experiences feel familiar and relatable. Did any of your own memories or experiences make it into the book?
I have vivid memories from my own childhood, which definitely help when I write from a child's perspective. I also visit schools as an author and get to speak to children and young people regularly. I could definitely relate to Jasper's feeling like an outsider at school, as I was also bullied. In my early years, school was an ordeal and I dreaded going every day. Like Jasper, there was a bully who used to wait for me at the school gate and I used to run home to get away from him. Taking up martial arts as an adult has helped boost my confidence and I'm now a black belt in karate.

You've also worked as a journalist, specializing in education reporting. What skills from journalism are useful to writing fiction? Did reporting help you develop Jasper's keen observational voice?
Working as a journalist has taught me to rewrite, rewrite, and rewrite again—also to meet tight deadlines. I worked for many years as a general news reporter before specializing in education, and I needed to be able to describe different scenes for newspaper readers. That skill certainly helped me to develop Jasper's character. I'm still very observant and carry a notebook around. I write down interesting descriptions of places, people, and snatches of conversations that I could possibly use in my books.

Did you grow up in a suburban neighborhood like Vincent Gardens? What inspired you to set the story there?
I grew up in a cul-de-sac in a suburban neighborhood, and from my sister's front bedroom window I could see into other people's houses. All the children played together on the street and the mums socialized at weekly coffee mornings. Growing up, it seemed idyllic to me. But I learnt from my parents later that we effectively lived in a goldfish bowl and secrets from inside the other houses eventually spilled out—from raging rows and marital breakdown to depression and even suicide. I live in a suburban neighborhood now with my husband and two young sons and often wonder about the secrets behind all those closed doors. It seemed like a perfect location for my novel, where my characters must fiercely protect their own secrets.

Crime TV shows are constantly referenced throughout the novel. Are you a fan of these shows yourself?

I'm a huge fan of crime TV shows and movies and watch a lot—*Criminal Minds, Cold Case, Sherlock, Department Q, Line of Duty, Broadchurch, The Fall*—too many more to mention! I also love reading crime thrillers.

What inspired you to weave *Alice's Adventures in Wonderland* into your story? Did you have it in mind from the beginning, or did you find a connection later in the writing process?

When I imagined Bee Larkham's first meeting with Jasper, I originally pictured her wearing a hair band like Alice's. I thought there was something almost childlike about Bee, a quality that would appeal to Jasper. The hair band could also help him remember her appearance. The more I thought about the Alice hair band, the more the themes and characters from *Alice in Wonderland* sprang to mind. I wanted to weave them in somehow, and the imagery eventually replaced the hair band. It also seemed particularly fitting in relation to Bee, given the background of Lewis Carroll and his well-documented obsession with Alice Liddell. The reading that Bee gives at the baby parakeet's funeral is at the heart of the *Alice in Wonderland* references. I found it terribly sad and poignant, reflecting Bee's quiet desperation.

In Bee Larkham, you've created a character who is both contemptible and sympathetic, both a villain and a victim. Or as Jasper thinks: "She was good and bad and thousands of shades in between." What was it like writing such a complex character? How did you strike the balance between the two sides of her?

I enjoy writing complex characters because people are complex in real life—they don't fit into neat, convenient boxes. Everyone has faults. Yes, Bee Larkham does terrible things, particularly to Jasper and Lucas, which I would never condone. But I don't believe she's a one hundred percent "bad person," with no redeeming features. I tried to show that, despite her flaws, she also has good points—she's mostly kind to Jasper and considers him her only kindred spirit on the street, despite eventually using him for her own purposes. She's also a victim herself and has never been truly loved, supported, or protected as a child. She wants to feel loved, but looks for love in entirely the wrong places. I think it's okay to feel sorry for Bee *and* be utterly repulsed by her manipulative, exploitative behavior.

This book takes many twists and turns and Bee Larkham's murderer can easily be many people throughout the book. Did you always know who it was going to be?
When I first gained the idea for my book, I didn't know who had murdered Bee Larkham or why. All the characters in my head had very good motives for wanting her dead. But when I started to write, two characters in particular jumped out at me as being the likely culprit. As my word count grew, so did my certainty about the identity of the killer.

What do you think is next for Jasper and his father?
I think Jasper and his father will build a happy, fulfilling future together now that they have truly bonded. Ed Wishart has accepted Jasper for who he is and will no longer try to force him to "act normal." Jasper has learnt that he can rely on his father and be completely true to himself in his company. By the end of the book, Jasper has allowed his father to experience his love of mixing colors and painting for the first time and hasn't been rejected or chastised. Their relationship is like the cobalt blue on Jasper's bedroom wall—it's optimistically bright and will withstand the test of time.

What do you hope will resonate most for readers about this novel?
Hopefully, the message will resonate with readers that we all perceive the world very differently and that diversity is a wonderful thing. It's okay to be different and to accept others who are. We shouldn't have to try to conform to society's image of "normal." What is normal anyway? We often confuse normal with average and who wants to be average?

Are you working on anything new? Can you tell us about it?
I'm working on a new adult novel. I can't say too much about it at this

stage, but it explores the aftermath of a tragic accident involving a child. I'm currently researching serious head injuries, comas, and post-traumatic stress disorder.

I also have lots of ideas for other adult novels and YA books bubbling away in the back of my mind.